The
Witch Hunter's
Daughter

Mount Orion Series
Book Four

Michele Baumann

ALSO BY MICHELE BAUMANN

Mount Orion Series

After Life

The Orchard

Haven

WWW.MICHELEBAUMANN.COM

This is a work of fiction. Names, characters, businesses, events, incidents, and towns are the products of the author's imagination. Any resemblance to actual persons, living, dead or undead, or actual events is purely coincidental.

No Artificial Intelligence was used for the creation of this book.

To

ALL THE STRONG WOMEN WHO
HAVE SHAPED MY LIFE,
AND
TO THOSE WHO DARE TO
BELIEVE IN MAGIC.

PART ONE

THE BEGINNING

MID-AUGUST

1

MIA

Mia Duran sped through the house with the envelope in her fist. She sprinted up the stairs, taking two at a time. She tripped. She fell and rubbed her knee. She started running again. Her pace was undeterred by the fall. Her long dark hair was pulled into a high ponytail that swung as she ran.

The carpeted stairs were freshly vacuumed by Mrs. Coolidge, a sweet older woman who came in twice a week to clean and do laundry. Mia had no feelings about Mrs. Coolidge. She was the same as every housekeeper, babysitter, or nanny employed by her mother since Mia was adopted. Nice, not overly talkative, and she kind of smelled funny. They all smelled funny.

Mia didn't know if it was medicine or really bad perfume, but the smell always turned her stomach. She never got attached to any of them. Whether it was the smell or not, Mia never felt a connection.

Mrs. Coolidge baked cookies a lot, which covered the smell, and Mia appreciated it. So far, she was her favorite, but she wouldn't be around for more than another month. They hired her six months ago when they moved to Forest Lake, and she knew her mother didn't feel comfortable having a stranger in her house, especially now that Mia was old enough to take care of herself.

The second floor of the house stretched out on either side of the staircase. The banister was dusted, the pictures straightened, and the carpet vacuumed. Her bedroom was directly ahead. With the door open, she could see the piles of clothes littering the floor and scattered over her bed.

It was the only room off-limits to Mrs. Coolidge. She pulled the door shut as she passed it.

"Mom!" she screamed between heaving breaths. "Mom!"

She banged on her mother's bedroom door. Listened and banged three more times. It was just after eight p.m. Sunset was sometime soon. She wasn't sure exactly but knew it looked dim outside when she checked the mail.

The mail was late tonight. The usual time the mail carrier circled the area was around four in the afternoon, but tonight they were really late. It was a lucky break that the letter she held clenched in her fist arrived today; otherwise, she would never have been able to wait four hours to tell her mother her good news.

Mia turned the knob and eased the bedroom door open. "Mom? You up?"

"After all that banging? How could I not be?" Bentyn Rae lay in the center of her king-sized bed. The covers were undisturbed and looked as if she hadn't moved at all in her sleep. She sat up and waved Mia to her. "What's all the excitement?"

"It came! It came! It finally came!" Mia jumped and danced in place just inside the doorway. She ran to the bed and dove beside her mother. Through her fits of giggles, she held up the letter in her hand.

"What's this?" Beni sat up and grabbed the letter.

"Only an invitation to join the…wait for it." Mia mimed a drumroll and rolled her tongue to simulate the sound. "The Magnolia Academy for Magical Arts." She held her hands out and made a sound like crowds cheering but sounded an awful lot like heavy breathing to her mother.

Beni dropped back into the mass of pillows behind her. "Mia…"

"No." Mia stopped her with an abrupt attitude. "You said I could go anywhere of my choosing for college. Well, this is my choice." She snatched the letter away from her mother and gazed at it like it was made of gold.

Beni closed her eyes, trying to hold back the tirade of hate speech that was sitting at the edge of her tongue.

"I hear you," Mia whispered, smirking. Her lovely young face was clean of makeup.

Mia could read minds and she could start fires. Neither ability was refined; in fact, it was the very reason she needed the Magnolia Academy for Magical Arts. If someone were to ask her what happened to the burned-out house across the street, it was her inability to control her fires that led to its untimely demise. Luckily, nobody was in it when it happened.

"So, stop listening," her mother snapped. She sat up again and rubbed her hands over her face and hair. "God, I need a drink. Hand me that flask on the nightstand, please."

"Eww." Mia stuck her tongue out. "Get it yourself."

Bentyn Rae was a blood drinker, an Ancient blood drinker whose age Mia could only guess. From what she could piece together from talking to Aunt Dyre and various conversations over the course of her life, her mother's age ranged somewhere between the Bronze Age and Cleopatra. Mia leaned closer to the Bronze Age, but it took coming right out and asking to know. That was difficult.

Beni hated talking about the past, hated laying her life out in timeline fashion. She said it made her feel old and insignificant. The things she'd done over the course of (only God knew how many) years never changed history. They never created societies or destroyed empires. Her life, though insignificant, was a string of failures and disappointments, she told her.

"Aren't you just a joy tonight." Beni dragged herself over the length of the enormous bed and wrapped her fingers around the metal flask. Unscrewing the top, she eyed her daughter, a bit dejected. She took a quick swig of the room temperature liquid and laid it back down on the table. She ran her tongue over her long white fangs as the blood relaxed her tense muscles. "Better. Now, let me see that letter." Her eyebrows arched as she waited for Mia to hand it over. Beni's long white fingers tickled the air, urging her daughter to obey.

She read it. "Dear Mr. or Mrs. Duran…" That's where she stopped. "Well, this is not for me. Miss Duran is dead, and there is no Mister Duran."

"Ignore that part. I'm sure it's a form letter."

"No, I think they knew exactly what they were doing when they wrote this letter." Her jaw swiveled from side to side, and she began reading again. "We are pleased to invite your daughter Mia Duran to join…blah, blah, blah. There's not much here to go on."

"It's an invitation. Starr said they would call to schedule a meeting for tuition and paperwork." Mia grabbed the letter again. "Can you believe it? I am going to be taught witchcraft by…" She took a deep breath. "Camilla Nolan. I can't believe it. I can't believe this is happening."

Mia screamed.

Beni covered her ears. Sensitive to high-pitched sounds, she hated when her daughter screeched. "I can't believe it either." She pulled a sour look and rolled her eyes. "Can we talk about this without you jumping down my throat?"

A knocking sound came from Mia's phone, and she held her finger up for her mother to wait. "April got hers too. Holy crap! I've got to call her." She sped from the room with the same ferocity she had sped in, and Beni found herself alone with the letter and a dark cloud hovering over her.

Beni pulled herself out of bed. She could hear her daughter talking and laughing through her bedroom door. The dread caused by that letter hung on her shoulders like lead weights, and she shuffled down the stairs into the living room. She dropped onto the sofa to wait for her daughter to finish her conversation, so they could finish theirs.

Somewhere in the house she heard Rosemary Clooney singing, and she followed it. Sitting on the kitchen counter, Beni's own cell phone sat playing the song "Sisters" from *White Christmas.*

"I already know," she answered in lieu of hello.

"And you're not letting her go, are you?" her best friend, Dyre Crane, asked. There was singing in the background.

"What other choice do I have?" Beni grumbled. "She's a witch and wants to go to witch school." The singing became louder and closer to the phone. "Is that Lulu?"

"Unfortunately." Dyre silenced her youngest daughter. "Sorry. Lulu being Lulu. Anyway, I intend to tell April no. I won't have her taught by Elena Nolan or—"

"Or Linus?" Beni whispered his name.

"Don't even mention him," Dyre snipped.

"Look, Mia and I have to sit down and discuss this."

"What are you going to say?"

"I know what I *want* to say. I want to say witchcraft is evil and practicing it is forbidden in my house, but even as I say it now, it sounds ridiculous. Given who her parents are and what she's capable of already." Beni could feel that dark cloud getting darker.

"And given that you are a blood drinker, who are you to say what's evil or not," Dyre pointed out.

"Thanks a lot." She ended the conversation abruptly.

Mia skipped down the stairs. "What'd Aunt Dyre have to say?" Knowing Dyre Crane since she'd been adopted by Beni, Mia treated her and called her aunt.

"Sit down." Beni pointed her long, thin finger to the armchair across from her.

Before she started, she looked at Mia. Her long, dark brown hair was full and often unruly. She was stubborn when challenged. Loving when supported and surprisingly courageous when cornered. Beni always attributed that to her upbringing and not her birth parents.

Her expressive brown eyes sparkled with curiosity, enthusiasm, and overwhelming interest in anything witchcraft related. Beni remembered those expressive eyes the day she snatched her out of her playpen as her birth mother lay dying in a pool of her own blood. Even at two, Mia looked like she was ready to drink in the world of mysteries surrounding her.

"First, I want to go on record as saying that I'm against this. I don't think you need to foster the gifts that come naturally to you. I think at this stage in your life, you should be expanding your mind and not your magical abilities." Beni tripped over the last words as they stuck in her throat.

"I will be expanding—"

"Let me finish. With that being said, you are eighteen in October and there is little I can do to stop you from attending the school that you wish."

Mia's eyes widened with excitement. "You're saying yes? Oh my God! Thank you." She jumped up and kissed her mother on the cheek, wrapping her arms around her neck. "You feel really cold."

"It's been a while." She thought the rest of her statement so she didn't have to endure her daughter's aversion to her drinking habits. *"Since I hunted."*

It didn't stop Mia's nose from wrinkling in disgust.

"Do you think my bio mom and dad knew Camilla Nolan?" Mia changed the subject.

"Why are you so hung up on this woman?"

Her mouth dropped open. "She was in the Great Coven." She ran out of the room and reappeared carrying a book. "Look, it says here that she is one of the greatest spellmasters of all time. That's amazing, don'tcha think?"

Beni's mouth twitched. "Where'd you get this book?" She flipped it closed to see the cover. The title was simply, *The Great Coven* by Penelope Press.

"Amazon. It outlines everything. The rise, the fall. How blood drinkers brought down the greatest coven of all time and how witch hunters killed three of its founding members. The leader was burned and came back from the dead. They call her the Phoenix. Did you know about any of this?" Mia turned to the center of the book where there were maps and photos of significant artifacts from the past.

Beni's mouth twitched again. "Kind of."

"Why didn't you ever tell me?"

"It's not exactly bedtime reading. There are lots of horrible things that happened in human history, blood drinker history, and witch history. History sucks."

"I think it's fascinating." Mia bit her lower lip. "So do you think my birth parents knew her?"

Beni took a deep breath. "Probably." That simple admission caused acid to sour her stomach, making her slip up in her thinking, and Mia heard her.

"My birth mother was friends with Elena Nolan? That's Camilla Nolan's sister." Mia slammed the book cover shut as she spoke. "She's the one who sent the letter. Do you think that's why she invited me to join the school?"

"Probably," she said without much enthusiasm.

"Would it bother you if I asked her about my birth mother?"

"Probably."

Mia's face dropped, losing all the excitement of the last half hour.

"Can we talk about this later?" Beni stood from her seat. "I really need a drink, and I can't talk about witches a minute more on an empty stomach."

2

GAIL

Stepping out of the cottage felt strange. The August night air, though heavy with the moisture of an impending storm, had a chill to it that made her uneasy.

Gail Andrews walked down the path from her front door. The flagstones were cool beneath her bare feet. Pinpricks of a million stars lit up the night sky. The moon hung large and bright. Two large long-haired German Shepherd dogs followed her, sniffing the ground as if they were searching for a lost child.

As she continued her trek up the driveway towards her mailbox, they darted into the fields to stir up trouble. The crickets went silent, and small animals scurried, looking for shelter as Thor and his brother Attila bounded past the three apple trees and into the field.

Dressed in yoga pants and a sweater, the pale skin on the blood drinker's neck glowed in the moonlight. Her long black hair was tied up in a bun as she walked the hundred yards to the mailbox near the road. Stopping to appreciate the silence, she looked back at the two houses behind her.

The cottage and the cabin.

The cottage looked like a shadow on the hill. She hadn't left any lights on when she ventured out. The fire her youngest blood child, Nadia, had burning drifted into the night air around the cabin. This was the perfect setup for the two women.

Separate yet together.

They were free to live any way they chose, while still enjoying each other's company. Perfect.

A branch cracked near the lake and her head snapped in its direction. She smelled a deer. The scent carried on the wind, making it easier to hunt when she was feeling lazy. As a blood drinker, Gail used her property as a convenience store. Traveling to the closest decent hunting grounds was almost ten miles north or thirty miles south. The deer inhabiting her property were perfect bounty for the lazy vampire.

Hunting humans was a challenge in this century. Gail remembered it being simpler when everything wasn't recorded by surveillance cameras, or the areas weren't so populated and hiding a body was easier.

Gail reached the top of her driveway. She looked up and down the road. Traffic around Mount Orion was thankfully light at night. The area did attract tourists visiting the Lake George area during the summer months, but she was far enough off the road not to be affected by their activities. An occasional hiker cut in and out of the trees on the west side, but they didn't come close enough to the houses to matter. A hundred acres was enough for everyone to keep their distance and stay safe.

The mail was minimal, advertisements mostly. She gathered what was there, along with a copy of the *Forest Lake Echo*, and headed back down the driveway. Thor barked in the distance. As she walked, she opened the newspaper.

Forest Lake, New York was a small out-of-the-way town that she adored. Gail grew up in that town and enjoyed the connection she shared with it now. The newspaper was filled with news for the impending school year, a harvest festival scheduled for next month, and local business news.

A witch shop, Raven's Corner, took out a huge harvest sale advertisement and listed their schedule for the lunar events as well. A coupon for a *Lughnasadh* tarot reading expired at the end of the week. Beneath the word was the pronunciation: *loo-nah-sah* in parentheses. The local witch shop had always interested Gail.

Her own mother celebrated the harvest holidays. She taught Gail to bake and harvest not only food but to take stock of her emotional, physical, and spiritual well-being. They would burn candles and gather leaves and berries for the neighborhood animals. Her mother taught her to appreciate the gifts of Mother Earth and to value her own gifts because they were fleeting and could be taken from her if the gods saw fit.

Lost in the memory of her mother, a truck's horn startled her. Stopping not five feet from her driveway, its air brakes hissed. Gail looked up as the driver rolled his window down.

"Can I help you?" She felt self-conscious, as she was wearing no makeup and little else in the way of hiding her pale pallor and the iridescent sheen in her eyes. She hoped the darkness would take care of it well enough.

The driver didn't seem to notice. "Got a delivery." He reached out of the window, handing her a bill of lading.

She checked it over and pointed down the driveway. "Just put it in the driveway, near the cabin." Her finger indicated the smaller and closer of the two houses.

"Yes, ma'am." The truck groaned as it turned down the steep driveway.

Attila and Thor sped to her side. Nadia Bishop opened the front door of the cabin just as the driver exited the vehicle. The small, Hispanic man was all business.

"What's going on?" Nadia scrubbed her fingers through the hair on Thor's massive neck. She was dressed in jeans and a Def Leppard tee shirt with her long blonde hair in a tight ponytail on top of her head. Her sharp features always held a look of accusation, but when she smiled, it brightened her face—as it did now.

Her feet were bare as she ventured off the porch. The whiteness of her skin only seemed noticeable on her feet. Her face and arms were hidden with sleeves and makeup, but her feet glowed in the darkness, and Gail wished she'd put on some shoes.

Gail shrugged slightly. "We got a delivery."

"At midnight?" Her youngest blood child looked at her in disbelief. "Do you often make midnight deliveries?" she called out as the driver dropped his lift gate with a resounding clatter.

"I do what I'm told." He pressed the button on the side. He rode the platform on the rear of the truck and lifted the sliding door. "I'm told this is important enough to be delivered immediately. The bill says they paid extra for discretion and speed."

Gail looked down at the bill of lading in her hand. *"The shipper's address is American, but it's billed to a Greek address. Mr. T. Adamos,"* Gail said with her mind so only Nadia could hear her.

They shared a unique talent of telepathy that spanned their family tree. Nadia was not only Gail's youngest blood child, but she was also her great-great-great-granddaughter.

Nadia laughed. "It's from Trevor," she said aloud. "Good lord, what could be so important that he would send it in the middle of the night?"

"And pay extra to rush it."

The driver pulled the pallet jack out onto the platform, dragging a large skid that contained one large square wooden box. He deposited it in the driveway as directed.

"Just need your signature." He thrust a pen in their direction, not caring who signed. A moment later, the truck was headed back up the driveway and they were left staring at the large wooden box that both dogs found incredibly enticing.

Thor sniffed the perimeter of the box, sticking his nose deep within the corners and on the underside of it. His long tan and black coat shivered as his excitement rose. His younger brother, Attila, smaller in size and darker in coat, threw his paws on the top, using his nails to dig into the wood.

"Do you have a crowbar?" Nadia asked.

"I'm sure between the four of us, we can open it." Gail giggled. "Attila is already working on it."

She grabbed one end of the top wooden planks, and Nadia grasped the other end. The two women pried the boards loose, until they could remove the top. After throwing the ten-pound lid to the side, Attila put his paws on the side, causing it to topple away from the box.

"Thanks, buddy." Nadia kissed the top of his head. "Now, let's see what our friend Trevor found so important." She dug through the mass of packing straw to find a large cardboard box nestled in the center.

Gail sliced the box with her fingernail and pulled it open. Before she could see what they received, Thor and Attila were inside the box. All four paws and all two hundred pounds of them.

"Out!" she commanded.

Nadia laughed, showing all four of her fangs as her mouth opened wide. "I'm getting the feeling this is for them." She pushed her way past the dogs and reached into the box. "Yep, it's for them alright." She pulled out two fifty-pound bags of food, the largest box of dog biscuits she'd ever seen, and a multitude of toys. A separate box contained brushes, shampoos, and flea medicines. "Have at it, boys." She stepped out of the way to allow both dogs access to their presents.

Gail didn't like it. "Why have it delivered while we're awake?"

"So we could sign for it. Who cares? He loves these two. I'm surprised he didn't ship himself." She laughed again and then noticed Gail's growing concern. "What's the problem?"

"It puts us in danger. I've lived here for over a century, and the closest anyone has ever gotten to my front door without being invited is the mailman. I have a word or two for your friend Trevor."

Nadia smirked with a dubious eyebrow lift. "Yeah, good luck with that. Hey, I'm going into town in a bit. Would you like to join me? I could use the help with sorting all that crap in the warehouse."

"I suppose."

Nadia Bishop worked for Haven. Over the past few years, the United Council of Blood Drinkers or UCOB, as they were known, had acquired the blood drinker safe houses that had been created during the vampire wars. Not so much safe houses anymore, these were places for the vampiric community to gather and find safety when they were lost. Over the centuries, Haven collected many artifacts and histories of blood drinkers.

When Nadia accepted the position as director of the Connecticut Haven, she found the storage for these artifacts was subpar and she aimed to change it. With the permission and complete funding of the Council, she found and renovated a warehouse in Forest Lake, New York to house the complete archives of blood drinkers. She called it the Annex.

Gail pulled her Jaguar into the empty parking lot. "So, this is it?"

"This is it." Nadia jumped out of the car with a ring of keys in her hand. She pulled the seat forward to allow the dogs to get out of the car. They jumped out and sniffed the ground. "Construction and decor are done."

She unlocked the glass door in the front of the building, and they walked into a small reception area that was not unlike a dentist's office waiting room. A few chairs and a coffee table sat to the left of the door and a reception desk to the right. Behind the desk, the word HAVEN was printed on the wall.

"Check this out." Nadia flipped a switch, and a water feature activated behind the letters with a light blue tone to enhance the visual appeal.

"A little garish for Haven, isn't it?" Gail cringed at the sign. Haven had a history of living secretly in plain sight. The neon sign seemed a bit flashy for her tastes.

The dogs circled the room.

"I wanted it to look like a normal business so the local chamber of commerce wouldn't blacklist us."

"Blacklist you from what? Do you intend to allow public access? Maybe give tours?"

"No." Nadia looked at the sign and switched off the light behind it with a dejected swipe of her hand. "I thought it was pretty. Anyway, there's a conference room, so there will be no need for the Council to use Mount Orion when they come to town. Upstairs is the storage, and downstairs are the docks and some rooms just in case they start using this as a backup Haven. I don't know. Jacenta thought it was a good idea, so I went with it."

Jacenta Brodie was the founder of Haven. She started the safe houses to keep rebels hidden from Council soldiers during the wars. Nadia valued and trusted her opinion a great deal.

"We just need to organize the massive amount of stuff upstairs and then get a director." She led Gail to the elevators and waited for the doors to open. "I should tell you before you see it and freak out on me."

Gail's shoulders slumped. "What did you do now?"

Nadia grimaced at the implication that she was always messing something up. "I brought some of the stuff from the barn here."

"My stuff?" Gail's hand flew to her chest like a Victorian widow in the grip of grief.

"*Our* stuff. It's my history too, you know. You keep forgetting that your family is my family too." Her jaw clenched. "I wanted our history, as thoroughly witchy as it is, to be part of the archives."

"But these are the vampire archives, not witch archives. And we're not witches, by the way." She stared at the door of the elevator just to avoid looking at Nadia.

"Whatever. I wanted us to have a small part of the bigger picture." She stepped out of the elevator.

Boxes upon boxes of artifacts lay in different piles throughout the room. It appeared to be organized, but Gail couldn't determine what that organization was. Some books had been alphabetized on metal shelving, but that was all.

"This is our stuff. I wanted to go through it together." Nadia's voice lowered to a more intimate tone that Gail found endearing. They knelt in front of the boxes and pulled out papers, books, and photographs. "I need you to identify some of the people in the photos. I obviously know who I know, but I'm not sure what your parents looked like or even your husband and children."

"My family were not vampires. Why would you need to include them?"

"You are a blood drinker. It's your story I'm telling here."

Gail smiled. "This is Virgil Andrews, my husband." She held up a photo of a handsome man in a suit. "You know this photo. All four of my children, just before Katherine died."

Nadia held up a photo of a woman in profile. Very sepia toned, very Victorian.

"That's my mother." Gail took hold of the thick card with the photo taped on. "I never realized how much you resemble her. Except for the blonde hair and blue eyes—I have no idea where the light coloring originated. I mean, look at me." She motioned to her black locks. "But your mother was light and some of your siblings too." She shrugged as if there was no explaining the unexplainable.

"Your family bible shows your birth year, old lady," Nadia teased.

Gail sneered at her, still staring at her mother's photo.

"Look at that gleam in her eye, you've got that and the way her mouth twists even when she doesn't smile." Gail dragged her hand down the photo. "Just like you. You'd never know she was a murderer by looking at her."

"Murderer? Who'd she murder?" Nadia cried.

"My father." The words slipped out a little too easy. Had the years dulled her emotions? "I was locked in a closet and forced to listen to him die."

It was Nadia's turn to grip her pearls. "That's horrible. You had siblings, right? Where were they? Were they in the closet too?"

"Nope, just me. Simon was married by the time Daddy died, and Edith died earlier that year. She fell down a well. She was two."

"How have you never told me this before?"

"I don't really like to discuss it. I think it was Edith's death that sent my mother into a spiral." Gail wrote *Marianne Payne died 1859* on the back.

"Hang on. That said your parents' names are Richard and *Mararis* Payne. What's up with that?" She dug through the pile to find the bible she buried.

"Must be an error on the church's part. I would know my own mother's name, wouldn't I?" Gail sounded offended.

"I suppose so."

The hours slipped by as they dug through Gail's boxes and then moved on to various artworks created by blood drinkers dating back to the thirteenth century. Attila and Thor found comfortable spots on the floor and had conked out hours ago.

"Did you know there's a blood drinker living in Forest Lake?" Nadia rested her head on a box and took a break. "I've only seen her once or twice. She feels old, so I'm not in any hurry to introduce myself, but I think she's been here for about six months or so."

Gail cringed. "Does she seem dangerous?"

Nadia shrugged. "No idea. I've just seen her in town."

"What's she doing?"

"Walking by herself. I did see her looking down at the Annex, but she never approached. She did give me her name." Nadia tapped her temple.

"She knows you can read minds?"

"You know me. I reach out as soon as I see someone. She must have felt me." She winced like the mistake hurt. "Bentyn Rae. I'm going to look her up when I get a chance."

Gail's phone rang. She smiled. "It's Jordan. Hello?"

There was something uncanny about her relationship with her sire. Perhaps it was their shared gift of telepathy, but he always knew when she needed him.

"You okay?" he asked.

She thought about it. "Yes." She paused, wanting to add more but didn't.

"But—"

"Isn't it morning in Italy?" She grew concerned.

"I'm inside." He sounded unfettered by any worries of dying by the rays of the sun. "Now, tell me what's wrong."

"No, I'm just in my own head. Going through some family pictures with Nadia for the Annex. You know how I am."

"Come here. Tuscany is beautiful this time of year."

When was Tuscany not beautiful?

"I can't. I promised Nadia I'd help her here."

"Ask him about Bentyn Rae," Nadia urged.

Gail didn't want to but allowed herself to be easily swayed. "Do you know anyone named Bentyn Rae?"

A deep pause followed her words. "Why?"

"She's in Forest Lake. Nadia and I were curious about her." She paused and listened to his silence. "Why? What'd you do to her?"

Gail learned two years ago that if Jordan didn't like someone, it usually had to do with his treatment of them during the wars. He made many enemies when he ruled the United Council of Blood Drinkers.

"She did spend time in the cages if I remember correctly." He chuckled, knowing how Gail felt about his wartime exploits. "But for centuries, she hunted witches. You think the wars were horrific? Look her up in the archives database. Her murderous tactics were legendary. Trevor could tell you stories about the Blood Cults that will turn your hair white. She has some connection to the Bloody Nun too. I just can't remember how?"

Gail's mouth dropped open. "What the hell is a Bloody Nun?" She looked at Nadia and watched her jot the name down.

"Now I'm really worried about you. I want you here with me." His tone sounded like an elastic band ready to snap.

"Worry wart. I'm fine. We're both fine."

After Gail ended the call, she pulled out a flask of blood she kept in her purse for just such a stressful occasion. She took a hearty swig from it and in her clumsiness ended up spilling the rest on the floor.

"Got something to clean this up?"

Nadia took the flask from her and drank what was left. "In the utility closet, down the hall."

Gail went to the utility closet for a mop. When she opened the door, the startling image of a young girl sitting slumped on the floor overtook her. No brooms or mops, no buckets or dust cloths. The black-haired teenage girl didn't look up at her. She simply sobbed, knowing there was no one who could help her.

Gail slammed the door shut and placed a shaking hand on her heaving breast. She was no longer that teenage girl, helplessly locked in a closet listening to her mother and father die. That was 165 years ago. Her mother was long dead, and Gail had been a blood drinker for 140 of those years.

She readied herself and opened the closet once more. The brooms and mops returned. The slop bucket sat on the floor instead of her fifteen-year-old self. She grabbed the handle of the mop and dragged it to the blood spill on the floor, all along reminding herself that those demons had no power over her anymore.

Those demons were dead and buried, along with her mother.

3

RAVEN'S CORNER

Rayne Grey looked up from the books she was unboxing. It wasn't something she ever thought she'd see herself doing. Stocking shelves at a second-rate witch shop for no pay wasn't a dream, but might as well do something productive. At least that's what Malcolm Brenig kept telling her. He disappeared over an hour ago, grumbling about faulty wiring and unboxed inventory.

"Did you call her yet?" she asked Iris.

Rayne looked around the shop, Raven's Corner, with a critical eye. The shop held potential but in the twenty years it had existed in the town of Forest Lake, she hadn't seen that potential developed. What she expected was tarot readings, classes, and book signings with a small retail side business. Their online presence was minimal, and their clientele were locals who wandered into the shop rather than called in by a need for their services. In the short time she expected to be in town, she hoped to change that.

"Not yet." Iris Chauncey, the manager, placed the cash drawer into the computer that masqueraded as a cash register. The petite woman pushed back her short brown hair as she pressed a few buttons on the machine. The jingling of her bracelets and multitude of necklaces reminded Rayne of the tick-tocking of the crocodile from Peter Pan. You could hear Iris coming a mile away.

Nothing was like Rayne remembered. She hadn't worked in a retail store in almost eighty years, and cash registers had come a long way. In her own witch shop, the register was large with ornate wood details that she liked to run her fingers over during a transaction. The keys stood up off the machine and were hard to push. She remembered them jamming if she pushed too many too quickly. There were no bells and no mechanical sounds at all from these new machines. Just a large computer screen and a cash drawer that opened with little noise or prompting.

"What are you waiting for? Camilla Nolan is not just going to come walking in here on her own." She swiped her hands together, freeing them of dust. She hated manual labor.

"You'd be surprised. She's in here quite often." Iris picked up a cloth to wipe the countertops. Her sharp features pursed as she tried to keep her temper in check. "She was just in a few days ago with a list. This time of year, she's distracted with the new semester starting, new students, new curriculum. She always makes sure I have a full stock of crystals, herbs, and the like for her new students. She won't return for a few weeks. Besides, she's also probably aware that you're in town."

Rayne glanced up from the box she was digging through with an air of satisfaction. Her long black hair fell from its confines, and she swept it behind her ear. "Why should my presence keep her away?" Her sly smile gave Iris pause.

Loud music pounded from the upstairs rooms. Rayne ignored it.

"Are you kidding?" Iris laughed. "The only person Camilla hates, more than you, is Seth Dallis. She has good reason to hate him." She laughed again in a cynical way. She kept wiping the glass cases behind the register that held tarot cards.

"That fool." Rayne made a sour face. "How Penelope didn't kill him for his crimes, I have no idea."

"She wasn't in charge then." Iris dismissed her attitude. "The Phoenix led the Great Coven—and rightfully so."

"The Phoenix. There's another fool I'd like to see in a long pine box." Just saying the name felt like tasting bitter medicine and she scowled. "Penelope has three times her power."

A sarcastic laugh came from behind the curtain in the back of the shop. "Don't allow your love of your mentor to skew your judgement." Malcolm poked his head out of the curtain. "The Phoenix's abilities far exceed anyone on the Board."

The Witch Board was a council of witches that Rayne had fought her entire life to join. Only in recent years had her mentor, Penelope Press, given her an opportunity to showcase her talents in leadership. "Dark magic does not belong on the Board," she always told her. And if Rayne was known for anything in the witching community, it was her ability to wield dark magic.

Malcolm grunted as he disappeared behind the curtain. "Jesus, Iris, what are you storing in these boxes?"

"Rocks," she said simply.

She walked past Rayne towards the rear of the shop. Malcolm threw back the curtain, almost pulling it from the rod that extended the width of the shop. His eyes widened while Rayne laughed.

"Did you say rocks?"

"Yes. Well, crystals. I buy in bulk to save money."

Malcolm raised an eyebrow towards Rayne.

"Hey, don't look at me. I didn't tell her to buy five hundred pounds of crystals. How is that saving money?"

"The last time I submitted my budget to the Board, I was told that I was spending too much on inventory." Iris crossed her arms over her chest. She hated that she had to get the Witch Board's approval on her spending. "Buying in bulk is cheaper."

The music pounded louder.

"Opal," Malcolm shouted.

Rayne raised her hand to silence the music. She calmed her mind and licked her lips before speaking. "No, you were told you weren't bringing in enough on classes and readings to support your excessive inventory costs. I can't imagine how this ridiculous purchase got past the Board." She motioned to the large box at Malcolm's feet.

Iris kept the sharp retort that bristled on the tip of her tongue to herself.

Malcolm struggled with the box again.

"You can use magic to move it, you know." Rayne looked at him in disbelief. When he didn't answer, she turned her attention back to Iris. "Are you going to call Camilla today or not? If you leave it to me, I promise you, it won't be well received."

"I will. But I want to speak with her alone. You, both of you, need to find something else to do while she's here. The last thing I need is for her to get angry and call her cousin." Iris pulled a book from the shelf and flipped through it as she spoke. "The Phoenix has never been in here and I'd like to keep it that way."

"So, it is true? She lives in Forest Lake?" Malcolm asked.

"Getting nostalgic, darling?" Rayne teased him.

"How long has she been here?" He ignored Rayne.

"For almost two hundred years, she's lived in the same house. The story goes she moved here to kill someone," Iris explained.

Malcolm's eyes widened as he finally found something interesting in this dull little town. "Who'd she come to kill?"

Iris shrugged. "It's never been clear, but I do know, or I've heard, her best friend died under mysterious circumstances. Her best friend, her best friend's husband, and I believe a child died too. The child fell down a well if I'm not mistaken. I wasn't here then, obviously." She paused. "This all happened over a century ago."

"Makes you wonder what her best friend did for the Phoenix to murder her and her family." Rayne commented in an offhand-ish way, pretending that none of this mattered to her. "I must ask Penelope if she has any details."

"Maybe I'll—" Malcolm started to say.

"Don't get any bright ideas." Iris stopped him short. "You already intend to stir up a hornet's nest by calling Bentyn Rae. The last thing I need is the two of them in here messing up my business."

"Wait, who called Bentyn Rae?" Rayne pushed herself up on her knees and then onto her feet.

"I haven't yet but I want to see her." Malcolm didn't hide the truth.

"You're going to call a witch hunter and invite her here? Are you mad?" Rayne threw a book at Malcolm. He deflected it with his arm. "Why would you do that?"

"If I'm going to see Mia, I need Bentyn Rae's permission."

Rayne closed her eyes, trying to compose herself before she screamed at him. She could hear Opal's footsteps on the stairs, coming to see who turned off her music. "We should sit and talk about what we're doing, exactly."

"Not now. It's almost ten. I've got to open. Clean up those books, please." Iris straightened her shirt and ran her fingers through her short dark hair. The bangles on her wrists jingled together as she moved to unlock the front door as if there was a crowd gathering outside. She pushed open the door and the bell rang out. "Opal, please, give me a hand."

The waifish girl slalomed through the tables to reach the front of the store. The tables held candles, crystals, books, and various metaphysical adornments. She waited for Iris's direction and then assisted her in pushing library carts of discounted books onto the sidewalk in front of the shop.

"Now that you've opened, can we talk?" Rayne glared at Iris.

She nodded but remained near the front entrance. "First, Bentyn Rae is an immediate danger to us. We must address her presence in town and attempt to push her out."

"Why?" Opal Vanyo snapped her gum. "I thought she was retired," she said in a soft Russian accent. She was a young witch, still mortal despite Rayne's repeated attempts to teach her to find an immortality spell that would hold. Her slender form looked more emaciated than stylish; bones pushed against her skin like she had not eaten in weeks.

"Have you ever heard of a retired witch hunter?" Iris couldn't believe what she was hearing. "Isn't that why you want me to call Camilla? You don't want her to allow Bentyn Rae's daughter to attend her school, right?"

"Yes, exactly," Rayne agreed.

"Mia is my daughter, not Bentyn Rae's daughter." Malcolm tossed a few crystals in the air and juggled them playfully. "I need to speak with her about seeing my daughter and possibly tutoring her in magic myself. There is no need for her to learn from someone outside of the family. I believe in the old ways. Magical practices are handed down, and I would like to hand down my family's practices to my daughter."

"Your brother works at Camilla's school," Iris reminded him. "He could teach her."

"Iris, please. If you don't wish to speak with Camilla, I will. Just say the word," Rayne barked.

"It's not that. I would just prefer not to be disemboweled by a witch hunter. What's to stop Bentyn Rae from calling Asher Delger and continuing their reign of terror?" Iris held her hands out to calm herself and exhaled audibly. "The less cold bloods in this town, the better."

"That could be a problem, seeing as how they are opening a Haven down the street." Opal raised a finger in the air.

"That's not a Haven. Is it?" Rayne looked at Malcolm for an answer.

"How the hell would he know? He arrived with you all hot and bothered about his daughter being in town. I'm the one who's been here for twenty years. I'm the one who's been watching their trucks go in and out all night for weeks." Iris's brow lowered over her dark eyes. "It's a Haven. Not a traditional safe house but some kind of archives."

"I knew you had an issue with us being here." Malcolm sneered.

"I have an issue with you inviting cold bloods into my shop and potentially angering one of the most powerful witches I've ever met. That's what I have a problem with." She only glanced in Rayne's direction, knowing she was staring her down. "Look, I know you're here to see your daughter. And that's great, but please, for the love of all that's holy, do not piss off Bentyn Rae or Camilla Nolan in the process."

"I'll do my best." His eyebrows rose on his forehead. "I just need to see Mia," Malcolm defended himself.

"A foolish endeavor."

"Rayne," he warned.

She waved him away like an annoying fly. She bent to pull more books from the box on the floor. The top one was an autobiography by Penelope Press herself. Rayne opened the book to read the table of contents. Most of the chapters dealt with the fall of the Great Coven.

Elder Path Circle, also known as the Great Coven, was the beginning of the unification of witches. When it fell over a thousand years ago, it took years before another attempt could be forged. Penelope Press, a founding member of Elder Path Circle, refused to allow witches to fall victim to hunters and hysteria. She established the Witch Board only two hundred years ago. Her biography inspired the younger generation.

"Opal, please finish this." Rayne waved her hands around the books she'd been unboxing. "I've got to go inspect the expense logs. After hearing her ridiculous rationale for saving money, I need to make sure Iris is still in the black."

Iris flexed her jaw, trying not to respond with a sarcastic or caustic answer.

The next hour passed without incident. Opal not only finished the box Rayne had been working on but emptied at least three more boxes of new merchandise as well. She was a good employee. Shy and reserved, her abilities revolved around healing and reading energies. Iris was glad to have her help in the shop.

Several people came and went before lunch. Purchases were made, a tarot reading done under Rayne's watchful eye, and Malcolm entertained a few customers by juggling crystals before putting them in the tower display. Not a usual day by any means.

"You could have invited them back for a follow-up reading or perhaps offered her a discount on her next reading," Rayne huffed. "You're not doing enough to create return customers."

It was a little before noon when the bell on the door jangled. Iris looked up from Rayne's berating. As the door opened, Rayne slipped behind the curtain in the back of the shop to continue scrutinizing Iris's inventory books.

"Lilly." Her lovely, young, part-time cashier, Lilly Pershan, pushed open the door followed by three girls. "What are you doing here on your day off?" A smile stretched across Iris's face from ear to ear.

"We're going to lunch and then a movie. I just need to check my schedule."

"You could have called." Iris smiled.

"No sweat. We were in town anyway."

Her friends scattered as Lilly rushed behind the black curtain into the stockroom.

"Hello, Starr," Iris called from the register area. "How are you coming along with your dream journal?" Starr Moreau was the tallest of the four girls that entered the store. Her plain face, gangly body, and frizzy hair made her appear mousy. Iris knew her abilities, though untrained, lay in seeing futures, and she was an empath.

"I keep forgetting them. I remember feelings but not details." The girl's head hung lower than her shoulders.

"Log the feelings. Eventually you'll remember the details." Opal overheard the conversation while she stocked candles on the wall. "I used to hate journaling too, but when I went back and reread my entries, even if they were single words, I started noticing a trend or pattern in my dreams."

Having someone understand the madness in her head made Starr happy.

"Starr, this is Opal Vanyo. She will be working here for a while. She's still learning like you." Iris introduced them.

"Are you a seer too?" Starr pulled her hair out of her face.

"Nope. I'm a healer but as a fellow empath, I get the vivid dreaming. It's like other people's energy clings to me and effects my dreams."

"Yes, exactly." Starr realized her response was a bit too boisterous and cringed slightly. "How'd you know I was an empath?"

"Because I am too. Can't you feel the difference in energies?" Her bony hand moved back and forth between them to illustrate the transfer of energy.

"Starr is still in school. Learning is important at this stage," Iris added. "Speaking of, can you give Camilla a note for me?" Iris scribbled her invitation for Camilla Nolan, the headmistress of Magnolia Academy for Magical Arts, to join her for tea and handed the note card to Starr. "Keep up with the journal. As Opal said, even a word or two can spark your memory." She glanced at the other two girls circling the store. "Who are your friends?"

"Oh, sorry. This is April Crane." Starr walked to the tall blonde standing in the center near the incense display. She wore amber-colored sunglasses and didn't make direct eye contact. Iris felt something off about this girl. She couldn't tell what it could be, but this girl was different. "Her and Mia are going to school with us this semester." She pointed to the other girl in the shop.

"You can read auras?" Iris asked April.

April's eyes widened behind her amber-colored glasses. A furrow deepened between her brows as she stared at Iris.

"The glasses, my dear. Most witches who read auras distract themselves with colored lenses. It helps but it also deters what nature is telling you." Iris touched her arm. "I understand wearing them in large crowds, but take it from me, when in close knit groups, you want to know if someone is lying to you."

April slipped the glasses off her face and into her pocket.

Iris got a good look at her now. She looked like Malcolm. Same eyes and straight nose. If she had the telltale shaggy hair, she would swear this girl was a Brenig.

"That's Mia Duran, over there. She's a bit of a bookworm and currently obsessed with the Great Coven." Starr giggled as she pointed across the room.

"Look, they have Penelope Press's autobiography." April stepped closer to Mia, pulling a book from the stacks on the wall.

"What are you reading?" Iris tried to regain Mia's attention.

The dark-haired beauty held up a book on medieval witch hunting. She could see in Mia's eyes the resemblance to her biological mother, Oriana Duran.

"Not the most historically accurate retelling." Rayne came out of the back room and stood beside Mia, making her feel uncomfortable. She grabbed another book from the table. "This one will cover more ground. Going from the first mass hunts in the twelfth century up to …let's see, this was published in 2013. This should include the Saudi healer executed for witchcraft in 2011."

"They're still killing witches?" Mia took the book from Rayne and flipped through it.

"We must always stay vigilant." Rayne raised an eyebrow as she stared down at the girl. "The Board carefully watches these activities and takes those responsible to task. We will not fall victim to hunters again."

"Are you on the Witch Board?" Mia looked at Rayne with a bit of curiosity and interest in her expression.

"I am."

"You must know Penelope Press. I'm reading her book, *The Great Coven.*" She was bursting to talk about the book and tripped over her words as the information exited her mouth.

"She is my mentor. Are you enjoying the book?"

"I'm loving it. I can't believe in a few weeks I'll be taught by Camilla Nolan and Linus Brenig." Mia shivered as if a chill had touched her shoulders. "I can't wait." She bounced in place.

Rayne made sure to protect her thoughts as she stared at this young girl. If she had slipped, Mia would have seen images of Malcolm in the forefront and questions as to whether she should just introduce them right now. She chose not to mention him.

There was silence in the shop for only a moment or two, when Lilly Pershan burst back into the room. "There's a strange man in your stockroom cursing at the electrical panel."

"That's Malcolm." Iris stopped and looked at Mia and then Rayne. It hadn't occurred to her until now that *this* was Malcolm's daughter. The biological daughter of Malcolm Brenig and Oriana Duran being raised by a cold-blooded witch hunter. Iris felt a chill creep up her back as she stared at the girl.

"Are you okay?" April whispered to Iris. A change in her aura color caught April's attention. She slipped the amber lenses back on her face as she moved closer to the front door. "Come on, Mia. Let's check out the books outside."

"Yes, you girls shouldn't waste your time here with us. Go enjoy this beautiful day." Iris's mouth was dry, and she tried to calm her racing heart.

Rayne glanced at each girl. Her eyes lingered on April longer than the others. The girl felt the hard examination and stepped closer to the front door, hoping for a quick escape. She looked at Mia, who was paying more attention to the book in her hands than the awkward silence that filled the room.

"Did you say Malcolm, as in Malcolm Brenig?" Mia asked Iris. "He was in the Great Coven too. Can I meet him?"

Iris's mouth dropped open, unable to formulate an answer. Rayne looked at Lilly, urging her with a simple mental suggestion to redirect her friend's thinking.

"Let's go. I'm starving," Lilly called her friends with no hint that she was being manipulated by magic.

Mia laid the book on the table and headed for the front door.

"No, please, take it. It's a gift."

"That's not necessary." Mia was polite.

"I insist. Education is essential. As a young witch, you should be educated on the dangers surrounding you every day." Knowing who Mia's adoptive mother was, Rayne's smile had a spiteful edge to it.

"Thank you."

The girls said their goodbyes, and the door jangled as it swung shut behind them.

"Should we tell him?" Iris hissed.

"That his daughter was two steps from him and we sent her away?" Rayne's eyebrows jumped on her forehead. "Absolutely not. And unless my senses deceive me, the blonde one was his niece. Did you see the resemblance?"

"Unfortunately." Iris cringed.

"Well, Malcolm is calling Bentyn Rae tonight. If all goes well, he'll never need to know she was here." Rayne straightened the books Mia had touched.

"Did you feel something from the blonde one?" Iris asked.

"She could read auras," Opal offered.

"Not that, there was something off about her. I didn't get my usual witch vibes from her."

"That's because she's not a witch," Rayne said. "I'll ask Malcolm, but I seem to remember something strange about his brother's ex-wife."

4

CAMILLA

Camilla Nolan circled her home. Room to room, she wandered. Straightening things that were left unattended for the last month and a half, picking up clothes and running a dust cloth over woodwork and tables. She avoided resentful glances from her sister and questioning looks from everyone else.

She tried to avoid using her magic as she cleaned. The simple act of dragging a cloth over furniture, woodwork, or precious family heirlooms was cathartic. It felt like by removing the dust, she was lightening her emotional load. The load seemed heavier when she returned from her vacation. Somehow, she'd lost her ability to push past those little needle-like irritants that kept her in a constant state of anxiety.

Her silver hair was tied back in a handkerchief she'd pilfered from Starr's room. A blue and white one that kept the strands out of her eyes as she moved quickly through the house. As she tied it to her head this morning, she studied the sadness in her own face. Since she'd returned from vacation, her eyes sloped slightly, and her mouth lost its upward curve.

She'd been gone for only a month and a half. Travelling around Europe, visiting old friends and places she hadn't seen in centuries made home feel different. Not wrong, just not the same.

Maybe it was the budding relationship between Elena and Linus. It had taken root in her absence, and she didn't know how to feel about it. They tried to hide it, sneaking around, making sure Linus was safely in his own bed by daybreak. This union felt unnatural. Elena was her younger sister, and she'd known Linus for so long, he was family. The thought of it caused a knot in Camilla's stomach.

Rayne Grey appeared in town two days ago. There had existed a simmering dislike between them for centuries. Not hate, just a distrust that festered for many reasons. Not the least of them being Malcolm Brenig. She hated a lot of women because of Malcolm but could never find the heart or strength to hate Malcolm himself.

She dragged her dust cloth over the hall table, frustrated by this strangeness she felt, this uncomfortable feeling in her own home. Moving a few knickknacks and pictures to capture the unseen dust, she found a pair of tortoise shell reading glasses hidden behind a frame.

Despite her discomfort, some things hadn't changed. One of her teachers, Kim Moreau, continued to antagonize Linus. Kim, a Black woman whose weight and style gave her a matronly feel, was a healer. An amazing healer if Camilla was being honest. And if Linus had one flaw besides his Brenig stubbornness, it was his failing eyesight.

His eyes had been damaged centuries ago by frightened villagers. Years before Elder Path. Years before the Great Coven fell. They blamed him for prophecies he'd only warned them about—as if by speaking the prophecies, he brought them to fruition. They bound him and poured poison into his eyes as a warning to keep his *seeings* to himself.

Camilla smirked as she was reminded of her cousin, Micah, burning the village to the ground as punishment.

As a healer, Kim hated that Linus refused to drink the tea she swore would fix his eyesight. She continually hid his glasses around the house. She hoped to frustrate him into drinking her tea. Seeing these glasses hidden behind the picture frame told Camilla that Brenig stubbornness was holding strong.

"Good morning." Pierce shuffled by her, still in his pajamas and slippers. His black hair stood up on his head and his eyes were barely open. He was a tall, Filipino man—yes, she had to remind herself he was no longer a boy. He turned twenty-five this year.

Linus and his ex-wife had adopted him fifteen years ago when Pierce's parents abandoned him on the doorstep of the school. They could not handle his seedling magical abilities. He was a handsome young man, and if he just learned to think for himself instead of depending on those around him, he would grow to be an extraordinary witch.

She often wished her cousin, Micah, could tutor him, not Linus. Micah was firm and commanding. Being the best spellmaster she had ever known, those spells did not save him from the flames the day Elder Path Circle fell.

She missed Micah.

"Here." She handed Pierce Linus's glasses. "Give these to your father before he crucifies Kim." She stopped, taking in his attire. "Did you just wake up?"

"Yes, ma'am." His eyes dropped away.

Camilla shook her head, still looking at him as a ten-year-old boy. "There's a package for you downstairs."

His eyes lit up and with a bashful smile, he thanked her.

For the last six years, a package arrived for Pierce every week. Occasionally, twice a week. The contents varied. Sometimes it was cookies, sometimes clothes, sometimes books, or supplies for school. Every box or package came with a letter containing money or gift cards. No one spoke of these mysterious packages or the equally mysterious benefactor, but they knew who sent them and why.

She let him pass. He disappeared into the bathroom as she continued to drag her dust cloth along the railing for the stairs. Her sister hummed somewhere in the house. Elena was up to something. She knew her sister enough to just hear it in her hum.

Camilla Nolan had given up watching her sister in the last few years. Given up worrying that she would do something dangerous or rash that would put them all in danger.

It's what Elena did, cause trouble. As witches, Camilla's abilities far exceeded her sister's, and Elena resented her for it. In the last eighteen or nineteen years, Elena tried to do better. But there was something in that hum that told her different. Camilla prepared herself for the worst.

An hour later, Camilla sat at her desk, scrolling through her phone, looking at pictures of her recent trip to Europe. A good portion of that trip she spent visiting friends in England and France, but her main reason for traveling brought her to the remains of a small area known over a thousand years ago as Elder Path. She and her family had settled there hoping to escape the persecution they encountered when they moved from their homeland near Mount Pelion in Greece. She still remembered the trek north as her family travelled hundreds of miles to avoid certain death.

It wasn't easy and she searched alone, but what she found was farmland on the site she called home. Where eight witches came together, embraced by the locals for their protection, to form the Elder Path Circle. Where her cousin and friends were burned to death for being witches. Where her husband betrayed the coven and led a cold blood to destroy the town and kill the villagers. Where she lost her baby daughter because her body was too frail to survive in this horrible world.

Camilla stared at pictures of rolling green fields and elderberry trees surrounding the land. Tears rolled down her cheeks as she swiped at the screen.

"Have you seen my glasses?" Linus Brenig entered the room. He searched the desk and beneath the stack of papers on the end table. His dark, curly hair held the telltale Brenig shagginess that she'd loved in his brother and adored in him.

"Kim probably took them again," she said without looking up from her phone. She carefully wiped away her tears so he wouldn't see.

"I'm trying to finalize the fall roster," he said. "Kim." He kept searching and waiting for her response at the same time. "What are you looking at that's got you so emotional?"

Camilla shook her head. "Nothing." She shut her phone off.

"Let me see. It's obviously something." He grabbed her phone. Pushing it away from his face with a futile hope that his eyes would focus on their own, his frustration grew. "Kim!"

"You bellowed?" Kim appeared in the living room.

"Did you take my glasses?" He stared at her with an unwavering gaze.

"Again," Camilla added in jest.

Kim reached into her deep pockets and pulled out a pair of wire-rimmed bifocals. "You wouldn't need to waste time searching for these if you'd just let me—"

"It doesn't work. There's too much damage. Just let me have this one weakness. I can't be strong twenty-four seven." An expression of despair crossed his face for only a moment before he caught himself and let it slip away. He pushed the glasses on his nose and looked down at Camilla's phone.

"Maybe you shouldn't look at that now," she said as Kim slipped out of the room to prepare lunch.

His thumb scrolled over the photos. "Elder Path," he whispered.

"Not anymore. I felt it but there's nothing to see." She gave him a pained smile, trying not to cry again.

"You could have warned me."

"You grabbed it out of my hands."

He took one more look at the remains of what used to be their lives and placed her phone down. "Well, since you're in such a great mood already. You might as well take a look at the fall roster."

She grabbed the packet of papers he thrust in her direction. "Why is Pierce on the list? I thought he would apprentice for you this semester?" Camilla started reading the list.

"We spoke about it, and he would feel more comfortable as a student who *helps*." Linus air quoted the last word. "He won't feel so much like a teacher's pet that way."

"No." Camilla reached for her red pen and scratched out Pierce's name. "He will apprentice. The girls will respect him if he commands it. Otherwise, he's wasting our time and his. And no babying him this year. He is old enough to handle these girls on his own." Her brown eyes glanced up at Linus as he agreed with a sharp, compliant nod.

There were five other names. Three of the students listed had been a part of the Magnolia Academy for Magical Arts for almost three years. All girls. Lilly Pershan, Starr Moreau, and Veda Kaur. All former students at the local high school. This would be the first semester in years that they had a course load with full-time students.

"Where's Betty Saris?"

"She hasn't confirmed yet. She's still in high school. Even if she attends this semester, it will only be part time."

"Call her mother. Confirmation should have happened weeks ago." Camilla dragged her pen to the end of the list. The last two names were new students.

April Crane. Mia Duran.

"No." She swiped her pen and Linus snatched it away.

"Too late. Both have been accepted." He tapped the pen on his palm as he stared at her defiantly.

"By whom?" Her brows lowered and then jumped on her forehead.

"April was approved by me, seconded by Pierce." He stared at her over his lowered glasses, daring her to object. "And Mia Duran was approved by Elena, seconded by me."

Camilla sat back in her chair with a huff. "I should have known. I felt something was off today." Her hands clawed, trying desperately to find something to grab on to but finding nothing but air. "Elena," she called.

It took a few minutes before her younger sister entered the room. She whispered to a small spider plant as she arrived. Elena was a lovely woman with dark brown hair that wisped around her face and shoulders. Her features, while severe when she was angry, softened easily with a simple smile. Her smile now told Camilla she knew why she was being called.

"Problem?" She placed the potted plant on the edge of Camilla's desk and straightened her pencil skirt with a quick jerk of her hands.

"What are you doing?"

"Fixing up the girls' rooms. Plants always bring such a homey feel, don't you think?" She caressed the leaves of the plant as she spoke.

"I suppose. Linus tells me you approved a new student without my permission." Camilla cradled her head with her thumb and forefinger, waiting for her sister's answer. "What made you think you had the authority—"

"Authority?" Elena held back a laugh. "I didn't realize this was a police state. Is that what you learned spending your summer in Poland?"

"You still haven't gotten over that I didn't take you, have you?" She clenched her jaw. "Regardless, I approve all new students. Period."

Elena looked at Linus with a conspiratorial laugh. "Can you believe her?"

He looked away, never wanting to take sides with the sisters.

"I've been doing it for over a century. What would make you think anything changed this year?"

"Because you up and left."

"I went on vacation. People do that. It's not unheard of."

"People do, but you don't. You haven't taken a vacation in…forever."

"Exactly. I was overdue. And it doesn't mean you can change our system while I was gone." She watched Elena fight through every possible retort or argument that bristled within her soul and successfully kept from exiting her mouth. "And Mia Duran? Really?"

"Linus can approve his daughter, but I can't?"

"Linus and I will discuss that too." Camilla looked at Linus as he actively looked away. "But Mia's not your daughter."

"Close enough."

"No, not close enough. She couldn't be further away. In fact, her mother is a cold blood. Did you forget that fact? Bentyn Rae is her mother now. A cold blood and a witch hunter."

"Exactly the reason we need to teach Mia how to control her natural born abilities. She should have come to us when Oriana died." Elena splayed her hands out to her sides. "With a cold blood for a mother, how is she ever going to grow into a proper witch? A witch Oriana would be proud of."

Camilla closed her eyes tight for a second. She did a round of square breathing and then said, "Oriana is dead. Let's just remember that too."

Oriana Duran was a witch with little to no power of her own, who enjoyed murdering and stealing the power of others. How Elena could love and defend such a person, Camilla could not understand.

"You love reminding me of that, don't you?" Elena's chin dimpled as she held back emotion. "I approved Mia's admission. I am still part of this school, aren't I?"

"Have you met with Bentyn Rae to get her permission for Mia to attend in September?"

Elena folded her hands together. "I left her a phone message an hour ago. If she doesn't cancel, you have a meeting with her tonight at eight."

"Terrific." She clenched her teeth as she concentrated on her breathing again. "Take your plant and get out of my sight. I need to yell at Linus now."

"Good luck," she sang as she left the room with her spider plant in tow. He swatted her behind as she left.

"April's in. No matter what you say." Linus stroked his beard as he spoke. "I want her here, and it's time that she and Pierce spent time together again."

He was a handsome man with dark curly hair that always looked in need of a combing. When not teaching, he wore nothing but jeans and a tee shirt or sweatshirt, depending on the weather. But standing in front of a class brought out the sophisticated side of him with khakis and button downs or a smart jacket with leather elbow patches. Camilla liked him better like this.

"Have you spoken to her mother yet or do I have another meeting I don't wish to attend?"

"She'll be here in fifteen minutes." He laughed. "I'm kidding." He held out his hands as Camilla slammed her fists onto the desk. "I'll speak with her."

She assessed him with the scrutinizing gaze of a detective. "Does April know that you are her father or is that to be a surprise for her first day of school?"

"Not yet. Dyre built walls and wiped both of my girls' memories of me and Pierce." His eyes dropped, dejected.

"Wiped or just blocked their memories?"

"Does it matter?"

Camilla was amazed at his naivety. "Do you really think Dyre Crane will allow her daughter to attend this school with my sister teaching? Did you lose your mind while I was away or are you thinking with another body part?"

"From what Starr tells me, April doesn't understand her abilities. She needs to learn. You know she does, and if Dyre is not willing to teach her, then I am." He crossed his arms over his broad chest.

"April's memories of you are one thing, and I fully support your need to be with your daughters…"

"Pierce needs them too. Dyre thinks some care packages are going to make up for abandoning him." His voice rose and he paused to calm himself.

"I understand and sympathize, but what Elena and Oriana did to Dyre's sisters is something you can't ignore. Whether it's been sixteen years since Oriana Duran was murdered or not, Dyre's memory is long, and her hatred of Elena is not unfounded."

"I know. I'll cross that bridge when I come to it."

"One more thing, tuition. Are you covering the cost, or should I draw up the papers for Dyre?"

Linus left the room, still looking flustered and unwilling to answer.

Camilla looked at her watch. Only seven more hours until she would sit face-to-face with one of the most prolific witch hunters in history and a cold blood to boot. She couldn't imagine how this night would end.

Promptly at eight, the doorbell rang. Camilla had sent everyone out of the house. When Linus objected, she pushed them out the door. She didn't wish to put anyone in danger.

Although she knew exactly who or what stood on her doorstep, she pulled the drapes back to get a preemptive look at her guest. Bentyn Rae stood at the edge of the porch, just inches from slipping down onto the step. Her long, voluminous, dark hair billowed around her shoulders, making her pale complexion almost ethereal in comparison.

Her witch hunting skills were so refined she didn't even know she was using them. She looked around for possible threats and she lifted her chin to sniff the air for approaching dangers. Her hand rested securely on a dagger in her waistband.

Camilla opened the front door with caution. She peeked out before swinging it wide. The women examined one another. "Bentyn Rae." It was more of a recognition rather than a question.

"Beni will do just fine," she said.

They stood roughly the same height, though Beni was a smidge taller. Her slender frame made her appear taller than Camilla from a distance. The black leather outfit also allowed her the benefit of stealth and intimidation. Otherwise, her face was lovely, and the iridescent sheen in her eyes was not unpleasant to gaze upon.

"You won't need that." Camilla motioned to the dagger.

Bentyn Rae looked down at her belt. "Old habits," she said, as if she didn't remember it was there.

"We can talk out here or you may come in and sit down. Whichever you prefer." Camilla stepped back from the door to allow the tall blood drinker access to her home.

Beni walked into the sitting room and then turned to face Camilla. As she passed, the magnetic force that was common among blood drinkers threatened to pull Camilla in until she stepped back.

She remembered the pull from the last time she spoke with her ex-husband, Seth Dallis. Standing in their home, tears streaming down her face, he moved in to comfort her and she found she had no will of her own as he came closer. That pull yanked her in, wrapped its invisible arms around her body, and kept her securely in place if he decided to kill her. She hated it then and she hated it now.

"We do need to set a few ground rules. First, no killing. I brought you here to talk and possibly sign papers. That's all. I have no intention of harming you for past behaviors or crimes."

"Okay." Her voice held a pleasing, feminine lilt that Camilla didn't expect even if it was shaded with sarcasm. Perhaps the image of a witch hunter came with a certain gruffness that extended to her vocal cords. "And I hope you understand that despite my attire and accidental arsenal, my witch hunting days are over." Her right eyebrow shot up as she waited for Camilla to challenge her. She pulled the dagger from her belt and laid it on the table beside the door.

Camilla nodded and slipped the knife into the drawer.

"Shall we sit?"

They crossed the room to the chairs and sat awkwardly facing each other.

"I wish I could offer you a drink…"

Beni raised her hand to indicate the offer was unnecessary.

"Let's get down to business. I'm sure Mia told you that we offered her a place this semester. It is customary for us to meet the parents and get their permission and assurance that they will foster a positive attitude towards their child's studies. I don't wish to be crass, but your history poses a unique set of issues." She studied Beni for a moment. Camilla attempted to read her mind. It was filled with possible excuses to get her out of this house. "Do you wish for Mia to attend our school in September?"

Beni didn't respond right away.

"I understand if…" Camilla searched for an easy way out for Beni.

"No," she spoke up. "She's eighteen in two months. This is just a formality. She doesn't really need my permission, does she?"

"Well, no, not really, but we do wish for you to accept this. We find parents that don't accept their child's natural abilities for magic tend to either deter them or discourage them."

"I fully accept Mia's natural abilities. Believe me. The fire department accepts them too."

Camilla's eyebrows shot up her forehead. "She's elemental?"

"Didn't she tell you?"

"The fire on Foxhill Drive?" Camilla and Beni shared a knowing look. "I was in Europe when it happened. Unfortunately, I did learn about it from other witches."

"You did?" Beni looked stunned.

"It caused only a minor stir," she assured her. "Unnatural energy of any sort will draw the attention of the Board. I suspect that's the reason Rayne Grey is in town."

Beni shifted uncomfortably in her seat, itching to leave.

Camilla studied her reaction and then noted the fire element in Mia's folder.

"Are there any other abilities, to your knowledge, that I should note?"

Beni licked her lips, taking a moment to think. "Mind reading, the fire thing, and she is intuitive."

"How so?"

"I don't know. She just knows things."

Camilla considered this with mild interest. "Could be that she's reading your thoughts without you knowing it or even without her knowing she's doing it."

"Perhaps." Beni cleared her throat. "I do have one question." She stood and walked to the fireplace on the other side of the room. Her long, slender, white fingers grasped the stone mantel. "Is it possible for you to foster Mia's natural abilities, keep her from burning the world down, controlling her need to read everyone's minds…"

Camilla chuckled.

"Without using witch paraphernalia?"

"Do you consider candles paraphernalia? What about crystals or herbs?"

Beni spun around and stared at her. "Not necessarily. But I draw the line at tarot cards, runes, pentacles or anything not natural in this world."

"Interesting." Camilla rubbed her chin with her thumb and forefinger. Bentyn Rae's hatred came from witches who didn't seem natural to her. Using *paraphernalia* was unnatural. Camilla had never considered this as a reason why she or anyone hated witches. "I'm sure an accommodation could be made."

"Fine."

"So, if you are okay with Mia's entry into our novice program, I need your signature on a few forms."

They sped through the paperwork. Beni signed where Camilla told her and handed her a check when tuition was mentioned.

"This is the curriculum and supplies that she'll need. Most are provided. Anything else can be obtained now and throughout the year at Raven's Corner. I'm sure you know of it, and I have no doubt that Mia has also visited with the other girls." She cleared her throat as Beni stared at her. "Is Mia aware of your…past?" She skirted the actual words.

"Does it matter?"

"In this case, yes. Your name is a big part of our history. I would hate for Mia to find out that her mother is a witch hunter in front of a classroom full of judgemental girls."

Beni rose to leave. "I'll handle it."

"If I may take one more moment of your time. Please sit down." Camilla held her hand out to the seat Beni had just vacated. "I feel I need to mention the elephant in the room. Oriana Duran is Mia's mother." She watched as Beni's expression tensed and her eyes hardened. Her jaw clenched but she said nothing. "My sister Elena will be teaching Mia and has already expressed an interest in helping Mia become the witch Oriana would be proud of."

"I would appreciate if that was a name not included in the curriculum." Beni glared at her for an uncomfortably long time. "Mia has shown interest in her birth parents more recently than when she was a child. Leave the life lessons to me and stick to doing what you do best." Beni looked at her from under a lowered brow.

Camilla offered a weak smile. "I want to assure you that she will in no way overstep your parental boundaries. The other teachers, Linus Brenig and Kim Moreau, are abreast of the possible issues, and we will guarantee that Elena does nothing that will jeopardize Mia's education or mental well-being."

Beni nodded, stiffly.

The front door swung open to laughter. Three girls came into the room. Lilly Pershan, Starr Moreau, and Mia Duran. Mia had a package in her hand.

"Mom?" Mia was the last to enter. "What are you doing here?"

Beni and Camilla stood as the girls entered. "Signing the papers for your education." The bit of bitterness in her words did not go unnoticed. "What's that?"

"Oh, it was on the front doorstep. It's for Pierce Brenig." She looked at Camilla and smiled.

"What are you doing here? I thought you were having lunch and going to a movie? It's after eight." Beni watched Mia hand the package to Camilla with undisguised awe in her expression.

"We went to Aunt Dyre's after the movie." She bit her lip in an apologetic manner. "I'm headed home now. Sorry, I forgot to text you."

Camilla's ears perked up with the mention of Dyre Crane and looked down at the package, knowing that's who sent it.

"I'll go with you." Beni turned and held her cool, white hand out for Camilla to shake. Their eyes met in challenge, both daring the other to go back on their word. "Thank you."

When the front door closed behind Bentyn Rae and her daughter, Camilla relaxed. Starr handed her a note. "Iris wanted me to give you this." She gave Starr the package to pass along to Pierce. "Can Lilly sleep over tonight?"

"Of course."

Both girls headed up the stairs, giggling as they went.

Camilla opened the note.

Camilla, I would like to talk to you. Please call me, so we can set up a time to meet. Best, Iris.

She frowned and thought, *What now?*

5

BENI

Mia slumped in the passenger seat, waiting for the barrage of hate that inevitably came with her mother spending any extended time with witches. She waited to hear about Camilla Nolan reading her thoughts or, god forbid, if Camilla commented on her sordid past and how it conflicted with the school's mission.

She didn't mean to, but her mom made her feel wrong. Wrong to be a witch, wrong to need to control her abilities, and really wrong to want to be a part of that community.

Mia's phone pinged. She read the text with concern laced with humor.

"Aunt Dyre changed her mind about school again."

Beni smirked without taking her eyes off the road. "Big surprise."

"Think she's serious this time?"

Beni thought before answering. "Maybe I should reconsider too."

"Can't." Mia jumped in her seat. "You already paid for the first semester."

"So, I lose twenty-five grand. It's better than losing you." Her grip tightened on the steering wheel.

Mia's eyes widened. "It's 50K for the year?" She chose to ignore her mother's emotional statement.

"Not including supplies or the brainwashing."

"Can you be a little supportive? Please?" Mia huffed. "I need this. My birth parents were witches. You knew that when you adopted me. You knew you'd have no way to help me learn. This will help me. Can you drop the little passive aggressive comments and have a decent conversation about this with me?"

Beni's knuckles turned white as she gripped the wheel like a vice. "I know what you are. I knew what they were." She could feel her stomach sour just talking about this subject. "And I know you don't like to discuss this, but you know what I am and what I used to do. I can't just forget a career I had for centuries. I'm sorry."

"Yeah, me too. I'm sorry I ever read that book on the history of witch hunting." Mia slid down in her seat, hoping to disappear.

The front windshield started to fog over as if the heat was blasting from the vents.

"Hey, quit it." Beni slapped her arm. She ran the wipers, hoping to clear the windshield, but it wasn't working. Her daughter was causing this, and she needed it to stop before she caused the car to catch fire. "I'm sorry, okay. I'm sorry for what I've done. I'm sorry for how I feel." She pulled over to the side of the road. "Look at me."

Mia reluctantly looked up at her mother from where she sat.

"I love you. Not because you're a witch. Not because of anything you do but because of who you are."

"Who am I?" Her eyes filled with water.

"My daughter. I accept you're a witch just like you accept that I'm a blood drinker. Do you hate me because I may or may not have killed lots of people?"

Mia laughed through her tears. "I guess not."

"And I don't hate you for anything you may or may not do with magic in the future." Beni chuckled. "I can't stop feeling uncomfortable around witches." She chose her words carefully. "But I promise you, I will not knowingly kill another witch ever."

"I guess that's the best I can hope for. Thanks, Mom." She kissed Beni's cheek, feeling the heat from a recent kill. Even though it kind of repulsed her, the warmth was better than the cold.

As they started driving again, Beni's phone pinged. She grabbed for it.

"Hey, eyes on the road, Missy." Mia mocked something her aunt always said. She took the phone. "Unknown number."

"Any message?"

"Just a name. Do you know Malcolm Brenig?"

"Why?" Beni's eyes widened in surprise.

Mia held out the phone for her to see the message. "He was in the Great Coven. I think he's working at Raven's Corner."

"Please don't tell me you went into that witch store."

"Just for a second…" The phone pinged again. "He wants to meet with you."

"What?"

Her mother pulled over to the side of the road. When Mia looked up from the phone, she noticed they were on Main Street, just before it turned onto Crow Court. Close to home.

"Why does a witch want to meet with you?"

"Here. Drive. I need to—" Beni reached for her phone as she switched seats with her daughter.

"You want me to drive?" Mia laughed.

That was unheard of. Beni was the driver. No one else drove if Beni was in the car. Period. Even when Mia learned to drive, it was Aunt Dyre who taught her. And that was an experience all by itself. Trying to get Aunt Dyre to allow her to make mistakes without autocorrecting her was impossible. If Mia was about to hit something, she would redirect the car or make the object disappear.

Aunt Dyre was a goddess.

Even thinking the word seemed strange. Goddess. The word was as fake sounding as *witch* or *spell*. When normal people heard those words, they laughed. They smirked or rolled their eyes as if they'd heard the most ridiculous notion of their lives. But it was true.

Dyre Crane, her mother's best friend, was a goddess. No one came right out and said it. It was never a conversation over Thanksgiving dinner. Aunt Dyre never walked around declaring how she missed visiting Mount Olympus or was fathered by Zeus. Mythology wasn't real in their world.

From bits and pieces Mia could put together from either walking in on a conversation between her mom and aunt or just from her mother's thoughts, Aunt Dyre was a goddess that had been cast out and forbidden to use her powers, although she often did. Mia always assumed she was forbidden to use her powers to change destinies or anything that would have a huge effect on mankind.

"Who are you texting?" Mia asked her mother as she turned onto Foxhill Drive.

Beni's phone pinged and she growled as she read the message. "Nobody."

"Are you texting Malcolm Brenig? Can I meet him?"

"Not now," her mother barked.

Her mother had spent a good part of her immortal life as a witch hunter. Mia couldn't fathom what that entailed. Did she burn innocent women at the stake because they were healers? Did she shame outcasts into admitting that they did the devil's bidding? What was her stance on the devil's mark? Why did she hate witches so much? What did they ever do to her?

These were questions Mia would never get answers to. Beni hated talking about her past. The closest thing to answers Mia ever got was from Beni's own diary. Tucked into the lining of an old steamer trunk in the attic—the attic that was "off-limits, no exceptions"—Mia found her mother's diary.

Written in her beautiful flourish-y handwriting, the diary recounted stories from something called *the tribes*, and she spoke in detail about her witch hunting days. Her feelings about why these people deserved to die, or rather, why someone named Asher Delger convinced her that they deserved to die.

From the stories, Mia got the feeling that if it weren't for him, Beni would never have killed anyone, except to eat. Whoever Asher Delger was to her mom, he had a hold over her that bordered on abusive.

Again, Beni never spoke of him, so Mia never knew if she was misreading her take on Asher Delger or not.

They entered the house in silence. Beni was still going back and forth with the mysterious texter. She walked into the house and disappeared into the basement in the same silence they'd shared on the drive home.

Mia grabbed her book on the Great Coven and sat on the sofa. She skimmed the first chapters for the name, Malcolm Brenig. He was mentioned as a founding member of the Elder Path Circle. The author spoke of him fondly as she detailed his physical description and his magical abilities, especially his ability to collect magic or redirect it.

"I've got to go out." Her mother appeared in the room, startling her. "Do you want to stay here, or should I drop you at Aunt Dyre's?"

"I'll stay here." Mia studied her mother, trying to read her thoughts. She was trying hard to block her and doing it admirably well. "Where are you going?"

Beni's eyebrows bounced. She felt her daughter rooting around in her mind, and she was proud of herself for successfully blocking her. "Just out. You know, doing stuff you don't particularly like to hear about."

Mia stuck her tongue out in disgust. She knew her mother was talking about hunting for blood.

"Be back soon." Beni blew her a kiss, and Mia went back to reading her book.

Beni ventured into the wooded areas that surrounded Forest Lake. Even if she didn't need the blood as often as she used to, she always enjoyed the hunt. It was the reason she'd kept up her part witch hunting. Killing witches wasn't always the fun part. For her partner, Asher Delger, it was, but for Beni, it was the hunt.

They'd hide and she'd seek. They'd use their magic to elude her, and she'd find them anyway. She got chills now just thinking about it. Killing them was just necessary. Hunting them was fun.

Beni stopped, sniffing the air. Her head lifted as she inhaled. Her dark eyes searched the darkness. It was a very canine characteristic. Most blood drinkers didn't use their sense of smell to hunt. Hearing was a big part of a blood drinker's abilities. Hearing a heartbeat from yards away. Hearing movement no matter how small.

She could smell pheromones, adrenaline, and any metabolic changes in a mortal creature. She could smell blood just as a shark can smell blood in the water. Using smell to flush out prey was a basic animal attribute that seemed to fade as blood drinkers became more domesticated.

Beni stepped off the path and into the brush. When she reappeared, her face was covered in blood, and she was breathing deeply. She wiped her mouth with the sleeve of her black shirt. With a deep, cleansing breath, she seemed to allow the blood to overtake her senses for a moment. Her eyes rolled back in her head, and she rolled her neck. When her eyes opened, a line of blood circled her iris until she blinked it away.

As she retook control of her senses and brushed away any leaves or deer hair from her black clothing, she stepped back into the bushes to take a final look at the large buck lying on the forest floor.

It was torn open from neck to stomach. Its face still held a surprised expression that appeared when Beni's capable hands twisted its head 180 degrees. Its eyes were black and lifeless like a deer head mounted on a wall. It had at least eight points on its antlers and had just begun to shed the velvet coating that covered them. Pieces peeled away where the deer had already started scraping it off.

She walked past the deer to the stream. Bending to the water, she cupped it in her hands, splashing her face until it was clean of any traces of blood. The cool water refreshed her as she prepared herself for what she needed to do next.

As Beni reached Main Street, her pace slowed. It was getting close to ten o'clock, and the only people around were closing their shops and heading home. The streetlights glowed, drawing moths to its light. The winged creatures darted in and out of the light like flecks of dust.

She looked down at the warehouse at the end of Perry Lane. Beni's nose wrinkled as she privately sneered at the building. Two cars sat in front of the building, and the lights were aglow in the reception area. She could see someone tapping away at a computer below the large sign reading *Haven*.

Beni didn't have anything against Haven itself. She remembered the safe houses from the old wartime days. She remembered the need to protect those hiding from the Council, hiding from death. Just thinking about the wars sent a chill up her spine and she shook it off.

She turned from where she stood to face three small storefronts. Haven was at the bottom of a driveway just off Perry Lane. On Perry Lane, there were three stores.

A vacuum repair shop, a witch shop, and a florist.

The witch shop was Beni's real destination tonight. The sign on the door of Raven's Corner was turned to CLOSED, and the light in the front window was out, but there were lights on inside the shop.

She pulled out her phone and typed, *"I'm here."*

The communication she'd received from Malcolm Brenig was a request to meet with him regarding Mia. She'd known for years that Malcolm was Mia's biological father. He had never tried to contact her before and it worried her now, after eighteen years, what he really wanted.

She pulled on the handle of the glass door and found it unlocked even though the store had been closed for two hours. The bells above her jingled, alerting those inside to her entry.

"I'm sorry, we're closed—" A short, attractive brunette popped her head out from behind a black bejeweled curtain. "Oh, it's you," she said with derision. She disappeared behind the curtain.

Beni wrinkled her nose at the overwhelming stench of scented candles. Her fingers fiddled with the table coverings and the small trinkets that littered them. Her eyes took in all exits or entry points. It was then she remembered the dagger she'd left at Camilla Nolan's house.

"Damn it," she whispered, raising her hands like someone was frisking her.

"Problem?"

Beni turned from where she stood to see a woman with long dark hair, a sarcastic smirk, and a knowing expression staring at her.

"Nothing." She stood up straight and threw her shoulders back. "Is Malcolm around?"

"He'll be out shortly." Without moving from her spot across the room, Rayne took in every inch of Beni. There was a hatred that burned in her eyes. A hatred so seething that Beni found herself second-guessing her choice to come here tonight. "You're Bentyn Rae."

Beni prepared herself for a possible attack. With no weapon, she searched the area surrounding her for something to grab. Something to defend herself, should it come to that.

"You are?"

The woman seemed surprised by the question. "Did I not make your list?"

Beni closed her eyes. Her jaw tensed and she took several deep breaths. "Enough with the games and just tell me your name."

The dark-haired woman laughed. "Rayne Grey."

The name tripped Beni's heart. She remembered searching for Rayne Grey two hundred years ago. Asher was obsessed with dark witches and according to him, Rayne Grey was the queen of them all.

A smile lit up Rayne's face, but the hatred kept its place. "He was right."

The black curtain in the rear of the shop shifted as Malcolm Brenig pushed it out of his way. The woman who rudely greeted her stood beside him. Her jewelry jangled like the bells on the shop door.

"Bentyn Rae." He smiled. "Thank you for coming."

Malcolm Brenig was a handsome man. Even if Beni didn't wish to admit it aloud, she couldn't deny it. He was part of the reason that Mia was a knockout. Oriana did have some DNA to contribute to soften Malcolm's hard features, but Mia bore a strong resemblance to her father. His light brown hair was a lot lighter than Mia's, but his eyes were the same chocolate brown. He had that telltale messy Brenig hair that she remembered from knowing Linus years ago. His expression was welcoming and warm with an apprehension that she recognized in Mia when she was unsure of herself. He gave off an air of calm that seemed to lull her into a false sense of security.

Her eyes darted to Rayne and then back to him. He understood.

"Rayne. Iris. Will you excuse us, please?"

"We're not leaving you here with a cold blood," Iris whined.

"Being a cold blood is the least of the atrocities she's committed." Rayne glared at her.

Beni cleared her throat in a loud manner that was a nonverbal version of *shut up.*

"I'll be fine," he assured them. He didn't give them much room to argue.

"Malcolm," she started when the room cleared.

"Let's sit down." His tone was friendly and for some reason put her on guard.

He led her to the corner of the shop behind the cash register where two folding chairs were set up and waiting for them.

"I hope you didn't go to any trouble." Her tone dripped with disdain.

Again, he laughed. It sounded like a joyful laugh and, unfortunately, a lot like the way Mia laughed. The sound of it soured her stomach.

"I want to see Mia." He got right to the point.

She knew this was the inevitable request when he called earlier. The thought circled around and around in her mind and heart. There was no way to say no without hurting Mia. It wasn't her fault that her biological mother was murdered and her father was a no-show for the last eighteen years.

"No." Beni tried it anyway.

"She is *my* daughter."

"She's mine, too."

"Only because—"

"Because you didn't step up to take her?" She threw his deadbeat dad ways at him.

Her words hurt him, and it showed on his face. It felt like she was hurting Mia too.

"How could I step up? Oriana was murdered." There was a pause that was full of accusation. "Then you take my daughter to places unknown."

Beni laughed.

"What's so funny?"

"Places unknown," she mocked him. "I took her because a sensible person doesn't leave a screaming child alone with a corpse."

"Whose fault was that?"

"Careful. You are speaking of things you know nothing about," she warned him.

"Enlighten me, Bentyn. If you didn't kill Oriana, who did?" He sat back and crossed his arms over his chest.

"Something large and hairy, I suspect." Her eyes met his and she didn't look away.

"A shifter?" He didn't believe it. "Why would a shifter kill Oriana and leave Mia untouched?"

She shook her head sympathetically. "Oriana made a lot of enemies. Any one of them could have put a hit out on her. We were hired to kill her, but someone beat us to it. Mia was screaming in her crib. I could have let Asher kill her like he wanted but I didn't."

"Now that you mention it, why didn't you? Why allow another witch to grow up in this world?" Those gentle chocolate brown eyes were full of accusation and hurt.

"I don't know. Part of me wanted to piss off Asher. Part of me wanted to give Dyre Crane the vengeance her family deserved. I'd let her kill Oriana's offspring." She stopped just short of admitting to him that she really took Mia because she was lonely, and having a child was something she'd never have in her life. An opportunity fell in her lap that she couldn't ignore.

His jaw tensed, and she watched his muscles pulse as he considered his options. A vein throbbed on his temple, and she felt a pang of hunger. "I don't care why you did it. I want to see Mia. I have a right to see her."

Beni thought about it. She could think of no way around it. She nodded. "Yes, you do, but…"

"But what?"

She searched her mind for the weakest of reasons. "I just signed her up for school." Saying the word *school* in reference to Magnolia Academy sickened her. "She's over the moon about being taught by Camilla Nolan." She noticed his interest and continued. "She bought this book on the Great Coven—"

"Penelope's book."

"Yes. She's read it cover to cover at least twice. She can't wait to learn from Camilla Nolan and Linus."

A look of pride lit up his face. "What better time for her to meet me?"

"She did ask about you tonight when your name popped up on my phone." She rolled her eyes. "I don't want you to distract her from school. I don't want her to be overwhelmed. She's dealing with issues."

"What kind of issues?" A look of paternal concern crossed his face that was endearing.

"She sets things on fire."

He laughed aloud at this, even jumped up and clapped his hands.

"What's wrong?" Iris sounded frazzled as she yanked back the black curtain.

"She's elemental. My daughter is elemental." Malcolm banged on the counter until Iris insisted that he stop.

"I thought I sensed something this afternoon," Iris slipped up.

"Wait, Mia was here this afternoon?" Malcolm's eyes widened with rage. "And you didn't tell me?"

"I'm sorry." Her words were barely audible.

Malcolm shook his head in an annoyed manner. His face reddened for only a moment and went right back to gushing about Mia. "Fire? Where did she get a fire element? My family's element is water, mostly. Linus and I got nothing." He laughed again; pride beamed from him. He banged his hands on the cash wrap.

Rayne Grey crossed her arms, watching his childish display. Iris was too worried about her countertops to show anything besides distress.

"I must see her now. I know you hate Camilla's school, and I do as well. Do you want her to be taught by Elena Nolan? Let me teach her." His face glowed as he thought of the prospects of tutoring his daughter in magic. "Fire. I cannot believe she's a firestarter. Just like you, Raynie."

Beni dropped her head into her hands. How was she going to explain this to Mia? Her thoughts and heart immediately went to killing them. Clean sweep. They'd all be dead, and she wouldn't have to explain anything to her daughter.

"Careful." Rayne read her mind. Her fingers moved in and out as if she was conjuring something.

Malcolm stopped dancing. His face hardened.

"I'll talk to Mia when I think the time is right. Don't even think of seeing her before then. She'll be well protected."

"And if she comes in here again?"

"You are not to speak with Mia until I do. Understood?" she reiterated with conviction.

Malcolm nodded, but she could see the cogs in his mind turning.

6

GAIL

Gail put her book to the side when she heard Nadia's car speed down the driveway. The sound of her footsteps coming up the hill drew the attention of Attila and Thor. They listened for only a second before dashing to greet her. Their long nails dug into the already shredded wood floor. Gail remembered having an area rug in the front entry, but after the dogs moved in, her rug lay in tatters in the garbage.

Their excited barks heralded Nadia's approach, and when she opened the door, they went crazy jumping up and down on and around her.

"Hello?" she called from the foyer even though she knew exactly where Gail was sitting.

"In here."

"Ugh, down," she demanded. "When is Trevor coming for these monsters?"

Gail walked into the foyer. "Never. I think they are officially our dogs. Maybe we should call him to collect them." Her eyes grazed the damaged wood in the foyer.

Nadia leaned to kiss Gail's cheek. "Nah, I suppose I'm used to them now." She ran her fingers through Thor's fur. "Got something for you." She thrust a large yellow envelope towards her.

Gail looked down at the envelope, seeing Nadia's flourished handwriting across the top spelling out her name. She didn't reach for it but only stared at it. "What's this?"

"Details," she said with a big, devilish grin. "All the dirt I could find on Bentyn Rae and that Bloody Nun. I didn't ask Jordan because...well, you know how he is. He'd be here in a flash, accusing you of stirring up trouble."

Gail didn't react but knew she was right. Her sire had a great talent in finding fault with her.

"Come. Sit down."

Nadia followed her into the sitting room with Thor and Attila pushing to beat her there. She stepped aside to allow them to find their place beside the hearth. Attila circled until he found a comfortable spot while Thor began chewing a new toy Trevor sent him. In the corner of the room, the box they received yesterday sat empty and half-chewed. The dogs found that box the most interesting part of their present.

Gail sat on her chaise and opened the envelope. Among the packet of papers were photos and photocopied journal entries that looked ancient. "Oh, she's really pretty."

"Yes, she is. I got in a lot of trouble getting those."

"What trouble?" Gail swung her feet off the chaise.

"Our esteemed leader, Kiernan. I'm guessing he set up an alert on his computer when his interests are investigated." Nadia's annoyed expression twisted her sharp features in a way that didn't sit well on her face. "He called and chewed me out."

"For what? What interest does he have in Bentyn Rae or that Bloody Nun?" Gail dragged her nails along the pillow beside her. She could feel the strain pulling on her nail beds. Any harder and she knew she'd rip the fabric.

"Read them." Nadia motioned to the papers. "She's one of Kiernan's own children."

"Bentyn Rae is an Ancient?"

An Ancient was a blood drinker who counted their lives in the thousands.

"Read it. It's all there. He told me to drop any investigations. I told him it wasn't an investigation, just curiosity. He didn't believe me."

Gail flipped through the photos and then looked back at Nadia. Their eyes met and a small glimmer of humor touched Nadia's pretty face. Gail smiled.

"Kiernan isn't usually this unreasonable."

Nadia shook her head. Her long blonde hair swung as she dropped onto the sofa. "If you think he was unreasonable about this witch hunter, wait until you hear what he said about that Bloody Nun."

"That name." Gail cringed. "What'd she do?"

"Apparently, she was a prisoner during the wars. He didn't tell me that. I got that from the database. He told me to butt my nose out of Council affairs. He didn't want me stirring up new trouble about an old war." Nadia shrugged. "He just about fired me for asking why. I promised him I would curb my curiosity. I assured him that I had only discovered these women while organizing the Annex."

"Thank you. Did you tell him Bentyn Rae is in town?"

"Are you kidding?"

Gail read a few passages of a journal entry. The original copy looked dried and yellowed. The pages looked like they had been pieced together over the years. "Jesus, this says they found Bentyn Rae under the altar of a small church. When they pulled her out, she'd been there for at least a century. Weak from hunger, they beat her severely and brought her to Jordan."

"Where he threw her in the cages?"

"It doesn't say as much, but knowing him, I have no doubt that's what happened." She continued reading. "They weren't even looking for her. They were hunting the Bloody Nun by order of Olivia Wilkes. There's a piece of her seal on the paper."

Nadia nodded. "Yeah, it was a piece of a wax seal, not much left of it."

"Did you read this?"

"Some of it. Why? What's it say?"

"It says this Bloody Nun killed the whole congregation or town. It's not clear. She was covered in blood when they found her." Gail kept reading and then laughed out loud. "They found her sticking out of the tomb beneath the altar. I'm guessing she was trying to hide. That's when they discovered Bentyn Rae."

Nadia's eyes widened. "That sucks. They would never have found her." She sat back on the sofa. "Bentyn Rae is pretty interesting. There's not much in the files about the Bloody Nun besides that, not even a name. Apparently, she was a favorite of Olivia Wilkes. Lots of torture and time in the cages. No notation as to whether she survived the wars or not."

Gail hated the thought of anyone rotting away in the basement of the old Council house. Anyone whom Jordan Glynn or Olivia Wilkes hated enough to be locked in the cages sat there for years, starving to death—some ate each other to survive.

"Bentyn Rae wasn't even mentioned as having been involved in the wars. I noted it because Jordan said so. She's got three big things that are mentioned. The Blood Cults. She apparently started them.

Some place named Harmonia that the Council burned to the ground after killing everyone involved."

"Except her," Gail noted.

"Kiernan's her sire." Nadia figured that was the reason for her survival. "And the witch hunting. It overlapped the wars, so I'm guessing she got out of the cages. Her file was linked to two other blood drinkers: Asher Delger and Marzuq Badru. No known whereabouts for either. The witch hunting lasted centuries. There are at least three known addresses for her. Forest Lake isn't one of them. I'll update that."

Gail cringed. "Is she still hunting witches?"

"I don't think so, but it could explain her appearance in town. The file mentioned a mortal daughter that materialized less than two decades ago."

"Strange." Gail flipped through the papers.

"I did say she was interesting."

They perused the file for another half hour before Nadia decided to leave. Gail walked her to the door and stepped outside into the warm August night air. They walked together to the small cemetery that sat to the right of the front door beneath a dying apple tree. Gail's family cemetery held the bodies of her husband, three of her children, her best friend, Tatianna, and Nadia's daughter, Renee.

"Do you think she's at rest?" Nadia whispered as she touched the top of Renee's tombstone.

"Who? Renee or Tess?"

She looked at Gail in disbelief. "Renee of course. Who the hell cares if Tess ever gets out of that damn realm I stuck her in. I hope she's suffering."

Nadia's daughter had the unique distinction of being a body housing the soul of another person. During a soul transfer ritual or transmigration, Gail helped remove the child's week-old soul and inserted the soul of a woman burned for witchcraft, Tess Pendle. Tess tortured Renee and attempted to murder Nadia.

"I believe Renee is at rest. Don't you?" Gail tried to take the conversation away from Tess. She remembered what it was like having to exist in a world where Tess dominated every waking hour. She hoped she was suffering too.

"I hope so." Her expression hardened. "Ugh, witches," Nadia growled. "Those witches in that shop near the Annex left me a note."

"Are they organizing a neighborhood watch?" Gail chuckled.

"Hardly. They said in no uncertain terms that they do not approve of our existence in town. But I got a feeling they meant blood drinkers and not Haven." Her mouth twisted with distaste. "Apparently, we can't cohabitate in such close proximity."

"Says who? Did you tell Jacenta?"

Jacenta Brodie had created the safe houses called Haven during the 125-year war between blood drinkers. She was still the go-to girl for any issues arising with Haven.

"Not yet. I didn't want to make too big a deal of it. I would hope this doesn't go any further than a one-time correspondence."

"Don't hold your breath. They may be lumping Haven in with that Bentyn Rae. I can see how having an Ancient in town would ruffle some feathers. I'd tell Jacenta just to cover your ass."

"I will."

Nadia kissed her cheek and headed down the hill to the cabin. Thor and Attila looked from Gail to Nadia and then sped down the hill to the cabin. Their choice had been made for tonight.

Gail returned to her chaise and her fire to read about Bentyn Rae and the Bloody Nun.

7

CAMILLA

The next morning just after morning blessings and breakfast, Camilla took a walk into town. The sun was shining, and the temperature was still in the seventies, making for an enjoyable walk. She came down Oakhill Drive onto Maple. The trees on Maple were oversized and leafy. The houses were set back on large properties. The whole neighborhood grew up almost overnight in the mid-1950s, and it could be seen in the design of the houses as she got closer to Main Street.

Oakhill Drive was older but not by much. Her house was a relic, left over from the late 1800s, but it was only one of three or four that were left from that era. Most of the larger, much older houses had been torn down during the fifties boom to make room for sleeker homes for growing families.

Her pace was leisurely, yet she could feel the tightening in her chest as she considered what Iris would want to discuss with her. She prepared herself for the worst.

She reached Main Street in no time at all. The traffic was light at this early time of day.

The bell jangled as Camilla pulled open the door of Raven's Corner. Beads tinkled on strings hanging from the top of the door, catching the sun as they swung like a pendulum as the door closed behind her. The counter to the right of the front door was empty, leaving the cash register unattended and, in Camilla's mind, vulnerable if a thief were to wake up early on a Tuesday morning.

"Hello?" Her voice wasn't loud. The silence of the shop and the beating of her heart caused an uneasy feeling like she was turning herself in to the police for some horrible crime she'd committed. The humming of the air conditioner was the only sound. There was no answer, but she was sure Iris was somewhere hidden behind those beaded velvet panels lining the back of the shop.

She browsed and waited. Her eyes scanned the books. Her fingers touched the candles, and her mind continued to wonder why

Iris wished to see her. Starr had a vision about rain last night as if it was about the weather, but Camilla knew Rayne was a person.

"Camilla." The sound of Iris Chauncey preceded her voice. Camilla could hear the jingling of her bracelets and the clinking of her necklaces. As she pushed back the beaded drape in the back of the room, the sound of jangling bells welcomed her as well.

"Is that new?" Camilla accepted the hug Iris forced upon her.

"The curtain? The old one was pretty but silent. Many a curious customer has peeked behind the curtain in the past while I'm up front. This way I hear the bells and the beads and keep them from rooting around my office."

Camilla rolled her eyes playfully. "A spell could do the trick without the need for those annoying bells."

"I've tried. I've never been proficient in spell work. I see, I read, I hear. When it comes to casting, my abilities are limited. I've heard over and over again from Rayne that I should close this shop and dedicate myself to my studies."

Camilla listened with the patience of a teacher. "I've always taught my students to nurture their given talents. Learning something new is wonderful, but never neglect what comes naturally. Rayne has always felt spells made the witch. She is wrong. Don't allow her to dim your glow. Your abilities would have been welcome in Elder Path."

Iris smiled. Her eyes sparkled as she appreciated and immersed herself in Camilla's kind words. "That would have been my dream come true if I was born then. You have such a good heart. Our young ones are lucky you've chosen the noble profession of educator."

"Thank you. So, what did you wish to speak with me about?"

Iris touched her hand tenderly. "Can I make you some coffee or tea? I've set the table in the back."

Camilla followed her friend to the back of the shop, keeping an eye out for any new trinket to purchase. "Will the shop be okay if we're back here?"

"Tuesdays are slow. Besides, Opal is somewhere around if we need her. Please sit down and I'll fetch the tea."

The small table was set with an antique embroidered tablecloth that hung to the floor. Two small, padded chairs with a delicate place setting faced each other. A porcelain plate, cup, and silverware were set with a plate of pastries between them. She ran her finger over the cup on her side of the table and found it chipped. She examined it. The chipped cup was just like Iris, she thought—beautiful but imperfect, exactly as Camilla liked her.

This table, so perfectly set for conversation, was Iris's tarot table. On a normal day, the cloth would be black, and the cards would be spread out facing down in a half-moon, waiting for the next guest to take a seat and have their futures read.

The tinkling of Iris's jewelry heralded her return. She carried a porcelain teapot in one hand and a carafe of coffee in the other. "I forgot to ask which one you'd prefer." Her face stretched easily into a bright smile. "Oh, let me get this first." She pulled back the curtain, revealing the store in front of them. "It still needs to be adjusted a smidge. I'll get to that later."

Camilla chose coffee and held out her lovely porcelain cup with a tiny chip for Iris to fill. She took a chocolate-filled croissant and placed it on her plate. Iris examined the front windows, making sure there were no customers just about to enter, and then took her seat. She grabbed a plain croissant and tore at it with her bejeweled fingers.

"So . . ." A cold chill streaked up Camilla's spine and she swallowed hard. "Opal is working here now?" She couldn't dive right in without a little small talk first.

"For three months. Penelope is lending her to me for three months." Iris tried to sound grateful, but it was difficult. "She's been a terrific help." She dipped her pastry into her teacup and took a large bite of it before continuing. "Lilly, of course, is always my salvation when I need her." She was speaking of one of Camilla's students, Lilly Pershan.

Camilla nodded and searched for something else to say. She couldn't find anything and knew Iris would just get to the point, even if she didn't wish it to happen.

"Rayne says hello. She stepped out for some breakfast with Malcolm to give us some time to talk."

Camilla nodded. Licking her lips, she touched the chocolate poking out of the pastry but didn't take a bite.

"She remembers you, of course. She mentioned something about a sun spell." It was more of a question or a guess rather than a definitive statement. "In any event, she remembers you fondly. Malcolm does too." She winked as she said it and ended with a giggle.

Camilla felt a warm blush touch her cheeks. She remembered Malcolm all too well. Their affair was potent. He was the first man she'd desired after her husband left her. She could remember the passion and the inability to contain herself in his arms. Relationships like that never lasted long except in memories, and she was glad to have them.

She cleared her throat and sipped her coffee. "What do they have to do with me?" She tried to hide her fear as best she could by stirring her coffee slowly and tearing a small piece off the croissant on her plate.

"Rayne came to Forest Lake for two reasons. Apparently, my shop is not performing as well as she had expected. She's here to *reassess* my business." She air quoted *reassess*.

"I'm sorry." Camilla was sincere.

"The second reason is grim. She learned Bentyn Rae is in town."

"How did she learn that? The Witch Board is in Italy, isn't it?"

"It's wherever Penelope wants it to be. I believe they've relocated to Budapest, but who knows how long that will last." Iris rolled her eyes. "But you know Rayne, she has spies everywhere. After that unnatural fire a few weeks ago, Rayne became a permanent resident in my shop." Her frown darkened.

Camilla took a bite of the pastry as she listened.

"So, to save my sanity and my business, I need your help in getting Bentyn Rae out of town." Her fingers air danced towards the door to illustrate her point.

Camilla laughed. "How am I going to do that?"

"By refusing to teach her daughter. Maybe if Mia can't go to your school, she'll search elsewhere. I hear there's a witch school outside of Portland, Oregon. She can take her daughter there, and Rayne will leave my shop."

"I'd love to help, Iris, but I've already taken her tuition check and we've signed all the papers. She's been accepted. Besides, that Portland school is run by Maude." Camilla's lip curled in disgust. "I wouldn't send my worst enemy to learn under Maude."

"Not even Bentyn Rae's daughter?" Iris's thin, light brown, highly arched eyebrows raised on her forehead as she waited for Camilla's response.

Camilla sat back in the soft padded chair and thought of the many people that had sat there before her, waiting to hear favorable news regarding their future. She could see Iris leaning over her spread deck of cards, turning each over slowly and precisely. Her short dark hair, peppered with strands of gray, falling forward as she read their energies and what the Fates were telling them.

She wished the Fates would send her a sign right about now. She found herself as lost as a small-town housewife sitting at this table, hoping to hear that her husband was not cheating on her.

"Sorry." Her voice was steady and sure, saying there was nothing she could do.

"Camilla," Iris warned. "You know the implications of Mia Duran attending your school. What about her real mother? Oriana Duran murdered for power. If she wasn't already dead, the Board would have strung her up themselves."

"If they felt like that, they were taking their sweet time with it. She killed Tera Pendle centuries ago. Mararis was killed only a century and a half ago. What are they waiting for?"

Iris closed her eyes. "Please, we don't speak their names." She looked around as if two of the Sisters of Fate would materialize. "Besides, did you want Elena connected to Oriana's crimes?" She sounded defensive. "That's what would have happened. You know that. Elena was right there hunting, trapping, and conspiring against beings far greater than herself. She and Oriana murdered beings so powerful that neither would have been able to control that magnitude of power had they acquired it." A shiver quaked over her shoulders.

"I know!" Camilla shouted. She held her hand up to stop her. "I know. But seeing as though Oriana is already dead and Elena is showing no interest in continuing her crusade, what's the harm in educating Mia?" She looked at Iris's dejected expression. "I mean, outside of getting Rayne out of your hair."

"And getting Bentyn Rae out of town. You obviously met with her. Did you discuss her witch hunting in your admissions meeting and the conflict of interest it poses? Will Asher Delger be available for show and tell?"

Camilla could feel the bile rising in her gut as she squashed down her anger. "Bentyn Rae is aware of my feelings for her. She will not in any way be involved in the lessons." She paused for a moment, remembering that Iris had ulterior motives. "What does Rayne have to say about it?"

Iris looked to the front of the store as two women stared at the window display from the sidewalk. They kept walking, and she brought her attention back to Camilla. "She is not thrilled. I'll tell you that. She knows of Elena's relationship with Oriana Duran and questions her intentions with her daughter. Her hatred of Bentyn Rae is no secret, but I'm sure that cold blood isn't losing any sleep over it. She was in here only last night speaking with Malcolm." She sipped her tea. "That's the bigger issue. He would prefer to tutor Mia."

"Malcolm." Camilla gritted her teeth. She clenched her jaw until her teeth hurt. "Is that why he's in town? What do you suggest we do?"

"Disallow Mia Duran's admission and allow Malcolm to tutor her."

"How will that get Bentyn Rae out of town?" she asked.

"He could take Mia away."

Camilla laughed. "And get himself killed in the process. I'm sorry. As I've said, she's already been accepted with my blessing," she lied. "I understand your concern. I have the same concerns regarding Bentyn Rae and her past, but I will not stop Mia from learning about her abilities. Goodness knows with a cold blood for a mother, she needs all the help she can get. I believe I'm in a better position to educate her than Malcolm. You can tell him I said that. Oh, and tell him I wouldn't tangle with Bentyn Rae either. She'd kill him just as soon as look at him."

"You will take full responsibility for any issues involving Bentyn Rae or backlash from Malcolm?"

"I don't expect any, but yes. Malcolm will do as he pleases anyway. He always has."

Iris blew out a deep breath. "Camilla, you know I love you and want you to succeed with this school. Goddess knows, we need it for the young ones, but if it is going to cause challenges in our community, we will have to close it."

"I beg your pardon?"

Iris's face whitened. She had overstepped and knew it. She scrambled to correct it.

"Rayne has expressed some concern that perhaps we were rash in accepting your petition for this school. She thinks that maybe this should be your last class of students."

Camilla couldn't believe what she was hearing. A small voice in the back of her mind wondered if it was Penelope who preferred to close the school and not Rayne. Penelope always hated her. "I never asked for permission to have my school. I never cared nor do I now care what you or your band of holier-than-thou witches think of what I am doing with my students or future students." Camilla got up from the table, causing the teacups to teeter in the saucers. "I can't believe what I am hearing. You just told me that you resented Rayne for questioning your ability to run this shop and you turn around and do the same to me. Maybe I should wait and speak with Rayne. Or perhaps call Penelope myself. Maybe we can end this battle of wills once and for all. And then maybe I'll see what or who is really behind all of this."

"Camilla, stop, please," Iris followed her to the front of the store. "I didn't want our talk to end this way. Please, I didn't mean to say or imply that we were acting as judge and jury over you. I'm sorry. I just wanted to make it clear where we stand."

"And where is that, exactly?"

"We stand with witches. We will not tolerate anyone who doesn't. And if you see or hear a whisper of Asher Delger in town, you are to tell us immediately."

Camilla waved her hand at the door, and it swung open. Iris gasped. The bells jingled and the beads tinkled around her. She thrust her hand into the air to silence them, receiving another gasp from Iris. The warm August air hit her hard in the face as she stepped out into it, and she could feel every muscle in her body vibrating.

A quick glance at the new cold blood warehouse was all she afforded them. She didn't care what Bentyn Rae thought or did, as long as she stayed the hell away from her. Strangely enough, she felt the same for the Witch Board too.

She crossed the street at the light and headed up Maple Drive towards home.

FIRST DAY OF SCHOOL

END OF AUGUST

8

MIA

During the summer months, Mia got up at five in the morning to spend extra time with her mother. The long days were a blessing unless you shared your life with someone who detested sunlight. Mia loved dark rainy days and long winter nights. Both allowed her more quality time alone with her mother, since the sun and blood drinkers didn't mix.

"Morning," Mia murmured. Even though this was the first day of school, five was still too early to be chipper. She shuffled to the kitchen counter to pour herself a cup of coffee. The pot was empty. She pulled out the pot and turned it upside down. She shook it at her mother. That's when she noticed Beni sitting at the kitchen table with her head in her hands.

Usually, her mother stood in the kitchen looking like perfection. Her long dark hair falling in voluminous waves around her shoulders and her porcelain skin allowed Mia to envision her as a perfect doll. Her long slender fingers were, usually, wrapped around a large coffee mug that she held out for Mia. She'd say, "Would you like some breakfast or is it too early?"

Then Mia would grumble, "Too early." And like today, she'd shuffle to the counter where she added lots of milk and sugar to her mug. Her mother would watch her motions with a look of amusement.

But not this morning.

"Are you okay?" She pulled a chair out beside her mother and sat down.

"I need to talk to you." Beni spoke from beneath her mass of brown hair as it billowed around her head and onto the table.

I need to talk to you usually meant trouble, especially in this household. Mia huffed and said, "Let me start the coffee first."

After the coffee was set to drip, she retook her seat and waited for the worst. "What'd I do now? You haven't changed your mind about school, have you?" Mia began gnawing on the skin surrounding her thumbnail.

Her mother's eyes were cast down at the table. The iridescence was dim; even that magnetizing pull seemed weak as Mia sat close to her.

"No, nothing like that. Still not thrilled, but I've had two weeks to sort it out in my head." Beni raised her head. "Your father is in town." She spat it out, hoping to never say those words again.

"Whose father? *My* father?"

It was the only thing Mia could think to say. She'd never met her father before. Beni had adopted her after her mother was killed when Mia was two. Her father never tried to contact her or find out what happened to her mother. He never cared whether Mia was safe or being treated well. In all fairness, Beni was a blood drinker. She could have killed Mia the night she found her.

"I've invited him over on Sunday night."

"My father is coming here? On Sunday?" It didn't seem real. *Who was he?* She didn't even know his name. She knew her mother was Oriana Duran. She'd given Mia her last name rather than her father's name. That always told Mia her mother didn't love her father. She didn't question it beyond that.

"How do you feel about that? I can cancel it. Believe me, I will have no issue cancelling." Beni's eyes glazed over, and Mia fought not to read her thoughts.

Mia believed her. If there was one thing she knew about Bentyn Rae, it was that she didn't like witches. She couldn't figure out how they'd ended up together, but being a mother to a witch seemed to work for Beni. They were a good team, at least Mia thought so.

She shrugged. She didn't know how to feel about meeting this man who called himself her father. So many questions swam around in her head. *Who was he? Where had he been for eighteen years? Was he a witch too? Why was he back?*

"What's his name?" she asked.

"Malcolm Brenig."

Mia Brenig. Mia Duran Brenig. Mia Duran Brenig Rae.

If she got married, it would be a long list to add her husband's name to the end.

"Wait." Something occurred to Mia. "Malcolm Brenig? My father is Malcolm Brenig?"

"Unfortunately."

"Malcolm Brenig, one of the founders of Elder Path Circle?"

"Yes."

The coffee pot beeped, and she rushed to pour herself a cup. She needed it this morning. Black with no heapings of sugar or milk. This was a lot to take in, especially on her first day of school.

"You've listened to me gush about the Great Coven for months now and you never thought to mention that my father was a founding member? When did you talk to him?"

Beni looked away from her daughter. "The same night I met with Camilla Nolan."

"That was like two weeks ago!" Mia raised her voice. "Oh my God, yes. He texted you. What the hell, Mom? My father has been in town for two weeks and you kept it from me?"

Beni tensed. "I don't trust him."

She sipped her coffee. Her heart raced and the pull from her mother yanked her in. She hated it.

"It's not for *you* to trust him. *I* have to trust him, and I don't even know him." She pouted.

Her mother's head dropped onto the table. It was meant to be comical, but Mia knew there was some truth in what Beni was feeling. Talking about witches was not a welcome subject, and Mia didn't want to upset herself or her mother this morning.

As Mia slipped a few slices of bread in the toaster, her mother changed the subject.

"First day of school." Beni tried to sound enthusiastic. "Feeling excited?"

"I won't know until tonight."

"What's tonight?"

"After the first day is over. I can't get excited until the nervousness goes away. Until then, I'm hyper-aware of each little twinge. I could set the whole school on fire and then where would I be?"

Beni frowned. "Don't stress about it. They are witches too. If you feel anything weird, tell them. Of course, burning down that school wouldn't be a terrible thing to do."

Mia's heart raced and she could feel sweat breaking out on her back as she thought of going to Magnolia Academy for Magical Arts.

Since she was two, she had exhibited certain talents that other children didn't possess. As a toddler, Mia had a temper. Like most two-year-olds, she was fussy and single-minded. She wanted what she wanted and that was that. With most kids, they threw tantrums or cried. Not Mia. Mia had an inherent ability to set things on fire. The sofa, the drapes, the dog, and Beni had pounded the cuffs of her pants more times than she could remember.

Mia had no control over this particular ability. Emotion seemed to be a huge catalyst but sometimes it would flare up if she sneezed or hiccupped at the wrong time. Once she had laughed so hard, she ignited her bedroom curtains. Most of her magical talents did not manifest until she hit puberty. After that, she could read minds and see futures.

That's when she found out what her mother did when she left the house at night. Up until then, Mia considered herself lucky to have a strong female presence in her life, but reading her mother's mind (and a history book on witch hunts) gave her centuries and centuries worth of trauma and blood she had to sort through.

"Look, it's only for one year." Her mother was always trying to distract her from witch school.

"Don't..." She knew where this was leading.

"Come next September, you could—"

"I said don't."

"There's nothing wrong with me trying to help you further your education. You're always saying I should be more like other parents. Isn't this what they do? Don't they encourage their exceptional children to pursue higher education?"

Mia regretted getting out of bed this morning. "College is not for me. At least not right now. I need to stop setting things on fire first, then maybe I'll go to college. Magnolia Academy will teach me what I need to know to blend in with *normals*."

"Normals? You're not normal?"

She wasn't and Beni knew it.

"Regular people." Mia rolled her eyes in true teenage fashion. "It's what Starr and Lilly call them. April too. Aunt Dyre hates the word, but I think it fits."

Beni studied her daughter's metabolic changes. "You're sure you're okay?"

"Yeah. First day of school nerves and now my father. I'm just trying to process it without starting a fire."

"Deep breaths. Go to Aunt Dyre's right after school and I'll pick you up from there."

"After *lessons*. And I'll have my car. No need to pick me up."

"I want to see Aunt Dyre. Is that a problem?"

"Fine. Just so you know, I'm thinking about applying for a job at Raven's Corner."

"No."

"But—"

"No. All day at that school and then working at night at that witch shop. No."

"Fine."

Beni looked out the window to the rising sun. Her face showed the sadness and worry that Mia could hear in her thoughts. She knew her mother had serious reservations regarding Magnolia Academy. She hated the teachers, Camilla and Elena Nolan. She hated the curriculum. She hated it all.

"Mom…"

"Just be careful, please." Her lovely face collapsed with concern.

"I think you're more nervous about school than I am?"

"If anything feels off, it probably is. Protect yourself and watch out for April too."

Mia nodded and squinted at her mother. "Can I ask you one more question about my father? Is he related to my teacher, Linus Brenig?"

"They're brothers," she muttered.

"Does that make me and April real cousins?" She bounced in her seat.

"You were never supposed to know that Linus is April's father. You took that information without my consent. If you betray my trust and, more importantly, Aunt Dyre's trust, you'll be in a whole heap of trouble. Do not tell April or Lulu."

"Yes, ma'am." Mia bit her lower lip. "That means Aunt Dyre really is my aunt, not just a friend of yours." She was bouncing again.

"I mean it, Mia." She dragged her pinched fingers over her lips and pretended to lock it.

9

AUNT DYRE

"Morning, Aunt Dyre."

Mia pulled open the sliding glass doors in the family room of Dyre Crane's house. She entered like she lived there. A large gray and orange cat pushed past her on its way out, and she happily moved out of its way. "Excuse me, Horus."

"Hey, Mia, ready for your big day?" Dyre Crane stood in the doorway of the kitchen with a cup of coffee in her hands. "Want some breakfast?"

"I can't eat."

"Nervous?" Dyre laughed and walked into the kitchen.

"Kinda." She shrugged. "Is April ready?"

"We're having some first day of school motivation issues." Dyre smiled.

Up until this morning, Mia thought Dyre wasn't really her aunt. Dyre Crane was Bentyn Rae's best friend. Her family became Mia's family when Beni adopted her.

Dyre Crane was beautiful. Mia knew that was usually subjective but not in Dyre Crane's case. There was something inside her that made her beautiful. Not her auburn hair, not her expressive blue eyes, but something that radiated from within that Mia loved. Her daughters had it too but not as strong.

Three pairs of metal scissors lay on the kitchen counter. Each intricately ornate and of different sizes.

"What's with these?"

"Just cutting…" Dyre touched the tissue paper beneath the implements with her right hand and the white moonstone pendant around her neck with her left. "Looking for guidance and grounding at the same time."

Before Mia could respond, Dyre looked at her watch. 8:15 a.m.

"Lulu, your bus will be here any minute. Get a move on."

Dyre's younger daughter sped through the house. The clomping of her sneakered feet and her backpack smacking into walls and furniture could be heard from the farthest end of their ranch style house.

"Why do I have to take the bus today?" Lucy Crane whined, dropping her backpack by the door for last minute mom-primping.

"Because today is April's first day, and I want to see her off properly. Just like I did for you on Monday."

Lucy huffed and brooded. "Hi, Mia." Her long blonde hair stood out from her head like a triangle with static. It always happened when she was upset about something. Dyre said that Lucy's abilities weren't defined yet. Her body was still sussing them out. Because of this, there were problems when she involuntarily used them.

"Oh, calm down." Her mother flattened her hair with a spritz of water and mashed her hands against the sides of her head at the same time. "It's only for today."

"But—" The girl looked at Mia, wishing she didn't have an audience. "What if I have an episode?" Her eyes filled with fear.

"Same thing you'd do any day. You know what to do." Dyre pinched her daughter's chin. "Deep breaths. And try not to let this one little thing upset you." She stared into her eyes and then kissed her cheek.

An uncertain nod and Lucy ran for the yellow school bus as it pulled into the cul-de-sac behind the house.

"Seems like we're all having a day," Mia said. "I'll go wake April and get our day started."

"Hang on for a second, Mia. I have something for you." Dyre went to the mantel over the fireplace and opened a small wooden box. She pulled out a gift box with a ribbon wrapped around it.

"What's this for?" She tried to hide the emotion in her voice.

"Just a little something for your first day." Dyre placed her palm on the side of Mia's face. "I know it's tough for your mom to understand what you're going through, and sometimes she's not … well, she just doesn't get it. Being different, I mean." Dyre smiled. "She's always been Bentyn Rae, you know?"

Mia nodded. She looked down at the small box in her hand.

"Well, this is something to let you know you are something special too. Being elemental is difficult. I know." Dyre returned to the kitchen. "You know I have two sisters. My sisters embraced their abilities sooner than I did, even though I was the oldest. Our powers and abilities were equal, but I was scared. I had control issues, temper issues, mixed with no patience in the least. But Tera, who was a bit younger than me, could cause rainstorms. Thunderstorms with lightning, torrential downpours. It always frightened me. Mother would tell me that once I learned to control my emotions, I would control my powers. Until then, I continued to set things on fire or accidently break something, and once"—Dyre laughed—"I caused all the flowers in the Garden Room to die from frost."

"The Garden Room?"

"Just my favorite place ever." Emotions thickened Dyre's laugh. "But Mother was right. When I learned to control my emotions, it was a whole different ballgame."

Dyre pulled the ribbon and opened the box, revealing a necklace. She unclasped it and slipped it around Mia's neck. "I want you to wear this, and anytime you feel your fire getting away from you, hold it."

"What will it do?"

"You'll see." She kissed her cheek.

Mia looked down at the charm hanging from the chain. It was a domed glass pendant with a yellow flame flickering inside it. "What is that? I mean, is that real?"

"Of course." Dyre winked at her. "Now, go wake April and let's get your first day of school started."

Ten minutes later, April sauntered into the kitchen dragging her fluffy socked feet and a blanket. "Lulu forgot her lunch." She dropped down into a kitchen chair and nestled her head in her arms.

"Shit." Dyre picked up the mushroom lunch box and slammed it down again. "I'll drop it off later."

Her daughter yawned and nodded, not caring in the least about her mother's problems.

"So much for an early start." Mia sat at the table to examine her pendant.

"Orientation is not for two hours."

"I know. I just thought we could explore the house a bit. I've only seen the living room, and I have so many questions for Camilla Nolan and Linus Brenig." Excitement bubbled in Mia's belly.

"What's that?" April changed the subject.

"A gift from your mom." Mia and Dyre shared a warm smile.

"Oh sure, we're just handing out gifts to Mia, but when I ask for twenty bucks for a tarot deck, you say no." April's muffled voice broke through the blanket.

"Waste of money. Your magic wouldn't work with tarot." Dyre swept through the room, hardly listening.

"You don't know that," she mumbled.

"There is one big reason it wouldn't work; you're not a witch." She stopped to sip her coffee.

"I know, but I have powers."

"I believe your father preferred to call them abilities," Dyre murmured.

"My father?"

Dyre froze with her coffee cup inches from her mouth. She hadn't realized what she was saying until she said it. She mentally kicked herself.

"Never mind."

Mia's eyes volleyed between her aunt and her cousin, feeling horribly uncomfortable.

"Typical," April huffed. "Anyway, the glows are not normal. Normals don't see people glowing."

"That word," Dyre huffed. "Stop calling people normals."

April pouted. "Whatever. I'm something that's not normal. I'm extra." April looked at Mia, who smiled sympathetically.

April could see what she called *the glows* on people. The books called them auras or energies, but April had called them *the glows* since she could talk. Which is exactly as long as she remembered seeing them.

The glows emanated from everyone. Good, bad, ugly, criminal, righteous—whatever. The glows were there. As much as she told her friends and especially her mother that she hated this talent of hers, she secretly loved it. The glows made her feel special. They helped her to know things. The glows had color and substance. The color showed emotion like a giant mood ring encircling a person. The substance showed intent. Were they lying? Excited? Murderous? The glow told all.

"You're perfect for who you are. Not a witch and not normal. Just perfect." Dyre pulled back the blanket and kissed her daughter until she giggled. "Besides, if Aunt Beni sees you playing around with tarot cards, she'll burn you and the deck." She laughed. "I just saved your life. You're welcome."

"Hardy har-har," April mocked her.

"She's right. Mom hates tarot. Any witch tools. Cards, cauldrons, pendulums, or wands. Natural abilities she can deal with, but don't *use* anything. Witch paraphernalia, she calls it." Mia palmed her pendant and looked to Dyre for help.

"She wouldn't dare." Her blue eyes widened in mock outrage and then she laughed again. "I'll make you girls breakfast before you go. April, take a shower and get dressed. I can't have your fa…" Dyre stopped short and summoned up a cough to cover her little slip. "I can't have your teachers think I don't take care of you."

She turned away to look out the window. She reinforced the memory spells she created almost six years ago. She knew they were weakening. April and Lucy wanted more information about their father, and their need far outweighed her magic. They were winning.

She knew that one day soon, she'd need to tell them. She touched her chest. The congestion and difficulty breathing told her to tell them, but she decided to wait and see what the doctor had to say.

"They really need to know," Mia whispered after April trudged out of the room carrying her blanket.

Dyre spun around to face her. Her mouth dropped open.

"Mom told me." Mia cringed in an apologetic manner.

"It's not that. I figured Beni couldn't keep her big mouth shut, but you just read my thoughts." A look of pride and astonishment made her more beautiful to Mia.

"I guess I did." Mia looked down to the tile floor. "I've been doing it for—"

"No," Dyre interrupted her. "You read *my* thoughts."

"So?"

"Only those who possess strong gifts can read my thoughts unless I let them in."

Mia swallowed hard, not knowing how to respond.

"Your mother was not a strong witch. She stole any power she possessed." Venom infused every word Dyre spoke regarding Mia's biological mother. "Your father is a strong witch. This came from him. The fire too, I would guess."

The girl's face became ashen. She stared at Dyre with a lost, hopeless expression.

"Beni didn't tell you, did she?" Dyre pulled out a box of pancake batter from the cupboard. She poured some into a bowl without measuring it.

"She told me he was in town but not much else. I'm supposed to meet him on Sunday." She nibbled on her bottom lip. "She told me his name." A bright smile lit up her face and she could feel a warm tingle slide up and down her arms. The fire pendant she wore sparkled but nothing more. "April and I are real cousins."

Dyre's face dropped.

"I won't tell."

Dyre's face lit up again and she grabbed Mia's face with both her hands. "Neither of you ever noticed the resemblance you share. It's in the eyes. You and April have Brenig eyes. I see it more in you, but April definitely looks like her father." She stopped and held her index finger in the air. "Do not breathe a word of this to April or to any of the girls at school. Linus will know the moment you walk into school. Just let me tell them in my own time."

"I promise." Mia sat back down at the kitchen table still examining her pendant. "Is this like yours?" She pointed to the moonstone pendant around her aunt's neck.

"No." Dyre looked down at her own necklace. "Mine is different." She kissed Mia's forehead and returned to making pancakes.

10

MAGNOLIA ACADEMY FOR MAGICAL ARTS

Elena swept into the kitchen with a joyful flourish, trying to bury her nervousness beneath her smile. "Good morning, all. First day, first day, first day!" she sang.

"You're certainly in a good mood," her sister commented with a glance at Linus.

"Coffee?" Kim Moreau offered.

"Please."

The cupboard beside the coffee maker opened on its own, and Elena pulled a cup from the shelf. She held it out for Kim to fill.

The cupboards did that. Everything in the house moved. The house was home to a spirit or two. They opened and closed cupboards and doors, moved knickknacks, and occasionally there would be crying late at night. It wasn't much, which is why Camilla allowed them to stay. There had been a few spirits over the years that were antagonistic, and she had promptly banished them, but the ones they had now were docile and friendly.

"Thank you," Elena said. The cupboard closed as she turned and joined the others at the kitchen table. She leaned to kiss Linus good morning.

"I love first days. And so do you." She pointed at her sister. "Don't pretend you are not just busting with excitement for homecoming." She looked around at everyone. "Speaking of, why are you eating breakfast? No breakfast buffet for homecoming this year?"

Linus ate his eggs, silently watching the two sisters talk.

"We're shaking it up a bit this year." Camilla winked at Kim. "We're having a big lunch. That way our new students can participate."

"Sounds great." Elena feigned excitement. Secretly, she wanted to keep April and Mia away from Camilla. Not forever, just long enough to gain their trust and affection. Yes, it was juvenile, but she knew her sister had a natural ability to draw people to herself. Elena just hoped for enough time to deflect some of the attention.

"I have to say, it will be nice to have a full house again." Camilla sipped her tea. "Lilly and Veda will be here full-time this year. Living and learning with us."

"Too bad April won't be living here." Pierce brought his plate to the sink and rinsed it before putting it in the dishwasher.

"Sorry, kid," Linus said. "We'll sort through this family stuff together. I promise. Because of April, I finally got Dyre to speak with me. That's the first step."

Pierce gave him a skeptical smile. "Didn't you say she didn't want Elena teaching April? How are you getting around that problem?"

Elena's mouth dropped open. "She can't still blame me for everything Oriana did, can she?"

Linus's face hardened. "You were right there with Oriana. You may not have pulled the trigger, but you hung the target."

"That doesn't make any sense." She frowned. "I didn't kill Tera or Mararis. That was all Oriana. She must know that. You told her, right?" Elena turned to her sister, who kept her mouth shut for now.

Linus shrugged. "This is one fight I'm not getting involved in. I'll keep you away from each other. That's all." He tried to kiss her forehead, but she pulled away.

Elena resented Linus's attachment to his ex-wife. No matter that she kicked him out of the house, kept his daughters from him, and wiped their memories, he still sided with her in any argument.

She huffed like she was done obsessing over this topic. "I don't wish to discuss Dyre Crane this morning." She buttered her toast. "Let's center on positivity today."

Camilla and Linus exchanged a look of concern. Camilla's expression showed more annoyance than his. "I should get moving. Homecoming is in a half hour. New student orientation is not until ten. That should give us enough time to get Lilly and Veda settled." Camilla jumped up from her seat.

Linus laughed. "No rush. Veda will be late as always."

"It was good luck for us that her parents let her stay here this year." Pierce chuckled.

"Luck had nothing to do with it. I insisted that if she continued her education with us that she either be on time or move in as a resident." Linus got up from the table and clapped his son on the shoulder. "You should get yourself ready for the day."

Pierce checked his watch and bolted from the room.

"He can hang out with me. Acclimate the new students, give them the tour, all the fun stuff." Elena placed her empty coffee cup in the sink. "No reason to stick him in a boring classroom on his first day."

Camilla, Kim, and Linus stared at her.

"What do you think being an apprentice means?" Camilla asked. "He will work under each of us in the classroom and then eventually lead his own class. He'll learn nothing giving tours."

"He'll do what I do. If you don't think what I do is important…"

"Oh Lord, here we go. I was wondering how long it would take you to ruin my day." Camilla glared at her sister.

"You don't just give tours." Linus caressed Elena's hand. "You teach. Pierce will learn under you in the classroom."

"Where is Starr?" Kim looked around the room as if she was hiding.

"Is she even up yet?" Elena frowned.

"Cover your ears." Camilla smirked. When they all followed her direction, she whispered a few words into the air and a siren echoed through the house. "That should do the trick." A smile brightened her face.

The cabinets opened simultaneously and slammed shut to express the spirits' displeasure with the noise.

Linus pressed on his ear. "I wish there was a better way."

"There is. It's called being responsible. Starr is as bad as Veda with time management. Maybe I should cover that during homecoming. A little refresher of the rules may be necessary. Don't forget to stress being on time to Mia and April today during orientation."

"I thought you were doing that." Elena looked surprised.

"I trust you." Camilla shut a cabinet door that swung open as she passed it and left the kitchen.

"She trusts me? That's new." She snickered.

"Don't look a gift horse in the mouth." Linus kissed her.

Homecoming went exactly as expected. Lilly Pershan was early, and Veda Kaur was late. Each girl arrived with massive amounts of luggage and overflowing with tales of their summer adventures.

Their parents seemed more than happy to get them out of the house for a while. They said their goodbyes and ran out the door. Veda spent a good portion of the morning showing off her new credit card and gushing about her full bank account. Her parents were celebrating her return to school with a month-long vacation in Australia, followed by a cruise. They wouldn't be back until late October, maybe.

Lilly's goodbye to her mother was brief. A quick kiss and an "I'll call you later." As a single mom of two daughters, Lilly's mother had to rush off to her job as a real estate agent. Money wasn't tight, but it wasn't as fluid as Veda's parents. Lilly supplemented her tuition with a part-time job at Raven's Corner and enjoyed a partial scholarship offered by the Witch Board, who also financially backed Iris Chauncey's witch shop.

Camilla's alarm did little to wake Starr. Kim tried rousing her with breakfast to no avail. It took Elena pulling off her covers and yanking her from the bed to get her up. She trudged down the stairs in her pajamas and slippers only to be completely awakened by squeals of delight coming from her two friends.

After a quick breakfast and settling the girls into their new rooms, as promised, Camilla went over the curriculum for the first semester. Starting with the first new moon of September and ending on the winter solstice, they had various classes that helped them learn their history and hone their talents. They would enjoy almost a full month of vacation and start the second semester on the first new moon in January (which happened to be at the end of the month next year) and then end the year on the summer solstice in June.

She reinforced the rules, including responsibility and time management. Veda and Starr felt singled out, but Camilla did not seem to care.

"We have new supplies, and a care package offered by the Witch Board," she announced.

"Penelope must be feeling generous this year," Kim murmured, and Camilla shushed her.

Camilla opened a large cardboard box and pulled out textbooks and other various supplies and handed them to the girls. One of two thick, hardbound textbooks covered all aspects of witch history, including the Great Coven, the witch hunts, and the newest reception into modern society thanks to social media. The second text covered the craft. It illustrated various techniques, even giving sample spells for novice witches to try.

"What's this?" Starr held up a leatherbound journal.

"I wasn't sure if she would include that, but it is intended to be a beginner's grimoire. This semester we will begin spellcasting, and you may use this book to jot down techniques that work for your unique talents or write your own spells. If you are not proficient in spell work, I encourage you to use this as a journal. Tarot journal, moon phase journal, set intentions. Anything that feels right to you. Remember, and this is the most important lesson you'll ever learn, your craft is your own." She looked at each of the girls in turn. "Never let anyone tell you what you are doing is wrong."

Veda moved to speak, but Camilla held her hand up to silence her.

"That doesn't mean you don't need to study. You can still fail a test. Learning is important even if you never use the information. We're here to give you options in your journey. You may have wandered in here thinking you are only a seer, but just wait until you cast your first spell…" A sly smile caused her eyes to sparkle. "What I'm saying is, if you believe in what you are, your magic will follow."

A single chime rang out on the doorbell, and Starr sprinted to the front door. Fatigue was gone. She upended the box of supplies and pushed Pierce to the side, calling out, "They're here!"

Elena collected herself before walking into the sitting room to greet her new students. She could hear Camilla welcoming them with less enthusiasm than she was used to hearing from her sister.

With any student in the past, Camilla gushed. She was thirteen again, pulling the student into the house, saying how excited she was to have them join this journey into magic with her. But today was different.

Today, there was no bounce in her step, no twinkle in her eye. No tears, no laughter. Just demure welcome. She did the introductions as usual, but they lacked any excitement or joy.

Mia Duran, Oriana's beautiful daughter, seemed too nervous to notice. Her long brown hair and pale complexion was so much like Oriana that Elena fought herself from running to her and hugging her. Her fingers fiddled with the strap of her messenger bag, and she changed her footing several times as her gaze darted to each of the new faces. Around her neck hung a necklace that appeared to have a flame dancing within it.

April Crane noticed Camilla's lackluster welcome. From her application, she knew April could read auras, and Camilla's was probably dim and flashing—an untrustworthy liar. She, too, looked nervous, but an air of caution hung heavy on her. Her fine blonde hair hung to her elbows, and when her hands weren't twisted together, they were twirling pieces of her hair into a braid. A set of amber tinted glasses covered her blue eyes and hampered her ability to see and be distracted by auras.

Elena glanced at Linus and wondered how his aura looked to April. She could only imagine that it was shining, perhaps too bright since April barely looked in his direction.

"Elena will lead you through orientation. Today, she will give you a tour, go over the student handbook and your syllabus. We have your supplies as well. The only real classes you will attend today and for the next week will be meditation led by Kim Moreau." Camilla held her hand out to where Kim was standing. She said hello and waved to the girls in turn.

"Okay, let's get on with our day. We'll meet again at lunch. We do have a part-time student who will be joining us after traditional school lets out." She held out her hands in a vain attempt to herd Lilly, Starr, and Veda out of the room.

"Wait, aren't we doing questions?" Starr asked.

"Oh yeah, that was my favorite part of orientation," Veda agreed.

Mia and April looked apprehensive. Mia grasped the necklace as if someone were about to grab it.

"Not today, girls," Camilla whispered.

It was one of the few times in her life where Elena saw her sister was nervous. What she could be nervous about was beyond her, but there it was, fear in her eyes.

"Oh, come on, Milly. It's always been fun and a great ice breaker." Elena smiled, knowing her sister wanted to punch her.

A squeal accompanied Camilla's reluctant nod, and the girls dragged April and Mia to the sofas to sit down and wait for the fun to begin.

"Okay," Starr started. "The way it works is you get to ask each of the teachers absolutely anything you want."

"And they in turn get to ask you something," Lilly added.

"When I started, the other students got to ask questions too," Pierce said.

Linus laughed. "We shut that down when the questions got too personal and inappropriate."

Mia's eyes shot up to see Linus slip his arm around his son's shoulder. Trying to conceal her thoughts, she looked away, hoping no one noticed her smiling. Her memories of Pierce were fleeting at best, but she knew Aunt Dyre kept a picture of him in her dresser drawer.

"Who wants to go first?" Elena smiled, feeling this could be interesting and quite educational. "Mia? How about you?"

Her eyes darted to each teacher. Her mind was clearly formulating and casting aside questions that Elena was sure Linus and Camilla could read.

"Anything," Veda urged. "You can ask *anything*."

"If you asked me yesterday, I had a million questions. But now my mind is blank." Mia bit her lower lip. She looked at Linus, dying to ask him about Malcolm, but refrained. Camilla shot an alarmed glance at him as she read Mia's thoughts. Linus cleared his throat as Mia formulated a question. "Do you fear, um, witch hunters?" Her eyes scanned the group. She stopped on Linus for a moment but then ultimately landed on Camilla.

"Me?" Camilla paused for a moment and then blew out a breath like she was thinking. She scanned Mia's thoughts for the reason for her question but found that it was from a book she'd been reading.

Her brow ruffled and a small smirk pulled up her cheek.

"Tough question. Yes and no. It's smart to fear anyone who has malicious intentions. Underestimating your opponent is a recipe for disaster. However, I have confidence in my abilities, and I trust that those who surround me will help protect me." Her eyes widened with certainty that her answer impressed Mia. "My turn." A sly smile brought out that twinkle in her eye that Elena wished to see earlier. "What is your biggest fear?"

Mia chewed on her lip until it tore. She lapped up the blood. "Um." Mia closed her eyes. "Accidentally burning my house down during the daytime."

April grabbed her friend's hand and squeezed it.

Camilla's eyes locked on to Mia with an intensity that made her wish to change her answer to Camilla being her biggest fear. When Camilla was satisfied, she nodded and stepped back to allow the other teachers access to Mia and her questions.

"I've got one." Elena stepped up. "What's that necklace you are wearing? It's unusual."

Mia's face brightened. "It was a gift from my aunt." Her eyes darted to Linus and then away. "She said it would help me when I need it." She looked down at the dancing flame. "I don't know what that means exactly, but I guess I'll find out eventually."

"Mia didn't get to ask you a question," Starr pointed out to Elena.

"Sorry, you are correct. Ask away." Elena flipped her hair out of her face and prepared herself for the worst.

"I heard that you knew my birth mother." Everyone in the room went silent. "Was she elemental?"

Camilla stiffened at the mention of Oriana Duran but when Mia's question ended up being harmless, her body relaxed like a deflating balloon.

"No," Elena whispered with a pained smile. "Your mother was not elemental. The abilities she possessed centered around kitchen magic. Cooking up brews and mixing potions."

Mia's face dropped and she could feel her heart speed up. Heat rose on her cheeks, and she touched the pendant. The tiny dancing flame changed color. The yellow flame became blue, and she could feel a chill begin where the pendant touched her skin. Mia snapped out of her thoughts and could think of nothing besides the icy chill spreading through her chest.

Camilla noticed the blue dancing flame and wished to speed up this process.

"Next question."

11

BENI

Beni drove to Dyre's house as soon as she woke.

"Knock knock," she called as she opened the front door.

"Who's there?" Dyre's youngest daughter called back to her.

Beni could hear April groaning in the other room. "No knock-knock jokes, Lulu."

April's little sister's name was Lucy, but she insisted on being called Lulu and would answer to nothing else.

"Aunt Beni." The child ran into the living room. "I've got a joke for you."

"Tell me quick before April hears." She wrapped her arms around Lulu and swung her around.

"Why did Dracula take cold medicine?"

Lucy Crane was a beautiful six-year-old child. A perfect blend of both Dyre and Linus. Her long blonde hair looked to be spun by silkworms, and her blemish free skin rivaled Beni's.

"Why?" She looked up to Dyre as she walked into the room to greet her friend.

"Because he was *coffin* too much." She shouted the answer between bouts of laughter.

Beni giggled at the joke.

"How about this one?" Lucy tapped her lips with her index finger, trying to remember another joke.

"No more. Let Aunt Beni come in and sit down." Dyre pushed her daughter out of the room. "Sorry about that. I made the mistake of telling her you were coming over, and she's been scanning the internet for vampire jokes."

"Did you feed my kid?" Beni joked.

"Fed and they are doing their homework as we speak." She hiked her thumb towards the family room.

"What kind of homework could they possibly get on the first day?"

Dyre shrugged. "Beats me, but they have been huddled together trying to figure it out for almost an hour."

"Are we sure they are doing homework and not fooling around on their phones?"

"I confiscated their phones before dinner. Go in and say hi and then come sit with me. I've got something to talk to you about." Dyre didn't look at her friend but walked back into the kitchen.

Beni knew she had a doctor's appointment this morning. There was a potential for bad news. From the look on Dyre's face and the scent she got from her blood, the news was not good.

Beni's sense of smell was exceptional. Her sire always joked that she was connected to the animal side of their nature. She could smell the sickness in Dyre's body from the first day she felt chest pains and wished she couldn't.

"What kind of homework has you two so engrossed?"

She walked into the family room, which was two steps down from the kitchen. April and Mia were sitting on opposite sofas, each with a journal opened on their laps. They were hunched over, scribbling in the books.

She leaned in to kiss Mia on the head. "How was your first day?"

"So much to tell you but later. We're writing a spell."

"Isn't it a bit early in your education to enact spells?" Beni tried to sound supportive, but inside she was fighting herself. Every impulse wanted to condemn spellcasting. She silently reminded herself to be patient and encouraging.

"They won't work." Mia laughed, reading her mother's thoughts. "Elena wants us to think of some dream or passion and write a spell that can make it happen."

"Like Elena Nolan knows anything about spellcasting. How is she even qualified to teach you something like that?" Dyre called from the kitchen where she was listening to the conversation.

"Why isn't she qualified?" April snapped back.

"She's a green witch and a weak one at that. All her magic revolves around nature. Her abilities are underdeveloped and limited. If she tried to cast, she couldn't do it. They should leave spellcasting to the experts, and she isn't one of them."

"Dyre," Beni warned in an easy, sing-songy way. She walked back into the kitchen.

"What about Linus, Mom?" April yelled across the room.

"What about him?" The bitterness in her tone was evident, and Beni hid a smile.

"He's a spellmaster."

"No, he's not. He's proficient in spell work but not a spellmaster." Dyre looked at Beni as if to say she already regretted sending her daughter to this witch school. Her friend responded with a sympathetic smile and a knowing giggle.

"Not to hear Elena talk about him," April chuckled. "Linus can do no wrong in her eyes."

"Did you see them today at lunch?" Mia whispered.

"What?" Dyre shouted and threw the sponge in her hand into the sink. "Are you kidding me?" Her hands were clawed as she marched around the kitchen, furious. A rumble of thunder rolled over the clear night sky. The pendant around her neck began to glow.

"Girls, watch Lulu for a few minutes. Your mom and I need to take a little walk." Beni grabbed Dyre's hand and dragged her out the sliding glass door in the family room.

She waited. Waited and walked. Waited for Dyre to start screaming or crying or whatever it was she felt like doing after finding out her ex-husband was dating her mortal enemy. It wasn't until the second turn around the block and some distant flashes of lightning when Dyre could find the words she wished to express her outrage.

"He's screwing Elena Nolan?" Her teeth were clenched as she spoke. Her pendant shone like it was lit from within.

"We don't know that. This is gossip from two teenage girls. Maybe he was just being nice, and the girls took that as affection." Beni was grasping at straws. "Maybe they heard rumors from one of the other kids. This doesn't sound like Linus. I mean, she's vile."

Dyre stopped walking to catch her breath. Breathing in was difficult, and breathing out caused her to cough.

"Slow down." Beni could feel the pain in her own chest as her friend wheezed and coughed again. "First things first. Are you okay?"

Dyre looked up to Beni with tears in her eyes. "You know I'm not." Her pendant dimmed as her anger lessened.

"Cancer?"

"That's what they're calling it. It's the only word mortal doctors have for a large energy sucking mass in my body that is growing at lightning speed. I know what it is. It is death come calling on me." She tried to hold back the tears, but it was impossible. "I tried cutting today to work out my anxieties, but it didn't help. It used to help."

Beni rubbed her back. "You're not dead, yet. And you are not without options."

"No." Dyre refused to listen to any options that included her becoming a blood drinker.

"So, you'll leave your daughters alone because of pride?"

"Let's go back home." Dyre started walking again. "I love you, but you know how I feel about that."

Beni looked away, annoyed. "Do the girls know yet?"

"To some degree. I still haven't told them what it all means to them. I don't even know where to begin. There was always the option of telling them about Linus and then having him raise them. But now that's off the table with him dating Elena Nolan. I know I promised not to kill her, but I'm telling you, it's looking more attractive in light of this information. That's the kind of cutting that could cure my stress."

Beni laughed.

Dyre wiped her face free of tears with a swipe of her hands. The house was in view, and she slowed her pace.

"Why'd you even bother going to a mortal doctor anyway?" The idea never made sense to Beni.

Dyre shrugged. "I needed answers from someone."

"They didn't question your blood work?" She laughed.

"They tried." She winked at her friend. "I made that go away."

Beni laughed, throwing her arm around Dyre. "Well, make this sickness go away too. I need you here."

"Who's going to take care of you when I'm gone?"

Beni put her hand to her heart. She could feel the tears queuing in her eyes and a tightening in her chest that meant it would be an ugly, gut-wrenching cry. "Let's not do this right now, okay?"

"Mia will not be with you forever. She's got her own life to live, and now that Malcolm is back..."

"I finally told her about him this morning."

"I know. She told me."

Beni raised her hand that covered her heart. "Why were you talking to Mia about Malcolm?"

"Why were you talking to Mia about Linus?" she challenged her friend.

"That was an accident. A slip of the tongue. And since puberty, I've been dodging her mind reading crap."

"She read *my* mind today," Dyre confessed.

"Seriously?" Beni knew the strength of Dyre's powers. Breaching them was almost miraculous. "Do you think Oriana did something to her? She's unusually gifted for having an inept mother."

"Malcolm is quite strong." Dyre kicked a stone in her path.

"Not really. He never made the list."

At the height of her witch hunting days, Beni made a list of witches she and Asher considered a threat due to the strength of their abilities.

"I'd forgotten about the list."

"You know who *was* on that list? Camilla Nolan. There was a time Ash would have given his eye teeth to bag Camilla Nolan. I sat right in front of her not two weeks ago. Do you know how difficult that was for me? Taking down the great Camilla Nolan, second in command of Elder Path Circle. Next to the Phoenix, she would have been one hell of a get." Beni sighed at the memory of the one that got away. "Asher would have been so proud."

Dyre gagged in response to the mention of Asher Delger. "That ass."

"He always treated you with respect."

"He feared me."

"With good reason. You tried to kill him."

"I would have succeeded, too, if you hadn't stopped me." Dyre sneered with a bit of humor in her expression. "I've never forgiven you for that. He went after Linus."

Beni smiled. "I know. I remember, but it's not like Linus couldn't protect himself. You were just starry eyed." She fluttered her eyelashes playfully.

Dyre cleared her throat, which became a hoarse cough. "That's all over now."

"He'd come back to you in a minute. It was you who pulled the plug, not him."

"He betrayed me."

"He got a job." Beni raised her hands in disbelief. "You blamed him for consorting with your enemies. And to be fair, he knew them before they became your enemies. With all that, you still let your daughter into the lion's den."

"I blame *you* for that." Dyre pushed Beni's shoulder, which barely moved. "Without Mia, April would never have cared to go to that school. Starr tried for months to recruit her. I'm guessing by Linus's insistence, and she never batted an eye. Now Mia wants to go—"

"Mia *needs* to go," Beni interrupted. "Do you think I want my daughter taught by witches? Do you think I'm over the moon about her spending time with Elena Nolan? I'll tell you something, if Linus wasn't there, I would never have allowed her to go. I know him. I trust him."

"You do?"

"Absolutely. He knew me and what I've done. He never had an issue with it, even when Asher almost killed him. But regardless of anything you say, I know it wasn't the Nolan sisters that split you and Linus up. It was Lucy."

Dyre frowned.

"If she wasn't your legacy, you would still be together no matter where he worked. You changed when she was born. He felt it. I know I did. You pushed him away because you were scared. Admit it."

"Do you blame me?" The tears started again, and Dyre coughed her way through them. "I still remember the look in his eyes the first time I sneezed. Lulu was no more than a month old. April and Linus were playing in the yard. I had Lulu on my lap. A breeze whipped up the pollen and I sneezed. That's it, but the look on his face tore my heart out. It was like I was dying. Right then and there, dead." She took a deep, labored breath. "It wasn't long after that we did the… you know, legacy spell."

"Was he happy?"

"Oh, yeah. Everyone was thrilled, but I couldn't get that look out of my mind. So, when he told me about the school, I used it to pull away. None of it matters now. My powers are weakening, and it will all be over soon enough." She trudged up the steps to her front door. "Can you stay here tonight?"

"Absolutely." She threw her arm around her friend's shoulder and pulled her in for a hug. When she stepped back, she said, "It's either stay here or go kill some witches, but I can do that anytime."

Dyre shook her head. "Did you see the new Haven in town? Have you been there?"

"I'm dealing with all this school and witch boloney, and you want to draw blood drinkers into my life?"

"What's wrong with that?" Dyre's eyes narrowed, trying to figure her friend out. "Being around your own kind is a good thing."

"When have you ever known me to want to be around my own kind?" Beni pulled open the front door. "I did see two women inside the other night. It would be nice to have another woman in my life. I'm getting a little sick and tired of your nonsense."

"Is that so?" Dyre raised her hand. The front door slammed shut before Beni could walk through.

"Nice." Beni rubbed her nose as if it hurt from the door hitting it. "I see your magic isn't as weak as you like to let on."

"It still works from time to time." Dyre looked pleased with herself. Her moonstone pendant was back to normal as she laughed.

When they entered the house, April and Mia were headed to April's room. Beni saw the fire pendant swinging from her daughter's neck. "What's that?"

"A gift from Aunt Dyre." Mia wrapped her hand around it.

"Did it work?" Dyre asked.

"I think so. Was it supposed to give me a chill?" Mia held up her two fingers crossed for good luck.

"It was meant to distract you from yourself and your anxieties." Dyre smiled.

"What is it? Let me see." Beni pulled her daughter's hand away from the pendant to get a closer look. "You gave my daughter magic without asking me first?"

"Oh, it's nothing. If she has a bout of anxiety, it will calm her before it gets out of hand. That's all."

"I almost want something big to happen just to see what it does." Mia laughed and followed April down the hall to her room.

"It was just a little trinket to help her relax and not set the school on fire."

"Damn, you thwarted my plans."

"Just consider it payback for getting in my way with Asher."

THE CALLING

END OF AUGUST

12

MIA

Mia pulled her Subaru up in front of Magnolia Academy for Magical Arts. The final day of orientation had finally arrived, and she was over the moon to start lessons. She jumped out of the driver's seat and grabbed her backpack from the back seat.

"You coming?" she said when she noticed April hadn't budged from her seat.

Her cousin dropped her head on the back of the charcoal-colored seats and shrugged.

"Are you okay?" Mia walked back to the car, dropping her backpack on the sidewalk. "Are you sick? Should I call Kim or Linus?"

April deeply sighed. "No. I feel off. Do you feel something is off today?"

It was Mia's turn to shrug. "Nope. Just a normal Tuesday."

"I guess." She scratched her head, sending her long blonde hair over her shoulder. "I feel strange. Like something's going to happen."

"Aren't *you* a joy today?" She repeated a phrase she'd heard her mother use frequently.

"Thanks, Aunt Beni." April sneered. "I guess we can go in." She shook her shoulders and then her whole body like a dog, hoping to shake off the unpleasantness looming over her.

As they reached the side door of the house, Veda barreled through, knocking them off the pathway. Pierce followed in a more respectful way, allowing Mia and April to pass first.

"We're going to the café for coffee. Want to come?" He was looking at April with a hopeful gleam in his eye.

"I'm good, thanks." She was polite. Without looking at him, she sighed in a forlorn way that was distressing to hear.

Mia noticed Pierce's dejected expression as he turned to leave. "Maybe you should have gone. Caffeine may help your mood."

"Nothing can."

When they opened the door, the smell of pancakes surrounded them. Kim stood at the stove with a spatula in one hand and a pitcher of pancake mix in the other. Her large body bumped up against the stove as she leaned in to pour the batter.

Starr stood beside her mother, looking a lot like a six-year-old waiting for Santa to descend from the chimney. "Do the thing," she urged, dancing in place.

Kim turned to look at Camilla, who was sitting at the kitchen table, scrolling her phone and sipping tea. "Would you mind entertaining my child this morning?"

She looked up and giggled. "Levitas," she said. She flicked her wrist in a Harry Potter type flourish that was not needed, but it added entertainment value that Starr appreciated. The pancake levitated off the pan and flipped onto the uncooked side. Starr clapped. Kim laughed.

"Awesome." Mia's jaw dropped.

"Good morning, girls. Can I get you some breakfast?" Kim asked.

"No, thank you." Mia looked on in awe as Starr attempted to repeat Camilla's spell. She whispered *Levitas* several times before the pancake rose an inch off the pan and then flopped back down without turning over.

April slipped in, hoping no one would notice her. Being inside the house did nothing for the unease she'd been feeling since she woke up this morning. When she opened her eyes, ten minutes following her alarm clock chime, her stomach twisted. Not in a sick way, but in a strange way. A way that made her want to stay in bed and avoid any possible impending troubles. In a way that made her comforter the perfect hiding place today.

She ate breakfast, and the twist moved to her spine where it slid up and down like a bead on an abacus. The feeling that a tornado was approaching and she should get her mother and sister into the basement seemed to accost her as the knot moved. Now it rested in between her shoulders and had intensified since she walked into the house.

The cabinet door opened as she passed, almost catching her in the head. She pulled away just in time to avoid contact and a serious bump on her temple.

"Whoa." Linus entered the room. "Watch yourself. The spirits are feeling jumpy today." He laughed as he rubbed his hand on her arm.

"They're not the only ones," she murmured.

"Something wrong?" His soft expression made the twist loosen for only a second, when April wanted to lean against him for support. He seemed to sense this and touched her cheek. "Do you want to talk about it?"

"I'm fine," she whispered.

The cabinet opened and closed abruptly again. April jumped.

"Are you sure you're fine?" His unruly hair bounced as he leaned down to look her in the eye.

April nodded.

"Elena's waiting for you in the solarium for your final day of orientation." Camilla stood from her seat and walked to the sink. She caught a cabinet door in her hand as it swung out again, stopping it from slamming shut. She placed her teacup in the sink. "Maybe you're just nervous about starting lessons." Her brows lifted in an optimistic manner.

Mia just about ran to the solarium, eager to finish orientation. April shuffled behind her, feeling the twist become a tight-fisted knot at the base of her skull. The solarium was in the back of the house, hidden from the outside world by trees and bushes. The walls were lined with windows, and inside, tables held rows of plants.

It was dome shaped and the sun shone through the glass ceiling, making for an uncomfortable heat building in the room. The floor was wet from a constant mist showering down from the ceiling.

The minute she walked into the room, Mia heard a high-pitched buzzing and pressure behind her ears. She pressed her ear with her fingers to try to block it out. No one else seemed to notice it.

Elena Nolan stood in front of the only wall not lined with plants. Behind her, a door stood open, allowing a gentle breeze to circulate, which the girls were thankful for. She was dressed in a simple black skirt and a black silk blouse that shimmered in the sunlight. A small table stood beside her, covered in a sheet.

With a warm, encouraging smile, Elena greeted them and asked them to approach the table.

"Sadly, today is your last day of orientation, and I must share you with the other teachers." She gave them a disappointed grimace and then smiled. "There are a few details and vocabulary words that we must cover before you can successfully blend into lessons without being completely lost." She giggled. "I do apologize for the mist. It should stop in a few minutes. It hadn't occurred to me that the entire room would be wet when I chose to conduct our final lesson here."

The girls pulled two chairs from the sitting area closer to the table. Elena handed them towels to wipe them off.

The new moon fell on the last day of orientation. For four days, Elena Nolan had lectured and led them through the rules of the school and what being a level-one witch entailed. During the lectures, she covered the first chapter in their history of witchcraft textbook.

The Great Coven became a large part of today's lecture, explaining how the acts of only eight witches determined the path witchcraft would take for the next thousand years. They were expected to memorize the names of the eight pivotal characters in the Elder Path Circle.

Mia participated with great enthusiasm, already knowing the names of all eight founding members. April wasn't as familiar, having been bored every time her best friend gushed about the newest book she'd discovered. Two were easy for her to remember, as they were people they saw every day and came to admire: Camilla Nolan and Linus Brenig. Malcolm Brenig was Mia's father. Another topic she wouldn't shut up about. The others and less familiar names were Penelope Press, Farryn Allard, Micah Allard, Amma Quincy, and Seth Dallis.

"Seth Dallis?" Mia whispered to April with her eyes wide with curiosity.

"Do you know him?" Elena raised an eyebrow.

Mia swallowed hard, feeling the fire necklace tingle cold on her chest. She didn't respond until April nudged her with her elbow.

"No, but he's responsible for the fall of the Elder Path Circle. Isn't he?" A nervous tremble shook her shoulders. The book alluded to Seth Dallis becoming a blood drinker. Mia didn't wish to mention this fact for fear that she would be opening herself up to questions regarding her mother.

Elena's whole body went rigid. She acknowledged her answer with a stiff nod. "His crimes ran far deeper than being responsible for its fall." She paled.

Mia could see images of a large man with a full beard marrying Camilla in Elena's thoughts. They looked happy, blissful. Somehow, it all went wrong. She was immediately sorry she'd mentioned anything.

"You probably already know this, but Malcolm Brenig is my dad." Mia could feel her heart racing. She had only just met Malcolm two days ago. He had never mentioned he was in the Great Coven, and she was too anxious to ask about it. She had so many questions for him that she felt her head would burst.

"I do know that. Perhaps we may have Malcolm join us for an informal Q&A while he's in town. He is Linus's brother." Elena smiled, thoughts of Seth Dallis disappearing from the forefront of her mind. "Get out your journals and write down the names of these eight witches. Before you join your fellow classmates in lectures, you need to understand certain vocabulary."

Both girls reached for their tablets to take down the vocabulary she dictated. Words like coven, spell, and enchantment were easy enough for them to figure out. Other words like *zemi*, *grimoire*, or *intention*, they needed to take careful notes.

Elena pulled the sheet from the table to reveal several items laid out on it. To the girls, the items looked ordinary: a leather-bound book and a few crystals and rocks.

"A zemi is an enchanted object." She held a simple polished stone in the palm of her hand. "It is endowed with magic. A zemi is one way a witch can obtain immortality." She handed it to April, who passed it to Mia. It felt like an ordinary stone, but April could see a golden glow surrounding it. "That's magic," Elena explained.

"An *intention* is essentially a goal, plan, or purpose for something specific you'd like to manifest. It is not a tangible thing. You set intentions in your heart and in your moon journals. Tonight is the new moon, the perfect time to set intentions for the moon cycle."

The girls took detailed notes.

"Next." She gave them a large toothy smile "This is a grimoire. A *grimoire* is a book of magic that includes how to create magical objects like talismans and amulets, how to perform certain magical spells, and sometimes how to summon or invoke supernatural entities or magical creatures." Her body shuddered as she placed her hand on the cover of the leather-bound book in front of her.

"Do you hear that?" Mia whispered to April.

"That hum or faint ringing sound?" April asked her. Mia nodded.

"You'll get used to it." Elena continued to smile. "Grimoires are filled with magic. Personal magic that the witch imbues herself. You may feel the energy from this book more than any other because this, Mia, is your mother's grimoire."

April's eyes widened. The knot tightened.

Mia didn't like the pressure in her ears. She squeezed her eyes shut and clenched her jaw, hoping it would stop. It didn't. No matter how uncomfortable it made her, she needed to see her biological mother's grimoire. "May I see it?"

"It doesn't open."

Starr entered the solarium from the house. "Excuse me. Elena, Linus sent me to get you. He's in his office." The tall young girl stood in the doorway, chewing gum and absent-mindedly pulled on the vines surrounding her.

"Very well. Girls, take a few minutes to get out into the fresh air. I'll be right back. Don't touch anything on this table. Starr, return to class," she instructed before leaving.

After Elena disappeared down the hall, Starr entered the solarium. "What are you doing?" She walked to the table to examine the contents. She picked up the zemi and threw it back and forth in her hands. "Is this Elena's grimoire?"

"It's my bio mom's," Mia offered. "Her name was Oriana Duran."

Starr pulled on the cover and it didn't budge. She pulled down the latch and it remained in place. "It's stuck."

"Elena said it won't open." April hadn't moved from her seat.

"Why not?" Starr snapped her gum. "What's the point of a grimoire if you can't read it? Is there a key?"

Mia shrugged. "Maybe there was at one time, but I guess they lost it after she died."

The cover was a lovely rich, warm mahogany color. It had a strap across the middle of the cover that was attached to the frozen latch. The initials *OD* were etched into the lower right-hand corner. The spine was a darker color, still in the brown family, but it was clearly a separate piece of leather. The pages were deckled and different shades of cream, ivory, and white.

She listened to the hum, imagining that it was creating a song in her mind. Like her mother was singing to her. The pressure intensified, pressing against her jaw muscle. She rubbed it with her fingers.

"You should get back to class before you get in trouble," April told Starr.

She didn't care if Starr stayed or not or got in trouble or not. It was the knot at the base of her head. It didn't like anything in this room, and the more Starr or Mia talked, the more it tightened. She could feel a wave of dizziness causing the room to spin.

Mia dropped her hand onto the cover of the grimoire as they moved away from the table. It was like she was telling it: *I'll be back for you.* A sensation ran up her arm like warm water in her veins. The latch snapped open with a soft click of metal like a key turned in the lock.

"No way," Starr exclaimed. "You're the key."

Mia stared at the open latch. Her heart raced in her chest. This book was the last connection she would have with her birth mother. With a shaky hand, she touched the cover, toying with the edge, daring it to move.

The cover jumped and thumped back down. The pages trembled.

"Aren't you going to open it?" Starr asked. She slid her fingers under the cover and flipped it open.

A strong wind blew through the solarium, knocking potted plants to the floor. One pot cracked, spreading soil under the tables. The wind sounded like it was caught within the glass walls of the room. The mist kicked on again, and it felt like they were caught in a rainstorm. The door of the solarium slammed shut.

A gasp squeaked from Mia's mouth.

"Mia, don't touch it." April couldn't stop herself. The knot at the base of her skull throbbed as Starr began to turn pages in the book. "You don't have to…you don't have to read that. I mean, we should ask Linus or Camilla first. Or wait for Elena to come back. Don't you think?" Her breathing accelerated as the knot spread. Fingers spreading around her neck like a strangler trying to kill her. Her hands instinctually clasped around her neck to stop the attack. It was no use. It was inside of her. "Aunt Beni wouldn't like it."

Mia stared at her, wondering if she was right. The wind died. The mist dissipated.

Starr continued to flip pages. Dried flowers were pressed into some of the pages. Doodles lined the margins of herbal remedies. Spells were written in a flourish of colored ink. Towards the end of the book, the margins of each page were filled with rantings about being followed or losing her magic.

"Look, it's baby Mia." Starr held a photo of Mia stuck in one page.

Mia chewed her nails as Starr commented on everything. It wasn't until the last page that she got what she sought for the last sixteen years. A small comment printed on the last page. Not a letter really, just a note to Mia. *Until we meet again. Be strong, my baby girl* was all it said. Mia touched the letters and felt the pressure her mother used as she wrote the words.

"No way!" Starr stopped on one page. "Your mom has a spell to summon the Sisters of Fate. That's amazing."

Still lost in a mist of tears brought on by her mother's words, Mia barely listened to Starr's excitement.

"We need to do this one. Come on, read it with me. *We summon the Sisters of Fate*," Starr began. "I can't do this alone, guys. You saw this morning. I can barely flip a pancake. Maybe between the three of us, we can make this work. Besides, I suck at Latin and the last lines are in Latin."

"I'm not summoning the Sisters of Fate." April stood. She stretched her neck from side to side and rolled her shoulders to free herself from the pain she was in. "My mother would kill me."

"Party pooper," Starr taunted. "Mia and I can do it then. You hold these."

She tossed April two chains: one strung through an orange gemstone pendant and the other was green. They looked a lot like the pendant her mother wore every day. The bezel on the orange pendant was tarnished and pitted like it had been burned, but the stone was immaculate. The green stone was perfect too, though the silver chain and bezel were a little tarnished.

April held them in her palm.

"Come on, it's just for fun." Taking Mia by the hand, Starr pulled her to the book. They recited the words. Mia was still only vaguely aware of what she was saying. Still lost in the wind that seemed to erupt when they opened the book. Still wondering if April was right about not reading from it.

Regardless of how she felt inside, she stumbled over the Latin phrases with Starr and then repeated it two more times.

"You're supposed to let the chains swing like a pendulum three times," Starr instructed.

April followed her direction and then gathered the chains in her palm again.

"Is that it?" Starr murmured. Her tall, lanky body bent closer to the grimoire to see if she had missed a step in the spell recitation. "Oh, we need the blood of Oriana Duran." She cringed as she looked at Mia. "Mind if I prick your finger?"

"What?" Mia seemed to wake from a daze.

"You're the closest thing we have to Oriana Duran. I need your blood." She said the last bit with a Transylvanian accent.

The humming she'd heard earlier seemed to surround her. The song that existed only in her mind lulled her. Mia allowed Starr to take her hand. The air felt moist and heavy. She expected to hear thunder in the distance.

Starr held a needle that was threaded into one of the pages of the book. Mia braced herself.

The minute the pin pierced her skin, Mia woke from her stupor. The humming ceased. The humidity in the solarium was oppressive. The needle dug into her index finger, sending a sharp, piercing pain up her arm. A bubble of blood pooled on the tip of her finger.

Starr turned her wrist, aiming the droplets of blood at the spell. Brown spots already darkened the spell from previous attempts, and Mia realized that her blood was mixing with her mother's blood on the page.

"One more time." Starr encouraged her to read the spell for the final time.

A low rumble of thunder shook the solarium. The door rattled and the leaves of the plants trembled as if an earthquake was causing this phenomenon. Mia pulled her hand back, no longer mesmerized by her mother's spell book. As she thrust her bleeding finger into her mouth, tasting the coppery blood, she thought of Beni. *What would she think of this?*

She knew Beni would be angry. But they had gone too far already.

As the thunder calmed and the earth ceased to vibrate beneath their feet, Mia slammed the book closed and latched it.

"We can't tell anyone about this."

They could hear running from down the hall. Linus and Elena sped into the room. He arrived before her, looking harried and out of breath.

"What are you doing?" he shouted.

A low rumble of thunder shook the walls of the solarium as a kind of answer.

Starr laughed.

April screamed out in pain. The pendants were glowing and became white hot in her hand. She shook them onto the floor. They took a layer of skin with them as they fell at her feet.

Linus ran to her. He examined her hand. "Starr, get Kim and hurry." His tone was angry and concerned all balled up into one, coming out as a frustrated shout. He pulled out a handkerchief from his pocket and pressed it against April's now blistering palm.

Starr bolted from the room.

Elena walked to the table. "What did I tell you? Didn't I say not to touch anything? Let alone read anything." She slammed her hands on her hips, her fingers tapping impatiently. "Casting without permission was one of the first rules we covered. Didn't we?" Her dark eyes moved from April to Mia and then back again. "You opened a book you had no right to touch and were strictly instructed not to do."

"It opened on its own." Mia's voice was no louder than the mewing of a kitten.

"What?" Elena snapped at her.

"It opened on its own. I only touched the cover, and the lock opened." Tears filled her eyes.

Elena glared at her, her eyes tiny fireballs of accusation.

"We didn't mean to…" Tears streamed down her face. She leaned on the table to support herself, and her hand accidentally touched the grimoire again. The lock disengaged. "See—"

"Mia, go inside and wash your face." Camilla Nolan seemed to appear in the exterior doorway of the solarium. She stepped up to the table and, without a word, reattached the lock on the grimoire. "After you do that, please wait in the kitchen."

Mia nodded. Looking at April, who had collapsed in Linus's arms, she sped from the room.

Kim rushed into the room, pulling April away from Linus. "Let me see your hand."

13

Mia

Mia stared at herself in the bathroom mirror for a long time. She thought of the grimoire, of her mother's beautiful handwriting, of the details drawn in ink along the sides of the pages. She thought of her blood melding with her mother's. Then the wind and the thunder. The vibration she felt under her feet like they had whipped up an earthquake.

As she stared at her long brown hair, frizzy from the mist and humidity, she remembered April's feeling this morning. *Do you feel something is off today?* Mia hadn't felt anything. But now, she knew April was right.

A few stress blemishes bristled to the surface that she hadn't noticed this morning. Her eyes were bloodshot from crying. The fire pendant around her neck flickered as she continued to examine her face.

"Mia?" A soft knock came at the door. It was Linus.

"I'll be right out."

She pulled out her phone. She texted her mother.

School is not going great today. (sad face emoji)

When she pulled the door open, Linus stood waiting for her. "Feeling any better?"

Mia followed him into the kitchen, where Camilla, Elena, and Kim waited. April sat with her hand lying on the table. Her palm faced up as Kim applied a salve to help with the burns.

"You okay?" she asked her cousin. April didn't answer but only shared a sad look with her.

"Where's Starr?" Elena started. "She started this."

"You don't know that." Kim defended her daughter.

"Did she?" Elena looked at Mia and April. Neither girl wished to throw their friend under the bus, but it was all Starr's idea if they were being honest. Camilla and Linus read their thoughts but didn't offer the information up as evidence. They would allow Kim to discipline her own daughter.

"Stop trying to place blame." Camilla spoke slow and calculated, trying to calm her sister down. "Let's just deal with the infractions. Shall we? Mia, take a seat." She motioned to the empty chair at the kitchen table.

The kitchen offered an informal mood to the proceedings. Neither girl felt as if they were on trial until they saw that Elena refused to sit and continued pacing while Camilla spoke.

"The biggest one I see is casting without permission. You both know that is not allowed. For safety reasons, mostly, but neither of you are in control of the abilities you've displayed up until now. Can we agree that adding spellcasting to the list of your abilities is well out of your wheelhouse?"

Mia and April nodded.

"Fine. There is still the matter of the spell you read and the house spirits you've upset." Her dark eyes widened as she pushed her gray hair behind her shoulders. "Apologies and making amends should appease the spirits. They are so temperamental, but that should do the trick."

"The spell you read…" Linus began. "You called the Sisters of Fate, correct?" His handsome face dimmed with disappointment for both girls. "What did you do exactly?"

Mia looked at April and realized she didn't intend to speak, so she started. "Starr…" Her voice caught in her throat, and she started again. "We read the spell twice. April had those necklaces that burned her in her hand. She swung them around a little and then Starr poked me with a needle. We read the spell for a third time. That's it."

"That's it?" Elena screeched.

A cabinet door swung open and slammed shut, displaying the spirits' displeasure at her volume and tone.

"Elena." Linus held his hands out to tell her to calm down.

"No, they used blood magic. They read a spell that far exceeded their magical range. They broke into a book they were forbidden to touch. What else?" She looked at the girls, who lowered their heads in shame.

Camilla sat back in her seat. She crossed her arms over her chest and waited for her sister to stop screaming. She didn't look angry. She looked curious as Mia watched her react to the list of infractions Elena had gathered. Her brows knitted together as her eyes narrowed. Her lips pursed and a small smirk curled her mouth.

"Kim, how is April's hand faring?" she asked.

"Should be good as new in a few hours. Just keep it clean." Kim winked at April and allowed her to hold a cloth over the wound.

"Linus, don't you have a class starting now?" Camilla gazed at Linus with humor.

"Magical Embodiment starts in about five minutes." He slipped his reading glasses on his nose to read his watch. He stood and slipped on a brown sweater with leather elbow patches and a suede collar.

"Take Mia and April to class with you. I think they've been oriented enough." Her eyes slid back to her sister with an angry glare. "After lunch, I want both of you in my office." She pointed to Mia and April as they followed Linus out of the room. "Kim, I'll allow you to discipline Starr unless you'd like me to do it."

"I'll take care of it," she assured her.

14

APRIL HEARS VOICES

The room Linus used as a classroom was a large library-type room that April adored. The smell of old books and an underlying scent of burning candles gave it a warm, comforting feeling that made her feel safe, especially after such a trying morning.

There were three comfy leather chairs and one sofa that faced the podium where Linus liked to stand. Each student had a favorite spot for whatever reason; it didn't really matter. April sat in the comfy leather chair closest to Linus's podium. The sound of his voice did something to relax her. Mia took the leather chair directly opposite her. Veda and Lilly sat on the couch. Starr sat on the floor even with one empty chair available. Pierce stood beside the podium, trying hard to look in control and authoritative.

"Immortality," Linus Brenig announced after he allowed the room to accept their two new students. That's all the group needed to snap to attention. "How does one gain immortality?"

"You tell us." Veda's snide remark got a chuckle from the novices.

Linus raised his eyebrow in response. He didn't comment but continued with the lesson.

Mia's phone sounded an incoming text, and she cringed when Linus raised an eyebrow at her. "Sorry." She quickly silenced her phone, noticing a text from her mother.

"There are three ways. Can anyone name them?" he pressed on.

Lilly Pershan sat forward. "Spells, charms, or amulets."

"How are charms and amulets different?" Veda snarked.

"Do you have a different answer?" Linus was growing tired of the constant attitude she injected into their daily lessons.

"Spells, amulets, and herbs."

"Correct." He looked impressed by her answer but equally annoyed by her self-righteous approach. "Mia, what kinds of amulets can be used?"

She froze. It was the first time she'd been expected to answer a question today. She'd been staring at the arrangement of dried flowers on the mantel, thinking of the mess they'd made of orientation this morning and the upcoming meeting with Camilla in an hour.

Mia shrugged sheepishly, actively avoiding Linus's intense stare. April nodded, trying to encourage her to answer, but fear kept her mouth shut. She could feel the heat rising in her cheeks and tried desperately to control her fear. Smoke rose from the dried flowers on the mantel, and she squeezed her eyes shut. The dancing fire charm chilled her as expected. The tiny flame danced blue.

Linus walked to her and touched her arm. "Breathe through it."

"What's wrong with her?" Veda's sarcasm didn't help Mia's anxiety.

"She's a firestarter," April offered.

Linus looked around the room. "She's elemental. Does anyone know what *that* means?"

"She can control elements." Veda didn't wait to be called on. She whispered, "Duh," under her breath.

"Veda, I don't wish to speak to you again," Linus warned her. "As for you, Mia, we just need to learn to control your fires. The proper name for it is fire elemental witch, but firestarter is acceptable. That's an interesting charm you have."

Mia smiled awkwardly. "It was a present from…"

Linus's eyes creased into a smile. He knew where it had come from. "Be cautious with unnatural flames. They don't extinguish easily." He placed a hand on the side of her face, and she saw her father in his mind.

She took a deep breath and blew it out. The flowers smoked but did not catch fire. The dancing blue flame returned to yellow, and the chill decreased as she calmed down.

"From where did she steal an eternal flame?"

A voice surrounded April. It sounded hollow like it was spoken in a large, empty room. She looked behind her and around to her classmates. No one had spoken or seemed to hear the voice.

Linus returned to the podium. "So, what amulets can be used? Mia, would you like to take another crack at this one?" He pointed to the charm around her neck.

"Um, I think anything can be used. Jewelry, crystals, personal items, stuff like that. The old-world term for them is *zemi*. It just means an item endowed with power."

"Excellent. Where did you learn about zemis?" Linus was impressed.

"Elena talked about it this morning," she said. "And from a book."

"That's good. Good for you. Education is important." He smirked.

"Especially when your mother is a cold blood." Veda giggled.

"Veda, after class." Linus glared at her until her smile disappeared.

"Fools. Her mother is not a cold blood. Her real mother is a cold-blooded killer."

It was a feminine voice, sour like vinegar but with a humorous undertone like everything she said amused her. The voice was dynamic and self-righteous. If this voice had ever lived, April knew she was someone who got things done without a care for anyone who got in her way.

"Let's move on. From your reading last night, you should already know the herbs that can increase immortality. Does anyone know the drawbacks of using herbs or even zemis?"

"They can be taken from you." The voice was closer now, almost in her ear. The hollow, echoing attribute still existed but didn't sound like it was all around her anymore. *"Say it."*

"They can be taken from you?" April raised a shaky hand. It didn't go past her shoulder when it rose, but Linus saw it.

"Excellent." He beamed. "Anything tangible can be taken from you, thus taking the enchantment away too. If someone steals your sachet or zemi, you lose your immortality."

"Why use them then?" Lilly asked. "Why not just use a spell?"

"Weakness." The voice sounded sickened by the notion of a weak witch.

April felt she had no choice but to repeat the voice's words. "Weakness?"

Linus was taken aback. Perplexed by her answer, he wondered where she'd gotten the belief that the inability to use certain magic denoted weakness. "Not necessarily. Some witches just don't have the ability to hold a spell or spells aren't their strength. Judging a witch by their abilities is not only prejudiced but also dangerous. Everyone is different. Everyone is strong in their own way."

April slid down in her seat.

"Your father is a fool. A weak-minded fool," the voice huffed, annoyed.

"What did you say?" April stood up. As she stood, hearing the words again, *your father*, a flood of memories filled her. She saw her mother with Linus. Pierce holding Lulu when she was a baby. A family trip to Disney World. April thought of the Disney pictures she had at home. Linus and Pierce had been removed from them, but in her mind, they were there smiling and laughing.

"Is everything alright?" Linus's eyes widened as he and the rest of the class reacted to April's outburst.

She stared at him. "May I go to the bathroom? I'm not feeling well." *Your father is a fool.*

Linus studied her, hearing the voice's words in her mind. A mixture of happiness, fear, and insult struck him as he heard them. He was unsure as to how to react or if he should mention it. He seemed to freeze as she waited for an answer. "Of course. Don't take too long."

Mia heard the words too. This was the last thing they needed today, after all the trouble they'd caused already.

"You are Dyre's daughter. Not the legacy." The voice followed her to the bathroom.

"Stop talking to me!" she shouted.

April splashed water on her face. She stared at herself in the mirror for a moment. The voice was silent. As she opened the bathroom door, she heard voices coming from the potions room down the hall. She stopped and listened.

"When *did* you think it was a good time to tell me?" Camilla's voice was unmistakable.

"Not today," Elena answered. "I planned to tell you when it was necessary. Up until now, I didn't deem it necessary."

"Well, you deemed wrong."

Clanging of metal instruments against glass echoed. It sounded like Camilla was preparing for a class in the most rushed and irritated way possible.

"What do you want me to say?" Elena's high heels clacked on the tile floor.

"I want you to undo this mess you made. Why did you show them the grimoire? Was a picture not good enough? Maybe take a blank journal and use it for practical purposes. No, you knew what you were doing?"

Elena sighed.

April could feel that knot in her neck grab hold of her shoulders. Her arms felt heavy as she stood listening to the sisters argue. A sour weight dropped in her stomach, and she felt nauseous. Her hands shook.

"I guess I wanted to win some points with Mia."

"Did it not occur to you that Mia would want to touch the grimoire? The only living being capable of opening it…no, you knew exactly what you were doing."

A resounding clang followed her words as if she threw a metal pan onto the floor.

"Stop saying that."

"It's true. Now, what do you intend to do about it?"

"What can I do?"

"I know what I can…" Camilla stopped speaking. She appeared in the doorway of the classroom. "April? Is there something I can do for you?"

"No, ma'am." Her throat filled with bile, and she swallowed it back down.

"Well, well, well. Nolan sister number one." The voice seemed to sidle up beside her as if she was telling her a secret. The voice was full of venom and humor.

"April?" Camilla walked to her. "You are white as a ghost."

"I'm fine."

"Milly, if we're done here. I'll go help Kim set up for lunch." Elena stepped out of the classroom, straightening her black skirt. She reached under her short black hair and fluffed it. The white streak blended into the rest of the hair and then reemerged like a buoy fighting fierce waves.

April froze. The nausea and trembling ceased, replaced with an unexplainable rage. She could feel it in every part of her body.

Every cell thundered, feeling a fire surrounding her face. Deep breaths did no good.

Elena stopped in front of April. "I'll be at the meeting after lunch. I'm still quite angry with you girls."

April could feel the rage building. Elena's fiery expression only fueled it. The way her hands fell on her hips in a maternal stance of irritation. The way her toe tapped as she waited for an explanation. April only became angrier. Her heart raced in her chest with such intensity that she thought it would burst.

Her hands clawed at her sides.

Camilla took in her physical changes and then read her thoughts. They weren't detailed, but she got the gist of what April felt. "Leny, go," she demanded. When her sister finally listened and continued down the hall, Camilla took hold of April's shoulders. She shook her several times.

"Linus," she called.

When Linus emerged from the library, only steps away from where they stood, the rage broke. April no longer felt the hatred burning in her stomach. The tension deescalated in her shoulders. She only saw the man who could be her father.

Both he and Camilla saw this in her mind. Linus smiled.

"Why don't you go get a quick drink in the kitchen—"

"No," Camilla interrupted. "Just use the fountain in the solarium."

April nodded without a word and walked down the hall.

"How did she find out?" Camilla asked.

"No clue, but whoever is talking to her is also draining her emotionally. I need to speak with Dyre." He rolled his eyes, knowing anytime he needed to speak with his ex-wife was an emergency.

"Well, whoever is talking to her also hates Elena."

"Do you think they really accomplished it? Calling the Fates, I mean."

"They did so much more." Camilla blew out a breath. "Would you like to join us after lunch? It promises to be one hell of a meeting."

In the solarium, April bent to sip the water from the water fountain. There were no buttons to press. The fountain was a continuous stream of fresh spring water that seemed to feed from an unknown source. She pulled her hair back and allowed the water to fill her mouth.

"You have no idea what that woman did to me. To my daughters. Tell your mother. She will deal with her properly." The voice sounded angry, frustrated, and frightened at the same time.

"She already knows." April didn't bother to whisper. She had a strong feeling that this would be her last day at Magnolia Academy. If her mother went through all the trouble of removing Linus from her life, she was going to be super pissed to find out her secret had been leaked.

"She knows and Elena Nolan is still alive?"

"What'd she do to you, anyway?" She circled the flower beds, touching the roses and the leafy vines as she walked.

"She killed me and my daughters."

"She killed you?" April stopped short as she weaved in between the tables. Curiosity outweighed surprise or revulsion. She wasn't sure she really believed it. Still wasn't sure she wasn't going crazy.

Hearing voices was crazy, right? There was still the chance that this was all a dream, and she'd wake up to her alarm clock in a few minutes.

Playing along with her temporary insanity, she continued to humor the ideas the voice placed in her head. Her mother said she hated Elena Nolan but still allowed April to attend the school. If she really killed this woman and her daughters, why wasn't she in jail? If Elena Nolan was a murderer, why did her mother allow her to go to school here?

It was all ridiculous anyway. She stared up into the blue sky beyond the glass ceiling panes, waiting for her alarm clock to start ringing or for her mother to tell her she'd overslept.

"If your mother refuses to do her duty, then I need you to do it."

April laughed. "I'm not killing anyone."

That was the deciding factor. Insane people heard voices that told them to kill, just like she did. She wasn't dreaming. She was insane. Her mother was right. Magnolia Academy wasn't the right place for her. She needed to be in a looney bin.

"April?" Linus stood at the door of the solarium. "Who are you talking to?" The concern in his face warmed her heart. She could see Lucy in his expressions. They did the same squinty thing with their right eye when they were figuring something out.

"Nobody, nothing. I was just…nothing." She tapped the toe of her sneaker in a puddle on the floor.

"How's your hand?" He stroked his beard as he asked.

April looked at the burn. The salve had softened it, and the edges were no longer red. She would have sworn the burn happened days ago instead of only an hour ago. "Fine."

"I think we should talk."

"We don't need to talk. Really. I'm fine. Mom has her reasons for doing what she did, I'm sure. Not that she's sharing them. Don't worry about me. I'm totally cool with keeping this hush-hush." She waved her hand between them, meaning their secret relationship. The speed with which she spoke caused her to stutter over her words. "I really think with everything going on today, I should go home. I don't feel safe. I feel…"

Unhinged, she thought.

Linus looked both confused and entertained.

"I really think we should talk," he repeated. "Sit down for a second, please."

April's head hung low as she sat on the edge of the white wrought iron chair near the center of the room. Linus stood and then thought better of it. He moved his hands in and out of his pants pockets as if he wasn't sure which way would be perceived less intimidating. April fiddled with the zipper on her hoodie as her eyes followed a line of water flow from the hose and down the drain.

"Is it true…"

"I don't really know…"

They started speaking at the same time and then laughed at the awkwardness of the moment. Linus urged her to continue. The voice laughed too.

"Is it true? Are you my father?" she said, feeling an awful lot like Luke Skywalker at the end of *The Empire Strikes Back*.

"Yes. Yes, I am. Pierce is your brother. Your mother and I adopted him when you were two or three, I think. He was ten. I don't suppose your mother mentioned anything about him." Linus looked defeated, like he couldn't fight Dyre's resolve.

April only shook her head. "Mom's really good at keeping secrets. Aunt Beni loves to say she could win an Olympic medal in secrecy." She giggled.

Linus smirked. "Aunt Beni." He said the name with affection.

"She told me I could trust you."

"Did she?" He laughed again. He slipped on his reading glasses and checked his watch. "Almost time for lunch and your meeting with Camilla."

"Will you be there?"

"If you want me to be, I will."

"I guess I need a parent present when I'm being reprimanded by the headmistress."

Linus's eyes lit up. "I suppose I should tell your mother."

April shrugged. "Good luck."

"Can we kill Elena Nolan now?"

"Shut up!" April found her internal voice and used it with authority.

"Pardon me?" Linus read her thoughts.

"Nothing." She smiled and followed him out of the solarium.

15

BENI

Beni stepped outside of her house and took a deep breath of the evening air. The day had been warm. She could still feel it in the dirt and on the rocks in her path. The warmth lingered in the air as she watched the sun fall behind the trees.

Mia was at Dyre's house. A message was left on her phone telling her so. Dyre sounded angry in the message. Beni didn't want to deal with whatever had gotten her dander up tonight. After Mia's text this morning, she knew bad news was on the horizon.

Her phone buzzed in her pocket, and she dug it out. Dyre's lovely face filled the screen. She thought she'd have at least an hour to appreciate the night before diving right in, but when Dyre got into a snit about something, there was no stopping her.

"Who did what?" Beni was in good spirits.

"Did you get my message?" Dyre sounded grim.

"Yes. I'm out now. I should be by in about an hour or so. Did Mia eat?"

"Come over now."

"What's wrong?" Beni stopped dead in her tracks, startling a scurrying animal behind her.

"Something's up. Neither of the girls is talking and they are both blocking me."

"Blocking *you*? How is that possible?" Dyre could worm her way into anyone's head. If they had a brain, she could infiltrate it.

"They're working together. I can't explain it. Just get here as soon as you can, please."

"What aren't you telling me?"

"Linus tried calling me today. Whatever it is, it's bad." Dyre hung up.

A growl rattled the back of Beni's throat.

"Mia?" Beni barged through Dyre Crane's front door without knocking. As she stood in the small vestibule, she saw her daughter sitting at the dining room table with her hands knotted in front of her. Dyre sat across from her, looking more annoyed than angry.

There was a strange odor hovering in the air. She raised her chin to sniff the air, wondering what it was and what was causing it. Mia and Dyre didn't seem to notice it.

The scent was hard to ignore and hard to describe. A natural smell, like lightning striking a tree. The smell of ozone in the air came in waves like caught on a breeze.

Mia sniffed her sleeve, and Beni knew she'd heard her thoughts. She gave her daughter a little shrug like it didn't matter and then turned to her friend.

"Where are April and Lulu?" She was unaccustomed to entering the house without being accosted by Lulu and a new vampire joke.

"In their rooms." Dyre spoke through clenched teeth. She didn't look at Beni but kept her eyes firmly glued to the table. Her leg bounced as her anger grew.

"Can I speak with Mia alone?" She glared at Dyre, whom she blamed for ruining what started as a decent night. Dyre walked into the kitchen without a word. "Did you eat dinner?"

"Yes."

"So tell me what happened?"

"I got suspended." Mia's voice sounded mousy and afraid.

"Already? Did you burn down the school?" A giggled bubbled in her throat and she knew this little blip had yet to ruin her good mood.

"There's a note for you."

"Where is it?" Beni's shoulders slumped. *Another damn note.*

"Aunt Dyre, where's the note for Mom?" Mia called as if her aunt wasn't listening to every word they said.

"On the mantel in the living room."

Beni only waited for a second before she realized Dyre had no intention of retrieving it for them. She stomped past her as she leaned against the kitchen counter with a glass of water in her hand. Her eyes followed Beni as she passed both times.

"Want to say something?" she challenged her.

Dyre's eyebrows jumped on her forehead. "We'll have our time to talk." Her jaw was set forward in a scowl Beni didn't try to interpret.

"Whatever." Beni threw her hand in the air and kept walking into the dining room. She pulled out the chair beside Mia and sat down. The crisp white envelope ripped easily as she slid her forefinger under the flap.

"*To the parents/guardians of Mia Duran.*" Beni looked at her daughter over the letter. "Jesus Christ, Camilla Nolan really is a bitch, isn't she?" She tried to keep hold of her good feelings.

"Keep going." Mia's voice shook.

"*Your child has been found guilty of casting without permission and ignoring the rules of the school. It is to our great dismay that we must take disciplinary actions. Mia will be suspended for a period not to exceed three days. On completion of her punishment, I ask that you and she meet with me to discuss how to move forward with her education. I hope we can put an end to this disruptive behavior,* blah, blah, blah. *Sincerely, Camilla Nolan.*"

A tear slipped down Mia's cheek.

"That's it?" Beni turned the letter over, expecting there to be more information on the reverse side.

"I really wanted to go there." Mia cried. "And I fucked it up."

Beni blew out a long breath and grasped her daughter's hand. "One day out of school and you've already acquired a potty mouth?"

Mia laughed through her tears.

Beni reexamined the letter. "Jesus, now I have to go back to see that witch. It's fine if you get in trouble. I've seen my fair share of trouble. I can't fault you for that, but now you've got me in trouble too."

Her daughter giggled through her tears. "I'm sorry."

"I'm sorry, too. If you just burned the school down like I'd hoped, none of this would be necessary." She pulled a handkerchief out of her jacket pocket and wiped her daughter's tear-stained cheeks. "This is not a big deal. You are a great kid, no matter what the Nolan sisters think."

"Thanks, Mom." Mia inhaled a shaky emotion-filled breath and let it out.

"So, what are you and April hiding from Dyre?"

Mia looked up to the kitchen door as Dyre Crane entered the room. She pulled out a chair across from Beni, placed her glass of water on the table, and sat down. Mia waited for her aunt to add to the conversation.

"I think April should tell you."

"She got suspended," Beni told Dyre.

"She told me that much. April did her one better. She quit."

"No shit?" Beni's eyes widened. "What prompted that?"

They looked at Mia. There was silence in the room. Dyre leaned forward towards Mia and then sat back. "How are you doing that?"

"Doing what?" Beni asked.

"Blocking me." Dyre spoke through her teeth in a frustrated tone. She looked down at the fire pendant around Mia's neck. "Take it off."

Mia's hand wrapped around the pendant.

"Take it off," Dyre demanded. "She's using my own magic against me."

"Who cares," Beni shouted. "The letter says you cast without permission. Casting is what?"

"We read a spell from a book," Mia offered.

"What book?" Dyre side-eyed her like she already knew what book they'd read from.

"Elena showed us…my mother's grimoire. I was the only one able to open it. When I did it, Starr read a spell and poked my finger with a needle." Mia looked at her finger. The place she jabbed her was still sore, but there was no mark left to see.

"What spell did you read?" Beni asked.

"They summoned the Sisters of Fate." Dyre frowned. "I heard them. Lulu came home from school early because she was sick. Not sick to her stomach, though. She was hearing voices. Two voices calling to her from Magnolia Academy for Magical Arts. Where the hell were your teachers when all of this was going on?"

Mia shrugged as she hung her head.

"Okay, fine. They read a spell. They need permission to do that?" Beni looked at Dyre.

Dyre laughed in a condescending manner that Beni hated. "How have you spent centuries hunting witches with Asher Delger and not know what witches do?"

Beni's jaw clenched. "Don't start with this again. I'm not going to make excuses for my life. You know that, and I know what they do. I just don't know the terminology."

"Well, learn it. Your daughter needs you to know something about her life."

"Because you've been so forthcoming with your own daughters, you can sit in judgement over me. So, please enlighten me, my Lady of the Fates." Beni kicked Dyre's chair leg like a petulant child. Dyre rolled her eyes as the chair moved away from the table.

"How mature," Dyre taunted her.

"You can give me crap about my past, but I can't give it back?"

"Stop it." Mia tugged on her mother's sleeve. "Can you two bicker another time? My life is dangling from a thread here."

"I'm sorry." Dyre lowered her eyes.

"Why are you so pissed at me tonight?"

"Not at you." She looked up at the ceiling as if she saw a bat flying above them. "This situation. What they did. Being reminded of what Oriana Duran did to my sisters. Everything. All of it." The glass of water on the table began to boil.

Beni glanced at the ceiling, knowing there was more to this story than just Dyre's temper issues. She grasped her friend's hand and squeezed it. The rolling boil in the glass slowly decreased. "What's this book they used?" Beni was almost embarrassed to ask.

"A grimoire is, in its simplest terms, a spell book. Mine also contains the history and stories of my sisters and our past. I've included directions to certain safe places and how to get home."

"You're not a witch. Why do you have a grimoire?"

Dyre groaned at her friend's ignorance. "Anyway… Oriana, being who she was, had a spell for summoning the Sisters of Fate, and the girls apparently homed in on that one right away. Naturally, I heard them read it, being the only sister still living. As my legacy, Lulu did too. I can't say if anyone else heard it. I don't think they caused any damage, but they got caught. April quit school. Thank the gods."

"What does Linus have to say about all this?"

Before Mia could answer, Dyre interjected, "Who cares. I didn't pick up when he called. I never wanted her there. Linus swears Elena abandoned her delusions of grandeur when Oriana died, but having April that close to that level of evil…" She stopped and closed her eyes. "Maybe now I'll be able to sleep at night."

"I think you should talk to April," Mia added.

"Is there something else I need to know before I move away and change my name?" Beni gave her daughter an exhausted glare.

"You're hilarious," Dyre snipped.

"You are joy tonight, aren't you?" Beni grimaced at her friend. "Give us a few minutes, please. Then you can unleash all the anger and blame you want on me."

After Dyre left the room, this time disappearing down the hall towards April's bedroom, Mia asked, "What does she blame you for?"

"If you hadn't wanted to go to Magnolia Academy, then April would not have wanted to go either. She can't blame you, so she blames me. Like she didn't foresee all this happening eons ago."

"Can she do that?"

An expression of amazement danced over Beni's face. "She can do anything. She's a goddess. If she chooses to bury her head in the sand, then horrible things will befall those she loves. If she opens her eyes and pays attention, she can protect us from anything. Guess which one she chooses more often than not?"

Mia's face collapsed into sadness. "Do you hate me?"

"Never. Just stop with all this witchy stuff for a while, please. Take these few days to reassess if this is the right place for you."

"Malcolm…I mean, my dad asked if he could tutor me. What do you think about that?"

Beni dropped her head on the table. "Can we discuss this later? Please." She leaned over and kissed her daughter's cheek.

Dyre appeared at the end of the hallway. Trying to control her anger, frustration, and fear drained her. She clenched her jaw as she said, "Beni, April would like to talk to you."

16

GAIL

The closet enveloped her. The shallow width and deep length held no air. Gail took short breaths as if it would conserve the little air that existed.

She stopped crying, stopped hyperventilating. Stopped banging on the walls and the door. Nobody was coming for her. Her father and baby sister were dead. Her older brother, Simon, moved away last year. He insisted he'd found love, but Gail knew her brother could no longer deal with the insanity that seemed to overtake the house since Edith's death. She'd written him a letter when Father died, to let him know. Poured out the heart-wrenching details on paper and received no answer back.

Nobody was coming to save her from this mad woman's torture. The mad woman she called Mother.

She sat in the closet, a pillow beneath her for comfort and a blanket for warmth. A single candle burned and the crack beneath the door offered light, but that was all. With her legs knotted in front of her, she listened. She listened for the sobbing and the breaking glass that invariably followed being thrown into the closet. Her mother's crying, sometimes screaming, but mostly just crying.

Her mother would apologize in her drunken state. Apologize and break things.

Plates, glasses, picture frames, furniture.

When the imprisonment ended, the cleanup began. Gail suffered many cut fingers cleaning shards of broken glass out of the living room rug.

The thin plywood door was indestructible. No matter how much she banged and pushed, it would not break. Through this magic door, she heard nothing.

Gail feared the worst. Had her mother fallen? Had she died? Would this tiny closet become her coffin when there was no one to rescue her? She heard footsteps outside the door. Not disoriented, drunken footsteps but sure, determined ones. She pressed her face to the floor and pushed her eye to the crack beneath the door.

First, all she saw was the kitchen's wood floor, then almost out of view, she saw her mother lying motionless. Her arms outstretched and her hair splayed across the rug. The hem of a dress swept past the door. The rustling of petticoats and rich fabrics denoted a woman of means. The light aroma of perfume and the clicking of heels on the hardwood caused more curiosity than fear inside Gail.

Miss Allard?

Gail already knew the answer. Their next-door neighbor and her mother hadn't spoken in weeks due to a falling-out. Besides, Miss Allard never wore a petticoat. Her clothing was simple, reserved, clean and respectable.

The strange woman with the silk petticoat pulled the necklace from her dying mother's throat. Gail heard whispering but neither saw nor heard another person. Within seconds, the strange woman was gone, leaving a trail of flowery perfume in her wake.

Gail banged on the door. "I'm in here."

She woke up.

The sound of her banging on that closet door jarred her from her sleep.

And then she heard it for real.

Gail Andrews opened her eyes and looked at the clock. Midnight. She scowled at the glowing numbers. Late summer nights left so little darkness for her to appreciate, and she had overslept. Bad dreams plagued her rest.

She stretched her arms over her head and reached for her phone. The weather app said clear, moonless skies. New moon. The image of a black moon sat at the top of her screen. She thought of the banging and looked at the window covered with heavy draperies, blocking out even the slightest sliver of light.

She rubbed her forehead and pulled herself from her king-sized bed. It was empty, something she'd grown unaccustomed to since having the dogs by her side constantly. But they had stayed with Nadia last night and the night before. She slipped on a light cloth robe and pushed her feet into slippers sitting at the foot of the bed.

Looking out the window, she could see the trees in the distance. The moonless sky left the field shadowy and ominous. Closer to the cottage stood the three apple trees sheltering her family cemetery. She could see the stones in the darkness, mocking her isolated immortality.

There was nothing that could have been banging on the door or wall. The yard around the cottage and the dark cabin were empty except for a few bats flying around the treetops. She could hear them as they searched for mice in the darkness.

Banging on the front door again.

Her gaze fell on the dark cabin. No lights. No cars. Nadia must be at Haven at this hour, tirelessly sorting through boxes of artifacts that meant nothing. If the place burned to the ground, would anything truly be lost?

Even her own memories, Gail thought, were not worth remembering.

Banging.

She went downstairs and stood in the vestibule, staring at the front door. The banging caused a vibration that rattled the pictures on the wall and the glass flanking the doorframe. She pulled on the front door. It opened as if caught by the wind. She kept her fingers laced through the latch to keep it from slamming into the wall.

"Hello?" she called. "Nadia? Is that you? This is not funny," she called into the darkness.

Back inside, she sat down on the sofa and picked up a book. Flipping the pages with her fingertips, she couldn't concentrate. Her eyes read words with no understanding of their meaning. She thought of the banging again. Thought of how similar it was to her banging on the closet door all those years ago.

Bang. Bang. Bang.

She opened the front door again to find nothing but darkness. Whoever was playing this prank on her, she was not amused.

Gail looked at the door. Using her inner ear, the ear that never deceived her, she listened. Since she was a child, Gail could read minds. It was a talent her mother revered but only when her father was nowhere in sight. Otherwise, she was chastised for using any form of telepathy.

She recentered her attention to the fool who dared to frighten her. Her senses—thanks to imbibing copious amounts of ancient immortal blood—were amazing. She heard the smallest pin dropping yards away. She could smell the blood of any living creature on her immense property.

She listened to the silence. Great hearing with nothing to hear. She closed her eyes for a moment and stopped. The silence seemed to press in on her eardrums. She listened farther. Listened to movement beyond the trees, somewhere other than in the empty cottage. She drew in a breath, hoping to smell the fool lurking outside.

Nothing. She pulled back the curtain in the window and peered into the darkness. Nothing. Her phone rang as she secured the door and drew the chain lock for good measure.

"Hello?" she asked cautiously into the phone.

"Where are you?" Nadia's voice sounded annoyed, but she could hear the sarcastic humor hidden in its recesses. "You promised to help me tonight. I'm drowning in tribes of Amazonian blood drinkers."

"I'm not coming." She followed her words with a shrug Nadia couldn't see. "I overslept and my mind is playing tricks on me." A solid knock on the front door jarred her. She pulled back the curtains beside the door. No one was on the stoop. She flipped the porch light, hoping to catch the prankster in the act.

As she returned her attention to the phone, there was a muffled argument on the other end of the line followed by barking. "Can you at least come take these beasts off my hands? They really need to go for a walk or something. They're antsy."

Gail laughed in a somber way that sounded forced. A heavy pounding on the door made her jump again. There was something in this last knock that frightened her more than it should have.

"I'll be there in twenty minutes."

She pulled the front door open for the third time and stood on the precipice of night. The porch light lit the area in a circle in front of her. Tiny insects flew in and out of the light. Movement in the trees stopped her for a moment, and when she was confident it was an animal, she returned to the house.

Pushing the door shut, Gail caught a shift of white light near the staircase. It flashed and she closed her eyes. Behind her lids stood the face of a woman standing in the light. She squeezed her lids shut and then rubbed her eyes with her fingers. When she opened her eyes, the light and the woman were gone. Her breath caught in her throat. Gail grabbed her car keys and ran from the cabin.

After picking up the dogs, Gail strolled the dark, nearly deserted streets of Forest Lake. It was much brighter the closer she got to town. Walking from Haven into the wooded areas surrounding the town, the light slowly disappeared. She listened to the scurrying animals and the screech of an occasional owl until her preternatural sight adjusted, and even at its best, the woods were still dark.

Attila and Thor were thrilled to run. Each took their own path, darting in and out of the trees. They would come together in front of her and then run away again as if chasing something. Thor repeatedly returned to her side to check on her. Gail appreciated the attention he paid.

Since she was far from Mount Orion and whoever or whatever had taken up residence there, Gail had plenty of time to think. She drove her hands deep into her pockets as she walked. Thinking of the banging on the door, of the bright white light and the face inside of it. Her mother's face, she would swear to it, but how and why now?

As a small child, years before her sister Edith fell down a well or was even born and before her mother heartlessly killed her father, Marianne Payne was wonderful. She carried a light inside her that lit up a room. She'd dance while she baked. She sang while she gardened. She also measured—everything. Gail and her older brother's height on a wall in the kitchen, the growth of the plants in the garden with wooden rulers, the length of time it took Gail to brush her long black hair (which measured twenty-two inches past her shoulders when she was ten years old). She'd even measure the length of Gail's father's sighs when she skipped about measuring everything in the house.

Later in life, she became a horrible drunk who would rant uncontrollably and shout at the ceiling or at the clouds if she happened to stumble outside while she was drinking. When she wasn't shouting at the heavens, she was shouting at their next-door neighbor, a lovely spinster named Farryn Allard. Miss Allard would not speak during these outbursts from Gail's mother. She'd listen with the most heartbreaking expression Gail had ever seen.

Shouting was the beginning, then she'd stop abruptly, and if Gail was in range, she'd grab her and throw her in the closet. Sometimes all Gail needed to do was read someone's mind (something she found to be a victimless crime) and her mother would know it, sense it somehow. Gail knew her view for the next few hours would be the four walls of the small kitchen closet.

Attila barked. Thor answered him. Both stopped and returned to her side. Thor's muzzle vibrated with a low growl.

In the distance, she could see the lights on Main Street. In that light, Gail saw the shadow of a woman. Tall and slim with straight shoulders that were thrust back as she pushed out her chest.

A blood drinker.

Could this be Bentyn Rae? Gail froze, knowing that if an Ancient wanted her dead, there was nothing she could do to stop her. She attempted to read her mind but was met with a solid wall. The stranger's head twisted with curiosity. Her hand settled on something strapped to her waist.

The dogs barked.

Gail shushed them. She searched the area for an exit. With one last look at the tall, strange blood drinker, she slipped through the trees, whistling for the dogs to follow. She sped down a non-existent path. Her hair caught on branches as she ran. With Thor behind her and Attila ahead, she felt confident they would lead her back to Haven.

She looked back only once, expecting to see the woman only steps behind, but there was only darkness. Her pace slowed. Her heart rate did too.

"Why did you run?" a voice echoed around her. It was a woman's voice that sounded outraged at what she'd just witnessed. *"Only a coward runs."*

Gail spun around. She searched the darkness for the owner of the voice. She didn't see, sense, or smell anyone in the vicinity. There had been no indication that Bentyn Rae possessed the same gifts of telepathy that she did and yet her voice was in her head.

"Bentyn Rae is as much of a coward as you. Her gifts are limited to murder and torture." The voice was bitter and angry.

"Murdering innocent creatures to satiate your own blood lust is cowardice. Severing a thread is not your job."

"Who's there?" Gail called out. Attila howled.

"I gave you abilities that brought you closer to the natural world. You spat on those gifts."

Gail spun in place as if the speaker would suddenly materialize. She stepped down the path as the dogs guided her away. Thor whined, pulling on her sleeve with his teeth.

"Go on. Walk away. I'm ashamed of you."

That tone caused a rage to build in Gail's belly. There was only one woman who dared to speak to her in that manner. Only one woman she had no ability to shut out of her heart and mind. And that woman was dead. Dead by her own hand.

Gail closed her mind to the voice. She tried to control her anger before she did something she would regret. Getting her bearings in the woods, she knew Haven was to the east and her old family house was to the north. The house with the closet prison.

She knew she needed to get out of these woods and go back to the Annex. If not, she would end up doing something she'd regret like killing the new residents of her old family home. They didn't deserve it, but there was something inside her that felt she'd never really gotten closure with what her mother had done to her. The trauma she endured over a century ago ached to be rectified.

"Typical." The voice broke through her walls, and she realized there was no blocking it out.

She turned and headed towards Haven only a half mile down the road. She looked behind her only once, making sure no one was there. The voice didn't speak again, and she was thankful.

17

BENI

Standing in the woods for hours offered Beni solace after listening to Dyre's anger, Mia's explanations, and that damned letter grated on her last nerve. It wasn't the words but the tone. God, that tone. Who did Camilla Nolan think she was? Did she think Beni incapable of killing a witch just because her daughter was a witch?

Beni growled in a frustrated manner that stirred the birds in the trees around her.

To the parents or guardians of Mia Duran.

It might as well have said, *To whom it may concern.* Like being adopted made Mia an eternal orphan who nobody cared about.

She silenced her mind for half a second and listened to the breeze as it stirred the leaves and ruffled her hair. A calmness washed over her, one she knew would not last long. It would only last as long as she remained far from witches of any kind.

That included Mia.

Her love for her daughter had no bearing on the fact that she was a witch. And a damn strong one too. She could read minds. She could create fire. She could probably see the future if she tried hard enough.

Honestly, Beni had no idea the depth of her daughter's abilities. She knew what she saw and ignored anything lurking beneath the surface. She knew Mia was a strong witch. She could smell the energy surrounding her as she slept, even as a toddler. There was an aura that surrounded her that emitted a strange metallic scent, like the smell of old coins in a sweaty palm.

She didn't want to know what power caused that kind of scent.

Beni took a few deep breaths and then growled again. It came from her throat, full of aggravation and stress.

She thought of her conversation with April. That strong scent of ozone attacked her the moment she opened her bedroom door. April sat on the edge of her bed with her palms sandwiched between her knees. Her long blonde hair hung over her face and only parted when Beni touched her shoulder.

"You wanted to talk to me?"

April's sad eyes filled with water, just as Mia's had, but there was no guilt in her eyes. It was fear.

Beni bent in front of her, falling on her knees as April cried. The strange smell was all over her like a cheap perfume. And even as she tried to hold her, Beni could feel something pushing her away like magnets repelling each other.

She sat back on her heels when April stopped crying. She waited for her to speak first.

April's blue eyes looked up at Beni with embarrassment. "I'm sorry. I can't stop crying." Her willowy hand wiped at her wet cheeks. "I quit school today." She smiled, thinking that it would please her aunt.

"Your mom told me. Why?" Beni frowned.

"I thought you'd be happy. Both you and Mom are so hard to figure out. Neither of you were thrilled when I got my letter, and now both of you are angry that I quit. I can't win." She raised her hands in a sign of surrender and then let them drop, defeated.

"We're not angry you quit. We're concerned because you were so excited to go. Is this because of that ridiculous spell? Because if it is, nothing happened. You irritated your mother and sister. When don't you do that?" She smirked until April smiled. "I still can't comprehend getting punished for reading a spell in a witch school. That doesn't even make sense. What are you doing there if not magic?"

April licked her lips and then wiped her mouth with her fingers. "It's more than that. After we read the spell, I started—" She stopped.

"What?"

"I started hearing voices."

"Well, you are Dyre's daughter. Is it possible the spell kind of reverberated on you?"

"No. That's not it. The voice I'm hearing actually *talks* to me. Like full sentences and thoughts."

"Man or woman?"

"Woman."

"Are you hearing her now?"

"Not since I came home."

"What'd she say?"

"Lots of stuff." April's head dropped, bringing her hair down like a teepee over her lap.

"Can you be more specific?"

"She wants me to kill Elena Nolan." April's voice shook as tears spilled down her cheeks.

Beni laughed and clapped her hands. "Okay, recap. You called the Sisters of Fate. Two of which are dead because of Oriana Duran and Elena Nolan. Now you're hearing a voice telling you to kill Elena Nolan. Correct?"

"She was also pissed that Mom hadn't killed her herself."

Beni nodded, mulling over the information. "So, this is why you quit?"

"I can't be within two inches of Elena without feeling this overwhelming rage. I have no control over it. What if I killed her?" April started to tremble. "I'm losing my mind. Only crazy people hear voices."

Beni held her hands out. "First of all, you are not crazy. Your family is special. Hearing voices kind of comes with the territory. Second, we need to tell your mother. This is beyond my expertise."

She got off the bed and walked to the door.

"Before we tell Mom, the voice told me something else today."

Beni looked up to the night sky. The moon was nowhere to be seen. She felt like she'd stepped in the biggest pile of dog shit and there was no way to wipe it off her shoes.

Dyre hit the ceiling when she learned about the voice and what she'd told April about Linus. Her shouting shattered the glass in the china cabinet doors. Beni left the house when Dyre turned her anger on her. Playing the blame game was a popular argument between them.

A growl rumbled in her throat, waiting to be released again. Dyre knew who the voice was and yet she blamed Beni for everything.

"How am I responsible for your sister's big mouth?" Beni screamed at her best friend.

"You…you…" Dyre held back her true feelings. She glared at Beni, her eyes shifting to Mia for only a second and then back to Beni.

"You adopted me," Mia explained. "If you hadn't adopted me, none of this would have happened." A sadness darkened her face, and she reached for the fire amulet around her neck. It was warm but hadn't turned blue yet.

"I'm sorry I ever gave you that necklace! One second she's blocking me and now she's in my head." Dyre's voice shook, full of guilt and regret.

"Aunt Dyre is angry right now. She doesn't mean what she's saying," Beni assured her daughter. "She's made many idiotic mistakes in the face of anger."

The chandelier above their heads swung, and the glasses in the china cabinet quaked.

"Mia, go check on April." Beni's brow lowered over her eyes as she stared at Dyre. Her fists clenched at her side. "Here's what's going to happen." She looked up at the chandelier as it swung precariously over her head. "You are going to calm down. Then you're going to apologize to Mia because what you said was unnecessarily hurtful. After that, find out why only one of your sisters was called back from the dead and what she plans to do."

"Don't tell me to calm down. Don't tell me what to do," Dyre shouted.

That's about the time Beni left. She didn't have it in her to argue tonight. Mia didn't seem as hurt by Dyre's comments as she should have been; maybe it was her intuition or that she was a smart, empathetic kid. Beni didn't know, but it made it easier to leave her there and escape into the woods for a few hours.

She thought of her options. Pull Mia out of school for good—*Yes.* Burn Oriana Duran's grimoire—*Yes.* Move away silently in the night—*Maybe.*

There were repercussions attached to the last one. Disappointing Dyre when she needed her most. Malcolm's disapproval and anger regarding his daughter's disappearance. Mia would suffer too. She'd lose the companionship of her cousins, her relationship with her father, and her education. There would definitely be some pushback from Mia.

Beni pulled at her hair as the growl turned into a scream.

The distant baying of a wolf accompanied her scream, and she didn't feel so alone all of a sudden. She lifted her head as she sniffed the air. The wolf was at least a mile off. Its proximity wasn't as big an issue as its species. Was it a normal wolf or a shifter?

She sniffed the air again. Normal. *Thank God,* she thought. With everything else going on in her life, having a werewolf in town would have caused a whole set of problems she wasn't prepared to deal with right now.

Now that she knew it was a normal, run-of-the-mill wolf, she was concerned. Seeing them farther up the Northway wasn't uncommon where there were dense forests and rural living. But being this close to Forest Lake felt dangerous.

Who was she to judge? She was dangerous, and no one was running her out of town.

The silence was disrupted again, this time by the shuffling of footsteps through the fallen leaves. The dry, dead leaves crunched as each unseen footstep stomped them to the ground. There were three sets of steps, two animals and one human.

Beni stood stark still, listening. She sniffed the air, wondering if she had been wrong about the wolf's distance from her. She slowed her heart rate to almost undetectable so she could hear the one coming towards her.

Not the wolf and not human. It was a blood drinker, and from the perfume drifting in the wind, she knew it was a female. There was not only perfume in the wind, but that all too familiar scent of ozone accompanied this woman, and Beni wondered if she was imagining it. Thinking of April's problems, she was sure she imagined the scent.

Up ahead, in the clearing, a woman came into view. She looked nearly invisible with her jet-black hair and dark clothing. If it weren't for her iridescent eyes and luminescent skin, Beni wouldn't have seen her as more than a shadow.

The wolf howled again, making the woman start. Two large dogs circled the area. Both felt anxious about the distant wolf and the nearby stranger. Both were good companions and protectors for this young blood drinker.

The woman and Beni stared at one another for only a moment or two. This mysterious woman's heart sped as she froze in place.

A whisper of pressure snaked its way up behind Beni's ear. Her neck twisted as if she felt a muscle spasm. But it was no muscle spasm, nor was it a mosquito tickling her ear; this blood drinker was attempting to read her thoughts.

Beni was quite familiar with the feeling. As Mia learned to read minds, Beni had gone through many of the telltale signs: the *Clunky Grab* that was unmistakable and easily deflected. The *Slide Job* that felt like vertigo and the *Creeping Charlie*, as Beni had come to call it.

Mia was at the Creeping Charlie stage. The Creeping Charlie felt like insects crawling around the base of her skull. She hated it. It made her itchy, which was a feeling, as an Ancient blood drinker, she never had to deal with anymore.

What this woman attempted was far more advanced than Mia. She wasn't as skilled as Dyre, but as a goddess, there was no detecting Dyre's covert tactics. Beni needed to come up with a name for this approach.

The Whispering Tickle?

Beni laughed. That was a good name.

She could feel the pressure again like someone was slipping their fingers under her scalp. She envisioned octopus tentacles as they crawled inside her skull and wrapped around her brain, sucking the information from it like a sponge.

Beni's mind went blank. She pictured the scene in front of her. The trees, the fallen leaves, the shadows as they danced around her. No thoughts or judgements regarding what was happening. Just a Polaroid image of this time and place.

It was a tactic she learned during the witch hunts. She called it building walls. The witch attempting to breach her mind would only see a mirror image of the scene before her. She would be blocked out of her thoughts until she allowed her in or they found another way around.

Beni placed her hand on the dagger in her waistband and straightened her stance. She knew this young blood drinker could sense her age, and that should be enough to deter her if she had any preconceived notions about attack.

Still, her abilities surpassed Beni's, and that made her a dangerous adversary.

As Beni held firm to the knife and the image in her mind, the dark-haired blood drinker darted in the opposite direction, followed by both dogs. In that second of flight, she sensed her age, which loomed somewhere just over a century, maybe more—definitely less than two centuries.

It was smart of her to fear Beni, who held the age, strength, and fighting advantage.

She waited until she could no longer hear the crunching of the leaves before she moved again. *What was a blood drinker doing in the woods surrounding Forest Lake?* Beni knew she was the only blood drinker who lived in the vicinity. Or at least she thought she was.

Could this woman be part of the team assembling the new Haven warehouse?

She decided to go home. She'd had her fill of witches for one evening.

18

MIA

After two days of suspension and house arrest, Mia was going stir crazy. When her father called, she jumped at the chance to escape captivity. The doorbell rang. She ran to answer it. If her mother heard it, she'd be in a mess of trouble. Swinging the door open, she found no one on the stoop. She stepped outside and searched the surrounding area.

"Come out, come out, wherever you are," she sang. "Dad?" she called as she looked around to the side of the house.

"Do you know how much I love hearing you call me that?" Malcolm Brenig came up the walk from his car.

"How did you do that?" Mia knew the answer before she asked the question.

He pinched his nose and wiggled it back and forth like in the old television show, *Bewitched.* Mia got him to watch it last night after very firmly believing that it was Hollywood trash that misrepresented witches. There were other movies she insisted he watch, but of the few he'd perused online, none of them sounded very believable.

Outside of their first meeting, their communication had been through text messages. Beni kept her on a short leash, especially when it came to Malcolm Brenig.

"So where are we going today?" She pulled the door closed and locked it.

"You're not inviting me in for a drink?" He feigned insult.

"You know how my mom feels about that. She doesn't even know I'm seeing you today. If she knew, she'd kill you and then me." Mia walked to Malcolm's car.

"Me first, I assume." He laughed.

"Oh, most definitely. Killing witches is her thing, and you are like a prize pig at the fair. You'd win her a blue ribbon." Mia laughed aloud.

"There are better, more worthy witches than me that she could kill." He walked her to the passenger side of the car and opened the door. As Mia slid into the seat, Malcolm stared down at her with pride. "I know you love her, but that mother of yours has killed many an innocent witch." He slammed the car door and walked around. "Let's not talk about death today."

"What shall we talk about then?"

"Do you want to tell me what happened at school?"

Mia slumped in her seat. "How about instead of that, you can tell me about what it was like to be in the Great Coven? You know, with the Phoenix and Camilla."

Malcolm squinted at her, trying to figure her out. "First tell me what happened at school and then I'll tell you about Elder Path. Kind of a quid pro quo."

"Fine. But nothing happened," she mumbled without looking at him.

"As much as I'd love to share the best years of my life with you, I'd like you to be honest with me."

She lowered her head.

"So, you were suspended for three days for nothing? Camilla simply doesn't like your face. Is that it?"

"We read a spell, that's all. Casting without permission, they called it."

"Is that so? What else?" He raised an eyebrow, knowing there was more.

"Um, Camilla said blatant disregard for the school's rules." Mia chewed on her lip and touched her flame pendant nervously.

"Really? What rule did you disregard besides casting without permission?" Malcolm folded his arms over his chest as he questioned her. He reminded her of Linus in that moment. That intense stare and authoritative demeanor intimidated her.

"Nothing. I mean, we opened a grimoire." She grimaced. "My mother's grimoire."

"Where the hell did Camilla get Oriana's grimoire?" he burst out.

Mia pulled back in her seat.

"Sorry, this is not your fault." He sat, facing straight ahead with his hands on the steering wheel. "What spell did you attempt?"

"We called to the Sisters of Fate." She didn't look at him as she spoke.

He thought for a second. It seemed strange that Linus's daughter would call the Sisters of Fate, when all she had to do was call her own mother on the phone. "And?"

"Nothing happened." She shrugged.

"Makes sense. I believe two of the three of them are dead."

"Really? How do you know that?" He waved her question away and urged her to continue. "Anyway, me and April met with Camilla and Elena. Linus was there because amid all the other insanity that day, April somehow found out that he's her father." She shrugged.

"I wish you'd called me. I could have been there to stand up for you too."

Her mouth shifted to the right. "It wouldn't have mattered. April quit school because apparently, we…never mind. I got suspended, but I'm not allowed to go back until she talks to Mom. That's never going to happen. Can you maybe talk to Camilla for me?"

Malcolm laughed. "Honestly, kid, I think you'd have a better shot with your mom. Camilla is not my biggest fan." Malcolm seemed to ponder the whole situation and then stated, "This is not for us to worry about. There's dinner to consider and then shopping. My little girl deserves something new. Some little bauble that when she wears it, it reminds her of dear old Dad." He tapped her nose with his finger.

"Wait, it's your turn." Mia sat up straight in her seat. "What was the Phoenix like?"

Malcolm laughed. "Ask her yourself. She lives less than a mile from here."

"She does not. Really?" Mia looked out the car window as if the Phoenix would materialize at the mention of her name.

Malcolm described the town of Elder Path as they drove into town. He had just finished explaining how the Circle connected its members magically as he pulled down Perry Way. Jumping out of the car before Mia, he grabbed the door for her. For a moment, he stared at Haven in the parking lot below.

"Mom says it's the archives for all blood drinker history."

"If I have my way, it won't be here long."

Mia jumped at the voice. A woman stood behind them, looking severe and a bit intimidating. She recognized her from weeks ago. Her dark hair was knotted on the back of her head with the length hanging over her shoulders. Her eyes opened just a bit too wide as if Mia had said something offensive. And her long slender fingers with blood-red fingernail polish lay on her hips, tapping away like an annoyed schoolteacher.

"Rayne, I thought you were going out." Malcolm took Mia's hand and pulled her past the frightening woman.

"Who was that?" Mia asked as they entered Raven's Corner.

"Rayne Grey." The woman entered behind them. "From the ridiculous expression of pride and joy on Malcolm's face, I know you must be Mia Duran."

"Brenig," Malcolm corrected. When Mia looked at him, he explained, "I thought you'd like to add my last name. It was just a thought."

Mia looked around at the faces staring at her. Her father, Rayne Grey, and Iris waited for her answer as if they were desperate to hear the outcome. "I'd have to talk to my mom first," she whispered.

"Shouldn't you be in school, Mia Brenig?" Rayne asked. "The new moon was two days ago. Classes started on the new moon."

Mia didn't know how to answer. Her fingers rolled over the stacks of candles and down the bumpy surface of an amethyst geode. When she got to the crystals, she dropped a polished stone into her hand.

"She's been suspended for casting without permission." Malcolm laughed as he turned to greet a rather waifish-looking woman in the back of the store.

"Congratulations." Rayne walked towards her. "Casting is your birthright. Don't let anyone tell you when and where you may cast your magic. Especially not Camilla Nolan."

"Well, she broke rules," Malcolm added. "She opened Oriana's grimoire after being asked not to touch it."

"Three days' suspension seems like a hefty punishment for flouting the rules." Rayne's suspicion was evident in her expression. "Was there more to it?"

"No." Mia's eyes shifted around the store rather than looking at Rayne. She began browsing the tables to distract herself from the attention centered on her.

Rayne sighed. "Those Nolan sisters are nothing but trouble."

"That's not fair." Iris looked up from her tarot cards. "Camilla has nothing but the best of intentions for all her students. If she didn't wish Mia to read from that grimoire, she must have had a good reason."

"Tell me, Mia, what reasons could Camilla have to keep you from your birthright?" Rayne drew Mia away from the display tables. She concentrated on her thoughts and saw the whole scenario as it played out two days before. She saw the three girls in the solarium. She watched as Mia's touch opened the grimoire. She saw the wind kick up as the book opened. She saw them struggle to read the Latin words in the spell. She heard the thunder and watched as April was burned by the charms.

Rayne didn't speak for a few moments. Her eyes softened as she analyzed Mia's thoughts regarding that fateful day in school.

"Rayne? What did you see?" Iris prodded.

"It seems Camilla had a very good reason for keeping that grimoire closed." She looked at Malcolm. He merely shook his head in response. She shook her head slowly, disappointed. "You used your blood to cement the spell?"

"You didn't?" Malcolm touched Mia's shoulder.

"Was that wrong? Starr said…well, she said I was the closest thing to Oriana Duran that we had, and the spell called for her blood." Fear and tears filled her eyes. "How bad did we screw up?" Her eyes were large as dinner plates as she stared at her father, hoping he would say he could fix everything.

Rayne walked to her. "When you opened that book, I saw, and you saw but ignored, a great amount of energy leave the book. The wind kicked up before you even read the spell, didn't it?"

Mia thought back to that unfortunate day. "I think so."

"I believe your mother's soul was locked in that book when she died."

"Oriana didn't have the power to accomplish it," Malcolm scoffed, not wanting to discuss this subject.

"I can't explain it, but she did it." Rayne looked at Mia. "She could have used your magic."

"I was only two when she died. I didn't have any magic yet." Mia looked around the room at the others surrounding her. Her gaze fell on her father's face. She knew so little about Malcolm Brenig. She only knew he abandoned her, leaving her in the care of Oriana Duran, who by most people's accounts was an unstable mother. Why should she trust him now to do the right thing for her?

He read her thoughts. Closing his eyes, a tension filled him. She could see his whole body go rigid. "I'm sorry," he whispered and walked out of the room.

"Let's stay focused." Rayne snapped her fingers in the air. "You did have magic. Untrained, raw magic that hovered in the periphery of your unspoiled potential. Oriana must have tapped into it somehow, knowing she couldn't harness it without killing you, but she could use it if she directed you properly."

"I locked my mother in that grimoire?"

"In a manner of speaking." Rayne grinned. "She must have known her time was short."

Mia's mouth hung open. Heat rose in her cheeks. Rayne Grey continued to stare at her as if she was speaking and she wasn't. Mia pulled on the collar of her shirt, hoping this would not progress any further than a hot flash. She touched her fire pendant, which seemed not to respond.

Rayne took a step towards her. "Are you a firestarter?"

Mia swallowed hard and closed her eyes. Tears lined her lashes as she fought the heat as it filled her neck and back with sweat. She searched for her father in the store and found he'd disappeared behind the black beaded curtain. Her breathing accelerated. She rubbed her hands together, hoping to distract herself from her fear. She tapped on the pendant. She drove her fingernails into her palms, drawing blood, but it did no good.

Smoke rose from the curtain, and following closely behind were flames licking the material as if it possessed an accelerant. Iris's head snapped up and she screamed. "Fire extinguisher. Malcolm, bring the extinguisher." Her cries hurt Mia's ears, and she clapped her hands over them.

"Oh, be calm, Iris." Rayne Grey walked to the curtain, grabbing a cup of water Opal left on a table. She held her hand up to the cloth and dragged it down slowly without touching it. The flames followed her as she contained it to a small area where she poured the water on it.

"I'm sorry," Mia whispered. "It got away from me. I'll pay for the damage."

Malcolm pulled back the curtain, glancing at it, and walked to Mia. "No harm done."

"Malcolm." Iris was irate.

"No harm was done, Iris," he insisted. "Stop making a mountain out of a molehill. It's a curtain, not your firstborn." He took Mia in his arms, and she stiffened. "It happens. Don't fret about it. It's the reason I brought you here. Rayne is one of the foremost fire handlers in the world."

Mia looked at the woman.

"Lesson number one, never let your emotions control your element." Rayne touched the black curtain and rubbed her fingers together. The material was charred and flaked off in her hands. "Lesson number two, where there's smoke, there is always fire. I saw that you were surprised by the flames. Always expect fire, even if you only see smoke. The fire is there inside you, ready to come out. The smoke is your stop sign. When you see the smoke, stop and assess your emotions. Take a step back, analyze what is causing you to cast unintentionally."

"I didn't…"

"Magic is an extension of us, of our intentions. Releasing intentions outside ourselves is casting, no matter what form it takes." Rayne didn't smile. She didn't warm to Mia's inexperience. She taught to teach and nothing more. She didn't wish to be friends or a mentor. She simply wished for Mia to control her abilities so she wouldn't burn down the world.

"This usually works, but it didn't." She touched her flame pendant, wondering why it failed her.

Rayne Grey approached her. "That's an interesting bauble. Where did you come by it?"

She looked at Malcolm before answering. "It was a gift from my aunt."

"Is this aunt a powerful witch?" Rayne held the pendant with her fingers, examining it. The tiny flame danced in its confines as she stared at it.

Malcolm nodded. "Her aunt is Dyre Crane."

"Oh. Her children are Brenigs, aren't they?" Rayne's smile was not pleasant. "Nevertheless, there is great magic in this little flame. It's not real fire. Did you know that? This is part of an eternal flame." Rayne looked into Mia's eyes, appreciating the fear and wonder that lived there. "Here, let me show you." She led her to the bookshelf where she pulled one book and opened it to the exact page she wanted. "The eternal flame or Prometheus flame is thought to be protected by the gods. It burns yellow and turns blue under great stress."

Mia clasped her hand around her pendant. "This turns blue when I'm stressed. It's supposed to, then it sends a chill through me. Kind of wakes me up and stops my fires."

"Interesting tactic." Rayne smiled a false smile. "Looks like it needs recharging. Maybe you shouldn't depend on it so much."

Malcolm took Mia's hand and led her to the front door.

"Do you think she's right?" Mia touched her necklace as she walked with her father.

"Yes, but don't let her know I said so."

Part Two

The Phoenix

September

19

FARRYN

Farryn Allard stopped at the end of the overgrown path in front of her house. She reached into the long metal mailbox and pulled out four letters and a copy of the *Forest Lake Echo*.

The largest envelope in her hand looked like a wedding invitation. The envelope was lined with handmade papers and embossed with the wax seal of the illustrious Witch Board. Placing her bags on the ground, Farryn rolled her eyes and slid her nail under the flap to open it.

Dearest Farryn,

The time of the year has come round again where I ask for your assistance, and you ignore me. I have felt the spells you've sent to deter my insistence that you join the Witch Board as I am sure you have felt my answer. We are two stubborn witches, you and I.

However, I must insist, nay, beseech you, to reconsider. There are many Board-related issues that have become far more than I can or wish to handle on my own. Oh, if only the Circle was still intact. But thanks to that odious Seth Dallis, we will never be able to join the Circle ever again.

Should we take him to task, finally? That question remains on my mind as it has for the last thousand years. That is a question only you can answer, my soul sister.

It was your leadership he usurped. Your brother he murdered. Your family he tore apart.

Imagine, turning his back on the Circle and his family for a cold blood. How has our beloved Camilla not torn him to shreds? Poor dear. My continued support and sympathy extends to you and your family for what that man has taken from you.

I have grown quite a militia to fight the cold bloods, should it come to that. I don't believe it would. In the last few years, I have begun meeting with the new cold blood Council, and they are just as ready to end our common yet seemingly unfounded hatred as we are.

Please, my beloved Farryn, I would love for you to join us. Your talents in leading Elder Path are what I feel is missing on the Board.

I implore you to respond to this letter so that I may move forward with building a stronger, more resilient coalition. It could one day, with your strong hand and dedication along with mine, be as strong as the Circle.

With my undying devotion—
Penelope Press

The Elder Path Circle was a coven of eight witches. Three witches were cousins, two were spouses of those three, and two were brothers. Only one witch stood alone, not sharing blood or bond with any of the others.

Penelope Press.

It was her name written in a flourished handwriting on the bottom of the letter Farryn Allard held in her hand. The letter she read and balled up to make perfect fodder for the waste basket.

She'd received the same letter once a year for the last decade. Before that, Penelope Press would take it upon herself to visit. Farryn was thrilled when the Witch Board kept Penelope so busy that she found no time to visit and instead wrote letters that Farryn could summarily chuck into the recycling bin.

The letter made Farryn's skin crawl. Every word was written in Penelope's sing-songy, sarcastic tone that sickened her. The subscript angered her. Penelope hated that Farryn led the Elder Path Circle, and when it fell, she was only too happy to rub it in her face. Building the Witch Board was her way of twisting the knife just a little deeper. Its intention was to make Farryn suffer. Each letter, not an invitation at all but a staunch reminder of who was in charge now.

She reached into the blue recycling bin and pulled out the balled-up piece of parchment. She opened it and smoothed out all the wrinkles and folds. She stared at the delicate lettering and perfect ink strokes. She took the top of the paper in hand and tore it in half. Turning it on its side, she tore it again and again and again until only a small stack of parchment remained.

Under her breath, she whispered her answer to Penelope. "I decline your invitation. I resent your continued interference in my life. I detest your snide judgement of my family."

Surprisingly, Penelope's signature remained intact, and after tossing the rest of the letter back into the recycling bin, she took that single square of paper and ripped it until there was nothing left of Penelope Press's signature besides some swirls and flourished loops.

It wasn't only the letter that had gotten under her skin this morning. It was Saturday morning, four days following the new moon and the fateful calling that Farryn was struggling to decipher.

She dropped three bags of groceries on the table. The three overfilled cloth bags toppled into one another as she stepped away from them. Usually, the grocery store was a pleasant distraction in her life. She loved searching for ingredients to cook interesting dishes and desserts. She felt content and happily anonymous within the aisles.

But not today.

Today, she saw a familiar face as she pushed her grocery cart around the produce section. Iris Chauncey. She ran a local witch shop on Main Street that Farryn had avoided for years. The shop was run by Iris but controlled by the Witch Board.

Iris's dark graying hair was pulled back in a bun, and her unimpressive style made her look as though she threw herself together to get to the store. Her harried expression and desperate thoughts were Farryn's one saving grace. She had no time to care who shared the aisles with her as she frantically threw items from her list into the basket dangling from her arm.

Farryn took the opportunity to study this woman's muddled thoughts, seeing the images of Rayne Grey in the forefront. An angry conversation was the reason for Iris's appearance and distracted mind. Rayne was demanding that Iris follow orders. Iris's eyes lit up, and she searched the area around herself. Farryn giggled softly as she turned her cart in the opposite direction before she gave herself away.

It had been years since she had cared to read anyone's thoughts, let alone someone that could detect her doing it. Iris had felt Farryn rooting around her mind, and even though she wasn't digging deep, she was out of practice and left a mark for Iris to feel.

Follow orders? She couldn't imagine what orders Iris would not follow, especially if given by the great Rayne Grey. Rayne was a sixteenth century witch who hadn't let go of the past. She spent all her time and energy making sure the witch hunts didn't repeat themselves. She'd been known to punish witches who showed any violence or wickedness toward other witches and kept a sharp eye on mortals just waiting to start building a funeral pyre or hanging a noose in a tree.

Farryn was not a fan of Rayne Grey or any witch who chose to follow her.

She wondered as she dug through the grocery sacks if these supposed orders had anything to do with the calling she'd heard this past week. She dropped into a red vinyl chair at the kitchen table.

The call didn't concern her. It wasn't intended for her; she'd just overheard it. Two distinct voices calling out to the Sisters of Fate. It was on the new moon, so whoever called knew when to do it. She heard only two voices but felt three novices involved. The words were carried on the wind as it blew through the trees around the arbor where she sat in the garden.

Farryn embraced the warmth the magic brought with it. In the afternoon sunshine, the warmth was like a hug, and she beamed with it. She thought of the words she'd heard. *We call to the Sisters of Fate.* Their voices were clear and carried from across town. She knew where they were, and it amused her.

Farryn giggled. She remembered the temptation of practicing her witchcraft as a child or even as a young woman with little experience. But it was the years that taught her that power was gained with patience and growth.

For hours after she heard the spell, Farryn called out to these young witches. If they heard her, they did not answer. If they did not hear her, she understood why. They were protected by powerful witches. Their coven was strong even if they were not.

On that day, she heard a voice, and that did concern her. She'd been knitting on the porch, watching the neighborhood children play next door. The voice sounded frightened and lost.

When the voice called out to her, she laid her knitting to the side and took up her prayer beads. She wrapped them around her fingers. As her fingers found each bead, she said a prayer and attempted to contact the spirit for guidance. Her hands worked on their own. Farryn's eyes were closed as her lips moved with prayer.

The voice materialized behind her closed eyes. It took the form of the great thread of life. The great thread held the lives of every living mortal being on the planet in its fibers. It connected every plant, animal, and human being. Farryn watched the thread dance around her spectral form and listened to the voice. She knew it. It was the voice of her best friend. One of the Sisters of Fate.

She opened her eyes and looked down at the beads in her hands. Her fingers were holding an omen bead. She knew this meant something—something she didn't understand. With the omen was a feeling she was getting a visitor. Farryn wondered what form the visitor would take.

That was four days ago, and she was still stewing over how her friend could be contacting her now. *Could that calling have been strong enough to wake the dead?* Farryn stood from her seat. She paced. She wrung her hands. She'd done all three things for four days now and nothing was coming to her.

She finished putting the grocery items away and knew what she needed to do. She needed to dig.

The warm September sun hung high in the sky. It wasn't an ideal time to garden, but she felt she needed to touch the earth. There was something in these happenings that were connected, and they had to make sense. And if the Goddess couldn't provide the answers, then she would dig in the soil until the answer presented itself.

Farryn walked out the kitchen door. Grabbing her hat and an empty basket, she followed the cobblestone pathway towards the small shed at the end of her property. Along the way, white and purple blossoms surrounded her. Blood-red roses lined the small arbor in the corner of the yard.

In her greenhouse, her vegetables were ripe. Several bright, plump red tomatoes, cucumbers, and a few zucchinis looked ready to pick. Placing her basket on the ground, she kneeled in the garden and pulled at the beautiful bounty growing in front of her. She smiled as her hand locked around each plant. She did this. She planted the seeds, tended to the garden, and helped them to grow. No magic needed. She could have used magic. It would have been easy. Making things grow was her specialty but she did nothing but love and tend to them.

When her basket was full, she whispered thanks to the Earth, brushed off her knees, and headed for the shed. She could feel the sun on her skin as she made her way through the greenhouse and the multitude of plants. The weathered shed doors stood open as she approached, and it concerned her.

"What are you doing in here?" She pushed back the large brim of her hat to look down at a small girl rooting through her gardening tools. The child's blonde hair was in braids that were pulled and frizzy from the afternoon heat and hours of playing with her brother in the yard. Her dirty, bare feet were perched on a wooden milk crate, much too high for the child to climb on her own.

"Ooh." The girl was startled and fell back on her behind.

"Violet." Farryn dropped her basket and helped the five-year-old to her feet. She brushed off her shorts and gave her a warm smile. "Are you okay?"

The child nodded, brushing away the tears the hard wood floor had forced out of her.

"Now, what are you doing in here? These are dangerous tools. You could accidentally plant yourself in the garden. And I wonder? Hmm, if I planted you—would violets grow?"

The child laughed, forgetting the pain in her bottom. "I want to plant seeds." She put her hands behind her back.

"Let me see." Farryn held out her hands. Violet looked down with guilt tattooed across her face. She held out her small hand. "Well, that's one big seed you found." Farryn laughed. "That's not really a seed, sweetie. It's a bulb, and it's a little late in the season for that to grow anything." She took the bulb from the child's tiny hand. "I don't think I had much luck with it anyway. And I can *make* things grow."

Violet giggled again, but there was a little fear in the periphery of the laugh. The neighborhood children were few, but they all knew the stories of Farryn Allard and her magical talents. On Halloween, hers would be the most popular house. Not because she gave out the best candy. The children gathered in hopes of seeing her flying on her broomstick or stirring a hardy brew in her caldron.

"Here. Take these. They will grow for you." She sprinkled a few seeds in Violet's open hand. "Plant them in partial sunlight—like near that big tree in your backyard. Water them every day and remember to give thanks to Mother Earth for allowing you the privilege of using her resources to create your own bit of beauty in this world." The warm smile returned to her lips. "Don't let Monkey in your yard or he'll dig up your seeds."

Monkey was Farryn's gray and white cat.

Violet nodded and looked at the seeds. "What will they grow?"

"Wonderous beauty."

"What kind of flowers?"

"That's a surprise." Farryn winked. "Now, out of my shed before I cook you up for supper."

Violet jumped down from the step and ran to the picket fence that separated their yards. She looked back at Farryn and waved.

She watched as the child returned to her house. Her backyard was trimmed with a swing set and jungle gym in the corner and a little patio just outside the back door. Farryn couldn't help but remember her best friend who lived in that house over a century ago.

The house was bad luck. It grew beautiful children, but the energy attracted death. Farryn felt it when she visited. Violet's father, Charles Barnett, died in a car accident. She tried to convince herself that the house had nothing to do with it. It wasn't working. The only thing she was convinced of was that the house brought death.

A hundred and sixty years ago, her best friend was killed in that house. Her husband died there too. Somewhere on the far end of the property beneath the ground was the old well that swallowed up her best friend's youngest daughter. Too many deaths. Now Charles was dead—only a year ago. It was the house, definitely the house.

She looked up at it. The two large bedroom windows formed eyes on the second floor. It stared down at her as she pictured her long dead best friend, Mararis Payne, standing in the window. She called her Marianne, a name she adopted to hide from witches that wished to kill her.

No, she wouldn't think of Marianne today. She thought of her often, and it usually led her into a descending spiral of depression that would last days. She shook her head. "No, not today."

Walking back to the shed, she remembered what brought her out here in the first place. The calling, the voice, and Iris. *The voice was Marianne's voice, wasn't it?*

Shaking the thoughts from her mind, the only solace she knew now was the earth. Only the soil could clear her mind and feed her soul. The soil and maybe some company. She wished she hadn't sent

Violet away. That little girl fed her soul as much as the earth and the moon fed her soul. Farryn fantasized about having a daughter of her own, one not unlike little Violet Barnett. She thought of the dresses she would buy her and the magic she would teach her. Violet was such a permanent fixture in her garden that Farryn sometimes pretended that she *was* her daughter. They baked together and gardened. She was teaching her to sew and make corn husk dolls for harvest holidays.

"It's thoughts like that, that give witches a bad name." A male voice surrounded her. *"Stealing children is a great way of propagating that myth."*

"I never said anything about stealing her." She spoke aloud as she returned to the empty shed to retrieve her basket of vegetables. "Why are you here, Micah?"

Monkey ran past the shed, heading for the shade beneath the arbor.

"Just visiting." He sounded hurt.

Micah was a witch from Farryn's old coven days and more importantly, her little brother. He was a casualty of fearmongering, otherwise known as witch hunters. Micah had been burned at the stake. It was a time that Farryn thought best left in the past. The Great Coven failed because of her. Being a solitary witch was easier, and she preferred being alone to having an entire coven depending on her.

"So, this little visit has nothing to do with a certain calling that's been circulating?" She grabbed her sheers and a garden trowel. There was still time to dig and then bake. Down the little pathway towards the trellis and rock fountain on the side of the house, she kneeled in the dirt, loving the smell and texture of the warm earth. The ground was soft from the recent rain, and she dug easily into it. The water from the fountain trickled down the rocks, and she felt the tension of the day slipping away.

First, she drove the trowel into the soil and then with her gloved fingers, she created a well deep enough to plant a bulb. Dropping into the soil the bulb Violet had hoped would bring her a giant plant, she covered it and tapped it flat with the trowel. With a few whispered words, she guaranteed the bulb would yield a lovely flower.

"I wasn't sure if you had heard it." Micah sounded distracted.

"I heard it." Farryn pulled at the weeds threatening to choke out her asters and marigolds. "I can't make heads or tails out of it. I was hoping the earth would lend me a hand in deciphering it."

"Has she offered any answers?"

"I just got started. Perhaps if I was alone—" She didn't finish the thought but left it up to Micah to get the hint. He didn't leave but also didn't speak. She could feel him hovering. His spirit glided as she moved from flower to flower with the hose and weeding sheers.

She blamed herself for his death for years. If only she had been with them when the witch hunters came to collect them. If she had used the breadth of her magic to protect the Elder Path Circle, would that have made a difference?

If she had—if she had—if she had only . . .

"Phoenix, stop blaming yourself." Micah read her thoughts easily.

Farryn could feel the tears coming. She could feel them filling her eyes and tightening in her throat. She could feel the scar that cut down the right side of her face pull taut. The scar no one could see thanks to her magic, but she could still feel it beneath the deception.

She fought the tears. "Don't call me that."

"You are the Phoenix. What would you have me call you?"

"Farryn. It's my name." She brushed the tears away from her red eyes with disgust.

"You are the Phoenix. You are what legends are made of. I don't care how many deceptions you use to cover your scars; you are the Phoenix."

"I need you to leave now." Farryn brushed off the dirt from her knees. Her gloves were covered in wet soil and were tinted green from pulling weeds. She took off her sun hat and pushed back her sweaty brown hair.

She could feel his departure. It was slow and resistant. He didn't want to go. She thought about it for a moment and felt she needed to tell him what she knew about the calling.

"I know where the call originated."

"Where?"

"Novices. I'm sure they didn't know what they were doing, but I have a feeling—a strong one—that this occurrence is the beginning of something bigger." She rubbed her stomach with her dirty fist, trying to say the feeling was deep in her gut. "I hesitate to say where they are—"

He hovered close and pressed in on her like a bully trying to get her lunch money.

She shook him off and walked back around to the shed. She stripped off her dirty gloves and tossed them on the shelf. "They are here in Forest Lake. Not far. In a school for witches."

"Where is there a school for witches, and why are you not teaching there?"

"Magnolia Academy for Magical Arts." She said the name as if she expected him to know it right off the bat. He didn't answer. "Milly's running a school. Did you know?"

"Doesn't surprise me, but no, I didn't know. A school, really? Makes sense why she didn't want you."

"I guess it's a coven for novice witches. I haven't been there. I have heard whisperings from others. The calling came from there." She shrugged.

"What else is bothering you?" Micah never missed a trick.

Farryn smiled. "Iris Chauncey."

"Is she still lurking around? What is with this town? Cold bloods, witches, goddesses."

She thought about it. There was something in Forest Lake that attracted extraordinary beings. Something in the energy that surrounded the town. Yet she couldn't pinpoint exactly what it was.

"What did Iris Chauncey have to say?"

"Nothing to me, but guess who was on her mind as always?"

"Rayne Grey. You didn't see her too, did you?" Micah sounded amused.

"Hell no, but I know she's in town."

"They should have killed her when they had the chance." Micah was not forgiving of the problems Rayne caused over the centuries. *"How did she slip through Bentyn Rae's fingers?"*

"Are you advocating witch hunting?"

"For the likes of Rayne Grey? Yes. Do you think she has something to do with the calling?"

"No, I'm sure it was novice witches. I can't say she won't use it to stir up trouble, though." She rubbed her dirty hand over her forehead.

"Do you think they actually called the Sisters of Fate?"

Farryn frowned. "Yes, I do. I heard Mararis reach out to me on the new moon."

"From the grave?"

"I didn't answer, but if she's back, maybe they called all three of them. No doubt Dyre heard it too." She closed the shed doors and locked them. "I believe she has a legacy."

"You think she would have learned after Mararis was killed," Micah said. *"Linus is the child's father, correct?"*

"Yep." Her answer was short. The topic of her former coven mates was unwelcome in any conversation to Farryn.

"Do you think the others heard the call as well?"

"If you mean Clotho, Lachesis, and Atropos, they won't answer even if they did hear it. They haven't cared about mortals for thousands of years. They never listened to earthly communication even in the best of times."

"What do you plan to do about this?" He loved to goad her.

"I don't want to, but I should tell Elena what's happening."

"Do you think Milly will allow that?"

"I just want to warn her. What's the harm in that?"

"I don't know. Milly's always held on to her grudges. Do you think she'll accept you back into her life?"

"There's only one way to find out."

20

FARRYN AND CAMILLA

Farryn stood staring at the house for almost ten minutes before she walked up the path. She saw the gabled roof and the turret that looked out of place in the neighborhood and this century. She saw the lace curtains in the windows and, peeking around the side, she could just make out the top of the greenhouse roof.

The gray siding saddened her. Mauve would have been better or maybe a dusty purple. Something as deeply personal as a house, where you kept your life, your secrets, and bared your soul. It should have wondrous color. If not in the paint, then in the flowers or decorations.

She studied the manicured lawn and the perfectly trimmed hedges. But nothing could disguise the deep sense of foreboding that hung over the entire property. A tingle wrapped itself around the nape of her neck and down her spine.

"Are you still here?" she said silently to her brother.

"If your intent is to surprise her, this form of communication is not advised," he said, sounding like a lawyer during a deposition.

"I don't care if she hears me." Farryn looked up at the house again. She wondered if anyone was staring at her from behind those lovely lace curtains. She searched for a shadow or the slightest movement but saw nothing.

"Feeling brave?" Micah goaded her. *"Let's knock on the door, then."*

She sighed.

The cobblestone path felt longer than it looked. With each step she took, Farryn wished to turn around. That bravery Micah assumed failed her. Each step to the door felt as if a weight was strapped to her ankle, making it incredibly difficult to move forward.

Had Camilla sensed her? Was she peering out of an upstairs window watching her struggle with her confidence and courage? Was this weight really the effect of internal doubt or contrived by a powerful witch's desire to keep unwanted guests at bay?

Finally, Farryn's foot hit the porch steps, and then the wood planks leading to the massive door. *"It's too much,"* she thought.

"What is?"

"This door. It belongs on a much larger house. I'm surprised it hasn't pulled the whole thing over." She ran her hand down the mahogany-stained door. Her fingers touched the brass details—the handle, the knocker shaped like a large teardrop, and the keyhole.

"Stop nitpicking and knock."

"I'm not—"

"You do this all the time," he quickly interrupted her. *"Whatever happened between you and Milly has nothing to do with this door. Finding fault in her home décor choices won't make this meeting any easier, Phoenix."*

"Don't call me that," she snapped.

"Complaining about nicknames is not helping your case."

She lifted the knocker and let it drop. She did this three times even though the doorbell was the preferred alert system with a camera and microphone. Regardless, steps echoed from beyond the door. Heels on hardwood—she knew it wasn't her cousin. Unless Camilla's tastes had changed in the last few centuries, she preferred comfortable attire. Which meant no heels outside of a dressy situation.

The door swung open to reveal a young Indian girl staring at her in an impatient and condescending manner. Farryn's tension lessened as the young girl spoke. "Can I help you?" Her large blue eyes were made even larger with eyeliner, and her dark skin made the blue sparkle. The perfectly tweezed eyebrows lifted to their full extent as she waited for Farryn's answer.

"I believe she's here to see me, Veda. You may return to class." Camilla stood in the hallway beside the stairs.

Veda shrugged and walked away without a second glance to Farryn or Camilla.

Farryn stood on the threshold between the past and present, lost in a blur of emotion. Veda's exit was humorous and left her with a nervous laugh sitting in her throat waiting to burst out. Seeing Camilla, however, pushed that emotion to the side, replaced by a tightening in her throat that refused to allow words to penetrate.

Tears burned the corners of her eyes, and she blinked them away, afraid the emotion would not be reciprocated.

"Would you like to come in?" Camilla straightened her shoulders as she pulled her silver hair to one side. She held out her hand to the sitting area just beyond the foyer. Her eyes never met Farryn's but instead searched the floor as if looking for a lost object.

The energy in the house pressed down on her. She could sense house spirits. Those ordinary spirits who called Magnolia Academy their home. They moved objects, opened doors, and maybe a time or two caused the electricity to flutter. Overall, they were ineffectual, harmless entities.

That was not the energy that concerned Farryn. There was something else hovering over the house. Something that frightened her.

"Milly, as much as I wanted to see you, I came to see…" she started talking but was quickly interrupted.

"Kim? Where the hell did you put my glasses? I just had them and now they're gone." Linus pounded into the room with no care for who was standing before him. He neither saw nor acknowledged Farryn or Camilla. "God dammit, Kim. I'm getting sick of these little games. It's not like I have a job to do that requires my sight." He pulled pillows off the chairs and tossed them onto the floor.

"Oh, stop your kerfuffling." A large black woman with a kind face and a head full of braids entered the room. Farryn could tell she was a healer the moment she arrived. "They are there on the mantel. Such a baby. And for the record, I did not hide them. You left them on the coffee table last night. I simply put them on the mantel."

"A likely story." He went to retrieve them, finally seeing they had company. "Farryn? My God, Farryn!" He could not contain his joy.

Looking at Linus, she wasn't sure if she should hug him or kiss him, so she held out her hand for him to shake. When he took it, his hand was warm, and he pulled her in for a hug that caught her unprepared. She surrendered and felt her body melt into his embrace. Her heart sped up as she clung to him.

He laughed as he broke from the hug. "I feel like if I blink, you'll slip away. I want to hold on tight, so you don't disappear again." That was Linus. His warmth and generosity defined him. His playful, curly hair danced around his forehead and ears, and she reached for his beard to scratch her nails through—just like the old days—but stopped herself.

He laughed that same boisterous laugh that she missed and didn't realize she had missed until she heard it. The tears she'd saved earlier showed themselves with two long streams slithering down her cheeks to her quivering chin.

"You heard it, didn't you?" Camilla approached as Linus held Farryn's face in his hands. His eyes were wet with tears. "That's why you're here."

"Yes," she answered.

Linus pulled her in again for a bear hug. "I don't care what brought you here. I'm just happy it's finally happened."

Camilla stared at him with an incredulous smirk. "Shall we sit down?"

After introductions, Kim brought tea and joined them in their discussion regarding Farryn's presence and the calling.

"We can't ignore the fact that it was the two Brenig girls who are responsible for the calling." Kim poured the tea, spilling it as she spoke.

"*Two* Brenig girls? You have two daughters?" Farryn was amazed.

He ignored her to lash out at Kim. "Starr was not exactly an innocent bystander."

"You know as well as I that Starr's abilities couldn't call someone across the street, let alone wake the dead." Kim reared up on him.

Farryn laughed. "This calling has riled you up quite a bit, hasn't it? So, tell me about these daughters of yours."

"I don't care who did the calling," Camilla interjected. She closed her eyes and when they reopened, she smiled at Farryn like she was embarrassed. "We have much bigger problems than worrying about Linus's daughter and his niece."

Farryn thought about it for only a second. "Yes, Malcolm has a daughter. I guess what they say is true."

Linus's brow knitted together, questioning her without words.

"Karma. What goes around comes around. You and your brother were flagrant womanizers back in the day. You two bedded half the town of Elder Path. And now you both have daughters. Seems fitting." She laughed.

Kim chuckled and sipped her tea.

"Why are you here, Fae?" Camilla sounded exhausted.

Farryn smirked, picturing her cousin when they were children. Her then-brown hair in braids, frizzy from running in the woods, chasing her sister or Micah. Her laughter echoing through the trees. The brightness of her smile and the positivity in her attitude was something Farryn wished to see again.

"I came to speak with Elena. Is she here?"

"She's in class," Linus offered. He turned his wrist to look at his watch. "She'll be another forty-five minutes. Is this about the calling?"

"In a sense, yes. I heard it. I prayed on it. Then Mararis called out to me on the new moon." She splayed her hands as if to say, *that's it*. "My fear…" She paused. Her eyes circled the room, ultimately landing on Camilla. "My fear is if she is back, then so is Tera. This calling was strong enough to wake the dead. They are not just going to waste it. I bet my life that they are going to kill Elena or want to, at least."

"What did Mararis have to say?" Kim asked.

"I didn't answer the call. Our history is muddy. I can't fall down that rabbit hole again." She bit her lower lip and chewed it.

"Typical." Camilla stood and walked to the fireplace. With her hands on the mantel, she closed her eyes.

"Am I to be expected to speak with every spirit who calls me?"

"Are we to believe your only reason for visiting is to protect Elena? You have never cared about Elena." Camilla didn't turn when she spoke. She was facing the wall.

"And you care too much."

"She's my sister. I *can't* care too much."

"You protect her from everything. That needs to stop. She's your Achilles' heel and you know it."

"Come on…" Linus tried to stop the fight.

"No, she's got something to say. Something much more important than her sister's life, apparently. So let her say it. Are you still angry about the Circle? Or is it Seth? Because I know you still blame me for both."

Camilla turned, having grabbed Linus's glasses from the mantel. She grasped them in her fist like a stress ball. Linus rose and snatched them before she broke them in her rage. The action deescalated the tension but did nothing to divert Camilla's anger.

"It's been two hundred years…" she began.

"Longer." Micah's voice filled Farryn's mind.

Camilla froze. "Is that…?" Tears stood in her eyes. "Is that Micah?" She couldn't hear him herself, but reading Farryn's mind was like second nature to her. She did it without effort. She looked at Linus. His eyes were closed as if in prayer. He was smiling.

"Hi, Milly. Give her hell." He laughed.

Farryn rolled her eyes.

A soggy laugh broke through Camilla's tears. She wiped her eyes and nose with the palm of her hand. A deep cleansing breath put her back on track.

"You've lived a mile away for almost two hundred years and it took *this* to bring you here. That's why I'm angry with you. I don't care about Elder Path or Seth or any of it. We all made stupid mistakes in the past. But what kept you away so long?"

"We had different agendas." Farryn's words were soft and non-confrontational. "We had to protect those we loved. We both failed, miserably."

Camilla nodded. "Yes, we did. I could have used you over the years."

"I didn't see you encroaching that mile gap, either."

"No, no, you didn't."

"Listen, I came here today for the same reason I came to Forest Lake two hundred years ago. I need to protect someone I love. Then, it was Mararis. When Oriana bought this house not two miles from Mararis and her family, I knew she was about to start trouble. I was right. I failed Mararis and her family. I admit that now."

She looked at Linus and smiled. "Then Oriana moved away, and you moved to town. And who did you bring with you? Dyre Brenig."

"Crane," he corrected her.

"Where'd she get that name from?"

"Something from our past. I'd rather not discuss this topic." Linus shut her down.

"Easy there, old man. Women were put on this earth to break our hearts. You had the misfortune of falling for a goddess. Double jinx. Consider yourself lucky that she didn't kill you," Micah teased, hoping to break the tension.

Linus made a derisive sound and let the matter drop.

Farryn put her warm hand over Linus's hand. "Well, I stayed in town to make sure Oriana didn't come back to finish the job. I'm here today because I believe Mararis and Tera are back to kill Elena."

"It's not Mararis or Tera that we're concerned with. It's Oriana," Kim slipped in her opinion.

"What does Oriana have to do with this…besides, I mean, starting it all?" Farryn looked flummoxed.

Camilla sat for a moment without speaking. She fidgeted in her seat, straightened her sweater, and pulled her hair over her right shoulder before switching it to the left.

"Milly…"

"The calling. The spell the girls read was from Oriana's grimoire."

"Figures." Farryn could feel the annoyance immediately overwhelm her. "I won't even ask how you came to have Oriana's grimoire."

Linus stood and started pacing.

Farryn continued. "The spell was the same one she used to find Tera and Mararis over the years. I remember Marianne, um, Mararis complaining about the pressure it caused in her chest. She hated it."

Camilla straightened in her seat again. "Yes, I understand. This, however, is a little worse."

"A little? Camilla, be honest. For once since this all happened," Linus shouted.

She reared up on him. "I'm not being honest? Who are you to talk?"

"This is not the same." He knew she was referring to his secrecy regarding his new relationship with Elena. "Since you got back from your little vacation, you've done nothing but lie and hide your true feelings." He wasn't shouting now but was emphatic.

Camilla sighed.

"I feel like I walked into the middle of something." Farryn's mouth pulled to the side as she tried to figure out what to do. "Linus? Kim. Could you please give us a moment?"

Linus left in an angry huff, and Kim followed without question or comment.

When they were alone, Farryn patted the cushion beside her. "Come, sit down."

Camilla dropped onto the sofa as if she were bearing Sisyphus's burden. Her shoulders dropped a few inches, and her head hung.

"What vacation is he talking about?"

"I took some time for myself, that's all. Apparently, it's upset everyone's equilibrium. Leny resents me. It's clear Linus does too. "

"Where'd you go?" There was a pause. A deep, hesitating moment that was filled with secrets. "Mil? Why are you blocking me?"

Camilla studied her hands. "I visited with some friends overseas and then went to Elder Path."

Farryn didn't answer. She didn't comment. She only waited.

"There's nothing there," Camilla continued. "Not one bit of the town standing." She turned her hands over and over. "I felt it, though, you know? I felt them. I felt us."

When she finished speaking, Farryn smiled. "It took you too long to go home."

"But now everyone is upset."

Farryn's smile didn't waver. "Leny's jealous. You're used to that, right? Linus…well, Linus is a different kind of jealous. He can't bring himself to go, so he resents you for going alone. It's a deeply personal experience. It's something you can't share with others. I know. When I went, I fell to the ground weeping for hours."

"Honestly?"

She nodded. "It was cathartic. I'm proud of you." She reached to hug her cousin, hoping it would be reciprocated. And when it was, Camilla held on to Farryn until they both laughed.

"There's something else…"

21

FARRYN

After a long discussion about the calling and Oriana's return, Camilla thought it best that they meet with Dyre Crane before Farryn could warn Elena. She felt there was no use unnecessarily frightening her.

Farryn spent the night going over possible scenarios in her mind. Having been one of the last people to see Mararis alive, she was sure Dyre held her responsible for her death. Not to mention, Dyre was the only creature on this Earth who could revoke Farryn's immortality spell. It was a spell that had remained strong for almost two thousand years, maybe more. She'd lost count.

Sleep didn't find her until well into the wee morning hours and even then, it was fitful and fraught with nightmares. Waking before dawn, she baked chocolate chip scones for her neighbor's children and decided to take a walk into town.

"Looks like you had the same idea I did." Linus stood at the end of the line in the bakery waiting to place his order as Farryn entered the shop.

"You always did have a sweet tooth." She smiled and slipped her arm through his. She laid her head on his shoulder.

"Everything alright?" His deep voice was soothing.

"No sleep. I keep thinking I should have spoken with Elena yesterday."

She stepped up to the counter beside him and allowed him to order her a coffee and a cinnamon roll. He ordered two more coffees, a Danish, and a bagel with cream cheese. They didn't speak again until they'd paid for their order and left the shop.

"Elena is happily oblivious right now. After the last few days of Oriana upsetting the house spirits and not knowing what she wants, she deserves a break." He sipped his coffee.

"So, Milly was right. You are an item. How did that happen?" She giggled.

"I'm not going to discuss my love life with you."

"Why not? You used to tell me everything. Not that I wanted to hear everything, but you told me anyway." She grimaced. "Between you and Malcolm, the competition between you two. Really icky." She stuck her tongue out. "He stopped sharing when he and Milly were a thing. Now, you're keeping your romance with Leny all hush-hush." She flicked her eyebrows and made a sound like she knew he was falling for her cousin.

"Speaking of," he changed the subject. "Should we include Mal in this?"

"You mean, going to Dyre's? Why?"

"Too many reasons to name but the big one being that his daughter is in potential danger."

They decided to have breakfast and broach the subject with Camilla before making any decisions.

When they entered the school, Camilla was sitting on the floor in the living room with Oriana Duran's grimoire opened on her lap. Her hands hovered over the summoning spell the girls used to call the Sisters of Fate. On either side of her sat two mason jars. On her left, a sprig of mugwort and in the other, a sprig of rue. Both, Farryn knew, were excellent for communicating with the dead.

Around her neck on a thin cord of jute was strung a mandrake root. Camilla's eyes were closed as she seemed to be in deep meditation and unaware of their entry.

Farryn sat in front of her cousin with her legs knotted in front of her. She took Camilla's hands as she shared the magic surrounding her. Taking a deep breath, she closed her eyes. The magic swirled around them.

Farryn could feel tingles on the back of her neck and crawling up her arms. She heard Camilla's thoughts as clearly as if they were her own. She heard her words as she called out to Oriana Duran, attempting to harness her spirit.

"Colonel Bradford, have you found her?" Camilla called out to the house spirits, and they replied using only the wind to slam doors shut and to move curtains. "They don't like her," she whispered to Farryn. "She upsets the energy in the house."

"There's like an orphic pressure closing in on us." Farryn could barely breathe as the house spirits attempted to rid Oriana from the house themselves.

"Oh, good, it's the Phoenix." A sarcastic voice surrounded them. The familiar voice of Oriana Duran. *"I'm so glad you could join us for my bodily return."*

"Pardon me?" Farryn said.

"My return. Didn't you hear? I'm back."

"Pul-lease." Farryn drew out the word, not holding back her annoyance. *"What can you possibly accomplish as a ghost? You can slam doors. Congratulations."*

"That will be remedied soon enough—"

A barometric pop seemed to fill the house, like the air had been pressurized and finally exploded. Farryn and Camilla braced themselves, holding their ears. Linus cringed as he, too, covered his ears.

"I thought only Mia could open the grimoire?" Linus asked as he extended his jaw to unclog his ears.

"When has a spell stopped me from doing anything?" Camilla smirked. "This one was weak enough that it only took a few words to get around it."

"Do you think they scared her away?" He raised an eyebrow and bit into his Danish.

"Doubt it," Farryn said. She unfolded her legs and stood.

"It shut her up, anyway." Camilla laughed. "I'd forgotten how much I hate the sound of her voice. What do you think she meant by *that will be remedied soon enough*?"

"I'd hate to speculate, but I think we need to protect Mia." Linus picked up his paper cup filled with coffee and sipped it. "We need to involve Malcolm."

"No." Camilla didn't hesitate.

"And Bentyn Rae—"

"No."

"Milly, it's important. Think of Mia. The universe has brought us all together for a reason. I think we should embrace it or at the very least, lean into it." Farryn looked to Linus for support.

"I'll do it for Mia but if Malcolm says one thing out of line, so help me Linus, I'll turn your brother into a toad."

Raven's Corner was not open when they arrived. Linus banged on the glass door, hoping someone would hear him. It was just after nine; someone had to be up preparing for the day.

"Linus, stop." Camilla touched his arm and smirked at him. "*Ephphatha.*" She touched the handle of the door as she whispered the word. The sound of the lock disengaging brought a smile to her lips, and she turned the handle on the door.

Farryn followed her in as Linus trailed, feeling humiliated.

"Breaking and entering so early on a Sunday morning." Rayne Grey came out from behind the velvet curtain. "Is that what we're doing now? Criminal activity is frowned upon in every society. I could call the town constable."

"Save it, Rayne." Farryn stepped in front of her cousin, just as she used to as children, always ready to protect her.

"Oh good, it's the Phoenix." Rayne Grey crossed her arms. "Have you come to deliver your answer to Penelope's letter in person? Goodness knows, she is waiting with bated breath."

"Is Penelope here or do you now consider yourself interchangeable with her?" Farryn glared at her. "I really have no care to speak with you. We wish to speak with Malcolm. Is he here?"

"I am."

Malcolm stood in between the slice in the curtain waiting to be acknowledged. Looking strikingly similar to Linus, his shaggy hair hung carelessly in curls over his forehead. No beard hid his handsome features or the look of concern on his face. An air of distrust surrounded him as his eyes scanned his three visitors.

The regret wrapped itself around Farryn's heart as he frowned at her. With disappointment in his eyes, his mouth twitched like he intended to say something but thought better of it.

When he looked at his brother, his right eyebrow raised. The men shared a silent communication that Farryn did not listen to. Linus walked to his brother, always the first to initiate an apology. They smiled awkwardly at one another before Linus took his brother in his arms to hug him.

They all could feel Camilla's unease, so Malcolm left her with only a glance and a toothless smile.

"Malcolm," Farryn started. "We need to speak with you about your daughter and hopefully get you to accompany us to speak with Dyre Crane."

His interest was piqued but he looked apprehensive.

"I am sure Mia has told you about the spell they read last week." Linus rubbed his hands together just as he did when he began his lectures at school. "They read from Oriana's grimoire."

"Yes, we know," Rayne interrupted. "Oriana was locked inside the grimoire. Have you come to warn us? You're too late."

"How do you know all of this?" Camilla spoke for the first time since entering the shop.

"Mia." Rayne splayed her hands apart. "We also know how Oriana accomplished it, but as I've been continually reminded my entire life, you are the more powerful witches. You were members of the Great Coven. Far be it for me to imply that I know something that you don't."

"Rayne…" Malcolm warned.

Farryn held her tongue. Every fiber of her wanted to scream at Rayne Grey. To scream at her for every stupid letter she'd received in the name of the Witch Board, for allowing Oriana Duran to live for centuries, all along knowing what she'd done to Tera Pendle and Mararis Payne. But instead, she chose to ignore it.

"Be that as it may, we spoke to Oriana this morning. She did say something concerning that I believe is in reference to Mia."

"What is it? What did she say?"

"Malcolm, please don't tell me you are entertaining any of their nonsense. Please tell me you have enough sense to see through this pathetic attempt to lure you away from the Board." Rayne tried to sound superior and assertive, but her voice shook as she spoke.

"Farryn goaded her for being a spirit and she said, 'That will be remedied soon enough.'" Camilla offered.

"That means nothing." Rayne laughed.

"It means she's planning to be flesh again," Linus shouted at her.

"So?"

"So, who better to house her soul but her own daughter. Flesh of my flesh," Camilla quoted the bible.

"We're going to speak with Dyre about her sisters. We would like you to join us. We need you."

"What about her sisters?" Rayne stepped in between Linus and Malcolm.

"Don't know everything, do you?" Farryn taunted her.

"The girls read a spell to summon the Sisters of Fate," Linus said. "Because of Oriana, two of them are dead, along with their legacies. They were called back from their graves, and we need to find out why."

"Just them and not their legacies?" Malcolm asked.

"As far as we know, just Tera and Mararis, but we'll find out when we speak to Dyre." Farryn headed for the front door. "Are you with us?"

He looked at Rayne and then at Farryn. "Just to meet with Dyre. I make no promises except doing what will protect Mia."

"Deal."

22

DYRE

The morning started out uneventful. Just a usual Sunday morning. Lucy ate breakfast, colored for a while, and then watched a little television. The day was overcast, the perfect fall day to stay in with her girls.

April hadn't left her room, but Dyre knew she was awake. She could hear Tera talking. April wasn't answering and yet she kept talking.

Tera hadn't spoken to Dyre directly, yet. No matter how much she engaged her. She wasn't sure if her sister heard her or was just ignoring her.

Tera was like that. As the youngest of the three sisters, she was, at times, impossible. It didn't surprise her that she was the first sister Oriana set her sights on. She broke the rules. She used magic. Oriana found her because of it.

Tera hated her punishment of banishment and being forbidden to use her magic, feeling it was rash and unjust to lump her and Mararis into Dyre's horrendous life choices.

She blamed Dyre the moment their feet touched the earth, the moment they found themselves tethered to the mortal world. Being immortal in a dying world was the worst punishment they could imagine.

Tera was the first to fall in love with a mortal man. The first to bear a child. The first to realize what birthing a legacy meant. It meant they would finally become one with the dying planet. Immortality separated from their souls. They aged, slowly but assuredly. Their powers dwindled. Their magic wasn't as effective as it had been before the legacy.

It took all three of them to decipher what was happening. From the moment Rose was born, Tera lost her immortality. That was easy enough to discover. As she grew, she claimed her mother's abilities. Tera felt her powers weakening. By the time the witch hunters caught up with her, she was too sick to fight them off.

There was the underlying hope that Rose would also be reclaimed by the gods. As she grew, sucking her mother dry of all her magic and disposing of any lingering culpability to Dyre's guilt, Tera hoped Rose could regain her place in the embrace of the Mother and the Father.

They never got the chance to find out. Rose died, tied to a tree and set on fire beside her mother and her sister, Tess.

When Mararis fell in love, she feared that she would create a legacy and thus lose her immortality as well. She held off getting pregnant for as long as she could, but her husband, Richard, wanted children. Simon and Gail were normal mortal children. Their family lived happily until she had an unplanned pregnancy resulting in Edith, her legacy.

That was when Mararis understood what it was like to be mortal. To feel sickness or bleed when she was cut. To attempt to protect her family and fail.

Dyre wondered where Mararis was. There were only three people she knew of that Mararis had any bond with: her daughter, Gail, her son, Simon, or her best friend, Farryn Allard. She knew where two of three lived. Gail lived a few miles north on a remote compound, and Farryn Allard was across town in the same house she'd lived in for two centuries. Simon was a mystery.

"Is my daddy visiting today?" Lucy asked.

"What makes you say that?" The last thing Dyre needed today was to see Linus.

"A feeling. He won't be alone." She spoke in a deadpan way that sounded creepy.

Dyre sat at the kitchen table and concentrated. Seeing futures wasn't as easy as it used to be. In her youth, all she needed was intent and she'd see someone's past, present, and future. Their life thread materialized, swirling around them like a magnificent metallic cord.

The cord looked different to each of the sisters. To Dyre, it glowed brighter than the sun and moved like it was floating on water. Easy to see, easy to cut. Mararis had described it as a living, breathing essence like a snake. Measuring it took concentration. Tera swore she'd spun rivers and vines.

Whatever they saw, Dyre could harness the thread. Listened to it, read it, manipulate it, or cut it if she wished.

Her cutting days were long over, so when the thread materialized, she simply listened. A multitude of voices surrounded her for only a moment before she waded her way through it, pushing unimportant messages to the sides.

She saw Linus, Malcolm, and Camilla. They were on her doorstep. Their presence angered her. She lost her grasp on the thread. As it swam away from her, awful voices filled in like a wave on the beach. Voices of murderers, child molesters, politicians, and thieves.

Hearing so much barbarism, knowing her own anger attracted the negative fragments of the world, her mind wandered to the drawer in her bedroom. The drawer full of scissors. Special scissors. Scissors designed to put an end to hatred, manipulation, and violence in the world. Scissors she was no longer allowed to use.

Steam rose from the pipes under the sink as she fought to control her anger. There were so many horrors in the world and her hands were tied. Her useless sisters, the ones appointed to replace her, ignored it—all of it.

More steam billowed from beneath the sink, seeping up from between the cabinet doors. The faucet creaked as the water boiled within the pipes.

Dyre grasped the place mat under her hands and squeezed it like a dish towel.

The pipe burst. The faucet flew, denting the wall as it collided with it. The hot water sprayed from the cracked pipe. Steam filled the kitchen. Dyre watched it for a moment as if she had no idea what she was seeing.

Lucy ran to the kitchen. "What's happening?"

This seemed to wake Dyre from her stupor. She held out her hand to her daughter. "Lulu, stay there."

Stepping into the scalding spray, she reached to turn off the valve under the sink. When the water was off, she was soaked. The damage to the kitchen was minimal, nothing a towel and a good plumber couldn't fix.

"Your arm…" Lucy cried.

Dyre looked down to the small cluster of blisters that bubbled to the surface on her forearm. "I'm okay, baby. Don't worry. Let's go bandage me up."

The burn felt like a sunburn, but the water-filled blisters looked a lot worse. She allowed Lucy to apply burn ointment to it and wrap it (maybe too excessively) with gauze. "All better." Lucy leaned to her mother's arm and kissed it.

"All better." Dyre gazed at her youngest daughter, loving every bit of the child. She was proud to pass on the breadth of her abilities to such a beautiful, empathic child. "Your father is coming today. He's bringing friends. April. All hands on deck. Company's coming." She pounded on April's bedroom door. "Let's call Mia."

Lucy nodded with vigor, all thoughts of the burn in the past. She ran for her mother's cell phone.

"I can't fix the pipe, but I mopped up the water," Mia told her aunt.

"Thank you." Dyre smiled and looked down at Lucy. "We dusted and vacuumed the living room. No thanks to April!" she yelled down the hall.

"Who's coming over?" Mia asked.

"My daddy." Lucy bounced in place.

Mia looked at Dyre with concern ruffling her brow. "Linus is coming here?"

The doorbell rang before she could answer.

"They're here. They're here." Lucy ran to the door.

"Lulu, don't open that door," Dyre scolded. Tearing the bandages from her forearm, she tossed them on the table. "I'll get it."

At the door, Linus and Malcolm stood shoulder to shoulder as if it was a competition to see who could enter the house first. Linus carried a pastry box, and Malcolm carried a box of coffee. Behind them, Dyre could see Camilla and Farryn standing a few steps back from the door.

"Come in." Dyre simply opened the door without speaking to either man directly.

"Dad?" Mia shouted and ran to him. She wrapped her arms around his waist. "I didn't know you were coming."

"That makes us even. I didn't know you were here." He laughed and hugged her again.

"Hi, Dad!" Lucy stepped up to Linus, mimicking Mia's greeting, and waved. His daughter was still unsure as to how to approach her relationship with him. He could see Lucy was itching to hug him.

Dyre smiled and took his pastry boxes.

"Hi." He returned Lucy's wave. "Do I get a hug?"

Her eyes went first to her mother and then to Mia. She nodded with quick motions and held out her arms for him to hug. He swept her up in his arms, swinging her around in the air, making her laugh out loud. After he put her down, he turned and saw April standing in the hallway.

"I'm not expecting a hug, but what about a hello?"

"Hi, Linus." She also had reservations about the man who'd been missing from their lives for six years.

Dyre watched him carefully. She could see the mixture of emotions that followed his daughter's lukewarm reception. His facial muscles froze, his eyes went glassy, and then he smirked. If she cared to read his thoughts, she probably would have seen him realize that April needed time to digest this massive drama that held her family tight in its embrace.

"I'll take it, I guess. But I'll give you a dollar if you'd call me Dad." He pursed his lips, hoping for a smile from his eldest daughter.

She studied him. "Make it a twenty and you've got a deal." She laughed. Her loud Brenig laugh made Lucy cover her ears and leave the room. Linus leaned in toward April and gave her a kiss on the side of her head.

"Pierce didn't want to come?" Dyre asked him, trying hard to hide the disappointment in her voice.

"Kim and Elena took the kids to the arboretum this morning. He doesn't know I'm here." He gave her a *this is hard for everyone* expression and left it at that.

"Why don't you girls put the coffee and donuts in the kitchen." Her expression hardened as Camilla and Farryn entered the house. Camilla's entrance was cautious, bordering on apologetic, while Farryn entered like she'd been invited. Her eyes took in the entire room before meeting Dyre's suspicious gaze.

"Mommy?" Lucy sidled up to her mother, looking frightened. "Who's that?"

"No one you need to worry about. Go inside with your sister." She urged her daughter away.

"Who's who?" Malcolm asked.

"There's a man in the front yard." She buried her face in her mother's back.

"A man?" Farryn looked out the door and saw nothing out of place. "What man?"

"You don't see him?" The child's shoulders began to tremble slightly, and Farryn could see water collecting in her large blue eyes. She looked so much like Linus. "He's right there. He's by the door." Lucy screamed, squirming into her mother's arms, until she held her tight. Linus walked to the door protectively, but he could not see the mysterious man either.

Dyre scowled at the man. "I said, he's nobody. Just go inside. April, come get your sister, please."

"What's the matter?" Mia stepped out of the kitchen instead of April. "Stop being weird, kid. Come and get a donut."

Lucy didn't budge. "There's a man…"

"There are two men. Time to get your eyes checked," Mia kidded her cousin.

"She's not talking about us, wise guy." Malcolm tapped her on the back of the head with his palm. "She sees someone else. I'm guessing I know who it is."

"Who?"

Farryn giggled to herself and decided to try something. She held up her hand to stop anyone from saying his name. She leaned close to Lucy. "Hi, Lulu. My name is Farryn Allard."

"You're the Phoenix," Lucy's muffled voice spoke through her mother's sweater that she used to hide her face.

"Call me Farryn," she said.

"What happened to you?" Lucy peeked out from behind the sweater and stared up at Farryn. Her eyes were wide with wonder.

A crease deepened between her eyes. "Can you see my scars?"

"Your face looks blurry on one side." Lucy touched her face with her hand to indicate which side looked off. Her little hand touched the left side of her face.

"I'm impressed. Most people can't see through my deception."

Having been burned at the stake may have gained her notoriety because she rose from the ashes, but the drawback was the scars were permanent. Farryn used a good deal of magic to cloak the disfigurement she endured over a thousand years ago.

"What's that?" Lucy looked intrigued.

"That doesn't matter now. What does matter is this man. What does he look like?"

She shook her head and disappeared behind the sweater again.

"Please, I am here to help you. I can't see them, but I can speak with spirits. If he is dangerous, he won't hurt you. I promise." She looked at Dyre, who was skeptical.

"If you can't see him, how can you stop him from hurting us?"

Us? She wondered if Lulu was an empath—just like Linus.

"I have magic, just like you. Once you learn how to use it, you won't be afraid anymore. Until then, you have your mom and Linus and me."

"And Aunt Beni. She can kill anyone."

Mia laughed and then covered her mouth.

Lucy's big, watery blue eyes met Farryn's with fear and doubt swimming around in them. She didn't turn her head but looked at this mysterious spirit from the corner of her eye.

"Yes, her too." Farryn tried to hide her annoyance at the mention of the witch-hunting cold blood. "Now, please."

"He's tall like Daddy. His hair is dark and long. His face is thin, and his eyes are brown." She moved her head slightly in the direction of the man. "He's just standing there."

"Listen to me, Lulu." Farryn diverted her attention away from her mother. "He won't move. Do you know why?"

She shook her head, returning her fear-filled eyes to Farryn.

"Because then I can feel him. He's trying his best to only see us, but he didn't count on you seeing him." She smiled brightly. "Want to know a secret? I know him. I'll prove it. Tell me this, now you may have to look directly at him to see this, if you can do that—tell me, does he have a scar over his right eye?"

Linus snickered. Camilla was transfixed.

"You swear he won't move?"

"I can't guarantee it now since we're onto him, but I'm pretty sure you're safe."

Lucy looked at the front door. The man stood with his arms crossed over his chest, looking interested in what was unfolding. She looked away quickly. "Yes. It cuts into his eyebrow a little."

Farryn stood and paced like she was giving a lecture series on spirits. "Can I tell you a story? I have a brother. His name is Micah, and when Micah and I were about your age—maybe a little older—I think I was ten and he was nine, he was practicing his magic—"

"He's a witch?"

"Yes, just like me. We come from a long line of very proud witches. Anyway, Micah wasn't supposed to use his magic except with an adult." She looked to the spot where she assumed Micah was standing. "Have you ever used your magic without permission?"

Lucy nodded her head sheepishly. Dyre chuckled.

"Me too. I think we all have, but this particular time, it got away from him. Do you remember this, Mil?" She smiled at her cousin.

Camilla nodded, enraptured by the story.

"You see, Micah was not very good at spells. He became one of the best spellmasters I've ever seen, but as a little boy, he couldn't control his magic. Does that sound familiar?"

Lucy cupped her hand over her mouth, hiding a giggle.

"Do you know what he tried to do? He tried to fly. Can you fly?"

Lucy's eyes were wide like saucers, but she didn't answer.

"Well, Micah could not fly. He did, with my help, I might add, get a few feet off the ground, but he couldn't stay in the air."

That was it. She stopped and waited.

"He came through the door. He's walking towards us." Lucy buried her head deep in her mother's stomach and wrapped her arms around her waist.

"Spoilsport." Micah was in Farryn's ear.

Farryn laughed and ticked her tongue in a disappointed manner. "Scaring an innocent child? You are the worst kind of witch, Micah." She smoothed back Lucy's ashen hair and kissed the top of her head. "Lulu, this is my brother Micah Allard. I promise he won't hurt you, but I really need you now. I can't see him, and sometimes he makes faces at me when I speak to him— faces I can't see. I need you to tell me when he is razzing me. Okay?"

Two curious wonder-filled eyes peeked out from beneath Dyre's bosom. "Do you see him?"

"Yes, sweetie, I see him." Dyre wasn't thrilled with having another witch around her daughter.

"Can you see him, April?"

April looked around to the curious onlookers surrounding her. "Kind of. I can see through him like he's projected on the wall."

"What happened next? Did he fall?" Lucy studied Micah as he sat on a chair beside her, unseen by anyone else in the room except her mother and April.

"I fell." Micah didn't sound thrilled. *"Hard."*

Farryn laughed. "He did fall, and he broke his arm in the process and got that lovely little scar on his forehead."

"I was fine."

"Only after Mama healed you," she retorted. "It was a blessing that she was a healer."

"Aunt June really gave it to you too." Camilla laughed. "The yelling she did. My ears are still ringing." She could hear her cousin through Farryn's thoughts.

After a moment of levity, Dyre looked at her guests. "Do you want to tell me why you're all here?"

"Mararis called out to me this week," Farryn started. "I wondered if you'd heard from Tera."

"Yes," April shouted.

Linus laughed.

"I didn't engage with Mararis, but I believe they are intent on killing Elena." Farryn concentrated on Dyre only.

"See, I told you." April glared at her mother.

"What makes you say that?" Dyre played dumb.

Farryn's expression hardened with annoyance. "We were hoping to stop them."

"Aunt Tera says, 'Like hell,'" April responded.

"I heard." Dyre shook her head. "They are harmless without their powers. Like any spirit, they can manipulate others but do nothing on their own."

"Which brings us to the other reason we're here…" Farryn looked at Mia. "Opening that grimoire brought Oriana Duran back too. And she's not content with staying in the spirit world."

23

GAIL

Gail opened her eyes. Nadia lay beside her in a fit of dreams. Thor and Attila were at the foot of the bed. The room darkening blinds were securely in place. She reminded herself that she was at the Annex and not in her own bed.

The bedroom door to the director's suite was open, allowing the dogs the freedom to come and go as they pleased. The basement door was left open so they could relieve themselves near the dock area without interrupting their sleep.

The clock on the bedside table read four fifteen. It wasn't even close to sunset. There were two more hours to go.

"Gail," her mother's voice called out to her.

She'd realized it was her mother's voice speaking to her two days ago. The overbearing attitude was difficult to ignore, as much as she tried.

After seeing Bentyn Rae in the forest, Gail returned to the Annex. The voice antagonized her the entire walk into town as only her mother could. She nitpicked how she carried herself, how she wore her hair, how she lived her life. As if being a blood drinker was a choice she'd made and not the result of an unprovoked attack.

"Gail, wake up," her mother called.

"Go away," Gail hissed from her bed.

The dogs whined. Their tails thumped the floor as they slithered to her side of the bed. A wet nose touched her hand, urging her to run her fingers over the furry head connected to it.

Nadia mumbled in her sleep but did not wake. As a young blood drinker of just over thirty years, she needed her rest to rejuvenate her body. She still feared the sun as well.

"If you don't get out of that bed, young lady, I'll take you out of it."

Gail laughed. *Young lady?*

"I'd like to see you try."

In that instant, Gail felt her body lift, and she was thrown to the floor. Thor barked and Attila, who had been seated beside Gail's side of the bed, skidded across the tile floor to safety.

"Didn't think I would do it, did you?" There was humor in her mother's voice. It was something she hadn't heard in centuries, and she had to admit that she enjoyed hearing it.

Even with the bang her body made when it hit the floor, Nadia lay unperturbed in her sleep. Gail shook her head, clearly annoyed by the lack of concern from her offspring. She whistled for the dogs to follow her as she slipped out of the room, closing the door behind her.

With a quick peek around the corner, she checked to see how far the sunlight extended down the hall from the reception area. The large glass windows did nothing to protect her from the dangerous rays of the sun. Fortunately, only the reception area seemed to be bathed in sunlight.

Through the door behind her, the stairs snaked up two floors and then down to the basement. She made a quick decision that the basement was the safer bet and ran down the stairs.

The heavy metal door opened on the far side of the basement from the living area. She closed the door after Thor and Attila were inside. The cement floor was cold on her bare feet.

The dogs ran to the sofa in the common area just outside of the guest rooms. There were four doors leading to the guest rooms. Outside of them there sat a sofa, two chairs, and a flat screen television set. She remembered Nadia mentioning that this was not your typical Haven and shouldn't attract guests like the other safe houses did. The accommodations were meager but sufficient for a chance traveler looking for a place to stay for the night.

Gail sat beside the dogs, pulling her feet up off the cold floor.

"What do you want from me?"

"I need you to find your Aunt Dyre." That imperious tone her mother had been using was gone. Her voice was soft and pleading. Gail found it endearing to hear.

"You mean Sarah, don't you? Aunt Sarah died well over a century ago."

"Not Sarah. Dyre. I don't know what last name she has chosen, but I know she's near. I can feel her. I just can't find her. She will reunite us, and we will get our vengeance."

"Who is we? Who is she going to reunite, and who are you avenging?" Gail found some part of her was entertained by this strange narrative her mother was weaving. "Who is Dyre?"

"Dyre is my sister and your aunt. Tera is the youngest. I am the middle, and Dyre is the oldest of the sisters. I assume we were brought back to kill Elena Nolan and Oriana Duran, and that is what I intend to do."

"My, my, my. For someone who has spent the last two days judging *my* life, you came back from the grave to kill two women? Doesn't seem like you learned anything in death?"

Her mother was silent.

"You killed Daddy, now these women. I guess I learned from you, didn't I?" A small smirk pulled on Gail's mouth.

A high-pitched whine cut into her ear. Attila was not happy with her mother's presence.

"I didn't kill your father."

A smile of satisfaction crossed Gail's face.

"I didn't kill your father. His own ignorance killed him. Stubborn fool that he was. He never believed we were in danger. No matter that Edith was dead. No matter that I was clearly losing my powers. He never believed." She stopped speaking, and the four walls of the enormous basement seemed to close in on Gail.

"Mother? What happened to him?"

"Oriana Duran tried to poison me. They broke into our house."

"They?"

"Elena Nolan and Oriana Duran. They put wolfsbane in my tea. Your father ignored my warnings and drank the toxic herbs."

Gail couldn't believe it. "No, you murdered him. I saw you."

"You saw me put him out of his misery. I eventually took the poison myself."

"Why?"

"To protect you and your brother. I was dying anyway. I knew they would find my body and not you. You were protected by the closet."

"Don't speak of that closet. There was nothing protective about that horrid place. I was a prisoner in there." She shook her head, hoping to rid her mind of the images of the tiny room with only a pillow and a candle for comfort.

"It kept you safe from prying eyes. Thanks to Farryn."

"Farryn? Miss Allard? The lady who lived next door?"

"The witch *who lived next door."*

"You mean, Simon was right? Miss Allard was a witch?"

"A very powerful witch. She's still alive."

"Do you know where she is? Maybe if I speak with her, some of this will make sense." Gail's mind was working.

"She won't help you. I pushed her away too many times. I pushed Aunt Sarah away. I pushed Farryn away. I just couldn't drag them down with me."

"If she wasn't your sister, who was Aunt Sarah, Mother?"

"Sarah Bruckman was a strong telepathic witch. She was also a descendant of Magnus Anmar. I found and befriended her because of Tess."

"Stop." Gail held her hand up as if her mother was sitting in the room with her. "Aunt Sarah was a guardian before me. Why'd Tess skip you?"

Tess Pendle was a spirit that had plagued Gail's family as far back as the fifteenth century. The story Gail knew was that Tess was a witch who was burned at the stake with her mother and sister. She believed that Tess's soul was never at rest, and she vowed revenge on the man who was responsible for her murder, Magnus Anmar.

In Gail's family, Tess was known as *the woman*. They were told and wholeheartedly believed that saying her name would call her out. Tess attached herself to one person in each generation. They called themselves her guardians and when one guardian died, Tess would pass to the next.

Tess appeared in mirrors and in glass panes. Their communication was never verbal. She lived in a realm that allowed her to peek into the physical world. And over the centuries, she learned to manipulate the guardians. After a century, Gail detested her intrusion in her life and opted to find a baby and give Tess the one thing she really wanted—a second chance.

She attempted a transmigration to insert Tess's soul into a baby. But like most transmigration attempts, it failed, and Tess was sent back into the spirit world to await another chance at life.

Tess was passed from Sarah Bruckman to Gail, skipping her mother completely.

Mararis laughed. The sound came from every direction. The dogs howled as she laughed.

"Tess would never have chosen me even if she could. I knew where she was and why. I knew there was no hope for her on this side of the veil." Her mother sighed. *"I followed her. I befriended many of the guardians. I tried to communicate with Tess, but much like her mother, she was angry.*

"She was angry for what happened to her, angry that she hadn't passed on, angry that she was trapped. So much anger." Mararis went silent again, and Gail feared she was done speaking. Then she resumed. *"I promised her that you would be her next guardian. I knew you'd find immortality one way or another and you'd be her last guardian. I was wrong, wasn't I?"*

"Yes." Gail shook her head, annoyed. "She tormented me. That anger you spoke of never went away. She was manipulative and vindictive. She sought out my daughter and their daughters. Driving them mad in the process. I tried…" She didn't wish to admit her failure and the poor decisions that led to that failure.

"I know and I'm sorry you had to endure so much. Your great-granddaughter put her back into that awful realm, didn't she?"

"Nadia. Yes, Tess almost killed her."

"I fear Farryn was right. Dyre's deeds set us up for a lifetime of misery."

Gail stroked the dogs as she absorbed the information her mother had imparted. "How did you know I would find immortality?"

"You are my child. Immortality has always been yours to find. Somewhere in this world, Simon is enjoying his eternal life as well. In what form, I do not know, but it is a gift given to each child of the divine, no matter if you are the legacy or not."

She ignored her mother's words, distracted by thoughts of her brother, Simon. *Could he still be alive?* Gail shook her head. That was impossible.

"I think you mean improbable." Mararis seemed to pull up a chair in her mind, happily sipping tea and reading every thought she had. *"Considering that you're immortal, Simon being immortal is not impossible. Don't you agree?"*

Gail huffed.

"I need to speak with Miss Allard. Do you know where she is?"

"She still lives in Forest Lake. In the same house."

"At sunset, I will go," she said with a defiant tone.

Her mother laughed and the dogs howled again. There was something about the pitch of her laughter that seemed to aggravate them.

"You know, the sun cannot hurt you," Mararis said. *"It was Rafe's blood mixed with Dyre's magic that caused the reaction. You have my blood inside you. More so than that horrid man you call a sire. Direct sunlight may burn, but if you stay in the shadows, you are strong enough to live happily in the daylight."*

Gail was speechless. Questions kept queuing in her mind, but she was unable to voice them. Her mother's laughter told her she heard them regardless. *"Go find Farryn. She will calm your worries."*

"If you don't mind, I'll wait until sunset."

At sunset, Gail stepped outside of Haven. She shared the conversation she'd had with her mother with Nadia when she woke. With her usual dismissive attitude coupled with a healthy dose of skepticism, the conversation was short and heated.

Gail chose to take Thor for a walk, leaving his very unhappy brother with Nadia.

She shoved her fists into the pockets of her sweater and walked to the top of the parking lot. Thor darted up the pavement, dragging his leash behind him. Passing Raven's Corner, Gail glanced at the display window decorated with a large basket of harvest vegetables in honor of the upcoming fall equinox.

Inside, a dark-haired woman glared at her, sending a silent warning to keep moving. Not knowing the woman, Gail did not understand the animosity. Jordan told her once that witches hated blood drinkers and vice versa. She felt no such hatred for this woman but chose not to incite a race war for simple curiosity. She kept walking.

Coming to the corner of Perry and Main, she stopped and grabbed Thor's leash. The streetlights lit up the center of town. Teenagers, happy to be free from school for the weekend, filled the café, the ice cream parlor, and movie theatre. Several carried bags from various shops, including Raven's Corner.

She understood their excitement but had never experienced it herself. Having been sent away to an all-girls school, any breaks required her to come home to watch her mother's slow decline into madness. There was no time for shopping.

"How very dramatic." Her mother's sarcastic tone was new to her.

"What do you call ranting about protecting ourselves day in and day out?" Gail barked at Mararis in her mind.

"You're welcome." Again, there was that sarcasm that she didn't associate with her mother.

It occurred to Gail that she and her mother were the same age. If she was alive, they could be friends.

Gail found herself walking down Main Street in the opposite direction of the noise and chaos. She wasn't hungry, but the need for blood was strong enough when her mother hovered that she was afraid she would not be able to control herself if she got too close to the masses of teenagers.

She walked the length of Main until the bridge over Poplars Creek. She turned after the bridge and continued down the idyllic little street where she'd grown up. So much was different from how she remembered it. There were more houses, at least a dozen more. The road was paved. The farmland that surrounded it had been converted into backyards and a small community park with a few benches and a fountain.

Gail circled the fountain, touched her fingers in the stagnant water, and stood still. Thor sniffed the grass and relieved himself on the fountain.

"You're stalling," Mararis sang in a hushed voice.

"I don't know why I came here." She kicked the stones surrounding the fountain. *"It's not the same."*

"Nothing ever is."

Slowly, she made her way up the street. Most of the houses were maintained perfectly. Each with a manicured lawn with shrubs and flowers lining the walk. One house was different.
It was small with a mass of overgrown flowers choking the front
yard. The front walk was perfectly trimmed as if the plants knew not

to grow near it. The windows seemed to have eyes staring down at her, and the plum-colored door held a thistle wreath with white roses intertwined around it.

A white wooden vine-covered arbor welcomed her as she stood before the threshold. To the untrained eye, it was a mass of unkept weeds, but Gail could tell each plant was carefully selected and nurtured. Fireflies blinked amid the wildflowers, looking like magic.

"Do you remember Farryn?" her mother asked.

Gail did remember her. *Miss Allard.*

"She's a witch," her brother told her when they were children. *"Stop lying, Simon,"* she demanded. *"I've seen her stirring her cauldron. Cooking up spells. Eating little children."* Simon would laugh, knowing Gail believed him.

Next door to the overgrowth was her house. The keyhole doorframe brought Gail back a century to the house that sheltered her family of five. The house that heard her tears when her father and sister died. The house that listened to her screams as her mother fell to the floor, taking her last breaths.

"I don't want to go in." Gail looked at Farryn Allard's house.

"Why not?" A strange voice from behind startled her.

Gail swung around to find Farryn Allard standing in the middle of the overgrowth of her yard like a statue come to life. Dressed in a long sheer dress made of flowing fabric and her hair pulled back with a flowery wreath, she resembled the Ghost of Christmas Past.

Gail was speechless. She had not sensed or seen her. Neither had Thor. Had she been there the whole time?

"Farryn," her mother crooned.

"Miss Allard?" She walked down the sidewalk and stood in front of the white arbor.

A large gray and white cat darted past her as she took her first step into the mystical yard. He cried as if to warn those within they had a visitor. Thor stood stock-still. His head pulled back slightly as he looked down. The enormous dog looked more afraid than the cat.

Gail stooped to say hello. The cat rubbed her fingers with the side of his face and purred loudly.

"You've won Monkey's affections. If you have any catnip, he'll be your best friend for life." She stepped out of the wildflowers onto the path. "How am I looking at you right now?" Her fingers grazed Thor's massive head as he leaned against her leg.

Gail raised an eyebrow. "I think we both know how. You know what I am, Miss Allard."

"I think you're a little old to call me Miss Allard, don't you, Gail?"

"I suppose." She couldn't believe that Simon was right. Miss Allard was a witch. She wanted to share this information with someone, but there was no one around.

"Please don't do that," Farryn laughed. "I don't have many friends in this neighborhood. They are all convinced if they cross my threshold, I'll turn them into toads or something."

"Farryn," her mother said again.

"Why don't you come inside and talk about that weight you're carrying around with you."

Inside the house was just as chaotic and magical as the outside. Too many candles, plants, jars, crystals, and books shoved into nooks and crannies. The furniture was placed in small conversational groups and tables, draped with silk scarves. Farryn offered her a seat and then sat across from her.

She unhooked Thor's leash, and he went to town smelling every nook and cranny.

"I'd offer you something, but I don't believe in playing games. As you've said, I know what you are, and you know what I am. I don't fear you. Do you fear me?"

"Is there a reason that I should?" Gail asked.

"Not that I can see."

The two women stared at each other for a few moments, until Farryn broke the silence. "You look a lot like her, you know." Gail nodded, uncomfortable with the compliment. Farryn could sense her unease. "Why are you here?"

Gail studied her, wondering if she should trust her. "I didn't come to see you. I came to see my old house."

"Liar," her mother whispered.

"You've had centuries to visit the house. Why now?"

She could feel Farryn pushing at her mental vault, and Gail pushed back. Her eyes narrowed as she tried to figure out what this woman was doing. When Gail didn't answer her, Farryn continued.

"Have you heard from your mother?"

Gail's eyes widened.

"I'll take that as a yes. Is she here? Is that what that enormous weight you carry is? I can also see some kind of mirroring happening, especially when you speak. You look so much like your mother that I can't tell if I'm really seeing her or am I seeing you."

"Mirroring? What's that?"

Farryn overlapped her hands to illustrate what she meant. "Her aura is on top of yours."

"She remembers you. She sends her love," Gail lied, hoping to appease this woman and hopefully assess whether she could trust her or not.

Farryn laughed. "You lie. Your mother hated me before she died. If she sends her love, it's only to say she loves that I ended up alone just as she predicted."

"I was frightened at the end. Pushing her away was all I knew how to do."

Gail repeated what her mother said.

"Do you know if my mother had a sister? Not Aunt Sarah, apparently, I was wrong for years regarding my family tree. Do you know…what's her name?" she asked her mother.

"Dyre," she answered.

"Dyre."

Farryn smiled. Her eyes sparkled like she had a secret that she was busting to tell someone. "I've just seen her today."

Gail couldn't believe that her mother spoke the truth. The astonishment showed on her face.

"Didn't your mother tell you? Dyre Crane lives not far from here with her two daughters. Apparently, your Aunt Tera is communicating with *her* eldest daughter."

"How come you can't hear my mother now? She told me she called you first." Gail splayed her hands out in front of her.

"Maybe she doesn't wish me to hear her. Maybe since she is now attached to you, I can't hear her. I don't know." Farryn cleared her throat and adjusted the cushions on her chair. "I didn't realize you were still alive until Dyre told me today. Funny how the Fates brought us all together in the same day."

"Wait." Gail held her hand up to stop her. "How does my aunt know me?"

"Goddesses are like that. They are sneaky." Farryn laughed. "Do you mind if I have a drink? This has been one heck of a day for me." She went to the sideboard and filled a glass with amber liquid that smelled like whiskey.

"Of course," Gail said. She sat back on the sofa. She took in the room, enjoying the chaos. Thor found a cozy spot on the floor to lie down. To his dismay, Monkey chose to cuddle up beside him. He looked at Gail with concern that she laughed away.

"Wait, what do you mean…goddesses? Who's a goddess?" Gail asked.

"Didn't your mother tell you?"

"No."

"Yes, I did." Mararis was adamant.

"Your aunt is a goddess, just like your mother and their sister. You are a demi-goddess, Gail."

Gail laughed, feeling less like a goddess and more like a fool. She stood from her seat as Farryn returned to her own. "I should leave."

"It's true. I know you think I'm mad but I'm not." Farryn sipped her drink and cringed at the strength as she swallowed. "Dyre, Mararis, and Tera were the Sisters of Fate."

"From mythology?" Gail burst out. "Now, I know you're crazy." She headed for the front door. "I may be hearing voices, but you're the one who needs to seek help. My mother was no goddess."

"Why do you think she was immortal? For the first thirteen years of your life, did she age?" Farryn raised her eyebrows as Gail considered the question. "Tera and her daughters died in the fourteenth century. Your mother died in the nineteenth century, and here we are in the twenty-first century and Dyre lives across town. They are not blood drinkers, and they are not witches." She shrugged. "What are they?"

"I don't know but not goddesses." Gail opened the front door. *The sun will not harm you.*

"Ask your mother. Go visit Dyre Crane. They will tell you the same thing. Your mother was a goddess. I know it's a hard pill to swallow, but think about your own abilities. Why are you telepathic? Why is your great-great-granddaughter a spirit walker?"

"How did you know about that?"

"You don't know me beyond what your mother told you or the stories your brother told, but as much as I hate to admit it, I *am* the Phoenix. I've lived for centuries and even died once. I keep a close watch on those with a significant show of power. Nadia Bishop was a strong witch before you got to her. She's retained her powers, but the blood drinker lifestyle negates any connection she could have had with the magical world. It's a shame, really."

Gail's head was swimming. None of this mattered. She wasn't a demi-goddess. Her mother wasn't a goddess. Farryn Allard was insane, and Gail knew she needed to get out of her house before she drew her into her insanity.

She ran for the door and slammed it behind her, nearly catching Thor's tail in her rush.

24

BENI

Two hours before Gail woke, Beni lay in her bed, awake for almost an hour. Her phone told her it was only two in the afternoon and almost four hours before sunset. With Mia out of the house, she knew she'd be able to putter around in the shadows. When her daughter was home, she ran the risk of a door being opened or the blinds lifted, so she rarely left her room before sunset.

A text from Mia sent her eyes rolling in their sockets. *At Aunt Dyre's Dad's here Linus Camilla and the mf-ing PHOENIX I'm totally geeking out right now Love you. *Sorry for the language*

There was no context for the text, just who her daughter was spending her day with. Debating on whether to reply, she chose not to. Silence could be misinterpreted, but it could also be assumed that she was still unconscious. She chose silence.

It had been years since Beni slept through the day. It took hours for her to nod off only to wake just an hour or two later. Depression or grief were the only two spiraling emotions that kept her asleep, sometimes for years. Luckily, it hadn't happened in the last sixteen years. Mia kept her grounded and content.

Are you up? Dyre, this time.

She once again chose silence.

Coward. She could hear the sarcasm in Dyre's tone as she read it.

Beni tossed her phone across her king-sized bed and pulled back the covers. She pulled off the cotton nightgown. Looking down at it, she smiled. Mia invented an imaginary birthday for her when she was eight. This was her present. *"You have to have a birthday."* Beni jogged her brain, trying to think when she was born or perhaps when she was sired, but neither date held much importance to be remembered.

She ended up choosing the date she found Mia. The day had started miserably. Fighting with Asher. Breaking into a witch's house. Finding her lying in a puddle of her own blood on the floor. Arguing again with Asher about wasting their time. Soothing Mia as she screamed her lungs out in an adjoining room. Having an all-out brawl with Asher, trying to stop him from killing Mia. And finally, sending Asher away and taking Mia home with her.

A terrible day that ended in the best decision of her life. Definitely a day to be remembered.

Beni got dressed and slipped down the hall into the media room. It was just a large bedroom set up with a hundred-inch television, top-of-the-line sound system, and a comfy sectional sofa with speakers, a mini-fridge, and cup holders. The windows were permanently blocked off with false walls, so Beni spent a good portion of her time in this room.

She lay on the sofa, switched on Netflix, and settled in to binge-watch something mindless yet entertaining.

It didn't last long. Her thoughts kept going back to Dyre's house. Why was every witch in a hundred-mile radius at her house today? It had to have something to do with that damn spell the girls read. And, without a doubt, the return of Tera Pendle.

Beni could still smell that weird odor that accompanied Tera's presence in Dyre's house. Her thoughts switched to the blood drinker she'd seen in the woods. That same scent was attached to her. At the time, she thought it was her imagination, but was her imagination that good that she could actually smell something that wasn't there?

No, it wasn't.

She looked up to the enormous screen on the wall and realized she hadn't been watching the show she'd chosen. She hit the power button and sat up.

She considered the facts as she knew them. Fact: three witches used a strong summoning spell to call the Sisters of Fate. Fact: Tera Pendle and Dyre had heard this spell. Fact: Mararis Payne was a no-show. *Why?*

Promptly at sunset, Beni jumped into her car and headed to Haven. She didn't know where that blood drinker lived, but she knew she had to have some connection to the new safe house in town. The chances that she had no connection were slim.

She pulled down Perry Lane, slowing in front of Raven's Corner to give Raven's Corner the stink eye and kept going down to the parking lot of Haven. As she came down the hill, she saw Rayne Grey and Mia walking towards her. Beni slid into a parking space and jumped out of the car.

"What are you doing with my daughter?" Her glare was so intense that her eyes ached to sustain it.

"Leaving hate mail." Mia laughed like it was all a big joke to her.

"Hate mail?"

"We are making it clear to these cold bloods that they are not welcome in this town. They have yet to open their doors to us, so I've taken to leaving notes." Rayne kept walking. "Why am I explaining this to you? You are on the wrong side of right and will never understand our position."

Beni laughed. "What position would that be? What gives you any more right to be here?"

"Raven's Corner was established twenty years ago when this was still a tire warehouse. I can still smell the burnt rubber." She wrinkled her nose.

Beni smelled the air. She had noticed the odor but never paid it much attention or bothered to classify it. It just seemed to be what this side of town smelled like. She looked at her daughter, whose eyes shifted knowing her mother was preparing for a fight.

"Your argument is we were here first? Is that right?" Her face lit up with an incredulous smirk. "Haven has existed since the sixteenth century. They may not have squatter's rights in Forest Lake, but they preceded the Witch Board by almost three centuries."

Rayne's mouth puckered as she fought the comeback bristling on her tongue. "Regardless, this letter will be our last. I've made it abundantly clear that the Board will not allow a Haven to exist within such close proximity to a witch community and school. Measures will be taken if they refuse to comply."

Beni enjoyed this. "What do the Nolan sisters think of this ultimatum you've thrust upon your dangerous neighbors? Do you fear retaliation?"

"Is that a threat?" Rayne's eyes narrowed.

Footsteps on pavement drew Beni's attention from this asinine conversation. At the far end of the parking lot, a woman walked toward her with a dog. Her pace remained slow. She appeared to be lost in thought, not currently aware of their presence. Beni could smell the ozone odor even from a distance.

"I thought you were at Aunt Dyre's." She returned her attention to Mia.

She rolled her eyes in an exhausted manner. "Big fight between…well, everyone. Farryn went home. Dad and I stayed for a bit but then we got dinner and came here."

"Camilla and Linus stayed at Dyre's?"

"As far as I know."

She checked the dark-haired woman's proximity in her peripheral vision. "I've got to talk to someone here. Go back to Raven's Corner and wait for me. I'll only be a few minutes."

Beni watched the woman and her dog walk to the front door of Haven. She didn't show any signs of seeing her. The dog assumed a protective stance but never pulled or barked. The woman grabbed the note taped to the glass door and went inside.

After contemplating what to say, Beni went up to the door. She knocked.

A few minutes passed before a young blonde woman appeared in the hallway, flanked by two large German Shepherds. The one on the left was clearly the dog who had just returned from a walk with the other woman. The woman and the dogs approached the door bathed in the blue light from the Haven sign behind the reception desk. In her hand, she held Rayne Grey's note, which appeared unopened.

"May I help you?" She was guarded, both by the dogs and her own anxiety.

Beni couldn't help but notice she wasn't being invited in.

"I'm Bentyn Rae. This is going to sound strange. A woman with black hair just came in here. She was walking him." She pointed to the larger of the two Shepherds. "I need to speak with her, if possible."

"Why?" The blonde straightened her shoulders and stood tall with false courage.

Beni's brow rose. She could smell the connection these women shared. The blood that ran in this woman's veins belonged to the dark-haired blood drinker. Her sire.

"You don't need to let me in. If she could come out, I'd be more than happy to speak with her here." She could feel the woman rooting around in her brain for her real motives. Beni didn't have the energy to deal with this tonight. "Stop it. What do you think I'll do? Kill her?"

The blonde looked behind her, down the hall. "We know who you are." She whispered like this was a huge secret that no one could know about. "We know what Jordan Glynn did to you. I won't allow you to get your petty revenge on him by harming Gail. That will not happen again."

Beni stepped away from the door like she'd been shoved. She looked into the sky as if asking God, *why me?*

Two years ago, Aaron Carew had taken a woman hostage in a vain attempt at a revolution and revenge on Jordan Glynn. She didn't know until this moment that the woman she was following was that hostage. This Gail, having been sired by that piece of trash, Jordan Glynn, must be quite the hot ticket, Beni thought.

She laughed. "Oh, my God. This has absolutely nothing to do with Jordan Glynn. I promise you. If I wished to punish that monster, I have far better means than using his child against him." She laughed again in a derisive way that sounded like she'd given up. "Can you just ask her a question for me, then?"

The blonde's eyes narrowed. "I suppose."

"Ask her if she's been hearing voices lately."

The color bled away from this young blood drinker's face, and she looked fearful. Her fingers fiddled with the white paper in her hands. The dogs sensed her unease and adjusted their position to better defend her. "How did you know that?"

Beni's eyebrows jumped. "Okay. Now ask her if she knows the voice?"

The woman pulled the dogs back inside and closed the door. She locked it. As she stepped away, she dropped the unopened note on the reception desk. She sped down the hallway. Both dogs followed her.

Minutes passed.

Stop by tonight, Dyre texted.

Something up?

Just need some support.

When Beni looked up from her phone, the dark-haired woman stood at the door, staring at her. There was no humor, nor life in her eyes. No fear or anger either. Just dead gray eyes gazing through the window. Her long, slender fingers reached for the lock and turned it. She pushed open the door without stepping outside.

"Please come in."

The smell accosted Beni as if whatever was causing it filled the room. She stepped into the reception area and waited for her to close and lock the door again. Without speaking, the woman walked past Beni and down the hall.

She followed.

The hallway opened into a small, comfortable sitting room that attached to a kitchen area. The blonde stood in the kitchen with a large bag of dog food in her hand and two very eager animals at her feet. She poured the bag and then mixed it with soft, chunky, meaty food. When she was through, the dogs waited. After she stepped away, they dove at the bowls.

Beni laughed.

"Please sit down." The dark-haired blood drinker sat on the sofa, and the blonde took the chair directly across from Beni. "You are Bentyn Rae, correct?"

"Yes."

"Your sire is Kiernan," the blonde added.

"Yes." She wondered where these questions were leading.

"Sorry." The woman read her thoughts. "My name is Gail Andrews. This is Nadia Bishop." Beni nodded to each of them. "I have only one question. How did you know I was hearing a voice?"

She looked at them, both eager to hear her answer, both anxious and a bit afraid of her too. "I smelled it on you."

"I beg your pardon?"

Beni smirked.

"It's hard to explain. I have a refined sense of smell. When I saw you in the woods, I smelled it above the blood, the dogs, everything." She gauged their reaction and kept going. "The funny thing about that smell is a friend of mine smells like that too, and she's been hearing voices."

"Since when?" Nadia sounded defensive.

"Tuesday."

Gail closed her eyes and shook her head. "Me too."

"Do you know who the voice is or why they chose you?"

"I know exactly who she is. It's my mother and she chose me to torment me."

"Your mother? Who is your mother? What was her name?" Beni slid to the edge of her seat.

"Marianne Payne."

"That bible said Mararis Payne," Nadia corrected her.

Beni exhaled a long-relieved breath.

"Don't start with that again. I think I know my own mother's name," Gail snapped at her.

"Your mother was Mararis Payne?" Beni's jaw dropped open.

Gail searched her eyes with shock tinged with anger. She could read Beni's thoughts. "Oh, don't you start with that too. My mother was no goddess. She was a regular run-of-the-mill housewife with some sociopathic tendencies."

Beni couldn't help but laugh. "I've never heard her described like that before, but excellent description." She applauded her. "Except she was a goddess."

"No, she wasn't. You and Miss Allard—you both need to stop with that nonsense." Gail stood and walked from the room. Thor raised his head from his food bowl, but Attila kept eating.

"Why did it sound like you were accusing Gail of being a goddess?" Nadia asked.

"No, her mother was a goddess. Gail is only a demi-goddess." Beni found this whole conversation amusing. Was this how all goddesses found out about their lineage?

"You really are talking nonsense." Nadia got up from her seat and followed Gail's route out of the room. "Gail?" Beni followed.

They found Gail standing at the front door staring into the darkness.

"Who's Miss Allard?" Nadia asked.

"Did you see Farryn Allard about this?" Beni caught up with them.

"Unfortunately. My mother told me to find her sister. Not the sister I thought she had but a completely different sister who lives here in Forest Lake. Imagine, I had an aunt not thirty miles away all this time." She huffed in disbelief. "And then Miss Allard, who, by the way, is a witch. My brother warned me when I was five and I thought he was teasing me. Turns out he was right. She told me my mother was a goddess. Now here you are telling me the same thing. It's your turn to tell me how you know this impossible truth."

Beni giggled at the speed and ferocity of the rant. "I know her. Your aunt, not your Aunt Sarah but your Aunt Dyre, is my best friend. We've known each other for—I hate to admit the centuries, but yeah, let's just say before your Aunt Tera was killed."

"That's the other name Miss Allard mentioned. I don't know who that is." Gail threw her hands in the air and paced around the office.

"You really need to speak with Dyre about all of this. This is going to blow her mind. I can bring you to her, tonight. She wants me to stop by anyway."

Nadia's eyes widened. "Wow. Just wow." She walked to the reception desk and picked up the note left on her door by Rayne Grey. She absent-mindedly opened it, while watching as Gail considered taking this Ancient blood drinker up on her offer to meet her aunt who could or could not be a possible goddess.

"Dear God, not another one," Nadia complained. "Listen to this: *Dear Haven, As our previous communication has been ignored, I must insist on your evacuation of the warehouse on Perry Lane. As a member of the Witch Board, led by the esteemed Penelope Press, I feel it is my duty to inform you that if this letter goes unheeded, I will be forced to act. Sincerely, Rayne Grey*"

"What the hell does that mean?" Gail demanded.

Beni laughed. "Welcome to Forest Lake. Rayne Grey is only one of many witches who believe blood drinkers are an affront to their community."

"What can she do to us?" Nadia stared at the letter. "It says she'll be forced to act." She handed the letter to Beni.

"Just tell Jacenta about the letters. She'll handle it." She looked at the note, at Rayne's beautifully crafted penmanship and flourished letters, and chuckled again. "Rayne Grey is such a bitch."

"Do you know everyone?" Nadia's lip curled in disgust.

"Pretty much. So, are you coming with me to see Dyre or not?" Beni smiled as Gail nodded. "We just have to pick up Mia on our way out. She's at Raven's Corner. You can confront Rayne if you want to come with."

"Just tell her I'm passing these notes on to the Council. We'll let the powers that be hash this out." Nadia walked back down the hall as Gail and Beni headed out the door.

"Who's Mia?"

"My daughter." She saw the surprise on Gail's face. "Don't ask. It's a long, sordid story. Are you coming in or waiting outside?"

Raven's Corner was closing its doors for the night when Gail and Beni arrived. She caught Iris as she was pulling in the carts of discounted books.

"Is Mia ready to go?" She asked the question as if Iris knew what she was referring to. She didn't. "I'm picking up Mia," she explained.

"Mia left." Malcolm stood inside the store holding a box of incense. Beni could smell it from where she stood outside the shop. "Said you told her to meet you at home."

Beni gave him a sardonic laugh. "First lesson with raising daughters: they're all liars."

"She was probably just bored waiting for you," Iris commented as she pulled another cart in from the sidewalk.

Beni checked her phone. "The door camera hasn't picked her up yet. She must be still walking, unless she went back to Dyre's. We're headed there anyway."

"I'll text her." Malcolm put the box down and pulled his phone from his back pocket.

"Why would she lie?" Gail whispered.

"No idea." Beni felt like there was more to this than just wanting to walk home.

TRANSMIGRATION

SEPTEMBER

25

MIA

Mia found herself wondering if everyone was right about her bio mom's soul coming back from wherever a soul goes when the body dies. She had no idea about God or Heaven or anything like that. Beni never went to church and never spoke of anything after life. Mia didn't think she truly understood what it was like to die. She'd never done it.

Something nagged at Mia since Rayne Grey told her about her mother's soul locked in the grimoire. They sent her out of the room when they discussed it today. She assumed her father was bothered by the prospect of his ex-wife's return. Mia, on the other hand, was intrigued. It swirled around in her mind, creating hopes and possibilities that she could meet her *real* mother. She'd never say that word to Beni, never. It would crush her.

Real meant Beni wasn't enough. To Mia, Beni was everything she could have hoped for in a mother, except that she wasn't around during the day, but every parent-child relationship had its struggles. The idea of Oriana Duran had always interested Mia. Who killed her and why? If Camilla or Elena Nolan could speak to her, maybe these were answers she would finally get.

Magnolia Academy looked deserted. Mia checked her watch. It was just after eight. Linus and Camilla were still at Aunt Dyre's house, but Kim's car was gone too. Nothing about the house said anyone was home. She knocked anyway.

The front door swung open after four knocks. Mia jumped. She'd given up after the fourth knock. Pierce held the door open. "Mia, what's up?" He was in unusually high spirits and looked to be on his way out.

"Got a hot date?" she teased.

"My dad just called. He's letting me see Mom, April, and Lulu. The girls dragged Kim to the movies." He laughed. "Elena's home. She's in the kitchen scarfing down Starr's cookies."

He bid her goodbye and ran out the door.

She walked through the living room and headed to the kitchen. The house smelled of freshly snuffed candles and lingering incense. Most of the house lights were off. The kitchen seemed to glow as she got closer to it.

"Hi." Mia entered the kitchen.

"Mia?" Elena stood with a cookie in her hand. "What a pleasant surprise."

It was the cookie. No matter how warm her tone or how welcoming her words, it was the cookie that made Mia trust her. Her mother could tell her how evil this woman was, and Aunt Dyre could warn her to stay away, but seeing her munching on a huge chocolate chip cookie seemed to humanize her, and Mia wasn't afraid.

"I'm afraid you've missed the girls. They hustled Kim off to some ridiculous movie." She put the cookie on a plate.

Elena was dressed in a wide legged black jumpsuit that complemented her figure beautifully. Her dark hair was pulled back in a low bun, and the white streak in her hair slid across her skull and behind her ear.

"Pierce let me in. He's gone to April's house. Linus is there."

"Figures. I heard April discovered the truth about her father. Big warm homecoming at Dyre's tonight, I suppose." Her mouth twisted with a little tremble. "I guess that leaves me out in the cold. I'm glad you're here. Would you like a snack?" She stood at the kitchen island. An insecure smile graced her face, and Mia thought she looked lovely.

"Sure." She didn't know how to read this situation. Something felt off, but then again, it didn't.

"Milk?"

"Sure."

Elena grabbed a glass and plate. "Grab the cookie jar, please." She set them down on the kitchen table and pulled out a chair. "Now, tell me why you are here. You have one more day of suspension, don't you?"

"It's not about that. I wanted to ask you something."

"Of course, shoot." Elena sipped her milk.

"It's about my mother's grimoire. Did, I mean, was my mother inside it?" She cringed after saying the words. They sounded absurd, but there was no other way to say it.

"I believe so." Her voice was soft, soothing, and warm. They felt like a hug. "Your mother was a misguided witch, Mia. I don't want you to believe that you will in any way turn out like her."

"No, I don't. I just want to know if—can you speak with her?"

Elena reached over to grab Mia's hand. She squeezed it tight for a moment. "I don't think I could do that. I'm not a strong witch. Communicating with spirits is more my sister's department."

"Can't we try?" Mia's eyes lit up. "My father says that I am a strong witch. Maybe between the two of us, we can do it."

Elena got up from the table and walked to the island. "I don't think so. This seems like a bad idea."

"What's the worst that could happen? She doesn't answer us? Please?"

"I guess we could try. I do have some mugwort left in the solarium. The grimoire is upstairs in the sanctuary. Milly locked the room, but I know where the key is."

She described what mugwort looked like to Mia and told her how to cut it. She told her to meet her on the second floor, third door on the left.

When Mia got upstairs, Elena was just coming out of one of the rooms with a key in her hand. "She had it hidden, but I know my sister better than anyone."

As Elena unlocked the door, Mia's conscience started kicking in. The prospect of talking with her real mother was incredible, but was it worth breaking and entering? Was it worth stealing something Camilla thought should be locked up?

The door swung into a magnificent room. It was a round room, simply decorated but still lovely. Dark wood surrounded the walls with a small crystal pendulum light hanging in the center. Mia recognized the tabletop covered in candles, crystals, and other implements as an altar. She'd only read about them but was sure that's what it was. A pentacle was burned into the hardwood floor.

"What do I do with this?"

"I'll take that." Elena took the mugwort, placed it in a mortar, and used a pestle to grind it. "Sit on the floor in the middle of the star. Here, take the grimoire." She flung a sprig of yarrow across the room that her sister attached to the cover for protection. Elena then spread the mugwort in a small circle around Mia.

As she sat in the circle, Mia opened the grimoire. No wind this time, but something told her this was wrong. She swallowed hard.

"Chilly in here all of a sudden, isn't it?" Elena shivered. "What else do we need?" She turned away from Mia, facing the altar, and for a long time didn't move.

"Elena?" Mia started to get up. "You may be right. This is a bad idea."

She swung around to face her. "No, no. Don't get up. We mustn't break the circle. Let me just see what else we need."

Elena pulled back the cloth covering the altar and looked beneath it. Pulling out five mason jars, she started to place them on each point of the star. In each jar, she placed an item she found on or around the altar.

"What are you doing?"

"I'm sorry. I keep forgetting how little your adoptive mother has contributed to your education." A very un-Elena-like giggle fluttered in her throat. "You know what the pentacle is, right? Its five points stand for each of the five elements. Earth, water, air, fire, and the spirit. As you see here, each point has an element." She indicated each item as it corresponded to the element it represented. "Air, in this case, I chose a feather to represent air. Other items could be substituted. Fire is obviously a candle. That's an easy one." She lit it. "For earth, there are so many choices, but I went with the easiest one here and one of her favorites, a plant."

"Whose favorites?" Mia asked. "My birth mother's?"

Elena turned and winked at her. That trustworthy woman eating a cookie from earlier was gone.

"This is oleander. It was in the room—I don't know why."

"It's toxic, isn't it?"

Elena smiled. A devious smile that worried Mia. "You know your flora."

"My mom had a red oleander shrub, and it killed our cat when I was four."

"That's horrible. Is there nothing that woman won't kill?" Elena asked the question but showed no signs that she expected an answer or reaction. She began lighting candles and burned incense as she explained the items on the floor. "Where were we? Yes, water. I have used moon water for this, but believe me, my lovely girl, any water will do."

"What's…" Mia cleared her throat as she found it hard to speak. "What's moon water?"

"Water charged under the full moon. Very potent and this water was charged under a super blue moon. Only the best for my little girl."

"What?" Mia's body flushed with fear. Her muscles quivered and she needed to get out of this room now. Her cheeks went hot, and she could feel sweat collecting on the nape of her neck.

"This empty jar is you." Elena clasped her fingers together in front of her.

"Me?"

Elena stepped up to Mia and cut a strand of her hair. "That will do nicely." She sprinkled the strands of hair into the empty jar at the top of the star.

"Why is this all set up? It's like you were waiting for me." Mia tried to stand again.

"I've been waiting for you for sixteen years." The glassy expression in Elena's eyes frightened her. "You are the missing piece." She tapped her lips with her forefinger, pretending to consider how to continue. "Turn to any page in that book, please. Any page. It doesn't matter."

Mia didn't have a choice. The cover opened and pages turned as she rested her palm on it. "I really should be going. My dad's expecting me."

"Hush, now. Malcolm can wait. You wanted to speak with me." Elena stood with her hands on her hips, tapping her toe as she considered what was missing. "Give me your hand, dear."

Mia was hesitant. "This feels wrong."

"Come now, give it here." In her hand, a large knife reflected the candlelight across the room.

Mia tucked her hands under her arms.

"You wanted this. You walked into this house and just short of demanded to speak with your real mother. Now that it is all set and we are in the middle of it, you turn your back on me?"

Guilt offered her hand. Mia didn't intend to do it. Guilt motivated her limbs to move. And Elena slid the blade across her palm as Mia winced from the pain. A string of blood pooled in the wound and then spread across her palm. With blood pouring from her hand, Mia once again stuffed her hands into her armpits.

Elena grabbed her arm. She pulled it, wrenching it until Mia cried out, forcing her bloody hand to lay on the pages of the grimoire. When Mia pulled her hand away, a bloody print remained on the page.

Elena took the book and began reading in a language Mia had never heard before. She tried to stand but was pushed back down onto the floor. She tried to cry out, but Elena slapped her to shut her up.

"No," Mia cried, attempting to crawl out of the circle, only to be pushed back in.

The page Elena read caught fire, and she snuffed it out. She kept reading.

"No," she yelled again. The page caught fire again and the cloth covering the altar too.

Elena snuffed out the paper for a second time. The hem of her jumpsuit smoked.

The pendant around Mia's neck shot icy flames into her chest. She cried out. And when she thought she couldn't take the freezing pain a moment longer, it burst, shooting blue flames around the room. The candles blew out, the curtains ignited, and blue flames danced around Elena's bare feet.

Footsteps sounded in the hall. Banging on the door. Elena read faster.

Mia screamed for help. Tears poured from her eyes. She screamed louder.

The door exploded. It slammed into the opposite wall, creating a dent and a hole from the knob.

"What do you think you're doing?" Camilla stood in the doorway, out of breath and enraged. A growl accompanied her words like she was part beast.

Elena stared at her with contempt for only a second before she fell backwards onto the floor, unconscious. The grimoire collapsed on the floor into Mia's blood. Camilla doused her sister's pant leg with moon water but did nothing further to awaken her. She beat at the curtains until the fire went out. The blue flames refused to stop replicating around the room.

She poured the remaining moon water in a circle to contain the flames and then whispered, "Congelo." Ice covered the walls and the floor, snuffing out the remaining flames for good. She looked around the room, dazed, until she saw Mia cowering against the wall.

She ran to her, holding her tight.

"Mia, are you alright?"

26

MIA

Mia ran from the house. She didn't wait for Camilla to bandage her hand. She didn't wait for an explanation or an apology. She ran.

Only when she got to Main Street did she realize she was running in the wrong direction. She stopped, holding a stitch in her side, and winced when she accidentally pressed her wounded hand against her hip. Examining the wound was difficult through the dried blood. It had stopped bleeding but was open and stung when air hit it.

She looked around. Aunt Dyre's house was to the right, home to the left, and Raven's Corner lay straight ahead. Mia waited for the light to change and tore across the street, hugging her hand to her chest.

The door to Raven's Corner was closed. Inside she could see the carts of discounted and donated books that usually sat in front of the display window. The small table for the equinox raffle sat beside it. A large sign in the window instructed people to get their raffle tickets now before they sold out.

She banged on the door with her uninjured hand. The bells that usually heralded her entry shook with each bang she delivered.

"Hello?" she called. "Hello? Is anyone in there?" Her voice was louder and carried farther the second time. Just as she remembered she had her phone in her pocket, the curtain in the back of the shop moved. The black curtains she had set on fire had been replaced by red velvet with an interesting, braided cord design along the edges. There were bells lining the bottom that jingled as the curtain moved. A rustling came from the other side, and Mia could see the shape of two people standing towards the top of the curtain.

"Somebody get the door." Iris poked her head out. Opal's face peeked out, but when she saw who it was, she went right back to adjusting her side of the rod. "Malcolm." Iris struggled with her side.

Her annoyance was evident as she stepped off the ladder to open the door.

Mia stumbled in. "Is my dad here?" She could feel the tears well up in her eyes and tried to blink them away.

"I called him. Mal, you have a visitor," Iris called again. "He's upstairs. Your mother was looking for you. Are you alright?"

Mia didn't answer.

The sound of Malcolm's boots pounded on the wooden stairs. It caused a shudder in her chest, and she knew she'd cry the moment she saw his face.

"Where have you been? I've been texting you." He appeared at the bottom of the stairs in a rush, looking and sounding every bit the father she needed him to be. "Your mother was here. Where'd you go?" He pushed aside the heavy velvet curtain like it was a nuisance. The minute he saw Mia, he stopped. A quick study and he knew all he needed to know.

She ran to him crying as he wrapped his arms around her. Life was so much easier with a parent who could read your mind, she thought. No lengthy explanations, no reliving the horrible details.

"Opal, if you please. Mia is injured." He inspected her hand and then let it drop to her side. Opal climbed down from her ladder and took Mia's hand in hers. She walked into the back room without a word.

"What's all this?" Rayne Grey walked out of the office pushing a cart loaded with candles. There were many different colors and types. Tapers, pillars, votives, trick birthday candles, soy, and beeswax. The strong scent of them upset Mia's stomach as she came closer.

"I was just getting to that," Malcolm said. "Come upstairs. We'll get you patched up and you can tell me what's going on."

"Can't you just…" She tried to get him to read her mind, but he refused.

"It will be better to get it out of your system. Very therapeutic." He was careful to take her left hand as they climbed the stairs to the bedrooms. Iris came out of the bathroom with a handful of bandages and gauze. She held a bottle of peroxide under her arm and a tube of antibiotic cream in her pocket. Malcolm took it all from her and sent her downstairs. "Where's Opal?"

"Preparing a salve, I think."

"Send Rayne up, will you?" he said.

Mia watched as her father cleaned her hand with a wet cloth and then carefully applied ointment to the wound. He looked at the bandages and opted to wrap her hand in gauze instead. He put ointment on her chest as well. Until that moment, she hadn't remembered the pendant exploded.

She touched her chest and felt the ache of a first-degree burn stinging her skin like a sunburn.

"Keep it clean. After we're done, Opal's salve will do the trick. You'll be good as new in no time." He touched her nose with his finger, and she felt the tears build up again. "Now what happened?"

Rayne Grey walked into the room without speaking. She sat in the chair facing Mia and listened as she recounted the horrors she endured at the hands of Elena Nolan. When Mia finished, her face wet with tears and her voice hoarse from hyperventilating, Malcolm and Rayne stared at her. They both looked as though they were working out a puzzle.

Malcolm frowned and his eyes searched the room as if the answers he sought were hidden somewhere in the ceiling tiles or peeling wallpaper. Rayne smirked, but she looked like she was contemplating something devious. Mia simply sat and waited.

They looked at each other. It was like they were conversing aloud but had not spoken one word. Rayne rolled her eyes several times, and Malcolm continued to shake his head.

"What?" Mia couldn't take it a moment longer. She didn't have the energy to read minds or play magical parlor games.

Her father smiled in a comforting manner that was meant to ease her anxiety, but it didn't. "We don't think it was Elena who did this to you."

"Yes, it was," Mia snapped back. It was the first time she'd given her father attitude at all, for anything. He got the best of her personality. Her sarcastic retorts and annoying eye rolls were reserved for her mother. But even as she said it, she remembered the creepy things Elena said to her. *Only the best for my little girl.*

"Physically, it was Elena," Rayne said, "but I think you just spent the last agonizing half hour bonding with your biological mother."

A sick feeling washed over her.

"Did your fire work for you?" Rayne asked.

"Not well. I mean, I've burned down a whole house before. Today, I could barely scorch the paper she was reading from." Mia rubbed the burn on her chest.

"That's because you share your mother's magic. Let me rephrase that. You *have* your mother's magic. When she died, it syphoned from her into you. I guarantee it."

"How do you know that?" Malcolm asked. He sat beside Mia with his arm securely around her in a protective manner.

"It's a theory Penelope and I have been working on since Oriana died. It's a long, sordid story that I would prefer not to recount right now. I can tell you that Oriana died without magic. We searched her apartment and found nothing that could have absorbed the power. Penelope always believed it was stored in her grimoire, which was missing when we arrived. But after hearing what she did to Mia today, I'm convinced only her soul was stored in that grimoire. Her magic is in Mia. Coupled with Mia's own Brenig magic makes her a very strong witch."

Mia looked up at Malcolm and saw her fear and sadness mirrored back at her. "What does she want?"

Rayne laughed. "You and her magic back."

Malcolm closed his eyes as she spoke.

"She wants your body. From what you described, she was attempting a transmigration of souls. I haven't seen it done successfully—ever. Occasionally, someone attempts it, and it looks like it worked but in the end, the souls are locked in an internal war. If she wasn't interrupted and passed into your body, I'd say you'd both be dead within a week, give or take a day or two."

"No." Mia trembled at the thought. "We were only trying to speak to my mother. How'd she get inside Elena?"

"That's what spirits do. Elena was a willing participant, I'd imagine. So excited to feel or speak to her friend again, she welcomed her readily. Oriana took it a step further than Elena anticipated she would."

"So, she wanted to kill me?"

Both looked at her, confused.

"My mom—Oriana Duran, if she did this transmigration thing wrong, she'd kill me from the inside out, and if she did it right, she would have pushed my soul out to go where?"

"Into the ether."

"Rayne," Malcolm warned.

"She needs to know the truth," she huffed. "Mia, your mother was a vile, manipulative, ineffectual witch who used what little knowledge she had or could take to lure others into her devious schemes and traps." Rayne looked pleased with herself when she finished speaking. She sat back in the chair with her arms crossed over her chest. "Goddess knows, I'm not one to defend the Nolan sisters, but Elena has been a long-time dupe."

Mia looked at Malcolm. Tears lined her red eyes. "Is that true?"

"Seems you are destined to be raised by one monster or another." Rayne chuckled.

"Get out." Malcolm jumped to his feet and grabbed Rayne by the arm. He ushered her to the staircase and watched her go back down to the store. When he turned, Mia had her head in her hands, crying. "She's jealous and vindictive. Ignore her."

"It's true, isn't it? What she said about Oriana Duran, it's true?" Her voice came out in between hiccups.

He thought for a moment and then said, "Yes. Oriana wasn't a good person and an even worse witch." He hated telling his daughter these horrible truths, but it was necessary to save her life. "She took what she wanted without care for anyone's life."

"How could you love someone like that?"

He laughed, a sad, sardonic laugh. "That was a long time ago, but she gave me you. I'll be forever grateful to her for that." He wrapped his arms around her. "Out of curiosity, how did Camilla get that flame out? It's meant to burn forever."

"I don't know. She poured moon water around it, said one word, and everything turned to ice."

"Congelo?" He appeared impressed by Camilla's skill. Not many witches could have extinguished an eternal flame with only one word.

"Maybe," she said. "I'd like to go home. I don't mean to sound like a baby, but I really need my mom right now." She wiped her face with her palm.

"She's at Dyre's house. I'll take you." Malcolm kissed her.

27

Dyre

"She's coming. She's coming." Lucy ran through the house from her bedroom to the front door. Linus caught her before she bolted from the house.

"Who's coming?" he asked.

"You're supposed to be in bed," Dyre scolded.

"She is." Lucy pointed with desperation at the front door.

"*Mararis,*" Tera said to April, who was lounging on the sofa in the sitting room, talking with Pierce.

"Mararis," April said aloud.

"I heard," Dyre said.

"My cousin is coming." Lucy danced in place. "I can feel it. She's coming. She's coming."

Dyre's eyes shifted to Linus. "She has visions."

"I figured that one out on my own." He chuckled.

"When are they coming?"

"Now." Lucy jumped on the sofa and pulled back the curtains on the bay window. Headlights lit up the darkness, and a car parked in front of the house. Car doors slammed shut and they could hear talking outside.

"They're here." Her voice dropped from excited to dejected. She slumped on the sofa, defeated.

"What's wrong?" April nudged her sister with her toe.

"That's not what I thought she'd look like." Her mouth shifted with disappointment.

Dyre went to the window and peered out. A smile stretched across her face. "That's your cousin Gail, silly."

"You said she was much younger than Aunt Beni." Lucy pouted.

Dyre kissed the top of her daughter's head. "When did I say that?"

"In my dream."

"Well, she is. By about three thousand years." She laughed. "Does Tera have something to say before I invite them in?"

April's eyes shifted back and forth as she listened to the silence. "Nope."

Pierce chuckled.

"Good, let's keep it that way."

Dyre swung the front door open without allowing Gail the chance to come up to the porch. She wore tight fitting clothing and a beaded silk wrap thrown over her shoulders. Her long black hair billowed behind her like a cape in the wind. A smile touched her mouth as Dyre threw her arms around her with no fear and no apprehension. Tears burst from her eyes the moment she touched her, and a soggy laugh bubbled from her throat.

"Nightingale." Dyre wiped her face and stepped away.

Gail stood like a statue with her arms still hooked as if to catch something. The surprise she felt at first meeting her aunt, her mother's sister whom she had never known existed, was overwhelming.

She found herself studying every aspect of this woman and comparing it to her mother. The same eyes, the same hair color, the same strength that seemed to emanate from every pore. She wanted to hug her again, and just as she thought it, Dyre grabbed hold of her.

"Dyre," Mararis whispered.

"I don't want you right now," Dyre said to her sister. She pushed Gail's long black hair out of her face. "I can't believe you're here." More tears slid from her eyes to her lips. She kissed her and hugged her again. "Okay, I'm done." She stepped away, laughing. "Girls, come meet your cousin, Gail."

Beni stood behind them, watching the emotional family reunion unfold.

April stepped out the front door. She was apprehensive at the sight of an unfamiliar blood drinker.

"Careful, April. That pull can be strong," Linus called.

"I don't feel it." Dyre laughed, still holding Gail's hand.

"Me neither." April waved as Linus pulled her inside the house.

"That's my oldest daughter, April. Sitting over there, trying to disappear is my son, Pierce. And…I have another one somewhere around here. Lucy." Dyre waited for Lucy to appear in the doorway, looking grumpy and sullen. "Come say hello. She was so excited to meet you and then saw you were not her age."

Gail laughed. "I'm sorry. It's been a very long time since I was your age."

"Did you have a sister?" Lucy asked.

Gail looked at Dyre and then to Beni. "I did. Edith." She didn't like talking about her dead sister. She felt like she'd failed her.

"I have a sister too. I have a brother. Do you have a brother?" the child asked, without hesitation.

Gail couldn't help but notice that she asked about Edith in the past tense and Simon as if she knew he was still alive.

"Yes, I do. My brother, Simon, was two years older than me."

"He's a wolf." Lucy laughed and howled playfully.

Gail looked at Dyre for an explanation. "Her powers are untrained but quite strong."

"Can I speak now?" Mararis sounded offended.

"If you must," Gail and Dyre said in unison. They laughed and knew the ice was officially broken.

Stepping into Dyre's living room, Gail looked around at the pictures lining the tabletops and along the walls. Pictures of her children in various stages of their lives. Baby pictures and school pictures lined the hallway leading to the bedrooms. After she was done studying her family photos, she turned to the group behind her.

"What are you looking so grumpy about?" Beni flipped Lucy over her shoulder, sending the girl into hysterical fits of laughter. "Got a joke for me today?"

When she dropped her on the sofa, out of breath, Lucy slapped her hand on her head. "Um, wait, I've got one. Why are vampires bad artists?"

Beni looked at Gail with a smile on her face. "Why *are* vampires bad artists?"

"Because they always want to draw blood." Her peals of laughter made Beni laugh.

"Bedtime," Dyre instructed. "April, can you please put her to bed? I would really appreciate if you and Pierce would stay in your room for a while too."

As April slunk out of the room, Beni grabbed her arm. "Have you heard from Mia?" She said no. "She left Malcolm with no details except to lie and say I told her to meet me at home. Do you know why she'd lie?"

"I saw her at my house." Pierce held up his hand to get Beni's attention. "Elena's the only one home. I guess Mia's hanging out with her."

Linus frowned. "I'll text Elena and see if she's still there."

Dyre walked into the kitchen with her arm looped through Gail's arm. "Have you called her cell?"

Beni waved her phone in Dyre's face. "Twice. No answer. Malcolm tried texting too. Nothing." Her mouth twisted in anger. "I'm going to kill that kid if she went back to that school."

"Shall we sit outside? It's an unusually pleasant night." Dyre ignored her.

Outside, only Linus took a seat at the table.

"Did Elena answer you?" Beni asked.

He shook his head. "Not yet."

"What did Lucy mean Simon is a wolf?" Gail splayed her hands out in front of her as if the answer would drop from the heavens.

This was not where Dyre wanted to start. It was times like these that she hated how strong Lucy's abilities had grown over the last few years. "Can we discuss that later?"

"I'd like to discuss it now," Mararis spoke up.

Beni laughed. "Your brother is a shifter? That's crazy. Blood drinker, goddess, shifter, and a spirit walker in one family? You should write a book."

Gail glared at her. This wasn't funny to her. This was her family. A family she didn't understand and who held secrets she couldn't comprehend.

"Both of you will have to wait. The more pressing matter is Oriana Duran and what we should do about her. And we need to find Mia."

They all finally sat around the table. Linus looked incredibly comfortable beside Dyre like he belonged there. Beni studied those surrounding her. A goddess, a witch, and a blood witch. It was an interesting combination. She was the only one in attendance that could not read minds. It put her at a disadvantage.

"Now that you three are reunited, what's the plan?" Linus asked, keeping an ear out for a text from Elena.

"From what I could decipher from young April, Oriana Duran is dead," Tera said.

"Yes." Dyre spoke as if her youngest sister was sitting at the table. When she realized she and Gail were the only ones who could hear her, she repeated what was said.

"That leaves Elena Nolan. We need to kill her," Tera continued.

"I concur. It was Elena Nolan who broke into my house to poison me. Oriana killed Edith. I know that much. I remember…" Mararis's voice broke.

Dyre repeated her sisters' sentiments.

Gail lowered her head, not keen on discussing Edith's death.

"That was a long time ago. Elena has changed." Linus stood as Elena's champion.

"Are you willing to bet your daughter's life on it?" Tera said.

His face paled when Dyre repeated her words.

"Dyre, you should kill her," Mararis said.

"You are both forgetting that I am still forbidden to use magic. The little I do use could bring the wrath of the heavens down on me. If I were to cut someone's thread, I don't want to even think about the repercussions." Her head swung back and forth in a definitive gesture.

"There are other ways, and you know that," Tera barked.

"No."

"What are you so afraid of?"

"What if the repercussions are killing April? Or taking Lucy away? I am not willing to sacrifice my daughters' lives for petty revenge on Elena Nolan." Tears filled her eyes, and she wiped them away like they offended her.

"I could do it." Beni held her hand up like she was in a classroom.

"Do what?" Linus was ready to fight.

"Kill Elena Nolan." She laughed as his eyes became two little fireballs burning into her forehead. "It's what I do, Linus. Don't act like this is a big surprise to you. I kill witches. Just give me the word and Elena…" Beni stopped talking. "Wait, damn it."

"What?" Linus snapped at her.

"I promised Mia that I wouldn't willfully kill another witch, ever." She cringed. "I just can't break that promise. I really am sorry."

Dyre's smile was warm and understanding. "I knew you wouldn't be able to do it. You are not the witch hunter you were five hundred years ago. You are better now. Besides, I would never have put you in that position."

Beni frowned, not understanding what she meant.

"I don't need you to fight my battles for me. I don't know if I even want Elena Nolan dead anymore."

"Are you mad?" Tera shouted. Mararis agreed.

"Calm down. You both had the ability to see Oriana's plans years in advance. We all knew what we were signing up for when we had children. We all chose to ignore the facts. We all hoped for the best but never prepared for the worst."

"Gail can kill her." Mararis offered up her daughter. She seemed to not have heard a word Dyre said.

Gail looked shocked. "I cannot and will not kill someone that has done nothing to me."

Beni leaned towards her and whispered, "You do it every day." She chuckled as she sat back in her chair.

"True, but—"

"She did kill your mother and sister…" Beni was goading her now.

"I guess I can." She looked at Beni and then Dyre. "Why does it seem so wrong?"

"Because it is." Linus dropped his head into his hands.

A car pulled into the driveway, and they heard two doors slam shut. The front door opened and it, too, slammed shut.

"Mom?" Mia called out.

"Out here." Beni looked at Dyre. "It's about frickin' time."

Mia ran through the house, pulled open the sliding glass door, and threw herself into her mother's arms. She buried her face in her chest and held tight as if she might slip away. Malcolm followed her outside. The tee shirt he wore exposed his arms and for the first time, Beni noticed the tattoos that covered his upper arms. She saw part of a dragon that wrapped itself around his left bicep, and a family crest adorned his right arm.

"What's going on?" She cradled her crying daughter and spoke without letting her go. "Gail Andrews. This is Malcolm Brenig, Mia's father."

He smiled and held out his hand to Gail. She took his warm hand and shook it firmly. They both made eye contact and acknowledged they could read each other's thoughts. She nodded and smiled before sitting back down.

"Is there somewhere we could talk?" he asked.

"Here is as good a place as any." Beni motioned for Malcolm to join them at the table. She pulled Mia from her bosom. "Go inside and wash your face with cool water while I talk to your father."

Mia looked at Malcolm.

"April and Pierce are in the other room," Dyre offered.

Mia ran inside.

"What happened?" She glared at Malcolm. "Where was she?"

He looked around the table. Sliding a bit to his right, he removed himself from the pull he felt coming on strong from both blood drinkers seated beside him. "Elena Nolan happened. I'm not quite sure it was Elena, to be honest. Rayne and I believe that Oriana was possessing Elena when she attacked Mia."

"She did what?" Beni jumped up. The patio chair flipped backwards as she stood.

Malcolm held out his hands to calm her. "Let me explain before you start killing witches." He watched as Beni picked up her chair and then proceeded to explain exactly what Mia told them earlier today. He told her his theory about Oriana's soul being held in the grimoire and then described the pentacle on the floor. He also made a point to mention that Camilla Nolan rescued Mia and had she not interceded, Mia could have died.

"Sounds like a transmigration," Gail said.

"Yes, it does," Malcolm agreed. "How do you come to know about transmigration?"

Everyone was interested to hear her answer, except Beni.

"Some years ago, I was part of a process that eventually went horribly wrong." She twisted her hands together as she spoke. "From my experience, it can't go right."

"Very wise. If you don't mind my asking—"

"Who cares," Beni interrupted. "What about Mia? Is she alright?"

"Yes. Thanks to Camilla, she is perfect. She refused the salve Opal made for the wound on her hand and the burn on her chest, but I brought it with me. If you'd like to apply it, it will heal her."

Beni sat frozen for a minute. Almost like marble, her body did not move as if a switch had been flipped, and she powered down.

"Beni?" Gail whispered.

"This is what we've been talking about," Tera spouted off. *"Alive or dead, Oriana Duran will exact havoc. This time she used Elena Nolan to do her dirty work. A willing participant, I'm sure. Next time, who knows who she'll almost kill using some other fool."*

"Beni?" Dyre touched her hand.

"Can you keep an eye on Mia?" She came to life and jumped from her seat, startling everyone.

"Beni, wait." Malcolm jumped up. Gail, Dyre, and Linus followed.

She was at her car when they caught up to her. Her speed was dizzying even for Gail. She couldn't imagine how Malcolm or Linus were dealing with it.

"Mom? What are you doing? Where are you going?" Mia called from the front door. She seemed to regain composure of her emotions.

"Mia, stay here," Beni barked.

"Beni, this is not the answer." Dyre crossed her arms over her chest.

"What would you do if she'd done that to April?" She slipped into the driver's seat. When Dyre didn't answer, she said, "Exactly. You want her dead…" She looked to the sky as if she was talking to Tera and Mararis. "You just got your wish." She slammed the driver's door closed.

When she looked beside her, Linus jumped into the passenger seat and Gail slipped into the back seat.

"We're going with you."

"If only to stop you from doing something you'll regret," Linus added.

"Fine. I have to stop at home for something first."

28

GAIL

They pulled into Bentyn Rae's driveway and sat for a minute or two before getting out. Linus didn't move, but Gail could hear the never-ending thoughts cramming his brain. Thoughts of Elena and how he could protect her. Thoughts of his daughters and how allowing Elena to live could jeopardize their lives.

Gail stared at the enormity of the house, thinking how unlike Beni it was. The solitude of the cul-de-sac did impress her. Its location seemed idyllic with no nosy neighbors to worry about. The only neighboring house was a burnt-out shell that Gail could see all the way through to the backyard.

Beni froze again, much like she did at Dyre's house. Her body seemed to solidify like drying cement. She stared at the house in front of her. Her hands held firmly to the steering wheel. Then, without warning, she opened the car door and ran to the house.

Linus and Gail were close behind.

"Beni, what are you doing?" he shouted as she left the front door ajar and bolted up the stairs to the second floor. "Wait."

She was already on the third level of her house when he caught up to her. Her speed amazed Gail. The steep third-floor staircase led to a single door at the top. The glass doorknob twisted easily and without a sound, as if it was regularly greased.

When they entered the room, she could hear Beni rooting around in the darkness. Metal objects clanged in the large attic room. The hinges of a trunk creaked as it opened. Gail flipped a switch on the wall. Just as their eyes adjusted to the darkness, they were blinded by the light.

Linus rubbed his eyes.

As she stepped into the room, her jaw dropped. The walls were covered with weaponry. Augers, brush axes, spading forks, various maces, mallets, torches, and several variations on the noose. Every conceivable form of medieval weapon either hung on the wall or lay on the floor. In the corner lay a metal contraption that resembled a collapsed dog crate. Beni stood beside an old steamer trunk that looked like it had been built a hundred years ago. She held a sword in her hand.

"What is all of this?" she whispered.

"What do you think?" Linus spoke with disdain and anger. "Her arsenal. Apparently, your witch hunting days are not that far behind you."

"I haven't hunted in over two decades. Truly hunted in almost a century. This is just memorabilia."

"Such warm, fuzzy memories," he grumbled under his breath.

"What are you looking for?" Gail could feel her heartbeat accelerate as she thought of all the witches who had spent their last moments feeling these weapons upon their flesh. Her eyes misted, yet she could not look away.

Beni groaned as she pulled something deep within the trunk. "This." She pulled a dagger buried beneath tomes on witches and effective hunting practices. The blade was longer and wider than the one she had carried with her to visit Camilla Nolan almost a month ago. Pushed out of the way were pieces of burnt fabric and a jar of eyes floating in formaldehyde.

"That's disgusting." Linus's hate-filled expression frightened Gail. She could feel static itch the back of her neck and knew he was about to cast on Beni.

She knew it too.

"Calm yourself. These were a present." She shook the jar, making the eyes bob in the yellowed liquid. A giggle bubbled in her throat as she watched them staring out at her. She tossed the jar on top of fabric remnants.

"A present? A jar of eyes? Those swatches... What are those?"

Beni pulled one out and inspected it. "Okay, fine. This *is* a little creepy. I admit it."

"What are they?" Gail asked.

"Never mind. You don't want to know."

In the early part of the sixteenth century, Beni found a piece of fabric mixed in with the ashes of one particularly brutal burning. It had amazed her that it didn't burn. The flames and heat consumed the body, the kindling, large logs of wood, and yet this little piece of fabric survived. She had kept it as a souvenir. And then any others she found after that.

Both Gail and Linus read Beni's thoughts clearly.

Gail shivered at the thought of women tied to a stake, begging for their lives. Fear. Fire. Death. She thought of what Beni said about her Aunt Tera and how she was burned at the stake. No matter if it was true or not, it gave her the willies to think about it.

"It is all true. She and her two daughters were killed by Magnus Anmar," her mother informed her.

"What?" Gail said aloud.

"What?" Beni repeated the question.

"Nothing." She thought about what her mother said. Magnus Anmar killed Tess Pendle and her mother and sister, Rose. Did he also kill her aunt and two cousins? The man was a monster, Gail thought.

"They are one and the same. Your cousin Tess and her sister, Rose, died by fire in the fourteenth century. Magnus Anmar was bribed by Oriana Duran and Elena Nolan."

"What good do you think a dagger will do?" Linus spoke as if Mararis was not speaking too. He didn't hear her.

"I thought you were a man of the world, Linus. A dagger is used to pierce the skin and cause the intended victim to bleed out." Beni wiped the blade of the dagger on her shirt. She returned it to its protective leather sleeve.

"Killing Elena won't solve the bigger issue."

"Tess was not my cousin," Gail argued with her mother silently.

"It will stop her from hurting Mia." Beni started walking towards the door.

"Yes, she is, dear."

"Are you saying Tess was Tera's daughter?" Gail asked.

"Yes."

"It will stop her, but what will stop Oriana from possessing someone else and trying again?" He huffed and then wheeled around on Gail. "Will you stop talking to yourself, please?"

Beni scrunched her face in a confused frown.

"Sorry. My mother…" She waved her hand in front of her to sweep away the insanity that seemed to surround her these days.

"She's insane. Are you going to kill this woman? Because if you're not, maybe we can return to Dyre's house. I have so many questions."

Linus deflated. "No, *I'm* sorry. Just seeing this museum of murder. I-I-I want to burn it down. What the hell?" He picked up the dome-shaped cage sitting on the floor. The steel trap was used to cover a woman's head with a firm piece of metal thrust into their mouth to keep them quiet.

"Like you've never seen a *scold's bridle* before." Beni rolled her eyes.

He lowered his head and closed his eyes to refocus his attention on the more important issues. "Killing Elena is not a solution but a bigger problem." His eyes searched the room. "Why not just put her in this cage? That will stop her."

"It would, but that's not for her." Beni stared at the cage and then looked at Gail.

"Brilliant." He threw his hands in the air. "Once a witch hunter, always a witch hunter."

"It's not for a witch," Beni shouted. "If you must know, it's for Jordan Glynn."

Gail cringed, while still understanding her reasoning for wanting to torture Jordan.

"Great. I'm so glad you're an equal opportunity murderer." Linus slammed the trunk shut. "Look. If we spoke with Camilla together, maybe we could come to an agreement."

"No."

He pushed past her and stomped down the stairs.

"I'm going to kill Elena with or without you, Linus." Beni followed him into the second-floor hallway. "Stop thinking with your dick and start thinking about your daughters."

"I am thinking of my daughters and Dyre." Linus kept walking. "If you kill Elena, we'll have bigger problems." Gail and Beni stared at him from the landing, waiting for him to continue. "You kill Elena. That solves your problems for now, but then Oriana finds another person to possess and kills Mia. What do you do then? Who do you kill then?"

Beni gripped the handle of the dagger in her hand tighter. "We need to kill Oriana." Her voice was low and uncertain.

"Now you're talking," Mararis chimed in.

"Quiet," Gail scolded her mother.

"What's your plan?" Beni knew she was out of her depth. Killing witches was one thing, but killing a spirit was another. How did you go about killing something that was already dead? "Does any of this involve an exorcist?"

Linus's laugh was annoyed and full of disdain. "Just stick to what you do best, and I'll stick to what I do best."

"You won't let me do what I do best."

Linus chuckled. "Just take care of Mia and I'll rally the troops to banish Oriana."

Beni's lip curled with disgust. "I'll go along with this for now. But if Elena makes one more move towards Mia, she's dead."

29

MAGNOLIA ACADEMY

The next morning was packed with lessons at Magnolia Academy. Due to the recent problems concerning Mia, April, and Starr, the lessons today centered on the goddesses called the *Sisters of Fate*. They were just starting the lesson when the sound of arguing rose from down the hall.

Finding it difficult to concentrate, Linus tried to teach his class as if he didn't notice the shouting. His glasses were perched at the end of his nose as he looked over them. "History tells us the Fates or *Moirae* were named Clotho, Lachesis, and Atropos. The stories leave out an original group of sisters. Three sisters that were cast out and then replaced with the three remembered in our textbooks. As daughters of the great Father and Mother, they are revered for their ability to harness the powers of all four elements and wield them to their whim. Each sister had a job. Does anyone know what these jobs are?"

Lilly's hand shot up. "One spins the thread of life, one measures the thread, and one cuts it." She sat back, proud of her accomplishment.

"Very good. Can anyone tell me what that means?" His eyes searched the group, finding Starr trying desperately not to be noticed. "Starr? Would you like to take this one?"

She sat up and cleared her throat. "The thread of life is what binds us all together. It's our lifeline, and the *Moirae* determine how long we will live."

"Is that all they do?" He dragged his fingers through his hair as what started small with a few raised voices had turned into an all-out brawl between Elena and Camilla. He tried his best to ignore it and continue with the lesson.

"They are said to determine our destinies as well, but that has never been proven." Starr held a piece of string in her fingers and twirled it around her index finger repeatedly.

"The Moirae are beyond reproach. It is not for us to judge…" He stopped dead at the sound of a crashing vase, gave directions to Pierce, and went to investigate.

"If they can use all four elements at once, they must be able to destroy the world." Pierce continued the lesson in Linus's absence.

"Like they really exist," Starr mumbled. She slid down in her chair like a sullen child.

"They existed enough last week when you got in trouble for calling them." Lilly snapped her gum. She was still a little miffed that April, Starr, and Mia had not included her in their secret spell.

"Shh, we can't hear." Veda shushed her and crept to the closed door.

"Vee, sit down. Linus wants us to keep reading." Starr pulled the string tight so the tip of her finger turned purple and looked at Lilly. "Did they show up?"

"Will you two shut up. I'm trying to listen." Veda spoke in a hushed but annoyed voice.

"We were clearly told not to interfere with whatever is going on." Pierce tried to exert some authority. It wasn't working.

"I'm not interfering. I'm listening. Pierce, can you…" Veda didn't finish her thought, but it was clear she wished Pierce to use his magic to get the details from down the hall.

"I can try." Knowing he wasn't getting anywhere trying to teach, maybe he would gain their trust using his abilities.

"No, you can't. We're not supposed to cast without permission." Starr slunk down in her seat farther. "I'm not going to get a double punishment because of you."

"Not casting, listening." Veda pulled one of the leather chairs closer to the sofa and sat down in front of Pierce. "Now, shush so he can concentrate."

Starr's foot jumped in place as she waited for Linus to return.

Pierce closed his eyes as Veda held his hands firmly.

"They are back in the meditation room. Camilla is holding something in her hands, a book or something. Elena looks confused but she's grabbing for whatever Camilla's holding. Oh, she just tripped Elena without touching her. My dad is…" He stopped short. "I think I'm in trouble. Damn it." He pressed his fingers into his temples as a sharp pain streaked behind his eyes.

"What?"

"I got shut out. We better go back to our lessons." Pierce grabbed his books from the coffee table and began flipping back to the pages they were reading before the shouting began. He flipped his black hair off his forehead and lowered his eyes. "The Moirae—"

"Camilla really tripped Elena?"

Pierce cringed. "Laid her out flat."

Lilly laughed out loud.

"Did they say anything worth hearing?" Veda persisted.

"Vee, stop." Starr opened her book too. "It's clear Linus does not want us butting in."

"You look tired." Lilly put her feet up on the coffee table, snapping her gum. Her barely-there reddish blonde eyebrows knitted together.

"Yup." Starr stretched. "Thought I saw someone in my room last night."

"Who was in your room?" Linus appeared in the room with no sound from the door or his boot heels on the hardwood floor. Starr jumped as he spoke.

"No idea. She wasn't very nice, whoever she was."

His brown eyes studied her affectionately with a bit of worry in his ruffled brow. "A seeing?"

"No, she was really there, I think."

"Stay after class. I wish to explore this in more detail," Linus said.

Starr nodded but could feel her heart rate accelerate.

"Everything alright with Camilla?" Lilly asked.

"Right as rain." Linus's thin lips smiled through his thick, dark beard. "I trust you all finished the reading this time. If not, do it tonight for a quiz tomorrow. I'll dismiss you now. Meditation will be held on the back lawn today."

Linus stopped Pierce at the door.

He dropped his large hand on Pierce's broad shoulder. "In the future, no more interfering. You lost control of the class." His dark eyebrows raised on his forehead above his intense glare. Pierce nodded guiltily and apologized. "Curiosity is one thing, but intruding is quite another. Understood?"

"Yes, sir." Pierce slunk from the room.

Starr remained in her seat. Her leg bounced nervously as she waited for what Linus was going to ask her. After talking to Pierce, he took his time collecting his papers and books. When everything was squared away on his podium and tucked into his satchel, he pulled a comfy chair close to her and smiled. His handsome face was serene as he allowed her a few moments to relax.

"First, this is a spirit you saw, correct?"

Starr nodded.

"Did this woman speak to you?"

"Not to me exactly. She just kind of spoke." She gnawed on the cuticle of her right thumb.

"What'd she say?"

Starr thought of the woman standing in the middle of her bedroom. Her dark hair was tucked behind her ears like she'd had a long day at work and felt exhausted. She wore large dangling earrings. Her clothes were dark and nondescript. "She was looking for something. She kept saying, *'where is it.'* I tried answering her, but she didn't hear me or wasn't paying attention to me."

Linus nodded, stroking his beard as he thought.

"Have you seen her before?"

"Not seen her but I've heard stuff. Some of the stuff on my dresser fell a couple nights ago."

"When?" he asked as if he already knew the answer.

"I noticed it on Wednesday morning. Pierce thought one of the house spirits did it." She looked away, knowing what he was about to say.

"You told Pierce?"

"He came into my room when I was picking everything up. We figured maybe reading that spell might have upset one of them."

"Perhaps, but they usually don't do much more than open and close doors. Kind of a boring bunch, aren't they?" he joked, hoping to get a smile out of her. The house didn't attract spirits as much as it used to, but they did have three unimaginative spirits who opened things that were closed and occasionally knocked the vase on the living room mantel over, but Linus was sure they did that just to annoy Camilla.

She didn't smile but continued to chew on her thumb and think. "Do you think we did this?"

"Possibly." He didn't spare her feelings. "Delving into magic that far exceeds your abilities before you are capable of controlling it can lead to grim consequences. Be thankful it's only a random visitation and you didn't really summon the Sisters of Fate. They are not as lovely as the storybooks make them out to be."

Linus chuckled in his deep masculine way, and Starr's twitchy nerves started to calm.

"So, what did the first group of sisters do to get cast out?"

"That's one of my favorite stories." He beamed. "It tells of the sister who fell in love with a mortal man and gave him eternal life and fortune beyond imagination. Everything his heart desired. He was weak, as mortal men are, and was seduced by another goddess. When the sister found out, her wrath turned him into a monster. He fed on the blood of living creatures, and he hid in the shadows away from one of the Great Father's most powerful gifts—sunlight."

"The Sisters of Fate created cold bloods?"

Linus nodded. "One of them did, yes. His hunger was so great that he could not be controlled. She was forced to contain him in a prison of hellfire. The story goes that his cold blood saved his life. He adapted and created a race of monsters. The immortality that she had given him passed through his blood into the blood of his progeny. Together they broke out of the hellish prison and now roam the Earth in the shadows, feasting on the blood of man."

"What happened to the sister that cursed him?"

"After being cast out, forbidden to use her powers to determine fates or help mankind in any capacity, she and her sisters learned to live normal lives." He smiled as Starr devoured the information. "They say our magical abilities were their gift to us. Each sister was given a sacred scarf from the Great Mother, and they cut them up and shared them with the world. Each piece was endowed with a special talent or power. If you were lucky enough to catch one, the power was yours."

Starr laughed. She loved the story and knew she would write it in her journal when she got back to her room.

"Go on to meditation. You can use it. Clear your mind and focus on your healing and not that woman. If you see her again, let me know."

"Who are you seeing?" Camilla met Starr as she walked from the library.

"Go on, Starr," Linus instructed. "Kim's waiting for you."

"What's going on?" Camilla asked.

Linus walked past her without answering.

"I understand that you're angry with me, but this behavior is immature." She slammed her hands on her hips.

"You're calling me immature? You threw your sister to the floor with magic. I should ground you for casting with intent to harm," he growled under his breath.

"I've apologized to Leny for my behavior. I lost my temper. It's something I do when one of my teachers attempts to murder a student. Everything is out of control. The students are casting without permission, Rayne Grey is breathing down my neck, and now Elena is aiding Oriana, who still thinks she can kill Dyre Crane even though she's dead."

He sat in one of the chairs near the podium. "Seems all the ideas we worked on just yesterday were all for naught. We gained a new member for our cause."

"Who? And if you say Rayne Grey, I will set you on fire."

"Seems a little harsh." He grimaced. "No, Mararis's eldest daughter. Her name is Gail, and she is a cold blood." He spoke slowly, making every word count and assessing which one would make Camilla blow. So far so good, he continued. "She's lived not far from here her entire life. She's pleasant enough, I suppose."

"Great. Just what we need is another cold blood." Camilla dropped into the chair facing him, covering her face with her hands. "What you're telling me is all three sisters are reunited and Oriana just tried to harm Mia. Just tell me one thing, and I need you to be honest with me. How long does Elena have before they kill her?"

"I think I successfully talked Bentyn Rae down from her murderous spree. The sisters, I don't know. Dyre only wants Oriana gone. Elena is not really in her sights unless she hurts April or Lulu. In that case…"

"In that case, what?" Elena stood in the doorway listening.

"In that case, I don't think I could protect you." He rose and walked to her. He wrapped his arms around her, and she leaned against his chest. "You need to stop being so available to her. Start building walls and keep her out of your head."

"She's not in my head. She's everywhere. For the record, I didn't invite her in. I was helping Mia speak to her mother. The moment we entered the sanctuary, I felt woozy. I should have left but I didn't. That was my mistake. It won't happen again." She looked at her sister. "I promise."

30

LINUS

Later that day, Linus held the two necklaces in his fist. The balled-up chains bit into his palm, but it was better than feeling the strange pulsing in his pocket. Both vibrated when he picked them up and emitted an odd hum. In his fist, they felt like bees fighting to get out.

They fell from the grimoire as Camilla and Elena fought earlier, and he wanted to know what they were. He knocked on Elena's bedroom door with the knuckle of his forefinger.

"Come in."

The heavy wood door swung into the room with little effort. "May I speak with you?" Without thinking, he scratched his beard, and the necklaces buzzed against his palm. He tightened his grip.

"Of course." Elena sat at her desk grading papers. "Did you know Veda's grandmother studied under Rasputin?"

"Yeah, she tried to sell me that bunk last semester. I told her if she tried it again, I'd fail her. Give her an F."

"I give her points for creativity." She laughed.

"There's a fine line between bullshit and creativity. Veda's been walking that line for too long. Give her an F. No, give me that paper. I'll talk to her myself." His temper was short this evening.

Elena handed him the paper. "Are you alright? You're not yourself."

"I have a few questions. Do you have time?"

"For you? Always." A smile brightened her face. When she saw he was not returning the gesture, she frowned. "What's wrong?"

"What are these?" Linus opened his fist only inches from her face. The two necklaces lay in his sweaty palm, leaving their mark in his skin.

Guilt and embarrassment colored her expression. "Where'd you get them? I was looking all over…"

"They burned April. They fell from the grimoire this morning." He fought not to shout at her. "What are they? They hum. They also vibrate when aggravated."

Her eyes dropped to the paper in front of her. She fiddled with the pen between her fingers.

"Don't act as if I haven't seen the same necklace hanging around Dyre's neck for centuries. Why do you have these?" Linus sat on the edge of her bed, still holding the necklaces. He looked at the pendants in his palm and then back to Elena, waiting for her to continue.

"It's their power."

"I'm sorry?" He was sure he'd misheard her.

She looked down into her lap, her mouth moving back and forth nervously. "It's their power. Tera and Mararis. After Oriana killed them, or had them killed, we stored the breadth of their power in those amulets so we wouldn't lose it."

"Is this what they want? Is this why they're back?" His brown eyes widened as he dragged his clawed hand through his wavy hair.

Elena's shoulders rose in an exaggerated shrug that he thought worthy of one of his students.

"How?" He glared at her. "How did you and Oriana accomplish it? Neither of you were ever proficient in spells. You can barely hold a deception. She was worse. If it weren't for zemis gifted to you, neither of you would have obtained immortality. So, you need to tell me what witch assisted you in killing Tera and Mararis?"

Her face paled. Tears filled her eyes. His words hurt; no matter how much she tried to hide it, they hurt.

"Malcolm."

Linus's expression hardened. He threw the chains onto the bed as he stared at the ceiling, trying to maintain composure. "Where is it?"

"What do you mean?"

"The witch ball he gave you. Where is it, Elena?"

Even during the years of the Great Coven, Malcolm was a troublemaker. He chose his hobbies by how outlandish or unlawful they were. He chose his women by how much they were feared, hated, or unattainable.

Magic was a game for him. Traditionally, witch balls were used to ward off evil or ill-intent. He saw them as a vessel to harness magic or enchantments. Using his unique abilities to separate a soul from its body without killing either, he studied and experimented with separating the body from its magic.

The ball was meant to contain the power, and eventually the magic would be syphoned into another person. He had only successfully accomplished it twice, before Farryn forbade him from attempting it again.

"How did you know—"

"He's my brother. I know him better than anyone. Where is it?" he shouted.

"I don't know. Oriana had it. She kept the amulets and the ball when she moved out." Tears rimmed her reddened eyes. "I was happy to be rid of them."

He stood and walked past her. He listened to her sniffle and wipe her eyes as he opened the door. "Just one more thing, how'd you get the grimoire? She had it in California. Where did you get it?"

After a long pause, she said, "I was listed as her next of kin. They called me to identify her body. When I got there, her house was swarming with police—just like in the movies. Missing child reports, dusting for fingerprints. They found animal hair everywhere. They questioned me about Malcolm and where he lived. Lots of questions. None that I could answer." She took a deep, trembling breath. "It took weeks, but they finally allowed me into the house. I collected anything I thought was valuable. The grimoire wasn't evidence, so I took it. It's still technically a cold case, but nobody cares anymore."

"Mia cares, and how does her mother repay her? She tries to kill her." He glared at her.

She didn't look at him. "I sold the house and furniture. The money is in an account for Mia. There's quite a lot."

"Was the ball among her possessions?" He didn't wait for her answer. "Go find it." There was nothing loving in his tone. He was hard, crass, and unfeeling towards her. "I've got to talk to Farryn and punch my brother in the face. I'll be back later."

"Linus," she called him back. "I'm sorry."

"I'm not the one you should be apologizing to."

31

GAIL

Gail sat on the porch with Nadia, talking about anything but her mother and the fact that she was presumably a demi-goddess. She could feel every time Nadia wanted to ask about it and then detoured her mind and the conversation to some other trivial matter.

They spoke of Haven, both in Forest Lake and Connecticut. At different points in the conversation, they each questioned whether Haven mattered as much as it did during the wars. Neither had lived through the wars, but for some reason, it was a question that mattered to them.

"I gotta ask," Nadia burst out. "How could you not know Tess was your cousin?"

"I didn't. The same way I didn't know my own mother was a goddess." She picked at a piece of lint on her pants.

"I'm still not so sure about that." Nadia rolled her eyes.

"Who asked you?" Mararis spoke up. Gail chuckled.

"If any of this is true, that means I watched your Aunt Tera and her daughters burn to death."

While battling wills with Tess several years ago, Nadia became a victim of her own abilities. Tess dragged Nadia into her spirit realm and forced her to relive the pain she endured at the hands of Magnus Anmar and hordes of terrified villagers. Nadia was raped alongside Tess's sister, Rose, and watched as Tera was beaten severely before being tied to a tree and set on fire.

"We saw it too," Mararis confessed. *"Dyre and I..."*

The dense forest made it easy to hide without being seen or detected by anyone. Dyre stood without cover, watching. Just watching. Watching as her sister was dragged from her home. Dragged for no other reason than fear. Their leader did it for money. Paid off by Oriana Duran. Fear and money, a dangerous combination.

"Witch." They chanted. They cursed. They spat.

Each man and woman had visited Tera and her daughters for treatment. They called upon her when their crops died, or their cows gave sour milk. They sought them out for fertility magic or help with their sex life. Not one of them stood up for her now.

They dragged her on her back, by her hair, and at times, by her feet. Behind her they dragged her daughters. Dragged them for the same reasons, dragged them in the same manner.

When they were done dragging, they stripped their clothes from their bodies. Men and women beat and humiliated them. They were led by the old judge, Magnus Anmar. They followed his lead as he beat them and violated them.

Not good enough to live but good enough to rape.

Mararis felt sick as she watched. There was nothing she could do.

That wasn't true. There was plenty she could do but didn't. Fear that her fate would be the same.

"She doesn't deserve this." Mararis was the compassionate sister. "Those girls don't deserve this. If we are to punish anyone, it should be that witch. You know it as well as I. Magnus Anmar is not smart enough to do this on his own. She is pulling his strings."

"Whoever is to blame does not matter now." Dyre watched through the branches as the women were dragged again. "They will burn for what they've done."

"They've done nothing. You will watch them burn for nothing." Mararis's hands were trembling. "We must stop this."

Dyre grasped her sister's arm, stopping her from bursting through the trees.

"You'll end up right beside them if you do. You know we are forbidden to use our powers, especially here. This is Clotho's land. She will have your head if you do anything to stop this. If she wishes this to end, she will end it." Dyre locked her sister's gaze with her own.

"She hates us, especially Tera. She will never stop this." Mararis was hysterical.

The screaming and crying escalated as the three women were tied to trees in a clearing. The raping and beatings left them weak and bloodied. Rose, a woman of twenty, was the first to be set aflame. Almost unbearable to hear, Mararis held her hands over her ears to muffle her screams.

Their sister was next. Naked and praying, they tied her to the second tree, screaming at her to shut up, but she wouldn't. Finally, Anmar hit her with a hammer on the head, and she was silent. Dyre could feel her life slip away before the fire touched her flesh.

They didn't stay to watch their second niece die. Tess died alone with no one to witness her death.

"Can I kill Oriana Duran now?" Mararis asked.

"Find Elena Nolan. She'll return to her and then kill them both." Dyre closed her eyes as the final screams could be heard from yards away.

Gail stared off into the darkness.

"What is Oriana Duran's problem?" Nadia wiped her tear-stained face, remembering Tess's trauma like it was yesterday.

"She was a weak, power-hungry witch," Mararis said. *"I may not love that Simon is a werewolf, but I'm proud that he avenged our family."*

"You never killed them yourself, why?" Gail asked her mother.

"Fear. Dyre was right. We would have been killed if we did anything." Regret and bitterness colored Mararis's words.

Gail wiped at the tears in her eyes. "I want to help Dyre and her family. We can't let them die."

"Me too." Nadia sat up. "What can we do?"

"Let's go talk to Bentyn Rae. Maybe she has some suggestions."

32

THE GARDEN ROOM

Gail drove up to Beni's house. Nadia decided to remain at Haven and allow Gail some time to assess Beni's willingness to accept help. The house was just as intimidating as it had been the previous day. Gail could still visualize the room of weapons in Beni's attic. Her long driveway wound down to a large two-and-a-half-car garage. Sitting halfway down were two cars. Neither seemed like anything Beni would drive.

Yesterday, she drove a Porsche. Even if she did have multiple cars, a Subaru Crosstrek and a Toyota Grand Highlander didn't fit the bill. She crossed her fingers that she was at home.

After she rang the doorbell, footsteps clomping on tile gave way to Dyre's youngest daughter, Lucy.

"Gail! Mom, Gail is here."

With no evidence of fear or apprehension, Lucy took Gail's cool, white hand in hers and pulled her into the house. The scent of warm chocolate filled the air, and Gail couldn't determine what form it took: hot cocoa, cookies, or cake.

"We're making brownies," Lucy announced, having seamlessly read Gail's thoughts, leaving no sign that she had done so. "Come into the kitchen. April, Gail is here."

"I see." Dyre's oldest daughter stood on the stairs looking down at them. Beside her stood Mia. Both girls gave her a half-hearted hello and watched as she allowed Lucy to pull her into the kitchen.

"What are you doing here?" Dyre's lovely smile reminded her of her mother. Her long hair was tied up in a bun with pieces pushed behind her ears, just like her mother did when she baked. Her apron hung crooked on her waist and her feet were bare.

"I came to see Beni. Is she here?"

"Sorry. She and Malcolm are doing reconnaissance at the school." She continued to stir the large bowl of brown batter with a bamboo spoon. "Did you grease the pan, Lulu?"

"Reconnaissance?"

"I got it." Lucy held the glass baking dish in her hands. "Don't forget. I get to lick the spoon."

Dyre smiled and tapped her daughter's nose with her finger. "That's what they said. I think they're hoping to sniff out whether Elena is a willing participant in Oriana's games or not. Seems fruitless if you ask me."

Gail nodded, not sure what to say. She thought about the vision her mother created of Tera's death but had no clue how to broach the subject. Having just met this woman, she didn't wish to insult her or accuse her of letting her sister die.

After filling the baking dish, Dyre and Lucy placed it into the oven. Lucy set the timer. "Go play," she told her daughter. "Stay out of Aunt Beni's bedroom."

Without question, Lucy bounced out of the room.

Gail watched every movement with interest and curiosity.

Dyre began cleaning up the kitchen, throwing utensils into the sink and rinsing the mixing bowl. She stopped. Bracing herself on the edge of the sink, she lowered her head. "Yes, I did what you're thinking. I'm not proud of it. That's all I can say. My sisters suffered because of my anger. They would have spent their lives in paradise if not for me."

"Your anger?"

"I got us banished in the first place. I can blame Oriana Duran or Elena Nolan all I want, but I signed Tera's and Mararis's death warrants the moment I condemned Rafe to his fate."

"Rafe? Was he the first? I mean, he was like me?" She stuttered over her words, feeling awkward and thoughtless.

Dyre turned to face her. Her cheeks were red and her eyes watery. A cough bubbled up in her throat, and she fought to suppress it.

"Do you miss it?" Gail couldn't think of anything else to say, trying to change the subject. "Paradise."

"I miss my family. I miss the Garden Room." Dyre took a shaky breath and exhaled. "Let's look on the positive side. Aside from the obvious, my sisters' dying and all, I wouldn't have Lulu or April if I hadn't been banished. Beni would never have lived beyond the middle Bronze age. You would never have been born. There's a glimmer of light within my failings."

"What's the Garden Room?" Gail tried to push aside the ache in her chest caused by her aunt's objectivity.

"Oh, the most beautiful place that ever existed."

Dyre seemed to glow as she spoke of the Garden Room. Her words were transformed into thoughts and then into dreams. Taking Gail's hand, she urged her to follow as she visited this place of wonder. Dyre's breathing slowed and her hands dropped from Gail's grasp.

Gail found it impossible to open her eyes. Panic wrapped around her lungs, and she was sure she lost her aunt.

"Gail, follow me," Dyre's voice surrounded her.

"Why can't I open my eyes?" she asked.

"Fear does that. Fight through it but don't be afraid when you can't see anything." She spoke as if she was instructing her children.

The darkness was not frightening, but the weight it carried terrified her. Gail felt it closing in on her. The only thing she could see was Dyre. There was a strange glow that encircled her, and when Gail looked down at herself, she had the glow as well. It lit up nothing besides their bodies, but she was thankful not to feel alone in the darkness.

"Where are we?" She was exhausted. The simple act of opening her eyes took all her strength, and this oppressive darkness was hard to bear.

Dyre looked at her. She was unaffected by the darkness. She could feel the light on the other side of the barrier. She smiled. "Shhh. It gets easier as you walk."

The darkness closed in on her as they continued down a long corridor of nothingness. There were no windows, no pinpricks of light, no hope for anything beyond here.

"Cast your eyes down. If you don't—well, just do it." She looked back at Gail.

Dyre reached out into the darkness before her. She questioned whether there was something there, as she always did. It was a question that never went away. *Do I trust myself enough to know when the end is near?* Dyre took a step and still felt nothing. Another and her hand touched the hard surface of a door right in front of her.

She took another look at Gail to make sure it was safe to open the door.

"Here we go."

The door opened silently as if it wasn't there at all. It swung away as Dyre pressed her hand onto the hard surface. She was used to seeing nothing after the door opened. As a child, she remembered her sisters daring each other to run into the blackened room. They touched their toes into the room and waited for something to happen.

"I remember doing that." Mararis's voice surrounded them. In the darkness, her voice calmed Gail.

Dyre touched her toe into the room, mentally daring herself to run in. *"Dare you,"* she heard Tera whisper and a muffled giggle from Mararis. Both sisters had joined them on this journey.

Her toe touched the nonexistent floor, and her body moved past the nonexistent doorframe. Still nothing happened. She looked around, knowing the light should come on, but it didn't.

"Follow me," her voice wavered as she instructed Gail.

They both entered, and still nothing happened.

Dyre thought of those times running around the room, waiting for Mother to join them. Waiting and playing, running in circles in the darkness. Mother would step into the room and…

Dyre swung around.

The door stood not more than a foot behind Gail. She didn't see it but could feel that it was open.

Close the door, Dyre, Mother would instruct as she entered.

"Close the door, Dyre." Tera echoed her thoughts.

She heard it again. *"Close the door."* This time it was Mararis.

"Make sure your eyes are shut and close the door," Dyre instructed.

The minute the door shut, the light came on. Gail's eyes were pressed firmly closed. Through her closed eyelids, she could see the light fill the room with the intensity of the sun shining on Mercury. Even with her eyes closed, she groaned. Pressing them shut harder, she covered her face with her arms. It worried her that this light could kill her just as the sun could.

"Slowly, open your eyes. Let them adjust to the light. You are safe."

"It's so bright, Mother," her sisters would declare as children. She remembered holding her arms out as if the light radiated heat.

"Your father smiles on you, my lovelies. Bask in His glow." Mother's voice was hypnotic. Dyre closed her eyes as she felt her

father's love in this bright light and the warmth of Mother's words. She and her sisters would dance for Father. They loved the light and craved his attention.

"What now?" Gail blinked and squinted, trying to force the adjustment on her eyes. As they adjusted, she could see the most miraculous light illuminating the room.

Dyre stood in the center of the wonderous light, and beside her stood Tera and Mararis. Seeing the three sisters standing side by side, Gail could see their resemblance better than ever. Each of their faces was marred by the lives they'd lived, but their eyes, smiles, and mannerisms were the same.

"I know this place," Gail whispered.

"I took you here as a child, against your father's wishes, of course." Mararis smiled. "I wondered if you'd remember." Her voice sounded just as Gail remembered, not the ghostly voice she'd heard for the last week.

Gail looked at the ceiling and walls that were white. A long hallway was the only exit besides the door they had entered from. It was a circular room with windows that looked out onto a beautiful garden. The flowers in the garden were perpetually in bloom, and Gail knew that if she wished to see a certain flower—no matter what flower—it could be found in that garden. The flowers framed the windows. She could see every color of the rainbow out the window.

The women gazed into the beauty beyond the window, unable to speak or breathe. They stood shoulder to shoulder, enjoying the peace just looking at such a miracle brought to them.

"Heaven," Gail said.

Her skin glistened in the heavenly light, and her form was vaguely translucent, as was Dyre. Tera and Mararis were solid forms. Their souls were not attached to some distant body, keeping it from the wholeness of this place. Being alive kept the others tethered to their earthly forms, only visitors in nirvana.

"I've missed this. Death didn't bring us back here. Why?" Mararis asked.

Dyre had no answers.

"This is our fault." Tera smiled in her hard, unyielding way. "If I had not ignored the danger signs, I could have warned my own daughters, and they would be alive today. Not rotting in the ground because of some weak little witches playing games with power."

Mararis huffed in a sarcastic yet agreeing way.

"Tess is still around." Gail squeaked, afraid that this was not the right time to mention this fact.

Tera's head snapped in her direction. "What do you know of my Tess?"

"I know Tess Pendle attached herself to my family for generations."

"Actually, not our family, dear. We've discussed this." Her mother touched her arm, and her image flickered. Gail pulled away. "Aunt Sarah's family were descendants of Magnus Anmar."

"That vile pig of a man," Tera spat.

"Tess followed his family bloodline until she found us. You were the only one left alive when Sarah died. She naturally went to you."

"Naturally." Gail's eyelids lowered with rage.

"You knew my Tess hadn't moved on and didn't tell me?" Tera shouted.

"I'm telling you now." Mararis showed no fear.

"Enough." Dyre stepped in. "We are not here to fight. I didn't even invite you. I only wished to show Gail the Garden Room." She touched Gail's arm. "We may leave now."

As they turned to leave, a tall, elegant woman with long, straight, bronze hair stepped out of the long white hallway behind them. Her gown covered her from neck to toe and looked like it was spun from gold. She appeared from nowhere, and Dyre couldn't believe she didn't expect her.

It was Dyre's sister, Atropos, and Gail didn't know how she knew that either.

"What do you think you're doing here? You know you are not permitted in the Garden Room. Wait, why are you not here? Why is only a projected image of you before me?"

"My physical form is no longer able to fully enter. You know this." Dyre's mouth twitched with humiliation. Her hand touched the moonstone around her neck. It was that stone that enabled her to cross worlds. Since her banishment, it lay inactive on her chest, only a reminder of what she once had and what she had lost.

Atropos smirked. She looked at Mararis and Tera. "And you two? Have you separated from your physical forms indefinitely?"

"We have," Tera answered.

"They were killed by a hateful woman seeking to steal their power." Gail couldn't believe the words had passed her own lips. This woman frightened her.

Atropos scoffed. "A goddess?" She expected an explanation from Dyre.

"A little behind on the affairs on Earth?" She couldn't help letting her sister know that she thought she was doing a poor job as a Sister of Fate. "No, this woman capitalized on a bad situation. You wouldn't know this, but having a legacy removes our immortality. This woman killed both Tera and Mararis after killing their legacies."

"Yes, yes, yes. We know all of this. Edith and Rose are with us here."

"Edith *and* Rose are here?" Gail burst out. "May we see them?"

"They don't leave the main house. They both fear the outside world for obvious reasons, and we would prefer to keep their time here as peaceful as possible. I assume you are here for help with this woman."

"It was not my intention to speak with you at all." Dyre's face hardened. "However, I would appreciate…"

Atropos's eyes shifted to Gail. "You dare ask for help after bringing others into our home without permission." The woman sighed in a disappointed way. Her hands were laced together in front of her. Her face soured. "And you brought one of your abominations with you."

Dyre's head lowered as shame washed over her like icy cold water.

Gail stiffened at the insult.

"You are Gail." After having just insulted her, the woman smiled. She saw recollection in her smile, and somewhere deep inside her heart and mind, Gail knew her too. "Mararis's daughter."

She nodded without looking at her mother. "Yes."

"You have retained your powers through this ghastly transformation?" Atropos asked. She took Gail's hand in hers and stroked it lovingly. "You were elemental if memory serves."

"I was?"

"Dear Mararis brought you and your brother—is he one of you?" Her hand slid up and down Gail's form, and she knew what she was asking.

"No, Simon..."

Atropos already knew Simon's fate. Her face soured before Gail could continue.

"Atropos, don't pretend you don't know why we are here." Tera, it seemed, had courage the others lacked.

Atropos's eyes rolled to meet Tera. "Like your sister, you are no longer welcome here either, dead or alive." She held out her long, slender, white hands like a gateway blocking the rest of the hallway. "Go now. While Father is somewhat forgiving by nature, Mother is not. Seeing you will only anger her. There are more than enough natural disasters on Earth as it is; let's keep Mother happy, shall we?"

Gail chuckled under her breath until Atropos glared at her. The giggle was sucked back in and replaced with a guilt-ridden frown. Without realizing it, Atropos was pushing them back towards the door.

Atropos paced the room. Her golden gown trailed behind her as she moved past the windows. "It is amazing to me what Mother's magic has produced. As you know, the Earth was a gift to Her from Father. She spun wonderous beauty in his creation. Her magic is in every living organism in the world. She *is* the thread. The end and the beginning. She is in all of us."

Gail nodded suspiciously, not knowing where this conversation was headed.

Atropos rubbed her palms together. She turned around and found Dyre standing submissively near the door. She smiled with contempt.

"You are dying. I can feel it in you. The thread has connected with you, hasn't it? Showing you your end?"

"No, it hasn't. But, yes, I am dying."

Gail looked away.

"How soon?" Her tone was cold and without sympathy.

"Soon." Dyre looked away, out into the garden. A tear slipped down her cheek, and she brushed it away.

"I will help you."

All three sisters stared at Atropos in surprise. Gail stepped away from the group to allow them to negotiate a deal.

"Under one condition. When you die and the full breadth of your power passes to your legacy, I want Lucy—here with us until she is ready to join her brethren using her skills as she was meant to use them. Your transgressions will not pass on to her.

"Her cousins are here. She will be raised, as she should be, by the gods that raised you." Atropos continued without looking at anyone but Dyre. No one else mattered in her mind, and Dyre knew it. Atropos was Dyre's equal. They both possessed the same job, both the oldest of the three sisters. Tera and Mararis didn't matter in her mind. And even though Gail was a demi-goddess, she was a monster, nothing more than a speck of dust caught in the wind. This was Dyre's decision and one she had assumed would happen anyway.

"If I agree, it will be with conditions of my own."

The women stared at each other for a long time, each considering the consequences of their actions and whether any of this was worth doing.

"Agreed." Atropos smiled. "Bring this woman to us. Banished or not, we must protect our family and avenge misdeeds at any cost."

"What will you do to her?" Gail asked out of curiosity.

"Just bring her to us," Atropos snapped. "Edith and Rose deserve retribution."

"We should go," Dyre whispered. She touched her sister for the first time in thousands of years. Her hands were warm, and she missed the closeness that had once existed between them.

Gail opened her eyes, finding herself back in Beni's kitchen. Dyre's face paled, and Gail could hear her heart racing in her chest. "Was that realm jumping?"

Dyre looked at her in a dizzying state of confusion. "That's not how I expected that to go."

33

BENI

The car ride to Magnolia Academy was somewhat entertaining. After they decided how they would approach this conversation with Elena, both Beni and Malcolm relaxed. It was Dyre who suggested they use Malcolm's abilities to sniff out Oriana in the house. And if they could, they should get the grimoire and her sisters' necklaces that had burned April during the calling. Dyre knew those pendants held significant power, more than Elena Nolan deserved to possess.

"So, what do you know about those necklaces?" Beni's fingers gripped the steering wheel.

"What do you mean?" His aloof manner didn't fool her.

"When Dyre mentioned them, you chilled and then you began to sweat." Beni's right brow raised. She lowered her chin as she glanced at him. She tapped her nose. "You may be able to read minds, but I can read your body. Don't lie to me, Brenig."

"I don't know for sure, but I think those are the vessels Oriana chose to store Tera and Mararis's power."

"And you would know this…how?"

"Why don't we just concentrate on protecting Mia? Looking for blame only aggravates our relationship." He shifted in his seat.

They pulled up in front of the school and walked side by side to the front door. Beni could feel the tension surrounding this situation. She could smell incense burning from inside and hear someone approaching the front door before they knocked.

"Come in." Camilla opened the door and stepped out of the way to allow them entry. "Linus has been looking for you." She didn't smile at Malcolm but only delivered the message with the impersonal tone of a stranger.

"We're here to speak with Elena," Beni said.

"No, you're not." Camilla chuckled in a cynical way. "You're here to speak with Oriana. Well, she's not speaking to anyone. We've tried countless times to contact her, and she's holed up somewhere in this house with her lips zipped."

Beni rolled her eyes.

"How is Mia?" Camilla asked.

"She's fine." Beni didn't wish to build a relationship with this woman, but she knew if it weren't for her, Mia would be dead. "Thank you for what you did."

Camilla nodded, understanding how difficult it was for Beni to say that much.

"Well, if we can't get Oriana out, Dyre wants the grimoire and those necklaces that were with it. She says there may be a way to bind her, if we can't get rid of her completely." Beni's face twisted with her ignorance. "I have no idea what that means, but if you're willing, I'd like her to try it. For Mia's sake."

"Of course." Camilla smiled for the first time since she broke in on Elena standing over Mia with that grimoire in her hands. "Let me go get it."

When she disappeared upstairs, Beni slapped Malcolm on the arm.

"Ouch! You pack one hell of a punch, lady." He rubbed his upper arm. "Go easy, will you?"

"What the hell is up with you? Are you just going to stand here and not say anything? And I could smell your adrenaline pique the minute those necklaces were mentioned again. What did you do?" Through clenched teeth, she chastised him.

"He helped Oriana collect Tera's and Mararis's power with this." Linus stood on the stairs with a glass orb in his hands. He tossed it in the air and caught it with ease.

Malcolm looked away from his brother. He stepped towards the door as if he was preparing for a quick getaway. Beni was way ahead of him. She grabbed his arm.

"Not so fast, Brenig. Explain yourself."

He glared at Beni. Spells collected in his mind as she tightened her grip.

"What's going on?" Camilla stood behind Linus on the stairs. "Malcolm, don't."

"Are you really trying to put a spell on me?" Beni took his arm into a firmer grip and dragged him back into the room. He pushed him towards his brother. "What'd you do?"

"He taught Oriana how to collect magic in the witch ball."

Malcolm held his hands up like he was being arrested. "In my defense, I had no idea what she was using it for. This was back when Mil and I were still a thing. I was helping her little sister. That's all. I thought it was a good thing." He shrugged sheepishly.

"You never thought to ask why the sudden interest in this type of magic?" Camilla approached him with the grimoire in her arms. "It wasn't a secret that both Oriana and Elena resented the Circle because they lacked the more refined abilities. You didn't think that they had some ulterior motives?"

He ran his hands through his unruly hair and laughed. "Honestly, when they asked, no."

Linus slapped him in the back of his head. Beni did the same from the other side.

"What the hell…" he yelled.

"You were trying to get into her pants, weren't you?" Linus accused his brother. "Why is your taste in women so appalling?"

Camilla's face twisted in disgust. "Thanks."

Malcolm scoffed as if it weren't true. "Why did *you* hit me?" he asked Beni.

She glared at him. "Because it's fun."

Camilla pushed past him, wanting to hit him too but choosing to be the bigger person. "Here's the grimoire." She handed it to Beni. "The necklaces were not with it. I'll find them."

"I had them earlier," Linus said. "I must have left them in Elena's room."

A scream drew their attention away from the snide remarks or veiled threats. From upstairs, in the back bedroom, Starr sounded like she was being murdered. Linus was up the stairs and running before anyone could figure out what was happening. Malcolm followed close behind.

When the men burst into the room, Starr was flailing. She pushed Kim away from her repeatedly and she screamed words that stopped Malcolm short. He ducked before being hit with a lamp.

"Oriana," he cried out. "Stop!"

Kim struggled to hold Starr. She pulled her arms down and wrapped her in a tight embrace. Starr cursed and pushed her away with force. It was taking its toll on Kim every time she was pushed to the floor.

Malcolm stepped up, pushing Kim to the side. Linus stood beside him. Starr stopped flailing. Her curly brown hair was tangled and stood up in different places. Her bloodshot eyes stared him down.

"Starr, I want you to be calm. Can you do that?" Linus didn't take his eyes off hers.

She whispered words under her breath. She reached out. "Malcolm," she said.

Her face hardened as if she had aged years in a day. Her mussed hair and disheveled clothes stunk of incense. She clawed her fingers and dragged them down his face, leaving long red marks on his cheek.

He winced. It wasn't Starr's voice that spoke but the voice of a much older woman.

"Where is she? Tell me." Her eyes were ringed red with tears swimming in them. From experience, he knew those tears were from Starr as she cowered in the periphery of this spiritual onslaught on her body.

"Oriana, let her go. You have no right to harm this girl."

"You speak of rights, Linus. What rights do I possess now? In death. My life, my power, sacrificed. Robbed from me. Tell me where my daughter is."

"Why, so you can try to kill her again?" Malcolm yelled.

Linus smirked. "Some things never change. Your dramatics won't work, Oriana."

The bedroom door swung open. Camilla and Elena burst into the room, followed by Beni.

The split second Linus had to react was not enough. Oriana saw Beni and lunged at her. She screamed again. Beni and Camilla were quick enough to step away, just missing Starr by inches. Elena wasn't so lucky.

Starr leapt at her, knocking her to the floor.

Elena went down hard, banging her head on the doorframe and then again on the hardwood floor. She screamed out as she fought the young girl with an enormous amount of strength. Starr punched and scratched at her. She pulled her hair. "You betrayed me."

Elena continued to scream in pain and fear. "I didn't mean to."

Camilla grabbed Starr and pulled her away. She pushed her to the floor and lunged again towards Beni.

"You stole my daughter! Where is she?"

Linus tried to stop the fight and was thrown down as well. Camilla tried again. As she grabbed Starr's arms and Malcolm fought to hold her shoulders, Elena reached into her pocket. She pulled out the necklaces and held them up in front of Starr's crazed and angry face. "Stop!" she shouted at her. A minute froze in time as Starr didn't move, Oriana didn't speak, and everyone waited.

Then Oriana laughed. "You'd use my own power against me?"

"It's not yours." Elena closed her eyes and extended her arm farther.

A force of air, powerful hurricane force wind, pushed through the room. Elena's hair was swept up in the force of it and seemed to billow above her head, but nothing else moved. Her eyes remained closed.

With a look of horror and outrage on her face, Oriana—with Starr hovering inside—was thrown back. Her body lifted from the floor and into the air like a great tornado had picked her up. It lifted her and slammed her against the wall with enough force to knock most of the pictures down and the trinkets off the top of the dresser beside her. Her head slammed into the wall, making her eyes spin in their sockets and a bloodstain appeared on the wall as she slid down. She was left huddled on the floor like a sack.

Camilla and Linus stared at Elena in shock and horror. Kim ran to Starr.

"Starchild, speak to me. Please," she cried. "Lilly, run a hot bath," she called at the top of her lungs. Footfalls could be heard outside their door as Lilly ran to the bathroom, followed by water filling the tub. "We need to get her into the tub. I need my herbs. Camilla, I know you said you'd never do it, but—"

"What do you need?" Her voice trembled with emotion and lingering horror from what was unfolding.

"Stop her from leaving. Build a barrier for me. I can help her if she stays with us. Stop her departure so I may—" She wept. "Just keep her with us."

"I'll do what I can. Get your supplies."

Kim darted from the room. Linus sped to the bathroom to gather towels and other supplies needed to save Starr. Beni and Malcolm were left staring at Camilla holding the dying child.

She held Starr's hand and cradled her bloody scalp. She kissed her forehead.

"Milly, don't. It's too dangerous." Malcolm crouched beside her.

"Should I just let her die?"

She closed her eyes and centered on the energy in Starr's body. There was a strong presence that hovered over her, leaving the dying form with no remorse for what it had caused. A sliver of dim essence remained in Starr's young body, but it was itching to go. It pushed against the lifeforce Camilla used to surround it. She spoke words of power and light. She wrapped it in her essence and held it fast, forbidding it to exit her body.

"Stay with us, Starchild," she whispered as she pulled away, leaving a bit of herself to carry Starr into her recovery or to carry her into the next world. Camilla refused to let her go alone. This was not her battle to fight; she was a pawn that had become a victim. She opened her eyes to face Malcolm's concern.

"Get her into the tub," she told him.

Malcolm pushed Elena out of the way as he carried Starr's battered body out of the room. Pierce, Veda, and Lilly stood in the hallway watching everything unfold.

Camilla found it impossible to stand. She fell to the floor with each attempt, and debilitating dizziness engulfed her. She remained on the floor, concentrating on her breathing.

Elena tucked the amulets into her pocket and looked at her sister with a smug look of satisfaction. "At least she chose someone besides me this time." She wiped at the scratches on her face and neck and touched the tender spots on her scalp from Starr pulling at her hair.

Beni held her hand out for the necklaces. "Hand them over."

"And if she returns, who will protect me then? No, these amulets will be with me always."

Beni stepped closer, ensuring the pull did its work. Elena froze in place. "If she returns, you deserve everything she gives you. Give me those necklaces. They belong to Dyre."

Elena's hand reached into her pocket and pulled them out. She handed them to Beni without meaning to, without wanting to, but the pull gave her no other choice. Beni stepped away.

"Are you good?" she asked Camilla, who nodded. Beni left the room.

"What did you mean when you said *I didn't mean to*? Didn't mean to do what, Leny?"

"I didn't mean to…" Elena looked as if the wind was taken from her sails. All the arrogance she possessed before seemed to disappear. In a whisper, she said, "I didn't mean to abandon her. I knew someone was following her. I did nothing to help."

Camilla felt herself falling and couldn't respond to her sister.

Beni returned to the room. "The girl is rebounding." She stopped as she watched Camilla's eyes close. "What did you do to her?" she barked at Elena. Dropping the necklaces on the dresser, her strong, capable arms lifted Camilla and laid her on the bed.

"Me? I've done nothing. Leaving a part of her soul to protect that child is what cripples her."

"Leaving what?" She brushed Camilla's hair off her face. With her palm, she tested the temperature on her forehead. She could hear the whisper of a heartbeat in her chest. "Malcolm!"

He rushed back into the room.

"She's dying."

"Goddammit, Milly." He grabbed her hand, feeling for a heartbeat. "It's faint. I don't think I can bring her back on my own. Get Linus in here," he shouted at Elena, who ran to fetch him.

Linus pushed the bedroom door open. His usually playful curly hair was damp and pushed off his forehead, and his sleeves were rolled up to the elbow. He dried his hands with a towel as he entered the room. The tender, understanding expression Elena had grown accustomed to seeing every day was gone. In its place was anger and frustration until he saw Camilla lying in Malcolm's arms.

"How are you at creating barrier spells?" Malcolm asked.

"Not good." Linus sat on the bed, touching Camilla's arm with his fingers. He listened for her heart and looked into her eyes as a mortal doctor would do. "There's nothing to do but wait it out. This is the reason she doesn't do this and should never do it again. To stop

Starr's soul from leaving her body, Milly had to leave a part of herself inside Starr. Her lifeforce was what will save that girl's life," he said.

Beni watched Camilla fade in and out of consciousness. Her heartbeat, what little there was, ebbed and flowed as she kept a tentative grasp on life. Camilla's eyes opened for only a second, and Beni knew what she should do.

"Enough of this." She pushed the men away.

Pulling Camilla into her arms, she raised her wrist to her mouth and grazed it against one of her fangs. The blood pooled for only a second before she urged Camilla to drink it.

"What are you doing?" Elena shouted. "Linus, stop her. She's killing her."

After only a sip or two, Beni pried her wrist from Camilla's mouth. It was no easy feat. Her mouth made a popping sound as she was forced to release her wrist.

"What have you done?" Malcolm asked Beni. He pushed her aside and took Camilla in his arms again, cradling her like a child. He brushed back her hair and touched her cheeks with his hand.

"Blood therapy. It's an ancient practice. My blood will speed her healing time. You were going to lose her tonight."

"Witch hunters don't save witches. They kill them. Do we look stupid to you?" Elena's voice was whiny and piercing. Her fists clenched as she screamed.

"Elena, calm down," Linus spoke over her. Elena's brow creased as she looked at him. "What side effects will she endure?"

"Endure?" Beni asked. "Give her a few minutes and she should be fine. I can hear her heart getting stronger. Her breathing is more even, and I can smell the rush of hormones in her system."

"Minutes? That's impossible." Malcolm's eyes widened.

"It's not possible for a witch hunter to save a witch." Elena wouldn't stop.

"Do you know what I find impossible?" Beni bellowed back at her. "That you're still breathing."

"You don't have the guts—"

"Leny, shut up." Camilla fought for breath and collapsed in Malcolm's arms again. "And get out so we may speak privately." The healing was slow, but she could feel it happening already. A little sleep was all she needed. Sleep, a bit of Kim's special tea, and more of Beni's blood.

"Fine, talk about me all you want. Your precious Elder Path connection no longer bothers me, Milly. And remember I didn't cause this situation. That honor goes to your precious Mia and her friends." With that, Elena glared at Linus. She knew which side he'd chosen. She breezed out of the room, slamming the door shut as she left.

"One spell, Camilla." Malcolm's jaw tensed as he spoke. "One spell and she'd be a flower in the garden or a crystal on my shelf. Just give me your permission and it will be done."

Beni laughed. "I'm starting to like you, Brenig."

Camilla laughed too. She coughed, wheezed, and laughed some more.

Beni studied her for a minute and then nodded. "Get some rest now. My blood is potent. You'll be feeling the effects well into tomorrow."

34

COMING TOGETHER

The next day, Dyre sat in the backyard of her house watching Lucy play frisbee with Mia. The sun was shining, and she felt the strongest she'd felt in days. Between the sickness growing in her lungs, the calling, her daughters' memories being restored, and the reemergence of Oriana Duran, she was drained. The simple effort it took to get out of bed had her wishing to return as soon as she rose.

The visit to the Garden Room had worked miracles on her mental and physical state. Whether she was welcome there or not, she couldn't deny the healing powers of the place.

Lucy screamed as she dove at the flying disc and missed it. She ended up face down in the grass, laughing.

"Be careful, Lulu," Dyre cried over the radio blaring beside her.

April didn't want to join the fun. It took all three of them to coerce her into sitting outside with them. The only thing she really wanted to do was listen to music at a deafening volume to drown out the constant, intrusive voice of her Aunt Tera. Her dark sunglasses hid the circles under her eyes from lack of sleep, and deep breaths covered her constant yawning.

"April, lower the music," Dyre shouted. "April," she repeated when she got no reaction. "April." She glared at her daughter. Throwing her right hand towards the small Bluetooth speaker, it went flying. Next, she clenched her fist and the music cut off immediately.

April looked up at her mother and then grabbed her phone. The screen was black and refused to come back to life when she pressed the buttons.

"What'd you do to it?" She continued to tap on the black screen. "You busted it."

"Good. Next time I speak to you, I expect an answer." She took her glass of lemonade from the table and sipped it.

"You don't understand. None of you do." She looked at Mia and Lucy. "She's always in my head. I don't get a minute of peace. Just blah blah blah. Kill Elena Nolan. Blah blah blah."

"How dare you—"

"Shut up, Tera," Dyre snapped. She looked at April with sympathy. "I do understand. I hear her too. So does Lucy."

"Then why can you sleep? Why aren't you going insane?" she cried.

"I think we're just better at blocking her out."

"How do *I* do it?" April sat up in her chair. She looked down at her broken phone and discarded it on the end table.

She had no answers for her daughter. Dyre didn't fully understand what her sisters meant to accomplish in this world. She thought of Atropos's words and promises. She also wondered how she would get Oriana to the Garden Room for judgement.

Gail returned to Haven, promising she'd visit tonight to help figure something out. Mararis went with her. As much as Dyre felt for April or Gail, she was thrilled her sisters hadn't fully embraced her just yet.

The rest of the day, they enjoyed the sunshine and played a few more lawn games. April tried to participate, but anytime Tera had something to say, she lost her concentration and retreated to her seat on the patio.

"What should we have for dinner?" Dyre asked when all three girls gathered around the patio table.

"My dad invited me to dinner with him. If that's okay, I'd like to go." The soulful expression on her face tugged on Dyre's heartstrings.

"Invite him here. We can order in." She looked at her own daughters, and something in her heart broke enough to go against everything she believed was right. She smiled. "How about we invite your father too?"

Lucy cheered. April did not. She was still uncomfortable with the idea of Linus Brenig as her father, and with Tera in her ear, it didn't sit well with her that he was dating Elena Nolan.

After Dyre called to invite Linus to dinner, Camilla knew this would be a good opportunity to speak with her about what transpired last night and what they both needed to work toward never happening again.

She was also hoping to find something that would allow her to release the fidgety feelings that had been building. Bentyn Rae's blood felt like a dozen energy drinks topped off with a healthy dose of cocaine. She asked Linus if she could accompany him to Dyre's house.

"We should bring Elena," Linus suggested. Pierce stood beside him, excited to see his family again.

"And get her killed? Absolutely not. She's safer here than anywhere near Dyre Crane." Camilla grabbed her car keys and headed out the door.

"Maybe I should stay here." Pierce held his father back from the door. "I'll take Elena out for dinner. She could use a night out after everything going on here."

Linus sighed, knowing he should include Elena. "That would be nice. Thank you." He hugged his son.

Across town, Beni lay in bed going over and over the details of the previous night. She and Malcolm drove to the school. They even shared a little flirtation. They entered the house, and she ended up saving Camilla Nolan's life. How exactly did that happen? She pulled the blankets up over her head and closed her eyes.

She missed having a man lying beside her, missed feeling a body leaning against hers. The bed was too empty with only one person, and with the events of last night churning around in her head, she wished she had someone to hold on to for support.

"Mom? You up?" Mia's soft knock put a smile on her face.

"You bet. Come on in." She pulled herself out from under the sheets and sat up. Her umber hair stood up with static from the blankets.

Her daughter peeked into the room like she felt she was intruding.

"Get in here," Beni insisted. She held her arms wide, and Mia climbed on the bed, falling into her embrace. Maybe she didn't need a man after all; maybe all she needed was her daughter.

The gentle scent of lavender from Mia's hair filled her nostrils, and she buried her face in her silky brown waves. "I hate to say it, but you've got your father's hair." She noticed an unruly wave filtering beneath her mass of brunette hair.

"I hate it. Don't tell him. I've dragged the flat iron over those waves at least three times. They won't budge. I'm going to cut it all off if it gets any worse." She pulled her hair to the side and tried to smooth it out. "How did April dodge the Brenig bullet?"

Beni laughed, loving the term *Brenig bullet*. "Aunt Dyre's genes run deep. A goddess needs to have long flowing hair." She mimed brushing back the flowing tresses of a Hollywood starlet. They laughed together. Beni loved Mia's laugh. She was glad to hear it after the last few days of trauma she'd endured. "I thought you were at Aunt Dyre's tonight?"

"I was. I slipped out because I wanted to talk to you." Mia's face dropped. She looked scared. "Dad told me what happened last night. How you saved Camilla's life. He said Oriana Duran hurt Starr."

Beni stared at Mia. "What do you want to know?" She cut to the chase.

"Just—" She stopped and chewed her thumbnail for a moment. "I think we should concentrate on..." Tears filled her eyes, and the emotion stopped her from speaking. Beni didn't interrupt but allowed her to continue in her own time. When the emotion subsided, she resumed. "I think we should get rid of Oriana Duran. I think she's the problem, not Elena. Rayne said Oriana Duran tried to kill me. She also possessed Starr. I don't think killing Elena is the answer."

Beni didn't answer her right away. She thought of her words. She wondered where they were coming from. Was this Malcolm's agenda she was reciting or were these her own feelings?

"Think about it." Mia gained confidence. "She's been the problem since I opened that grimoire. Elena hasn't bothered anyone before that, and when something goes wrong, Oriana Duran is there."

She couldn't help but notice that Mia only spoke of her mother as Oriana Duran. She never once referred to her as *my mom* like she had up until today. She also only used her full name like she was someone she didn't know. Beni knew she was distancing herself from the woman who'd given birth to her, and she didn't know how to feel about it.

"I understand what you're saying. I do." She placed her hand on top of Mia's. "But Elena Nolan did a lot of horrible things in her life. Horrible things to Aunt Dyre's family. I don't think she should get away with that." Beni stopped and assessed Mia's reaction. "Is she to blame for what's happening now? No. I agree with you there. But is she innocent? Absolutely not."

"Can't Aunt Dyre take care of her then? Why do you need to get involved?"

It became clear that Mia wasn't trying to save Elena's life. She was trying to keep Beni from killing another witch. She smiled and nodded. "Fair enough. I am no longer a witch hunter. I promised you that I would never do that again. I *will* assist in getting rid of Oriana Duran to keep you safe. I will allow Aunt Dyre and Gail to decide the fate of Elena Nolan."

Mia dove at her mother, wrapping her in her arms with a great bear hug. Beni laughed. All she had to do was figure out how to get rid of Oriana Duran. "I better get back to Aunt Dyre's. Camilla brought dessert."

"Camilla's there?"

"Everyone is there." Mia giggled. "Come with me."

"Who's everyone?" Beni hated the idea already.

"Dad, Linus, Camilla, and Rayne."

"That's everyone, alright." Beni's face soured. "Let's pick up Gail. Maybe if we're all in one room, we'll be able to figure this thing out."

35

THE PLAN

Dinner went as well as any one of them would have expected. Lucy was thrilled to have Linus in the house. April stayed silent, hoping to keep her aunt's voice quiet too. The group discussed recent events, Dyre's recent meeting with Atropos, and Camilla asked how Mia was feeling since the transmigration.

"How do we proceed?" Camilla dared to ask when the girls left the table. "Do you think your sister means what she says?"

"I don't know. It doesn't matter. I can't even fathom how to entrap and deliver Oriana to her." Dyre held in a cough. The pain was minimal, but she could feel the tumor amassing itself. Each breath felt heavier. She wondered if Atropos could help her with that as well.

"Where'd Mia disappear to?" Malcolm asked.

As they all thought their own private thoughts and Malcolm went to find Mia, a car approached outside.

"Expecting someone?" Rayne turned to Dyre as if this was a closed meeting.

"It's Beni." Her eyes searched the air as she felt the approaching visitors. "And Gail…and Mia. Mal, Mia is outside."

Linus smirked. "Your powers aren't waning."

Dyre's eyebrows jumped on her forehead.

"Could you imagine what she could see if they weren't?" Rayne sniped.

A moment later, Lucy opened the front door.

"Where do vampires live?" she said as soon as her aunt entered. Mia groaned as she slipped passed her mother into the house.

Beni picked Lucy up in her arms, loving the way the child smelled. It was a mixture of watermelon shampoo and crayons. "Where?"

"On a dead-end street."

"Lulu, I've got one for you." Gail came up from behind them. She waited in the doorway to be invited in. "What kind of rocks do vampires collect?"

Still snug in Beni's arms, she gazed in awe. "What kind?"

"Tombstones." She laughed.

Beni faked a laugh, and Dyre joined her. Giggling like schoolgirls for a minute, Dyre grabbed Lucy from Beni and hugged her. When she placed her on the floor, she ran to Linus to repeat Gail's joke as if he wasn't only steps away when it was first said.

"Go tell your father you're here," Dyre told Mia. "He's been looking for you."

"Oops." She cringed and disappeared down the hallway to the bedrooms.

"Gail told me you saw Atropos?" Beni looked astonished. "That's kind of a big deal."

"For whom?" Dyre grimaced. "I hate to be the one to suggest it, but should we call the Phoenix? We have so much to discuss, and I think we need her."

An hour later, they sat together at Dyre's dining room table. Dyre served drinks and the cake Camilla brought.

"Any suggestions on how to capture her?" Beni spoke up first. April and Mia weren't at the table, but they sat within earshot so they wouldn't miss anything.

"Mal?" Linus glared at his brother. "You've had moderate success with your orbs. Do you think they could work?"

Looking at everyone staring back at him, Malcolm considered the idea. "Absolutely. I don't have one. Fae? Do you have a witch ball?"

"Why would I have a witch ball? The ridiculous notion that you can collect magic in a glass ball—really, Malcolm." Farryn shook her head.

"It's been done," Beni said. "That's how they stored Tera's and Mararis's power before shoving it into their necklaces."

"Why can't we just use the one they used?" Linus asked. "We have that one at home."

"I never reuse a witch ball. God knows what divine power did to the orb. If Oriana finds a way out before we can get her to

Atropos, I guarantee you, it will not be pretty." Malcolm sipped his coffee.

"There are plenty at the shop. Iris went on another one of her spending sprees. Take your pick. We can cleanse it before you use it." Rayne reached over to cut herself a slice of cake.

"We?" Camilla couldn't help herself.

Rayne stopped. She licked her hand free of icing. Her eyes danced over the assembly, falling on Farryn finally. "I'd like to help. My abilities can be of some use to you."

"We need to trap her, somehow," Linus continued.

"I've been thinking about that. The best way is the Circle. If we close the original Circle, we can use our collective abilities to keep her tethered until Dyre can put her into the orb." Farryn sat back in her chair as she spoke.

"I can't do that alone." Dyre looked into her lap, ashamed of her waning powers.

"Can't Mararis and Tera help?" Beni asked.

"Possibly." She glanced at her friend with gratitude.

"We're still short four members for the Circle," Malcolm pointed out. "We could tether her with a pentacle. It's not as sure, but with Rayne, we have five strong witches to hold her here."

"Too risky. She could slip through and then where would we be?" Farryn sighed. "No, the Circle is our best bet. We need four witches to close the circle and act as proxy for our missing brethren. We are four, with Rayne, five."

Rayne Grey beamed.

"I think we should consider including Elena," Linus spoke up.

Everyone objected, but none more than Farryn. "Are you crazy? She'll sabotage us."

"That's not fair," Camilla jumped in to defend her sister. "She's as much a victim as anyone."

Beni raised a finger in the air. "Not as much as some." Her smile was bitter as her eyes shifted to her daughter sitting in the other room.

"Including her will keep her out of Oriana's line of fire, don't you think?" Linus continued to campaign for Elena.

"Sorry, Linus. It's far too chancy, and she's never had the strength to join the Circle." Farryn shook her head.

"Why must you do that?" Camilla argued. "Leny has plenty of strength and magic inside of her. She's just had too many people telling her she's not enough all her life." Her eyes dropped to the table. "Including me."

"She's not enough and never has been," Farryn snapped. "She will never be in the Circle."

Before Camilla could fight back with centuries of examples why her cousin was wrong, April and Mia jumped from their seats and ran to the dining room. "How about us?"

"Absolutely not." Beni didn't hesitate.

"I'm afraid I agree with Aunt Beni, girls. That's a no from me too." Dyre gave her a thumbs-down.

"Me too," Linus joined in.

"No go, kid." Malcolm turned his thumb down too.

"I'm a witch, you know," April shouted. "You keep telling me that I'm not a legacy or Aunt Tera keeps saying I'm a spare. What does that make me? To you guys, I'll never grow up. Mia is a witch too."

"Mia knows better than to ask. After what happened the other day, she's not going within thirty yards of that woman." Beni's jaw tensed as she spoke.

"This is my chance to be a part of the Great Coven," Mia whined with a hearty slap to her mother's arm.

"No." Beni stood firm.

A silence fell over the group. Every moment filled with tension.

"It might be the only hope we have," Farryn offered. "We may not be able to do this without them."

Mia quietly cheered, bringing out a laugh in Malcolm.

"Even with them, we're still short one," Camilla added.

"What about Iris?" Linus suggested. "She is the consistently ignored witch in our midst."

Rayne and Malcolm exchanged a glance. Neither could disagree with Linus's assessment. They'd lived with her for over a month now and neither thought to include her.

"Yes," Camilla spoke up. "Iris is a fine choice."

After the coffee was gone and the cake eaten, April and Mia went to bed. The adults took their conversation outside. It was unseasonably warm for September as they sat around Dyre's patio table drinking.

"Does anyone else think it's strange that Oriana Duran was killed by a shifter and Simon—Mararis's son—just happens to be one?" Beni spoke up.

"It's not strange. I completely believe he was the shifter that killed her." Gail sat back in her chair. "Makes perfect sense to me."

Farryn nodded.

"Wait, I thought *you* killed Oriana Duran. That's always been my understanding," Rayne cut in, pointing to Dyre.

"I thought I did too." Dyre was embarrassed that she had failed in her first murder attempt in centuries. "I cursed her."

"You attempted a spell?" Farryn looked amazed and a bit impressed.

"Not exactly."

"What did you do, exactly?" Rayne leaned in, as if it were a criminal offense for Dyre to practice magic against a witch.

Dyre glared at her until she leaned back. Her powers may have been waning, but everyone knew she was still capable of cutting a cord when she needed to. She suppressed a cough. "I frayed her cord."

"Pardon me?" Beni chuckled.

Dyre narrowed her eyes as she looked at her best friend. "If I cut her thread, Atropos would have been alerted immediately and then I'd be dead. So, I frayed it. I shredded it down to the finest strand. It drained her energy and her magic, *and* if she tripped on a curb, it would have killed her."

Farryn's wonder grew.

"Who hired the shifter?" Malcolm asked.

"I did." Farryn made her drink stirrer move with magic. Her finger moved in a circle as the stirrer followed her movements.

"Why?" Dyre asked.

"Why?" Farryn was amazed at the stupidity of the question. "To finish the job. I knew what Simon had become, Gail too. She was different than him. She had no memory of her past."

"No knowledge," Gail corrected her.

Farryn nodded, accepting that answer but not truly believing it. "But Mararis had spent years priming Simon. Prepping him for the fight he would one day fight. Following his transformation, he became distracted. I guided him in the right direction." She looked around the yard until she found Malcolm.

He tried to stare her down, tried to hide the truth. After only a minute or two, he bowed his head. "He nearly found her a few times," he said. "Good thing shifters are easily distracted." He looked around at the curious faces. "I threw him a bone."

Linus snickered. He always loved his brother's warped sense of humor no matter what the circumstance.

"What does that even mean?" Rayne was annoyed at his attempt at humor.

He cleared his throat. His form of apology in a tense situation. "I usually sent him in another direction. This one time, though—"

"Look, I don't care about the specifics." Dyre cut him off.

"Why send Simon? If you knew where she was, why not just kill her yourself?" Beni stared daggers at Farryn.

"Contrary to popular belief, witches don't enjoy killing people. Do I have the capability? Of course I do. Do I have the inclination? Absolutely not. I don't want to kill anyone. Shifters, on the other hand, are born killers. You should know that." Farryn returned Beni's scowl.

"How the hell would I know anything about shifters?"

"Aren't you one and the same? Didn't shifters come from some twisted form of cold blood?"

"You have no idea what you're talking about." Beni looked at her like she was crazy.

Beni and Farryn frowned at each other. Beni could feel the energy building around the Phoenix and could smell the electricity sparking between her fingers. She looked at her hands and instinctually grabbed for the dagger strapped to her waist.

"Sit down," Dyre demanded. "Both of you. It doesn't matter who called who. Farryn called Simon. I frayed Oriana's thread. None of this matters now."

"How did you come to find Mia?" Rayne directed her interest towards Beni.

"Honestly, I'd like to know that too," Gail added.

Beni shifted uneasily in her seat as all eyes turned to her. "Asher said he got a call. Wouldn't tell me who it was but he was being paid handsomely to kill Oriana Duran." She shrugged. Her mouth twisted with doubt. "I had one foot out the door at that point. The life wasn't as thrilling as it used to be. He offered me half to help him."

"And?" Malcolm urged.

"And she was already dead when we got there. Not more than a few hours but still dead. Mia was screaming her head off with a full diaper. Ash wanted to kill her. I mean, she was a witch, which usually was a good enough reason for him, but he also had this thing about wasting his time. He was there to kill Oriana and since he got cheated out of that, he needed to kill something."

"You protected Mia, a witch?" Rayne found some cosmic satisfaction in a witch hunter protecting a witch.

"I protected an innocent child. She didn't deserve to die just because her parents were rubbish." She didn't look at anyone after she spoke.

"It's strange," Gail said, finally. "That you all chose to act at the same time. You called Simon. You frayed her cord. You took a job to kill a witch. What drove each one of you to want her dead at that particular moment in time?"

"We've always wanted her dead," Farryn said.

"Yeah, she had it coming for centuries." Beni shrugged.

"But you could have frayed her thread centuries ago. And you and Asher Delger could have hunted her down whenever. What happened that put a flame under your ass?"

"Mia," Farryn said.

"Yeah, I'd have to agree," Dyre chimed in. "When I heard Mia was born, I knew I couldn't leave her in that house with Oriana Duran. The woman was a lunatic."

"Is that why you hired Asher Delger? Sealing Beni's fate as Mia's mother?" Mararis whispered in her sister's ear.

Dyre looked to Gail, the only other one at the table who could hear Mararis, and smiled.

36

ELENA

The next day at Magnolia Academy, Elena looked at her watch. Nearly four thirty. She didn't smell anything cooking in the kitchen, and her stomach was rumbling.

"No dinner tonight?" She peeked her head into Linus's study.

He sat at his desk with his laptop open, his glasses perched at the end of his nose. His hair hung carelessly over his forehead, and she felt the desire to touch the curls. It was something she enjoyed doing, particularly after sex, and he was too sleepy to care. She'd bounce a curl on her finger like a spring, giggling as she did it.

"It's Lilly's birthday. Her mom took Starr, Veda, and Lilly out to a show and dinner. I think the girls are staying with her tonight. And considering what's been going on here, I didn't argue." He dropped his glasses on top of the keyboard, looking exhausted.

Elena nodded. It was a jab at her weaknesses that she didn't appreciate.

"No, it's not." He frowned, reading her thoughts. "I'm just glad to have a quiet house tonight. That's all. The house spirits are calm, which means Oriana is hiding in her hole somewhere. Kim didn't feel like cooking. We'll probably order in."

"Where's Milly?"

"With Farryn." He gauged her reaction. "And before you freak out, it was my idea. They have some serious wounds to heal. Leave them be."

"Fine." Elena stalked out of the room in a huff.

The house was eerily silent without the girls chattering in their rooms or a television blaring in the media room. She looked in on Pierce as she passed his room.

"Hi." He offered her a thin smile. Their relationship had changed since his reunion with his mother. He pulled headphones from his head when he saw her. In his hands, he held a video game controller. "Need something?" He attempted to get up from his gaming chair when she stopped him.

"No, just checking in. It's just us tonight. Your dad, me, you, and Kim."

"Kim left." His eyes darted to the large television screen in front of him.

"What? When?"

"Like ten minutes ago."

"Did she say where she was going?"

"Nope, and I didn't ask." He slipped the headphones back on to let her know he was done with the conversation.

"I guess I'll take a bath. We can order food in about an hour. How does that sound?" She smiled, hoping to keep Pierce on her side. She knew it was a lost cause.

"Yeah, whatever." His attention had already diverted back to his game, leaving her a distant memory.

Elena returned to her bedroom to collect the items necessary for a relaxing bath. A few candles, music, and the foamiest bubble bath she owned. As she shifted bottles on her makeup table, Tera's and Mararis's necklaces vibrated as she pushed them out of the way.

They sat on her vanity for the last two days, unperturbed. She neither had the care nor the inclination to touch them or use them. Seeing them, in her current mood with everyone either ignoring or shunning her, Elena picked them up.

The vibration tingled into her fingers and up her arm. She wondered if she held them and whispered the Sisters' names, would they answer her? She wondered if she returned the power to the orb, could she transfer the power to herself?

It was Oriana who craved the entire power of the three sisters. Elena would have been happy with a fraction of that power. She would have been happy if her family would have accepted her with the limited abilities given to her at birth.

She carried the pendants into the bathroom. She knew she'd never give in to that kind of thinking, but feeling their purr in her palm calmed her. She laid them on the edge of the tub as she filled it.

Ten minutes later, Elena slipped into a piping hot bath, bubbles six inches deep. Her muscles relaxed. Her mind wandered. She fell asleep.

The forest twisted around them like a blanket in a fever dream. It welcomed them and then sent them in all directions until they didn't know how to get out. It squeezed their bodies so tight they lost their breath.

Bits of sunlight peeked through the canopy of branches, and knotted roots waved in their path like an angry ocean.

Up ahead, twelve-year-old Camilla laughed as she ran, darting behind trees and diving through vines. Ahead of her, her cousins, Farryn and Micah, yelled for her to keep up. Elena trailed, struggling and lagging behind.

The wind burned her cheeks, making them red and sore. She hadn't noticed this until now. Her long brown hair caught on brambles as she left the path, cutting the distance between her and her cousins. Elena's legs tired and her heart pounded in her chest.

In her mind, she heard her mother caution her sister, "Keep an eye on Elena."

Camilla stopped dead. Her bare feet, black from mud and forest debris, slid in the dirt. She looked around, listening to the forest. The birds in the distance. Her cousins ahead of her, laughing.

"Leny," she called. "Leny, where are you?"

Elena didn't answer.

"She'll get lost," her mother reminded her this morning. "She'll lose herself in the woods."

Elena sat amongst the trees. The forest felt alive around her. Unseen creatures scurried, snapping branches as they ran. Leaves rustled; birds called from above.

"Leny!" her sister cried out. "Answer me."

Footsteps crunched in the fallen leaves.

"Mil? Are you coming?" Farryn stood on the path close enough to see but far away from her.

"I've lost Leny." Camilla wore her loss on her face, worry and panic darkening her expression.

Farryn stood with her hands on her hips, always acting as an adult when there weren't any around. Her toe tapped. From where she sat hidden in the overgrowth, Elena could see her foot moving in the leaves.

"Leave her. She can't ever keep up. Just leave her." Farryn turned away and disappeared over the embankment.

Elena watched as Camilla turned again to where she'd come from and realized in her harried sprint to join her cousins, she didn't know from what direction she'd come. Elena could be anywhere.

"Leny," she called at the top of her lungs, until her throat ached.

Elena refused to answer. If she answered, she would be forced to join Farryn in one of her ridiculous games. Games she could not participate in. Magic games. She preferred the warmth of the sun and the acceptance of the trees.

"Mil." Farryn's voice seemed to be carried by the wind.

Elena watched her sister pull her hair ribbon from her head and tie it to a branch, knowing when Elena saw it, she would know she was on the right path. As she tied it to the branch, she whispered her sister's name into it. It would continue to call out to Elena, guiding her in the right direction. With one last look behind her, she ran to catch up with her cousins.

The ribbon called to her. She could feel her sister's untrained yet strong magic surrounding her. Elena walked to the tree where her sister had tied her ribbon and pulled on it. As it fell into her hand, she lifted it and allowed the wind to take it.

As her sister and cousins reached the cliffs, Elena looked at the sky. Clusters of birds swarmed above them, screaming and darting in and out of the trees.

Micah watched the birds. He took in every movement and sound. He studied the circular flight patterns and watched as they seemed to speak to each other. Farryn paid them no mind. She set off to collect branches and rocks. She wouldn't deviate from her purpose.

"Milly," he called. "Look."

A group of blackbirds continued to shriek in the sky. They dipped and chased each other and then dove into the trees. One bird, the largest one, held a ribbon in its talons. Camilla's ribbon.

She bent down to pick up a rock and threw it with great force at the bird. She missed. She bent for another one.

"What are you doing? Stop." Micah ran at her. He forced the stone from her grasp.

"They have my ribbon. That was for Leny to find." She bent for the stone again.

"No," he yelled at her, knocking another stone from her hand. "They found her."

Camilla stared at the damnable crows as they circled overhead. She heard movement in the brush, and she kept her eyes on both the trees and the sky. It made her dizzy. A moment later, her sister pushed her way through the overgrowth, tripping on roots and dodging tree branches. Her dress, her legs, and her face were muddy. She held her apron out as she carried something.

"Leny," Camilla shouted. She ran to her. Micah followed. Camilla threw her arms around her.

"Careful." Elena pulled away.

"What have you got there?" Micah plucked two mushrooms from her apron and tossed one to Camilla. "Mushrooms." He attempted to pop one into his mouth.

"Don't eat it." She grabbed his hand.

"Why not?" He sniffed it and tossed it back in her pile.

"They're poison."

"Why did you pick poisonous mushrooms?" Camilla dropped hers on the ground and wiped her hand on her sister's apron.

"Magic. Aunt Junie told me where to find them, and she's going to show me how to use them. These are the biggest I've ever seen." Elena beamed with excitement. She held one up in the sunlight. "There's a patch of clover at the bottom of the hill. And I found a fairy circle…"

"You didn't disturb it, did you? To get your ridiculous mushrooms." Farryn appeared before them. Her hair was littered with leaves like she was rolling on the forest floor, and sticks were cradled in her arms.

"I'm not senseless. I know not to…"

A knocking at the bathroom door awakened her.

"Elena?" Linus poked his head into the bathroom. "Did you fall asleep?"

A wave of dizziness washed over her as she tried to stand. Linus caught her with a towel in hand.

"Are you alright?"

"Yeah. Fine," she lied.

She wasn't fine. She felt small. Weighted down. She could feel herself being pushed down and she fought it. Like trying to lift an arm underwater, a force held her back. Her body felt like the ocean. She struggled and kicked to reach the surface. She swam, but it felt as if her legs were tethered. It drained her, all this fighting. The faintness was the result. If Elena stopped fighting, she knew Oriana would take hold.

She just couldn't maintain her hold much longer, and there was no way to let Linus know.

"Here's your robe." He wrapped it around her shoulders. "Want to order tacos?"

"I could think of something much better to eat." She heard the words, knew they were coming from her mouth, but it wasn't her who said them. *What the hell did Oriana think she was doing?* she thought.

"Having some fun before I kill his wife," Oriana told her.

"Stop it. He's mine. Not hers or yours to play with. Hands off." Elena couldn't believe her nerve, but Linus was off-limits. There was no way she'd allow Oriana to manipulate him.

"Imagine sleeping with another Brenig man after all these years. My heart is all a tingle, as well as other places." Oriana was just as unscrupulous in death as she was in life.

"Pierce is still home." Linus slowly closed the bathroom door.

"He's busy with his game. We'll be quiet." She reached up to kiss him. Her tongue forced its way into his mouth as it rolled with his. Her fingers touched the necklaces lying on the edge of the tub.

As the robe hit the floor and she pressed against Linus naked, Elena struggled to communicate with him. She screamed his name. She fought the pressure Oriana used to keep her drowning.

Her hands, controlled by Oriana, unbuttoned his pants. Her fingers clawed through his hair, rougher than usual. He noticed her ferocity and ignored it.

Elena swam like her life depended on it. She reached the surface for only a moment. She pushed Oriana away, down into the depths. "Linus, don't do this..."

She only managed to say four words before Oriana's fingers closed around the amulets. That warm, pulsing purr felt like a sudden jolt as she held them firm in her fist. Elena felt the water close around her again, and everything went black.

PART THREE

THE BEGINNING OF THE END

SEPTEMBER 9

288

36

APRIL

The next day, after spending the day lying around on the couch and binge-watching TV shows, Dyre threw April out of the house.

"If you're going to waste the day away, you could at least help me out. Go pick your sister up at school." Her mother sat at the kitchen table, trying to decipher the scribblings in Oriana Duran's grimoire. She hoped to find a way to keep Elena out of Oriana's clutches and possibly find a reason for Oriana's madness. She hadn't found anything after hours of searching.

April called Mia and headed for Lucy's school on foot.

"Why are we walking?" Mia groaned. Her dark hair was pulled back in a plastic clip, and she wore an oversized hoody and sweatpants.

"My mom told me to take my time. I think she's sick of me hanging around the house."

"We could take Lulu to Raven's Corner after we get her from school."

"Yeah, maybe." April turned her phone on and off, looking disappointed.

"New phone?"

"Yeah, Linus got it for me. I've been texting him and he's not answering." She shrugged.

Lucy was thrilled to walk home with her sister and her cousin. She was even more thrilled to experience Raven's Corner. It was a store that her mother refused to let her enter, and she was dying to know why.

She skipped ahead of her sister, dragging her backpack on the ground as she went. They walked over the bridge into the large, spacious park. People walked dogs, jogged, rode bicycles, and children played in the playground. The afternoon air had a chill to it, reminding everyone that summer would soon be a distant memory.

"Can I swing for a little while?" Lucy asked her sister.

"I thought we were going to Raven's Corner?" Mia asked.

"Just for a little while. Please." She dragged out the *please* for almost a full ten seconds.

"Yeah, go ahead." April didn't care either way. She just knew she needed to keep an eye on her little sister.

Leaving her backpack at her sister's feet, Lucy bolted toward the swings littered with three or four other kids around her age. April watched Lucy wave to one girl and stand shyly in front of her grandmother. The woman bent towards her, asked her questions, and then looked around for April. The woman waved and she waved back. Mrs. Stekel had been teaching in the Forest Lake school system for as long as April could remember. She'd keep a close eye on Lucy and her grandchildren.

April walked towards the lake with a large fountain in the center. Pulling out her phone, she texted her mother. *At the park for a bit. Be home soon.*

Her mother's response was immediate. *I want your eyes on Lulu the entire time.*

She sent an okay emoji and slipped her phone into her back pocket. "Still nothing. I hope he's okay. I'm getting a strange feeling, yah know?"

"Like the one you got the day we read that spell?"

"Kind of." April looked like she'd eaten a large, juicy beetle. Her face soured.

"Maybe we should go home." Mia searched for Lucy in the crowd of kids. On the far end of the park, a man stood with his hands in the pockets of his jacket as he stared at Lucy.

"There's a strange guy over there."

"Which guy?" April didn't look at her. She checked her phone again. "Can you text your dad and see if he's heard from him?"

"Who?"

"Linus," April snapped at her. "Who do you think I'm worried about?"

"Obviously not the man staring at your sister."

April searched the area. "That's just Micah. Who cares about him? Lucy can see him. If he gets too close, she'll scream." She looked away from her phone and found Micah standing only feet from Lucy. His serene face was transfixed on her as she laughed with her friends. He seemed to be mesmerized by her energy and ability to flip her body over her head with ease. "Wait, how can you see him?" April's mouth hung open.

"I don't know. I couldn't see him before. I can't see Oriana Duran or your aunts. Do you think that transmigration thing did something to me?"

"I can't see my aunts either." April shrugged. "Maybe we should go home." April called to Lucy as Micah approached her.

"Why are you here?" April asked Micah.

"Keeping an eye on Lulu," he said.

"Katie and Mrs. Stekel are leaving. Can I play with Micah for a while?" Lucy ran to her sister.

"No, we should get home."

April looked to where Micah was standing.

"What are you staring at?" Mia felt uncomfortable being able to see Micah.

"Ah, there's the Brenig charm," he joked.

Lucy giggled. "Can she hear him?"

"She can see him too. Why can she see you now? Do you know?" April asked Micah.

"Compliments of the Phoenix," he said. *"She couldn't sleep last night. My dear sister worries about people. It's her weakness. She thought if you could see the other side, if only for a day or two, it would keep you safe."* Micah smiled. *"Has it helped?"*

"I don't know. You're the first ghost I've seen."

"That's disrespectful." Micah stepped away from her.

"I'm sorry. I didn't realize calling you a ghost was bad."

After leaving the park, the three girls walked down Main Street towards Raven's Corner. Lucy lagged behind, walking beside Micah. She marveled as he did sleight-of-hand tricks for her entertainment.

When they reached the intersection of Main and Maple, April looked down the street towards Magnolia Academy. Mia looked in the opposite direction towards Raven's Corner, hoping to catch her father coming from or going into the store.

"Looking for your dad?" April asked her.

"Yup. You?"

"Yup." April's mouth twisted. "I'm still worried about him."

"I thought we were going to Raven's Corner?" Lucy whined.

April looked at Mia. "I just want to see if he's home. Do you mind?"

"We shouldn't go this way." Lucy searched the area, feeling unsafe. "April, this is a bad idea." Her voice shook with fear.

Ignoring her, they turned the corner at the light and walked up Maple Drive.

"Looks kind of sad," Mia said as they stood in front of Magnolia Academy. "Well, what are you waiting for? Go knock, so we can get out of here. I'm getting a creepy feeling standing here."

The curtains in the front room moved.

"Someone's in there," April said. "Maybe it's him?"

"It's not Daddy." Lucy grabbed her sister's hand.

"I think it's Elena." Mia could just make out the outline of a woman standing behind the sheer curtains.

"I think you're right," Micah agreed.

April felt a sudden jolt of fear streak across her chest and up her neck. "We should go."

The front door of the school swung open as Mia was about to agree. Elena stood on the front porch. The silver streak in her hair glowed in the sunlight. In her hands dangled the two necklaces, and the healed burn on April's hand began to throb.

Lucy pulled at April's hand, dragging her away from the house. She didn't say anything. She only urged her sister to leave with a stern tug. Micah stepped up in front of them, blocking Elena—though she could not see him.

"Go to Raven's Corner. Get Malcolm," he ordered them.

Lucy ran first and April followed. Mia stood frozen in place.

"That's my mother," she whispered.

A flash lit up the porch, and Lucy screamed.

37

AT RAVEN'S CORNER

Chaos surrounded Dyre as she entered the store. April fell immediately into her arms, crying. There were no thoughts or words coming from her. Her mind was a jumble of chaotic images that included fire and screaming.

Beside the door, Linus held Lucy, looking as if he had been dragged up a chimney. Black dirt, blood, and water covered his white shirt. His usually calm face was frozen in an expression of bewilderment and confusion.

Micah stood beside her, having appeared in her kitchen to deliver the bad news only ten minutes ago. On the floor, Malcolm bent over someone.

"We need to move her." Iris was in the mess of backs that Dyre could see from the storefront. Opal's face was pale. Rayne kept a safe distance from the pack while still watching it unfold with great interest. Lucy held tight to her father. She was on the verge of tears as she watched the scene before her.

The pack began to move.

Iris raced to pull open the curtain. She pushed the tarot table and chairs out of the way and pulled open the door to the upstairs rooms. The pack turned and opened, revealing Malcolm with a body in his arms. A gasp caught in Dyre's throat as she saw what she already knew was true. The blackened, bloody body he was carrying was Mia. Dyre moved to the side without speaking; she could feel her body vibrating with fear.

Rayne followed Malcolm and Iris upstairs without looking back.

Dyre turned to Linus with tears in her eyes. His blurry visage mirrored hers. "Where's Pierce?" Her voice was barely a whisper.

"Farryn's." He leaned his forehead against Lucy's and closed his eyes. "I need to call her. Tell her what's happening."

"The Phoenix? Really? That's who you're concerned with right now? Your niece is burnt to a crisp and you care about preserving your connection to that ridiculous coven? That could have been one of your daughters. She could have…" Dyre stopped, holding back the tears. "She could have killed them," she whispered.

"I know. Don't you think I know? Don't you think I blame myself for all of this?" He took a shaky breath and buried his face in the crook of Lucy's neck.

"Don't cry, Daddy. She wouldn't have killed us. She only wanted to kill Mia." Lucy placed her small hands on his face.

"Lulu, how do you know that?" Dyre crouched beside her daughter at Linus's feet.

"She said it."

"Who said it?" Linus was inches from her as he spoke.

"The lady inside." Lucy pointed to her chest.

Linus looked at Dyre. "Elena. She must be reaching out from *inside*. Did she say anything else?"

"Just for me to run away. She said when Mia was dead, I was next." She turned to face her mother. "Why does the mean lady want to hurt Mia?"

"She's looking for a vessel." Rayne came out of the bedroom and walked into the store. "When the transmigration failed, Oriana, in her infinite ignorance, believed if Mia was dead, she would have a better shot at taking over her body."

"You can't reinhabit a dead body." Linus looked at her like she was crazy.

"I know that, and you know that, but Oriana Duran is desperate right now. She'll try anything, even if it means killing her own daughter to get it." Rayne handed Linus a wet cloth to clean the soot from his face.

"So, what happened?" Dyre asked.

"We were walking home from the park." April spoke through tears and uneven breaths. She wasn't making clear sense. "I had a strange feeling that something wasn't right with Linus. I just wanted to make sure he was alright. That's all. I just wanted—then Elena came out of the house and Micah told us to run." Dyre pulled Lucy from Linus's arms and held her as April was fused to her side, still crying.

"Are you in need of assistance?" Rayne centered on Linus, who looked okay, just a little singed. He held his hand up to say he was fine.

"How is Mia?" Dyre found her voice was failing her, and she could feel a cough bubbling up in her throat.

"Malcolm is tending to her. With our mixed talents, that child will survive. I will not face Bentyn Rae with the corpse of her daughter in my hands." Rayne's voice shook with fear. "You don't look well. Can I get you tea or water, perhaps?" Rayne touched Dyre's arm.

"Drink this." Opal snuck up behind Rayne and shoved a cup into Dyre's hands.

"Thank you." She sniffed it. It smelled fruity. Dyre didn't have much say in drinking. Opal waited until she emptied the cup and then took it back.

"Better?"

Dyre looked at Rayne and then back to Opal. "I suppose." She really did feel better. Her lungs felt lighter and the shortness of breath she'd been experiencing wasn't so short.

Opal nodded with pleasure and disappeared into the adjoining room without another word.

Rayne and Dyre exchanged confused looks.

"How did this happen?" Rayne folded her arms over her chest and centered her attention on April. "That fire that ravaged your friend's body was not natural fire. I can smell that much. Where did it come from?"

Linus looked up at them, dumbfounded. "Oriana's in control."

Fifteen minutes ago, Mia couldn't move. Linus carried her, she knew that much. Not because she could see him (she could barely open her eyes) but because Lucy kept crying, "Daddy, is she going to live?" Mia could hear the quick pitter-patter of her sneakers as she tried to keep up.

Now as she lay in bed, Malcolm hovered over her, giving her water to sip, and touched her brow with a warm, wet towel. Opal administered a drink that made her burns crust over, and even that intimidating Rayne Grey whispered foreign words that allowed her to breathe easier.

"Can I see her?" It was Aunt Dyre.

"Sure." Malcolm didn't speak louder than a whisper.

"I can't do a lot." Dyre choked back tears. "But I can do this for you, my dearest Mia." She bent and kissed her forehead. A rush of icy air washed over Mia, taking away the searing pain that covered her body. "Rest easy. I'll have your mom here the minute she wakes." She kissed her again and held her hand without speaking.

She thought of the scene at the school. Not April screaming at her to run. Not Linus fighting with Elena. Mia thought of Oriana Duran. When the front door of Magnolia Academy for Magical Arts opened, Oriana Duran stepped out onto the porch. This new ability to see spirits was unnerving.

She wondered if everyone else saw Elena Nolan standing in the doorway. Mia only saw her biological mother.

Dressed in a lovely flower-print white dress, she smiled at Mia. She waved to her to come closer, and Mia saw the two necklaces swinging from her outstretched hand. Her large toothy smile looked like something out of a horror movie, and Mia could not move.

Linus followed Elena out onto the porch. He looked dazed as he stumbled out the door. They fought. April screamed and Lucy cried. Linus shook Elena while Oriana stared at Mia, unfazed.

As Oriana lifted Elena's hand, Linus's eyes doubled in size. He wrapped his hands around Elena's shoulders and threw her to the ground.

It was too late. A blast of light blinded Mia, and she could feel heat surrounding her body. Linus ran to her. He knocked her onto the lawn, trying to snuff out the flames.

"Micah says to use water." Lucy's piercing voice broke through the chaos.

Mia threw her head back on the pillow and stared at the ceiling. "How long until Mom comes?" she croaked at Malcolm.

He held a glass of water to her lips. He looked at the clock. "Soon. Dyre just left for your house."

"Do you think Mom will kill Elena now?" The water did little to soothe her sore throat.

"If she doesn't, I will." His handsome face looked sad. There was no anger, only sadness. "She can't continue to channel Oriana and hurt you. This ends tonight."

"I was supposed to help. To be part of the Circle." If her eyebrows were still intact, they would have arched with despair.

"Don't worry about anything. You just rest." He touched the tip of her nose with the lightest touch that she didn't think he really touched her at all.

"I love you, Dad." Her voice rasped like sandpaper on metal as she closed her eyes.

He smiled. "I love you too."

38

BENI

Beni rolled over in bed, knowing what needed to be done tonight. She stretched out her arm, feeling the emptiness on the opposite side of the bed. Maybe today would be a good day to stay in bed, she thought.

"You couldn't be more right about that."

That sounded like Dyre, she thought.

"It is me. Wake up."

This can't be good.

"Get up. Mia's hurt."

Beni sprang out of bed. She hadn't bothered to change into comfortable sleeping attire. She wore the same jeans she had yesterday and the same tee shirt that read *My daughter is a witch.* Mia bought it for her made-up birthday last year.

"Where is she?" She didn't stop to talk with Dyre but sped into the hallway, calling for her daughter. Mia wasn't there. Beni knew this the moment she stepped out of her bedroom. "Where is she?"

"Raven's Corner."

"What happened?" She could feel the heat rising in her cheeks. Her fingers moved in and out of a fist. "Oriana, again?"

"Yes." Dyre remained in her bedroom. "Mia needs you right now, so I won't tell you any more or you'll go on a killing spree. Just come with me."

The drive to Raven's Corner didn't take more than five minutes, yet Beni wished she had run it. She was sure she would have gotten there quicker. The moment Dyre's car turned down Perry Lane, Beni opened the car door and jumped out.

"Where's my daughter?" she shouted. She tore the door off its hinges as she entered the witch shop and let it hang from the top hinge that kept it from shattering on the cement sidewalk.

Linus was the first to approach her. His messy hair and sooty shirt told her that Mia had set something on fire. "Mia is upstairs…"

He tried to explain further, but she pushed him aside and bolted for the door beyond the curtain.

Pushing past a few tables, she managed to take one down in her rage, throwing crystals and a few decks of tarot cards flying into a candle display. She didn't stop to assess the damage but continued her rampage through the tarot reading room. The curtain tore as she pushed it out of her way.

Iris followed her, whimpering about the destruction and broken merchandise.

The door opened as she approached it. Rayne Grey stood between her and Mia, and there was no way she could allow that.

"She's resting."

"Move," Beni barked.

"I just want to warn you. Right now, she looks bad. That's the healing process. Don't freak out."

"Move or I'll move you."

Rayne held her hands up and stepped aside.

Beni took the stairs four at a time, flying up like she had wings. Before she entered the room, she smelled burnt skin, and her heart sank. It smelled like an electrical burn, much like when Oriana Duran's amulets burned April's hand. She stepped into the room without speaking.

Malcolm stood over Mia with a cloth in his hand. He was swabbing her forehead with cool water as he spoke words in a foreign tongue that Beni only vaguely remembered hearing centuries ago. Five candles were lit in different places, and incense burned too.

"Mom?" Mia saw her. Her voice was raspy and broken.

"Baby, what did they do to you?" Beni sank down beside the bed, afraid to touch her daughter.

Her skin was raw and flaking. Her face was puffy and swollen. Patches of dry, broken skin covered her body. She tried to lick her lips, but her tongue was dry too.

"Do you have water?" Beni looked at Malcolm.

"Right beside you."

She held the glass of water to her daughter's lips, urging her to drink. Mia took a little and stopped. "Mom."

"Don't speak." She touched Mia's lips with her fingers. "Leave," she said to Malcolm.

"No," he said without a hint of fear.

"I want to be alone with my daughter."

"I know what you intend to do, and I won't allow it." He stood straight and crossed his arms over his chest.

Beni's laugh sounded caustic. "I don't remember asking for permission. Leave or I will kill you and give it to her anyway." She fixed him with a combative stare.

"And what good will that do? You think you're saving her, but you'd be hurting her."

"What do you know about it?" She dragged her hand over Mia's singed hair. It felt dry and brittle; clumps were missing in places over her head.

"Plenty. It will kill her." Malcolm stared her down.

"You know so little about blood therapy, I doubt that is true."

"There is a sizable amount of divine energy in her system right now. Your blood is pure energy. Did you know that?" He raised an eyebrow as he lectured her. "Pouring it into her system, especially *your* blood, could cause an overload and kill her. Also, she's a firestarter." Again, he waited for a response, but it was clear that he didn't want one. "As a firestarter, the fire that burned her wasn't natural. It may have shorted out her natural abilities. Adding something equally unnatural to her system could be catastrophic."

He turned. He walked to the pitcher on the dresser and filled another glass of water for Mia.

"May I try?" Farryn Allard stood at the head of the stairs. Dressed in a long broom skirt, flowers in her hair, carrying a drawstring bag and wearing dangly jewelry, she looked as mystical as a witch could get. She held her sandals in her hand as she swept across the room. When she got to Mia, she placed her shoes on the floor and kneeled beside her. "We're going to need some privacy and have Iris draw a bath."

"May I speak to my daughter before you turn her into a toad?"

"Yeah, because that's what we do. We wicked witches just love our toad potions," Farryn snapped back. "I can't believe the world isn't just overrun with them by now."

"Ladies, let's remember why we're here." Malcolm stepped up. "Beni, hurry up and say what you want to Mia. We've got a date to kill a witch. I'll have Iris draw a bath."

Beni told Mia she loved her repeatedly, until it was Mia who told her to leave with a smile. She met Malcolm at the bottom of the stairs. They shared a look of fear, anger, and defeat that only parents feel when their children are in danger.

Beni stood outside the bedroom door, listening to Farryn's calming voice as she spoke in the same foreign tongue she'd heard from Malcolm a few minutes before. A bell rang and the smell of incense filled her nostrils. In some distant room, she heard water running.

Every fiber of her body wanted to turn around and run up the stairs to her daughter. She wanted to hold her in her arms so tight that she would never feel unsafe again. She wanted to give her the blood that ran in her veins, the strongest blood she knew. She wanted to take Mia from these witches and hide her away.

"Are you ready?" she asked Malcolm.

"Ready for what?" It was Rayne. "To gather your rather large and scary collection of witch hunting tools and weapons?"

Beni's expression was a mixture of hatred and desperation. She had to do something. She couldn't allow this attack on Mia to go unpunished.

"What good will it do?" Rayne casually sipped a cup of tea as she waited for an answer that would never come. "You'll take a rope or mace or ax or even matches. You'll stomp over to the school and then what? Camilla has already gone to the school. She will have already fortified the walls with spells that *I* can't even break."

She studied Beni's body language and thoughts for only a moment before continuing. "You could break down the door. That is always an option, but I doubt you could. Go on and try. I'd love to see you flying through the air from a jolt so strong the heavens would quake. Or it could just simply turn you to ash. Either way, as much as I detest saying this, that young witch upstairs needs a mother right now. And you are not fit to kill a witch of Camilla's magnitude."

"I've done it before." Her voice wavered from stress and self-doubt.

"Have you?" Rayne's head twisted like an inquisitive dog. "By my count, you and your despicable spawn have murdered hundreds of weak or novice witches, one halfway decent one who had given up on her path…" She looked at Iris standing beside her. "Miranda," she explained.

Iris mouthed an *oh* and nodded.

"You are not capable, nor were you ever, of killing a witch as strong as Camilla Nolan."

"I don't plan on killing Camilla. Just her sister. Then returning those damn amulets to wherever they came from. And just for your information, if I can't stop Camilla, she can." Beni pointed to Dyre, who looked flabbergasted.

"So, you think she will simply step aside as you both disembowel her sister?" Rayne smirked.

"What's that?" Lucy asked in a hushed voice. Linus shushed her.

"Aunt Beni, I don't want Camilla hurt." April's voice shook. She was still visibly shaken by this whole ordeal.

"I second that," Linus spoke up.

"I just said I don't intend to kill her." Beni tried to retain her composure, but it was getting difficult with these people going on about their love for Camilla Nolan.

"Aunt Beni, is Mia okay?" Lucy gazed at her with large soulful eyes that she couldn't look away from. She sat on Linus's lap near the cash register. She'd give anything to hear a stupid vampire joke right about now.

"Thanks to you. I heard you put out the fire." Beni walked to Lucy and kissed her cheek. "Great job, Lulu." She raised her hand for a high five. "Without you, Mia could have died. You saved her life."

Lucy's face glowed. She looked at Linus and Dyre and then back to Beni with a light of pride beaming from her. "April pushed the mean lady."

"You did what?" Dyre's mouth hung open. Beni was equally amazed.

"When Lulu made it rain, I screamed. Elena went flying. It wasn't intentional. That's when we ran." April looked more embarrassed than proud as she recounted her part in the story.

"Well done. You're a badass with a temper, just like your mom." Beni smiled.

"Come on, let's go," Malcolm said. "Elena isn't going to kill herself."

"If words were wishes," Dyre mumbled.

The bedroom door opened, and Iris emerged.

"How is Mia?" Beni jumped. The need to hold her daughter was killing her inside.

"Bouncing back amazingly well. Farryn is putting her in the bath now. Her skin just drank in the cream she applied." A bright toothy smile stretched across her face. "To have that kind of power…"

Dyre breathed a sigh of relief, whispering thanks to the divine for their blessings.

Beni didn't want to think about anything besides Mia's recovery. But she knew part of Mia's recovery included taking those responsible to task.

"Do you have a safe room here?" Beni asked Iris.

"Any room I choose is a safe room," Rayne said. "The girls will be safe enough with us. Deal with this. Do not worry about your children."

As Dyre kissed both her daughters and reminded them to be careful, Beni handed April her car keys. "If anything happens, if anyone tries to break in here, take Lulu and Mia and run. Run to Haven or get in my car and go to Mount Orion. Gail will protect you."

April nodded, holding the keys like they were her lifeline.

39

MAGNOLIA ACADEMY

The walk to Magnolia Academy was a silent one. Linus and Malcolm led the way with Beni and Dyre behind them. They crossed the street together when the light changed, and no one paid them any attention.

The only thing that mattered was killing Elena Nolan. They followed the path to the porch and climbed the three steps to the door. Linus knocked. He couldn't feel or sense a barrier or a spell. There were no telltale signs that said he would be in trouble if he opened the door.

He tried the knob, and it turned. Looking back with a shrug, he stepped into the vestibule.

"Camilla?" He tapped his toe on the hardwood floor of the living room before entering.

"There's nothing, Linus. It is safe to enter." She sat on the sofa in the living room. A dark colored drink with ice cubes sat on the table next to her, and from the amount of condensation collecting on her antique end table, Camilla wasn't drinking it.

"How is she?"

"Resting."

"Is she herself or…"

"For now." Her voice was even and without emotion.

He'd seen her like this only once before, and it was just after she'd lost her baby daughter, Mary, ten hours after she was born. It frightened him then and it frightened him now. He opened the door and stepped out of the way for the others to enter.

Beni was the first one inside. "Where is she?"

Dyre was next, followed by Malcolm.

"Upstairs, resting."

Linus ran up the stairs, taking two at a time. He didn't look back at what was unfolding behind him. He didn't care. If he could talk some sense into Elena before Beni reached the second floor, he would consider this day a success.

Dyre grabbed Beni's arm before she followed him up the stairs. She shook her head, telling Beni not to go. "That's the room she protected."

"How is Linus getting in then?" Beni held her hand out towards the staircase.

"He's a witch." Dyre rolled her eyes. It seemed unbelievable to her that Beni still didn't fathom the power these individuals held in their grasp. After losing a significant chunk of her abilities to her daughter, Dyre found that she was jealous.

Camilla studied the movements of each visitor to her home and smirked. A mix of embarrassment and annoyance washed over her like a cool breeze, and she dropped her head with a deep eyeroll. "How's Mia?"

"Alive," Beni snapped. "Whose side are you on? Why are you protecting her?"

"I'm protecting my sister. Kill Oriana. I will gladly help with that, but leave Elena alone. She's a victim just as much as Mia."

"Don't you dare compare your sister to Mia. Elena has been a willing participant from the beginning. Mia is a victim. She didn't ask for Oriana Duran as a mother. She didn't ask to be set on fire either," Beni shouted. She stewed for a moment. Pacing back and forth in front of the staircase, her hand held the dagger in her waistband with a firm grip.

"Where is Oriana Duran?" Dyre asked to the surprise of everyone in the room.

Camilla's eyes widened and sparkled with tears. She pulled her lips in and closed her eyes, allowing a few tears to spill onto her cheeks. "She's here, but I don't know exactly where. There's a hole somewhere that she crawls into that I can't access."

Upstairs, Linus touched Elena's bedroom door with the palm of his hand. The cool wood seemed to pulse with Camilla's magic. He could hear voices coming from the other side of the door, and he leaned an ear close enough to hear but giving a little distance, so he wasn't shocked.

He could hear Elena arguing. He knew the tone. The high pitch to her voice and the short, annoyed tone told him she was angry.

"Elena?" His hand still rested on the door. He knew any quick or sharp movements would send a shockwave of magic through his body and most likely throw him down the hall. With his hand on the door, he thumped with his palm. "Elena," he said again with more conviction.

No answer.

He wondered if she could hear through Camilla's magic. Was the spell keeping everything out including sound? Linus grasped the doorknob and turned without stopping. He always knew that a quick, even motion was better than stopping midway through and overthinking. The magic worked with even strokes. It abhorred sloppiness.

The door opened with the magic causing only a touch of stiffness in his arm muscles. He could feel it shoot up his arm and into his neck, but he held on without pause. If he hesitated, he knew it would throw him from the door.

"Elena, what are you doing?" He closed the door behind him.

She stood in the center of the room naked, staring at herself in the full-length mirror. The bruise April had caused was still a large blotch on her chest but showed signs of healing with the blue and purple hues fading into yellow around the edges. One hand touched the bruise, caressing it as if she was trying to seduce him. The other held the glass orb in which Oriana had collected Tera's and Mararis's power.

"Why do you have that?"

She held it up to the light and looked into it. "I thought it might come in handy. After what happened, I figured a visit from Dyre Crane would be unavoidable."

"You are not going to kill her." He spoke softly, knowing he wasn't addressing Elena now. "What you did to Mia was not okay. You know that, right?"

Elena turned her head towards him in a slow, calculated manner that confirmed his suspicions that it was Oriana who stood before him and not Elena. He wondered if Elena could hear anything that he was saying. He wanted to tell her he loved her and for her to fight. He wanted her to know they wouldn't let Oriana win.

"Linus, that daughter of yours is a strong one. Far stronger than I had expected, especially for one who is not the legacy. That's the

Brenig in her. After what happened between us today, I know Brenigs are passionate." She raised her eyebrows at him, hoping to elicit a reaction.

He looked revolted.

"Anyway, Malcolm's magic is quite impressive, as is yours. April has the best of you and Dyre inside of her. If I punished my Mia a little too harshly, perhaps your daughter would serve as a suitable substitute."

Linus sneered. "You did punish Mia too harshly, Oriana. She nearly died."

"Nearly? Well, perhaps I won't need your daughter after all. Was it your magic that saved her? No, it was Malcolm. He dotes on that little girl of ours. Would have been nice if he showed a little of that when I was alive."

He didn't answer. He could hear the footsteps on the stairs.

"They are coming," she whispered. "Better get ready." She placed the orb on the dresser and walked into the bathroom. She slipped on a long silk robe adorned with cherry blossoms. In the pocket were Tera's and Mararis's necklaces. "Step aside, Linus. I have work to do." She held her hand up, but instead of using the amulets to kill him, she pushed him aside until he was thrown on the bed.

He knew then she was more in control of the amulets than they were of her.

Dyre, Beni, and Malcolm followed Camilla upstairs.

Camilla stood in front of her sister's bedroom door. "I'll knock first and then unlock it. She's probably sleeping." She held a large skeleton key in her hand.

"I don't hear Linus. Maybe he didn't get in." Beni leaned closer to the door to listen.

"No," Camilla sighed. "Linus knows ways around my magic. He always has."

"We all did," Malcolm whispered to Beni.

Camilla knocked in a kind of code and whispered a word or two before slipping the key into the lock. Dyre had been right. Camilla hadn't protected the whole house; she only protected this one room.

"Leny, are you awake?" she whispered.

When she swung the door open, the bed was empty. Camilla walked in first, and Malcolm followed. Dyre put her hand out to block the door, keeping Beni from entering. She didn't explain or speak; she simply blocked her. Beni pushed past her.

"Leny?" Camilla called again.

Linus lay on the floor beside the bed, writhing as if he were bound, but she could see no restraints. Dyre rushed to him. With considerable concentration, she waved her hand over him in a slow scanning manner. Once he was free, Linus grabbed Dyre and threw her to the floor.

The bathroom door swung open, and Elena stood holding the pendants out in her right hand. The bathrobe she wore hung open as she approached the group.

Just as Linus pushed her to the floor, Dyre saw another person superimposed on top of Elena. A woman with long dark hair that hung in waves around her shoulders, and what little she could see looked like Mia. Oriana Duran.

A flash of light took them all by surprise, hitting Malcolm first. He dodged a direct hit by throwing himself to the floor. The magic tore through his shirt and burned his arm. Camilla screamed as another flash lit up the room. She flew across the room. Her body slammed against Elena's dressing table and folded on the floor.

Beni ran at Elena, fast enough to take her off guard for only a moment. She wrapped her arms around her and drove her fangs into her shoulder.

Elena screamed. She closed her fist around the pendants and allowed the power to fill her body. Electricity shot through Elena's veins and into Beni. She was thrown into the bathroom, breaking the sink and the mirror as she collided with them. Beni lay dazed on the floor, covered in broken porcelain pieces.

"Where's Dyre?" Linus shouted above the chaos. Elena moved into the bedroom, looking around frantically.

"I'm here," she whispered.

Dyre appeared behind Elena, rallying what little power she possessed. The seconds moved slowly and just as she raised her hands, Elena swung around. Her mouth dropped open as she saw Dyre's body.

Her hands looked like a fireworks light show. Her fingers pulsed in and out like she was fingering a baseball ready for the pitch. She hadn't moved an inch from where she stood. When she raised her hands toward her, a wind kicked up in the room. Dyre's long auburn hair blew back from her face as her eyes locked on Elena. "You ruined my life. You took my family from me. You destroyed everything I loved."

The wind blew harder. Dyre's extended arms were laced with lightning and glowing with energy as it grew more intense. The balls of light in her hands sparked like they would explode.

Oriana looked at everyone around her indignantly. She didn't speak or try to defend herself. Her mouth hung open, trying to find a clever retort, but fear kept it from her. Beneath Oriana's overlay, Elena looked at her sister's body sprawled on the floor near her dresser.

The floorboards creaked as she took a single step back before Dyre screamed and hurled balls of energy at her. Her body vibrated as she stood frozen in place. A high-pitched, bloodcurdling scream filled the room.

Elena stood stiff and straight for only a minute before her skin blackened. It started in her limbs and then crawled up her face. Her body vibrated with electricity coursing through it, and a low, dull moan exited her mouth. It was the sound of a dying animal. Not will but gravity dragged Elena to her knees as her charred, smoking body collapsed. Her legs twitched convulsively before her body went completely still.

With no time to waste, Malcolm grabbed the glass orb from the dresser. One palm cradled the orb, while the other covered the top of it. He whispered words in an ancient language under his breath as smoke seemed to fill the orb. A soft vibration confirmed that Oriana was collected in the glass ball.

He tossed the orb to Dyre as she ran to Beni. Malcolm ran to Camilla. Linus, already on the floor, reached out for the blackened hand of Elena Nolan. A shot of electricity sped up his arms as he touched her, but he kept holding until the pain stopped.

"Are you alright?" Dyre said as Beni opened her eyes.

She looked up at her, then to the charred body on the floor just feet from where she lay. "Better than some." Beni rubbed the back of her head and sat up. "You haven't done that in centuries."

Dyre nodded. Her hands still shook. "I guess I should expect a visit from Atropos."

"Are my arms supposed to be tingling like this?" Beni asked.

"Considering the amount of divine power you just drank, you're lucky to be alive."

40

SAVING CAMILLA

A stillness hovered over the house. Linus lay weeping beside Elena's dead body. He held her until all of Dyre's magic had left her. He lifted her onto the bed and wrapped her in a sheet.

"Hang on." Beni stopped him before he could complete his task. "Has she still got those necklaces?"

He stared at her with despair and confusion.

She didn't wait for an answer and threw back the sheet, once again revealing the woman's charred remains. Wrapped around her wrist and fingers, the pendants were still nestled in her palm. With no care or respect for the dead, she yanked them from the corpse's hand, tearing it loose from her arm in the process.

A sob seemed to stick in his throat as Linus put his hand over his mouth. Beni threw the sheet back over Elena and walked away.

"These belong to you." She dropped them in Dyre's still shaking hands and left the room.

Malcolm followed her out of the room. "You can't leave."

"Watch me. My daughter needs me more than you do. I've done what I came for."

"Camilla needs help." He closed his eyes, not wishing to cry in front of Beni, but the tremble in his voice gave him away. "She's dying." His breathing sped as he fought the emotions that were about to overflow.

"I can't help with that," Beni found herself whispering.

He touched her wrist. "Please."

"You don't want my kind of help. You know you don't. She doesn't." She pointed to the room where Camilla lay dying and shook her head. "What do you want from me?"

"I don't want her to die." Tears filled his eyes as he continued to fight the emotion.

She watched him, feeling conflicted. Her brow lowered as she thought of reasons to refuse him. "Fine. But she needs to agree. I won't do this without her consent."

Beni went to Camilla. Her shaking hands lay on her chest where Malcom had placed them. Beni took them.

"Get out," she told Malcolm, Dyre, and Linus.

"Beni, you can't do this." Dyre stood in judgement over her. "This is wrong."

"Get her out of here. Go check on Mia." She didn't look at her friend but heard her arguing with Malcolm as he tore her from the room. Linus finished swaddling Elena like a makeshift mummy. He pulled back a few times as his fingers hit a bit of flesh that still sizzled with electricity and then slipped out of the room.

Short, uneven breaths made Camilla sound like she was crying when she was fighting for breath. She choked on blood in the back of her throat, and it seeped from the corner of her mouth. The weakness was something she was accustomed to feeling following any contact with a spell—the shortness of breath, inability to move her limbs, and the sluggish way her thoughts connected were all side effects of strong magic. Her immortality spell weakened in her mind. The darkness pulled at her like an undercurrent. She kept bobbing to the surface, only to be dragged back under again, helpless to stop it.

"What can I do?" Beni asked.

"You know what to do." Her voice cracked, and with what little strength existed in her body, she squeezed Beni's hand to ensure she understood.

"I must ask. Do you want the witch hunter or the blood drinker? They have very different skill sets."

Camilla thought about it. She stared at Elena's body lying on the bed. "I'm not ready to die."

Beni thought about it for a moment. She could hear every argument Dyre had given her over the years every time she chose to share her blood with someone. This was different. This was the first time she was saving someone by doing it. And a witch—if that wasn't redemption, she didn't know what was.

She bent over Camilla, smelling the death on her, and drove her fangs deep into her throat.

Before Camilla knew what was happening, Beni was all around her. Everywhere her lethargic gaze lolled, there she was. Thoughts of Elena were gone. There was only Bentyn Rae.

She felt Beni's teeth as they pushed deeper into the skin of her shoulder. She felt the blood rushing from her barely beating heart, from her veins and into her mouth. She felt Beni's heart as it pounded in her ears.

Her eyes rolled open. She was not in control of her body.

"Are you sure?" Beni pulled away for a moment as if to catch her breath, her mouth sodden with blood. Camilla could feel her intensity as she drank from her. "Are you ready?" Her voice banged around Camilla's head like a pinball.

"Yes," she hissed, eager to get it over with. Without the blood, only death awaited her.

Through a haze of weakness and increasing darkness, Camilla watched as Beni bit down on her forearm. The blood pooled on the surface immediately and she nearly jumped at it. Elena didn't matter. The Circle didn't matter. Camilla watched as Beni raised her arm to her mouth as she silently begged for it.

Beni took Camilla's face in her hand, pinching her slightly as she did it. Her voice was commanding, and Camilla found herself loving her tone and forcefulness as she told her to drink.

She obeyed.

Beni pushed her arm into her mouth. The blood was fluid and tasted sweet like the nectar of a ripe fruit. As it flowed into her system, she saw pictures like a giant movie screen had appeared in her mind. Flickering on the wall of a long-ago hotel room were pictures of a handsome man, of four handsome men. Camilla had no idea who any of them were. The pictures changed. There were images of burning witches in lines while crowds cheered. Looking out from within a cage surrounded by emaciated blood drinkers.

And finally, Beni with Mia as a baby. She saw a unique side of Bentyn Rae. The mother singing lullabies, feeding her infant daughter, changing diapers, playing pattycake.

So many thoughts and memories that were not her own, Bentyn Rae's memories. Through her blood, she shared a connection with her deeper than any magic; the blood was magic.

Camilla pulled harder on her arm until Beni resisted. Something was different in her body, something changed. A tingling in her fingers and toes, a numbness on her lips and tongue, and a feeling of floating that wasn't at all unpleasant. Electricity shot up her arms and legs. It fluttered in her chest as it seemed to awaken the dying soul that was ready to leave her only a few moments ago.

Her immortality spell slipped from her mind, replaced with the blood. Divine blood. Magical blood. Her head rolled on her neck as she opened her eyes. She lay in Beni's arms. Linus and Dyre were gone. She devoured every aspect of this woman's concerned face looking down on her. The iridescence in her eyes, the bounce in her long dark hair, the pale pallor that seemed to glow when she looked at her. Camilla reached out to touch Beni's face. Her fingers slid down her perfect skin, and she could feel the steel muscles of the capable arms that supported her.

"Can you stand?" Beni's voice sounded different to her ears. The hollow timber that always sounded like she was speaking through a microphone had disappeared.

Camilla wanted to touch her again. This time Beni grabbed her hand and laughed. "Come on. There is plenty of time to discover your new senses. Right now, we need to get a few things out of the way." She pushed her up so she was sitting without support.

When she sat up, the perfection of the moment ended. The scent of her sister's charred body filled her senses, and a deep churning in her stomach gave her pause. She raised her hand to her mouth. "I'm going to be sick," she managed to say before the bile forced its way to the back of her mouth. The fear that this was an allergic reaction to the blood swept through her and forced the vomit from her throat at a faster rate.

"This won't be pretty, but it will be over quickly." Beni laughed as she helped her to the bathroom. "You'll be here for a while. Consider the worst sickness you've ever endured and then multiply it by ten. You'll need a bath afterwards. I'll run one and lay out some clothes for you." Beni walked to the door and turned back. "You may also bleed." She pointed to her groin and grimaced playfully. "This change cleans out all the orifices."

Camilla thanked her as she placed her face in the toilet and vomited the contents of her stomach into the bowl.

Beni trudged down the stairs and turned into the sitting room. She wasn't ready to deal with the anguish she saw on the faces of the Brenig brothers. Linus didn't look up as she entered. He stared at the floor, twisting a piece of cloth in his fingers. Malcolm tended to the burn on his arm. He rubbed a salve on the wound through the tear in his shirt, and it was then Beni realized that it was his shirt Linus was mindlessly twisting.

Beni looked at Linus and then at Malcolm.

"How's Camilla?" he asked.

She glared at him, hating him for bullying her into turning Camilla. "She's having a moment with her sister."

Linus banged his fist against the end table, upending the picture frames on it.

"Camilla, I'm leaving," Beni called.

"Isn't she staying here?" Linus's voice sounded lost and hopeless.

"You have no place for her here. She has a lot to learn." She leaned around the newel post and looked up the stairs. Camilla stood at the top of the stairs looking down at her. She wore clean clothes and looked refreshed from the bath.

As she descended, Malcolm stared at her without speaking. His jaw dropped.

Camilla was always beautiful, but this transformation had increased it. Her movements were more fluid, her posture not so rigid, and she seemed relaxed—something Camilla rarely was. Reading everyone's thoughts easier than before, she smiled, showing her teeth for a brief second before pulling her lips over them, knowing they would upset everyone.

She waved his emotion away like it was insignificant. "I've anointed Elena's body and prepared her for her travels. I would like to…" She stopped, holding back a sob. "I would like to send her on her way with the appropriate memorial and festivity." She sniffed and dried her eyes.

"I'll notify the Board and make all the arrangements," Malcolm informed her.

"I'd like to keep it small but significant. She comes from a long lineage. She deserves to be honored. I've said my goodbyes. I doubt the Board will allow me to attend the service." She didn't look him in the eyes as she spoke and wiped the tears away when she finished speaking. She turned to look at Linus and saw the anguish in his face. He didn't speak or even look at her.

"Shall we get Mia? There is so much left to do tonight." Beni was exhausted. The smell of burning flesh infested most of the house, but below it, she could only smell four of them. There was no scent of ozone or static, and she knew Oriana was gone.

41

DYRE

Dyre walked into Raven's Corner, still feeling the tingling in her arms and hands. Her attempts to shake it off proved futile. Her sister's necklaces sat in her pocket, and she could feel a warmth emanating from them even through her jeans. She wasn't sure what she intended to do with them just yet but was grateful that her sisters' deaths had been avenged appropriately.

She held the smoky glass orb in her hand, feeling it purr just as the amulets did.

Seeing Elena Nolan drop to the floor, sizzling and black, was amazing. Even though her hands still shook, and she couldn't get the terror in Elena's eyes out of her mind, killing the woman that killed her sisters felt good.

She looked down at her right hand, trembling. She tossed the orb onto the counter. Taking her right hand with her left, she held it still. A shortness of breath bubbled up in her chest. A burning cough erupted, and she could feel the phlegm filling her throat. After she coughed, she felt better.

"I've mixed up some more." Opal appeared beside her with a cup in her hand.

Dyre took it and threw it back like a shot of whiskey. She felt better instantly.

"It's a bit stronger. I'm experimenting with the mix." Opal took the cup and walked away.

The necklaces burned Dyre's thigh. She pulled them out of her pocket and threw them on the counter beside the orb. A strange thing happened. They repelled each other. The orb seemed to push away from the amulets like the corresponding poles on magnets.

"I need to dispose of those properly, and I need to get this to Atropos." She spoke only to Farryn, who sat at the tarot table sipping tea. Micah sat beside her. "Is there something I can put them in until I figure it out?"

Rayne stepped into the room. "Of course." The look in her eyes told her she knew what happened even without the ability to read Dyre's mind. "Looks like we didn't need your sisters after all."

"Good thing because I haven't heard a peep out of them in hours." Dyre felt the exhaustion of the day wrap itself around her. She just wished to fall into bed and stay there for days. "Where are April and Lucy?"

"Upstairs with Mia."

Dyre nodded without speaking another word. She headed for the bathroom at the back of the shop. In the bathroom, she examined the burn on her leg. A red patch about the size of a quarter appeared on her upper thigh. She rummaged through the small medicine cabinet behind the mirror for ointment. She found nothing.

The light was dim, casting shadows on her already overwrought face. The circles beneath her eyes stood out like bruises, and her coppery hair looked dull and lifeless. The drink Opal gave her earlier didn't last long. She hoped this stronger blend was better.

Dyre ran the water until it was icy, holding her shaking hands under it until she felt nothing. No more tingling. No more tremors. She embraced the numbness.

When she returned to the sales floor, Farryn, Rayne, and Iris were arguing about something near the register area. Dyre looked at the three, reminded for only a second of when she and her sisters would stand and argue over ridiculous topics. She didn't wish to get dragged into their nonsense.

She headed upstairs.

"Well, you look better."

Mia sat on the bed, scrolling her phone like she hadn't been burnt just a few hours ago. Her long dark hair stuck out from her head, looking frizzy and sizzled. She looked up to Dyre with concern and fear in her eyes.

"I see you've finally acquired your Brenig hair." Dyre tried to keep the conversation light. She ran her hand over Mia's head, trying to flatten it. She looked around the room. "Where's April and Lulu?"

Mia pointed to the door, and then her pointer finger angled down.

"Are you okay?"

Mia only shrugged. Physically, she seemed fine. The burns were mostly healed. There were still a few pink patches on her face, neck, and arms. Her breathing sounded perfect, and her energy appeared strong.

Dyre kissed her forehead. "I'll be right back. I'll send your mother up as soon as she gets here."

Mia's eyes lit up at the mention of her mother, but her eyebrows still sloped with worry and her mouth pulled to the right as she fought tears.

As Dyre entered the tarot room, she saw the group of women had grown. Linus and Malcolm stood between Farryn and Rayne as they continued to argue as before. Micah stood to the side, watching. She looked at him.

"Your sisters' pendants are missing," he told her.

Farryn swung around to face Dyre. "You put them right here, correct?" She tapped her finger on the register counter.

"Yes. They were right next to the orb." Dyre looked at the others.

"The orb is still here." Farryn picked it up and immediately put it back down. She worked her fingers in and out of a fist and shook her hand out. "She doesn't like being in there."

"Check the floor. The orb was pushing itself away from the necklaces when I put them down. Maybe they fell on the floor." Dyre went behind the counter to check the floor. "Not here."

Malcolm huffed and pushed past the group to get to the bedroom door.

"She's not speaking," Dyre told him.

"That concerns me, but that could be the trauma," Rayne said.

He nodded and disappeared upstairs.

The door to Raven's Corner jingled, and Beni entered. Camilla stepped into the shop behind her. Mouths dropped open.

Farryn held back a scream by covering her mouth.

Camilla put her hands up. "Fae, be calm. In the melee, I was wounded. Bentyn saved me."

"Second time this week," Beni joked. "Is Mia upstairs?" She left the assembly to argue over the ridiculous topic of whether she should have let Camilla die tonight or not.

Farryn stomped into the tarot reading area. Her bare feet pounded the wood floor as she came face-to-face with Bentyn Rae, stopping her from seeing her daughter. Beni met her gaze, combatively.

"Fae, calm down," Camilla shouted at her.

"This is inexcusable. How dare you do this to her?" Her nose was inches from Beni's.

Beni smirked but didn't answer her. "You mean save her life?"

"Save her? Is that what you think you did?"

Beni laughed. Pulling on the door handle, it wouldn't budge. She knew the Phoenix was stopping her from opening it. "Let go." She kept her voice even, refusing to lose her temper.

"We're not done discussing this."

"Yes, we are. Now, remove your spell or whatever. I want to see my daughter." Beni stared her down.

"Let her go up, Fae. What the hell have you got to be so angry about? Did you lose your sister today? Are you an abomination of nature? Gee, in my estimation, that is Camilla two to Farryn zero." Camilla huffed again. "I feel like I'm floating. Is that normal?" She looked at Beni.

She nodded with a smirk. "And you're not an abomination of nature. Just differently abled." She gave one last glance to Farryn and went upstairs to see Mia.

"I lost my sister today. So, score one for the Phoenix." Farryn frowned.

"I'm right here. You just hate what I've become, and I get that. Believe me, I get that. But your anger is not helping anyone or anything." Camilla lowered her head as she felt the tears pushing to the surface.

"But—"

"No buts. I lost Leny today. I don't want to lose you too."

Farryn cried, sounding sniffly and relieved. She put her arms around Camilla and then pulled back in a sharp motion. "Oh, that magnetic thing. It's all over you."

"Yeah, apparently it's supposed to help me kill living things." She grimaced. "I don't think I can do that."

"Too late now," Iris laughed.

The group exhaled, and a chuckle worked its way through it.

"Enough of this warm fuzzy stuff," Rayne interjected. "We need to tear this store apart and find those necklaces."

"Where are April and Lulu?" Linus asked Dyre. His voice sounded sad and thick with emotion.

"Mia said they came downstairs a few minutes ago."

"I saw them playing around with the crystals. I shooed them away, but I thought they went back upstairs," Iris said.

"Where could they have gone?" Linus asked.

42

GAIL

Gail wandered from room to room in the cottage, hating the emptiness, the silence, and the echo of her own footsteps on the wood and tile floors. Her mother's voice was absent from her mind today. The constant commentary that encircled her last week had been silenced. When it was there, she hated it. Now that it was gone, she missed it.

Just as she thought it, she heard a car engine in the distance. Peering through the bay window, she saw Beni's Porsche come down the driveway. Gail's rigid shoulders deflated as she exhaled. Beni's timing couldn't have been better, she thought.

The car pulled up beside the cabin and stopped.

Nadia opened the front door of the cabin to see what was happening. Thor and Attila followed her out. Their heads hung at a low, steady height, and their tails were thrust firmly between their hind legs. Something was wrong.

The driver's door swung open to reveal Dyre Crane's oldest daughter, April. As Nadia approached the car, she glared at her. Her red-rimmed eyes rested above dark circles, and her skin looked gray.

From her perspective on the hill, Gail could see Nadia smile at her until April raised her hand. In her hand, she held the two necklaces containing the power of two of the three Sisters of Fate that Gail had only heard about. She stopped in her tracks. The pendants lit up as a powerful bolt of energy hit Nadia in the chest, sending her flying backwards into the rose bushes.

The dogs barked. Their teeth bared in response to the attack. They ran to Nadia.

Gail raced down the hill. "April? What are you doing?"

With no indication that she'd heard her, the girl pulled her young sister from the car by her long blonde hair and flung her on the ground. Lucy cried out in pain and fear. She scurried to her feet and ran to Gail.

She wrapped her arms around the child, feeling her tremble.

"April? Does your mother know you are here?"

"It's not April," Lucy said to her mind.

Rumbles of thunder rolled overhead as Lucy shook in her arms. Gail looked to the heavens. *"Mother. I need you."* She repeated the plea three times.

"She won't answer you," Lucy cried, hearing Gail's thoughts. "She's gone away." The sky rumbled with thunder again.

Gail studied April's movements. She seemed to be assessing the area and the situation with slow, calculated movements. The vacant look in her eyes was unnerving. She looked at Nadia.

"Are you okay?" She hoped she could hear her.

"I'm fine. I can't move. Get the kid to safety." Her answer was sure and immediate.

She watched April raise her hand once more. Lucy's body began to vibrate. Gail wrapped her arms tighter around her and stepped in front of her. She could see the internal struggle as April fought the woman inhabiting her body. The pendants bobbed up and down as she tried to protect her sister from certain death.

Against her will, April's arm raised again. She aimed the chains directly at Gail and Lucy.

"April," Lucy cried.

Gail could smell static energy all around her. That strange smell of ozone that Beni had described surrounded them. Lucy's body went rigid in her arms like she was having a seizure. Beni's car exploded. A fire ball towered over them. The car flew towards the cabin.

Gail and Lucy were thrown onto their backs by the force. The dogs scattered. Nadia scurried into the cabin as the car barely missed her. The front window of the cabin shattered. April was nowhere to be seen.

Gail grabbed Lucy and ran into the fields. Attila and Thor followed. She held the child's stiff body in her arms as she bolted across the open field in the darkness. Hoping that whatever had taken hold of April could only function on her limited human abilities, she gambled that they were invisible in the darkness.

43

SAVING LUCY

Beni drove to Mount Orion in her Bronco with Camilla, Malcolm, Rayne, and Mia. Farryn followed, with Linus, Iris, and Dyre in her Subaru. She had no intention of bringing Mia, but there was no time to argue. After Linus told them Oriana's threat of taking April in place of Mia, everyone jumped into the cars. They noticed April had stolen Beni's car and knew where they were headed.

The entrance to Mount Orion was black as pitch, and Beni nearly missed it. She skidded as she slammed on her brakes when the stone pillars seemed to jump out of the darkness. She saw her Porsche lying on its side, still burning. She raced to it. Farryn was right behind her.

As they pulled to a stop, everyone jumped out.

"Tell me again why you think Oriana took April? She's locked in that orb, isn't she?" Beni searched the darkness for some sign of April, Lucy, or even Gail.

"She probably got out," Malcolm said. "I told you I didn't want to reuse the old orb. It must have been damaged."

"What do you think happened here?" Linus looked at the cabin and Beni's burning car.

The front door was open, and Nadia staggered out. She managed to get halfway out the door, pulling herself up on her hands and knees.

"What happened to you?" Beni crouched beside her.

She sat on the ground, trying to catch her breath. "I got hit with some kind of magic. Sent me flying."

"It didn't kill you?" Rayne's jaw dropped.

"Almost."

Beni unbuttoned Nadia's shirt to reveal a huge burn on her chest. She bit down on her wrist and offered it to her. A collective groan from the witches followed her actions. She ignored them.

"Okay, okay. That's enough. *I'm* going to need a transfusion if I do this again today. Twice is enough for me." She collapsed in the dirt, trying to regain her strength.

Nadia dropped onto the ground, exhausted. "Your blood is miraculous. Thank you," she whispered. She fingered the burn on her chest and watched it fade. She got to her feet, offering more respect to Beni than she had when she first met her.

"We're wasting time," Dyre shouted. "Where is everyone?" She ran up the hill to the cottage door and tried the knob. When she found it locked, she banged on it, screaming for her daughters.

"Dyre." Linus was right behind her. He touched her shoulder. She wasn't thinking clearly.

Farryn stepped up and whispered a few words. The door opened soundlessly.

Mia stood in awe and whispered to her father, "Just like Harry Potter."

Malcolm beamed as Mia spoke, relieved.

They walked in single file. Dyre led, followed by Beni, Farryn, and Nadia. Linus and Malcolm were next with Camilla. Rayne remained outside with Mia and Iris, keeping an eye on the property and out of danger.

"Gail?" Beni called out. She was met with silence. "Hello?"

"Any idea where they could have gone?" Camilla asked Nadia.

"After the car blew, Gail took the little girl and ran."

"Lulu?" Linus stepped closer to her. "Where did she take her?"

"Mal! Dyre!" Rayne called from outside.

"We saw April." Mia met Beni as she came outside.

"Where?"

"She was walking in the field. Kind of dazed." Mia pointed into the field. "She had those necklaces in her hand. They were glowing. I would have called out to her, but..."

"Say no more."

Gail placed Lucy down in the field. Knowing the child couldn't keep up, she lifted her in her arms again. In the darkness, she could hear owls and small scurrying animals. The songs of frogs from the lake and crickets in the overgrown grass surrounded them as they ran.

A shed lay on the farthest edge of the property. The roof collapsed during a past winter storm and the walls had holes gnawed by mice. Piles of grass and leaves in the corners told her the mice were sharing this space. The stench of urine told her that as well. An old, rusted scythe leaned in the corner, and a shovel so pitted by the elements that it was no longer round with a jagged corroded edge hung on the wall.

She crouched beneath the collapsed roof pieces and pulled Lucy close.

"Lulu, do you trust me?" Gail placed her inside the shed. The child stared at the cobwebs and mouse nests around her. "Lulu, you know I would never harm you, right?" She shook her to snap her out of her fear-induced daze.

"Yes." Her answer sounded like a question, but Gail accepted it.

A mouse scurried past, making Lucy jump. She pulled back under the roof and kicked at the creature. Her foot slipped on the dirt-covered floor, making her stumble.

Gail caught her before she fell. She kneeled and pulled up the floorboards. The wood stuck in places, but she forced it until it snapped. "Get in here."

Lucy's blue eyes filled with water as her body quaked. She shook her head.

"Trust me. You hide here and I'll deal with April."

"It's not April." The tears spilled down her face as her hand grasped Gail's sleeve. "It's not April."

"I know. Please trust me. This is the only way."

Lucy looked at the hole beneath the floorboards and around the area for possible mice. She stepped in, using Gail's shoulder for support. Her white sneakers sank in the moist earth. She squatted in place and looked up to Gail. The dogs squeezed themselves in beside her. Lucy put her small arms around them like they were stuffed animals.

"Do you think I killed April?" Lucy's lips quivered as she spoke, and her chin hardened into a walnut.

"No, I don't." Though she wished she had. The explosion distracted her long enough for Gail to grab Lucy and run. April screamed like she was in pain, but she wasn't dead.

"How do you know?"

Gail wanted to throw her arms around the girl and protect her. "I still hear her."

Lucy's face went white.

"Lulu, where did Aunt Tera and my mother go? You said they went away. Where did they go?"

"To get help."

Gail thought about this for a minute, not really knowing what it meant. She nodded. "You need to lie down now." A shredded tarp lay in the corner, half eaten by mice and saturated by urine. She pulled it and laid it on the earth in the hole. She then pulled off her sweater and wrapped it around Lucy's head and shoulders. "No matter what you hear, don't come out. Promise me. Keep her safe, boys."

When Lucy lay down, she placed the scraps of wood over her. After it was done, Gail looked around for a weapon. A rusty scythe hung on the wall, and she grabbed it.

"Don't hurt April," Lucy whispered from beneath the wood.

"I'll try."

44

THE CIRCLE

Dyre took off running into the field when they saw April. Only Beni had the nerve and the speed to stop her. "You can't stop her. She'll kill you."

"Fine. Let her kill me. Let Lulu take my power. Give her the medallion." She reached for the moonstone necklace that had been hanging around her neck for thousands of years. "I need to get my girls."

Beni threw her arms around her friend. "I know, but this is not the way. You'll die and end up getting April killed too. Let's do that circle thing we planned on yesterday." She looked at Dyre. "Trust me. This is going to work."

Dyre pushed her away, embarrassed by the emotions she couldn't control. "How do you know?"

"Because you're glowing."

"What?" Dyre looked down at her hands, confused.

"Your medallion is glowing again. I'm guessing we're not completely alone anymore." Beni smiled.

Dyre wrapped her hand around the pearly white stone. She held it in her fist and wrapped her other hand around it too. *"Thank you,"* she whispered silently. She exhaled a long, exhausted breath and allowed Beni to lead her back to the cottage.

"They're in the shed at the far end of the property." Mararis's voice startled Dyre as they approached the three dying apple trees. She kicked the rotten fruit on the ground as she trudged through it.

"They're in a shed at the far end of the property." Dyre looked at Beni.

"What's the plan, witches?" Beni looked at all of them lined up, Mia included.

"Tera and I can stop her," Mararis said. *"Not for long but long enough."*

"If we join together," Tera chimed in, *"we will be able to free April and obliterate Oriana. We need our necklaces."*

Dyre repeated what her sisters said for those unable to hear them.

"How will you keep Oriana from disappearing again?" Beni asked. "If she can possess April, she can possess any one of us."

"She won't get past us." Farryn reached out her hands to Linus and Camilla. "Our combined strength will keep her in place."

"Elder Path was a circle of eight. We're missing one to close the Circle." Camilla looked around at those surrounding her. "Should we call Opal or Kim?"

"There's no time," Malcolm said.

"What about Nadia?" Micah suggested. Farryn repeated his words.

"I'm no witch." Nadia was adamant.

"What do you call a telepathic realm jumper with ties to the divine?" Micah snickered. *"You're a witch, whether you like it or not."*

Mia translated this time, still able to see and hear Micah for a little while longer.

"That will work. We can do it." Farryn looked at Dyre.

"No, we can't." Nadia was skeptical. "Do you people know what you're dealing with? I just got hit with twenty tons of power from that little girl. I seriously doubt a stupid circle is going to make a difference."

Farryn glared at her.

Beni turned to the group. "I will come up from behind the shed. My suggestion is to gather from all directions, so she doesn't have a clear target on anyone."

"Can I ask a question?" Mia held her hand up. "What's going to happen to April when Aunt Dyre rips Oriana out of her?"

"Micah will stay with April's soul to keep her here." Farryn looked at Dyre.

"What does that mean?" Beni stepped up, concerned for her nieces.

"If they are going to *obliterate* Oriana without the orb, Dyre and her sisters need to take her away so she will never return," Farryn explained. "April's soul will want to follow them. Her body will die if it's not tethered to something. Micah will take care of that. Hopefully, he can distract her soul with his presence."

Dyre swallowed hard. "Thank you."

"Wait, where are you taking Oriana? Are you coming back?" Beni asked Dyre.

"I can't promise anything." Dyre looked at Linus. He nodded, a stiff uncomfortable nod that told her he understood but didn't want to think about the consequences right now.

"Then, no." Beni could not allow her friend to die. "Your sisters will take care of this. I don't want you to…" Her voice quaked with emotion.

"Beni." Camilla took her hand with a soft squeeze. "She needs to save her daughters."

Dyre touched her glowing medallion as she considered the consequences.

Gail heard footsteps, and she readied herself. Silently, she told Lucy to be still as she raised the scythe. Her eyes closed and she concentrated on the thoughts of the one approaching. The thoughts were a jumble of images. Mia as a baby. Mia only a few days ago standing on the sidewalk. A dark-haired woman and Mia's father, Malcolm. Three women tied to trees as they were set aflame. The image of Gail's own two-year-old sister lying dead in a well. And Simon standing over Oriana as she died.

Anger burned her from the inside. She raised the scythe as the footsteps stopped. Gail scurried to the right side of the shed. The sunken roof blocked her path as she tried to step over it.

The shed door flew open. April stood in the doorway with her arm extended, holding two necklaces. The orange and green pendants glowed.

Thor's deep growl filled the shed.

"Oriana, stop!" Dyre's voice shouted from within the darkened field. The animals were silenced as her voice seemed to come from every direction.

"How many times must we continue this farce?" It was April's mouth that spoke the words but not her voice. The voice was Oriana's. "These are mine." She held up the necklaces. "Your daughter is mine. And in a moment, your power will be mine as well."

Dyre searched the darkness for the witches. Feeling for her sisters around her, she said, "Why are you doing this?" She took a step forward, and April took a step back.

Her slim, pale hand raised the chains into the air. "I just need one more for my collection. If you give me a minute, I need to dispose of this cold blood who wishes to hide your legacy from me." Oriana laughed. "Fire kills cold bloods, doesn't it?"

She aimed the glowing pendants at the door, and it burst into flames.

"Kill them." Camilla came up behind Oriana. "Kill them all, but what will you have then? Just the same as you do now. You have no ability to harness her power. You are weak, Oriana. You always have been."

Farryn stepped up from out of the darkness with Linus to her right and Malcolm to her left. They reached for each other's hands. Beside Camilla, Nadia, Iris, and Rayne linked hands. In front of Oriana, Mia appeared and joined hands with Malcolm. The chain circled Dyre and Oriana.

Micah stood beside Dyre, waiting for her to give him the okay to secure April's soul.

The shed leaned precariously to the left as wood snapped and flames crawled up the walls. The creaking of the structure frightened Dyre. She called out for Lucy. It sounded like something heavy fell inside, and the already dilapidated structure collapsed. Sparks from the fire soared into the air, lighting up the area. Dyre cried out for Lucy again.

April laughed. It wasn't the beautiful, youthful laugh of an eighteen-year-old but the cackle of the ubiquitous storybook witch. She approached Dyre. "You tried to kill me once and you failed. After trying to drain my life from me bit by bit, you sent Asher Delger and Mia's false mother to finish the job. But who sent the shifter? Was that you too? Getting desperate."

"No, she didn't. That was all me," Farryn called as she felt the Circle's power flowing through her. "You killed Mararis and Edith. It was his birthright to avenge their deaths."

Oriana laughed again. "Birthright? You are a fool." She turned to the others, looking for an ally in the group. Her eyes fell on Mia and Malcolm, holding tight to each other's hands.

"Oriana, stop!" Malcolm shouted. "You've been misappropriating what little power you were born with for years. Gaining the power of the three would be a disastrous mistake."

April's eyes settled on him. A look of hatred bristled under a lowered brow, and her mouth was a fine line of anger. She looked to the shed now lying in a heap of wood, fire, and smoke. A vindictive smile pulled on her lips.

Gail dragged herself from the burning debris as April raised her hand to Dyre. The pendants glowed, building up the energy that would be expelled. Dyre stood strong, knowing that if she died, Lucy would inherit the breadth of her power and immortality immediately.

They waited, all wondering if Oriana was considering this fact as well. She smiled, a heartless smile, and swung around towards Gail, standing just inside the Circle. Terror streaked through her. With the necklaces aimed directly at her, Gail raised the scythe and brought it down on April's wrist.

April's hand and the amulets fell to the ground as she screamed out. Her voice echoed over the property. Dyre ran to her daughter.

"Dyre, no!" Farryn yelled. "Grab the amulets. Finish this." She held tight to Linus as he attempted to break the Circle to go to his daughter as well.

April dropped to the ground. Blood pumped from her stump. Micah embraced her from behind as if to keep her in place. His hand, transparent yet strong, closed around her wrist, and the bleeding stopped.

"Oriana Duran," Mararis's voice filled the darkness. Gail could see a blur of energy swirling in the center of the circle. Like a tornado of wind, leaves, and power, Tera and Mararis held Oriana's spirit in place.

Dyre picked up the amulets, prying them loose from her daughter's disembodied hand. A sob escaped her as she held them up. The glow enveloped her. She held out her hands for her sisters to join the power. As they released Oriana, the glow followed each of them until Oriana was completely contained.

A burst of sunlight filled the night sky. It covered them, swelled like a bubble popping, and disappeared. The force pushed the Circle members flat on their backs. It sent Gail flying too. The night consumed them, and they searched in the darkness for each other.

Linus was the first one up. "Lulu?" he shouted as Farryn lifted April's arm and started working on reattaching her hand.

"She's here." Beni carried Lucy to the group. Both were covered in dirt and debris. Thor and Attila trotted beside them, looking pleased with the outcome.

Linus grabbed his daughter.

"Where's Mommy?" Lucy asked.

No one answered her, then Beni touched Lucy's head with her palm. "Do you feel any different?"

"No," she said, laying her head on her father's shoulder.

The group looked around in the darkness for some sign of Dyre or Oriana. There was nothing. They began their trek back to the house in silence. Mia held her mother's hand as they walked.

Linus helped April into a chair on the cabin porch.

"Will you be okay now, April?" Mia asked.

"Unfortunately," April groaned. Holding Gail's sweater that Lucy had used as protection, April's arm was tied securely to her chest. "I could have used another few hours of blackout time."

"Do you remember anything?" Rayne touched her forehead.

"Nothing until Gail started swinging an ax," April grumbled, not wishing to discuss what happened in the field.

"She'll be fine. She'll have scars but otherwise, good as new," Farryn said with a chuckle.

The group gathered inside the cabin, considering what they endured. "So does this mean that I'm part of the Great Coven?" Rayne joked. Iris laughed.

"Me too?" Nadia joined in.

"Hardly," Farryn snipped. Camilla laughed.

Outside, Mia and Lucy remained with April on the porch.

"Where's Mommy?" Lucy whispered in her sister's ear.

"I don't know." She sounded frightened.

The front door of the cabin opened, and Linus stepped out. "I guess you two are coming home with me. You can bunk in Camilla's room until we figure out this mess."

"I want to go home." Lucy's eyes filled with heartbreaking tears. Attila laid his head on her lap for comfort.

April put her good hand on her sister's shoulder. "Me too," she whispered.

"Me too," a voice called out from the darkness. "It's been a long night."

"Mommy!" Lucy leapt off the porch and ran to her mother. Linus escorted April out to the driveway, keeping his pace slow for her benefit.

Beni flew out the front door, followed by the exhausted group of witches.

"How are you, baby?" Dyre swung Lucy in the air.

"Gail shoved me in a hole," Lucy announced. "And she cut off April's hand."

Dyre looked at Gail with a chuckle. "Did she?"

Gail was mortified. She whispered her apologies silently to Dyre, who responded in kind. *"You saved my daughters. I am in your debt."*

"How are you here?" Beni asked. "You said…"

"Did you think I was just going to abandon my girls? I will be here for as long as they need me."

"How'd you get there with your body?" Gail was curious. "Last time…"

"Last time, I didn't have this." She held up her own amulet. The glow had diminished but still lit up her face in the darkness.

"And Oriana?" Beni asked.

"Not my problem anymore. Atropos, Clotho, and Lachesis took her, and they will punish her accordingly. I do have these." She held up Tera's and Mararis's medallions. "Gail, your mother wanted you to have hers. And April, Tera gifted you hers. She said she liked your spirit. She also apologized for driving you crazy this past week." She kissed her daughter as she handed her the orange medallion.

"Will they do anything?" Gail slipped the green medallion around her neck.

"I don't think so, but if they ever start glowing, you'll have a direct line to the Garden Room." Dyre beamed. "Oh, Camilla…" She turned to find Camilla standing at a distance from the group. She tossed the smoky orb to her.

Catching it with one hand, she looked at it. "What's this?"

"Elena. It seems Malcolm accidentally trapped her soul in the orb. She's been trying to get out ever since. She's been judged and absolved of her crimes by a much higher power. It's up to you what you choose to do. Set her free if you wish. Just remember there are some strict rules about playing God."

Camilla nodded, understanding what she meant.

"And your sisters?" Beni asked.

"Home. Welcomed back with open arms." Dyre shrugged. "Don't ask me. I doubt I'll have such a warm welcome, but they are at peace now. I did learn something from this little test." She kissed Lucy's head. "I'm not ready to die. Opal gave me a drink earlier that was close to miraculous. I suspect she used immortal blood in the brew. I'll take more of it. My girls are more important to me than my pride." She winked at Beni.

"Thank the Gods," Linus laughed.

"How's your hand, April?" Dyre asked.

"Miserable. Throbbing. Farryn said I'll have a scar forever." April lowered her head in a vain attempt for sympathy.

"Not that long, I should think. Here, let me see it." She took her eldest daughter's wrist in her hands. After stroking the red, swollen area where April's arm and her hand were reattached, Dyre placed her palm over the bond. She closed her eyes.

The moonstone around her neck glowed.

April pulled back her hand when her mother opened her eyes. "That's amazing." She inspected her wrist. The bloody wound was gone.

Beni smiled, looking at everyone gathered around her. "Looks like your powers are not waning after all."

"Their decline is inevitable, but I intend to use whatever I have left for as long as I can." Dyre winked at her friend with a smile.

ACKNOWLEDGEMENTS

This is my version of witchcraft and mythology. My version and no one else's. I thought to myself one day, what if there weren't just three Sisters of Fate. What if there were other sisters not written about because they were cast out? That is how Dyre, Mararis and Tera were born. That is how their legacies found their place in mythology and among the stars.

As for the witches: I make no judgement against anyone who practices witchcraft using tarot or any *paraphernalia*. That is a bias of Bentyn Rae and is not shared by the author. ☺

With that being said, this story was almost too difficult to write. The amount of drafts and edits it has endured is a testament to its need to live in the world outside of my head. Anyone who had lived these last few years between first draft and final draft has heard me say, "This book kicked my ass." It really did.

I would truly like to thank my sister for her honesty by telling me that certain details were unnecessary and distracting to the story. After removing many superfluous characters and streamlining the story to where Mia is the central character, I realized her criticism was spot-on and the right "kick in the ass" that I needed.
Thanks, Deb.

ABOUT THE AUTHOR

Michele Baumann is a four-time author of supernatural fiction. Her books captivate readers who seek stories beyond the ordinary, where the supernatural elements serve as a backdrop to explore themes of love, loss, and family connections.

She lives in New Jersey with her husband and daughter.

www.michelebaumann.com